Now, we begin our journey to defe Demon Lord—

Swordmaster | **Aria Rizas**

Priest | **Ares Crown**

Holy Warrior | Naotsugu Toudou

Mage | Limis Al Friedia

DEFEATING THE DEMON LORD'S A CINCH

IF YOU'VE GOT A RINGER

VOLUME 1

TSUKIKAGE

Illustration by **bob**

YEN ON

New York

Translation by Alex Kerwin
Cover art by bob

This book is a work of fiction. Names, characters, places, and incidents are the product of the author's imagination or are used fictitiously. Any resemblance to actual events, locales, or persons, living or dead, is coincidental.

DARENIDEMO DEKIRU KAGE KARA TASUKERU MAO TOBATSU
Vol. 1
© Tsukikage 2016
First published in Japan in 2016 by KADOKAWA CORPORATION, Tokyo.
English translation rights arranged with KADOKAWA CORPORATION, Tokyo through Tuttle-Mori Agency, Inc., Tokyo.

English translation © 2018 by Yen Press, LLC

Yen On
1290 Avenue of the Americas
New York, NY 10104

Visit us at yenpress.com
facebook.com/yenpress
twitter.com/yenpress
yenpress.tumblr.com
instagram.com/yenpress

First Yen On Edition: August 2018

Yen On is an imprint of Yen Press, LLC.
The Yen On name and logo are trademarks of Yen Press, LLC.

The publisher is not responsible for websites (or their content) that are not owned by the publisher.

Library of Congress Cataloging-in-Publication Data
Names: Tsukikage, author. | Bob (Illustrator), illustrator. | Kerwin, Alex, translator.
Title: Defeating the demon lord's a cinch (if you've got a ringer) / Tsukikage ; illustration by bob ; translation by Alex Kerwin.
Other titles: Darenidemo Dekiru Kage Kara Tasukeru Mao Tobatsu. English
Description: First Yen On edition. | New York : Yen On, 2018–
Identifiers: LCCN 2018023883 | ISBN 9781975327354 (v. 1 : pbk.)
Subjects: LCSH: Fantasy fiction.
Classification: LCC PL876.S853 D3713 2018 | DDC 895.63/6—dc23
LC record available at https://lccn.loc.gov/2018023883

ISBNs: 978-1-9753-2735-4 (paperback)
      978-1-9753-2736-1 (ebook)

10 9 8 7 6 5 4 3 2 1

LSC-C

Printed in the United States of America

Defeating
the Demon
Lord's a Cinch
(If You've Got
a Ringer), Vol. 1

TSUKIKAGE

CONTENTS

Defeating the Demon Lord's a Cinch
(If You've Got a Ringer)

Part One

Let's Begin

His existence was first confirmed twenty years ago.

He emerged as the enemy of humankind—those under the divine protection of the God of Order, Supreme Deity Ahz Gried. Darkness began to gather in the demon colonies, slowly at first and then with extraordinary speed, absorbing enormous amounts of energy until finally it gave life to a great power.

It was only when it was all over that humanity realized the danger.

This was the Demon Lord Kranos.

Cruel, cunning, and possessing great power. He who won the allegiance of the proud demons: their leader, the Demon Lord.

He made sure to conceal his presence until he had amassed a formidable store of power. Though he had grown strong, it was not until he had united the demons of the world—for the first time under one ruler—that he began to act.

Humanity became aware of his existence after a number of small kingdoms were destroyed, and even then, they could not band together as the demons had. This was because, compared to the demons and other races, the humans were much greater in number, and the destruction of small kingdoms was not uncommon.

Our kingdom first clearly understood the danger when one of the other major kingdoms fell. It was then that they began to invade.

The average abilities of demons are inherently far greater than those of humans. Nevertheless, in this world, humans thrived mostly because of the strength in their numbers and also because of the chosen few blessed by the protection of the gods, outstanding individuals who defeated multitudes of monsters and gained strength and skill rivaling that of the demons—these were the warriors.

Many kingdoms were destroyed. The demons, few in number, gathered together monsters to join them until their forces matched that of the humans. Having lost their advantage, the humans' defeat was inevitable.

The struggle went on for a long time. As the demons were set loose and scattered across the world, it became increasingly difficult for the people of each country to unite.

Humanity's greatest heroes, those possessing great life force and the strength of divine protection, went off to win their fame and fortune in battle with the Demon Lord. Most of them never returned.

The humans and demons each struggled to gain the upper hand in combat, but little by little, the humans grew weary. Serving the God of Order, the Church declared the demons enemies of God and performed miracles to hold back the invasion. However, these efforts did little to affect the situation.

Now, twenty years have passed since the Demon Lord Kranos was thought to have come into existence. At last, following the annihilation of a great ally, the vast Kingdom of Ruxe reached a decision.

To summon a hero.

It was the greatest miracle in the power of the holy god Ahz Gried and humanity's last hope. They resolved to perform this secret art and summon a powerful Holy Warrior from another world.

"The overdone sense of justice is a crime."

Prologue

The Hero's Party Assembles

Okay, this has to be a joke.

Looking at the faces around the table, I'm at a loss for words.

The only other male in the group, who's sitting across from me, stands and introduces himself.

"Hi. My name is Naotsugu Toudou," he says, somewhat shyly. "Nice to meet you. Um... It's kind of embarrassing to say out loud, but anyway, I'm the *hero*. I'm still training with a sword, so I don't have much experience, but I'm prepared to face any hardship to overthrow the Demon Lord. I look forward to working with you. Oh, and I'm level fifteen."

He has black hair and black eyes and looks sort of androgynous. I heard he's eighteen, but the baby face makes him look younger. Like he said, no experience in battle. You can't really call him a warrior, and he certainly doesn't look the part.

Level 15 is the level of a novice warrior, but I don't think he's quite there yet.

The *Holy Warrior*. The one called here by the secret art of the hero summoning, who has the potential to become the strongest person in the world. The one granted divine protection from the Three Deities and Eight Spirit Kings of this world. This is him.

He doesn't have the aura of a warrior, but I guess that's to be expected of someone from a peaceful world. Supporting him in battle is one of the tasks with which I have been charged.

Which is why this inexperienced young hero isn't the reason for my shock.

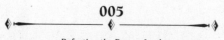

The problem is the other two.

The hero takes one more look around the table and sits down. Next, the girl sitting to my right stands up.

"Limis Al Friedia. Third child of the Prince of Friedia. I'm a mage, and I have some experience fighting monsters. Happy to work with you, Holy Warrior."

Blond hair, blue eyes. Flat chested but very pretty. Maybe a few years younger than Toudou. Her stiff expression and the tension in her eyes look more like nervousness than anger.

Her shining hair is visible under the white mage's hat. That sort of hair—perfectly groomed, flowing down her back—is never seen among commoners.

The high quality of her brown robes shows her status as well. They're the kind of robes an ordinary mage wouldn't be able to get their hands on. The staff she leans on is nearly her height and is inlaid with a stone the color of red lotus, an item that boosts magical power.

"Your level?" I ask automatically.

Her equipment is top-of-the-line, but it's obvious from her behavior that she's an amateur. The term *sheltered child* describes her perfectly.

Limis points a glare in my direction as she answers.

"…It's ten."

Why the hell is she a lower level than

"The overdone sense of justice is a crime."

our no-combat-experience Holy Warrior? Didn't she *just* say she has "experience fighting monsters"?!

Damn... This is a lot to take in.

Limis looks at my tense expression as if she's never seen anything like it and sits down.

As if I *want* to be irritated...

The House of Friedia has the strongest family lineage of mages in the kingdom. It is essentially the highest pedigree.

The founder was called the Mage King, and generation after generation, his blood relatives demonstrate a high aptitude for elemental spells.

There's no question about her natural ability. No question, but...

With the awkwardness still lingering, the third member rises.

"Aria Rizas. I am a swordmaster from the Mixirion school. Although I am still in training, I am honored to have been chosen as a member of this mission to defeat the Demon Lord. I hope my inexperience does not cause inconvenience. I put myself in your service. My level is twenty."

She has an excessively large chest. She's tall, has blue hair...and huge breasts. So large that your eyes are drawn to them even before her face. Or maybe I should say that I'm not interested in much else.

I can't take my eyes off her chest, and neither can the hero. Even Limis is staring, almost like she's annoyed.

I don't know if Aria is just used to it, but she only frowns and keeps standing tall.

"Your father is the great swordmaster Norton Rizas?" I ask, still staring at her breasts. I mean, I'm not trying to stare, but somehow my eyes just...

Aria hugs her arm over her chest as if to hide it. "That's correct," she answers sharply. "However, my abilities and my father's have no connection. I recognize my father's great skill and respect him, but I wish to be judged by my own merits."

"...I see."

What is going on with this bunch? Something just isn't right about it. Daughter of a grand swordmaster only level 20? Isn't that a little low?

I mean, c'mon, at least bring your dad along. That's another thing—the grand swordmaster is supposed to be the leading instructor at the Pramia school. So why is his daughter from a different school? Both are excellent institutions for swordsmanship, but I just don't understand it.

The talent is there, but to take down the Demon Lord... Her level is just too low.

The daughter of a prince and the daughter of a grand swordmaster. Aver-

"The overdone sense of justice is a crime."

age level…15. Regardless of the hero's level, with that kind of average, it would be suicide to battle the Demon Lord, no matter how you slice it.

Limis is narrowing her eyes at me. Could it be because I reacted so badly when she told us her level?

"So…what about *you*?" she asks.

"Right…"

What to do… This isn't what I expected. Raising the level of the hero is within the realm of possibility, but for the companions to be low level is no laughing matter. How can we possibly take down the Demon Lord?

I manage to avert my attention away from the doubt twisting around in my mind and start talking.

"Ares Crown. Reverend of the Church of Ahz Gried. I will function as the priest on this journey. My level is—"

I stop. The three of them eye me suspiciously.

It's not a good idea to be honest about it. After all, the average level of all three of them is 15. There's too much of a gap, and level gaps in parties yield need-less friction. The heroes could lose confidence in themselves. Most importantly, if they think they can rely on me in a critical moment, it will be a weakness in their minds. That is something we need to avoid.

Defeating the Demon Lord

Fortunately, only priests can measure a person's level—and in this party, that's just me. If I want to make something up, I can. Priests don't often lie, so they wouldn't suspect a thing.

I hesitate for a moment, then decide to reveal just the last digit.

"My level is...three."

"Three? Just three?" says Limis. "Hold on, can you even use healing magic at that level?!"

...Well, I said what I said and can't go back on it. Be that as it may, it is annoying to have that pointed out by *Limis*.

"Oh, I can still do all the basics a healer can do: healing, removing status ailments, level measurement. Nothing to worry about."

"Ahhh, so...we should just try not to get hurt then, huh?"

I can see in her eyes that she doesn't completely believe me.

Next to me, Toudou is looking at my weapon with curiosity.

It's a metal rod topped with a barbed iron ball. It looks like an ordinary blunt-force weapon, but actually, I had it made with a metal bestowed with holy power, so it's particularly effective against things that live in darkness.

"This is a mace—a priest's weapon. Priests of Ahz Gried are not permitted to have bladed weapons. I guess you could say it's like a mage's *staff*, in that it amplifies the effects of magic. Try not to think of it as something to be used in close combat."

"I-is that so...? Just what one would expect from a fantasy priest..."

Toudou gulps. Maybe he imagined the power of it. I suppose if you judge on appearance alone, it looks more dangerous than a sword.

There is a little tension in the air, and Toudou clears his throat as if to close the subject.

"Well, in any case, we will work together to defeat the Demon Lord! I'll need all of your support."

"I will show you the true power of the magic of Friedia, Holy Warrior!"

"My sword lacks experience, but I will use all my strength to serve at your side, Great Hero. We will overthrow the Demon Lord."

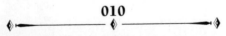

"The overdone sense of justice is a crime."

As I look at each of them, filled with eagerness, I breathe a sigh. At least they appear to be good people.

Everyone looks to me, so I speak my closing statement:

"I will do as God wills."

Heading out on a journey to defeat the Demon Lord with this completely underqualified party.

At that moment, I felt I'd reached the lowest point in my life. Things couldn't possibly get any worse...

I have just one thing left to say:

This world's a bitch.

On the Abilities and Disposition of the Hero

It was about a month ago that I received the order from Amen Creio, head of the Church for the Eradication of Heresy, otherwise known as Out Crusade.

The mission was to help defeat the Demon Lord Kranos, currently viewed by the Church as the greatest existing threat. I'm to accompany the hero.

The Church of Ahz Gried is the most widespread religious organization among humankind, and within the Church there is Out Crusade—an unusual organization that sets out to annihilate demonkind.

The primary component of this group is the *crusaders*, those who possess the power to cleanse the darkness that threatens humanity.

The *hero summoning*, which called Holy Warrior Naotsugu Toudou to this world, is one of the secret techniques of the Church, so it was expected that, when the time came, the Church would dispatch a capable person to challenge the Demon Lord.

If you compare the basic ability of humans to that of demons and other races, it is generally low. Nevertheless, the God of Order, Ahz Gried, one of the great Three Deities, bestowed upon humanity its greatest strength: the power to make rapid progress.

That power is *leveling up*, the phenomenon of life-force feedback. When a human kills a demon or other living creature, they can take a portion of its life force as their own. Leveling up also occurs in other races, but comparatively, humans have a significantly higher rate of growth.

The Holy Warrior possesses extraordinary talent and receives the

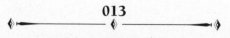

protection of numerous gods, but in the end, he is still a human. Not to mention that directly after he is summoned, he starts from level 1 and doesn't stand a chance against any demon.

Consequently, the true nature of our mission is to help the Holy Warrior Naotsugu Toudou raise his level in whatever way we can. We need to take action.

The Demon Lord is under the protection of an evil god, and only an attack by someone under unique divine protection will be able to cause him direct damage. That would be, for example, a hero—someone like me doesn't have that power, unfortunately.

What I'm saying is that just being high level doesn't mean anything on its own.

§ § §

When the introductions are over, I step out of the tavern where we're meeting and go around back where there aren't any people.

From noisy to quiet, from the hot air smelling of alcohol to the fresh air of the outdoors, I take a minute to catch my breath.

I check to see if anyone is around, then take out my metal earring with a black stone and put it in my right ear.

The earring is a magical tool used to communicate with the Church headquarters. It's a rare item, but I have it because, as a crusader, I frequently work in rural areas.

"Good morning, Ares."

Almost as soon as I boot up the device, a transmission comes in.

It's an operator on standby from headquarters. The familiar robotic voice is one I've had many exchanges with since becoming a crusader.

"Connect me to Cardinal Creio."

"…Certainly. Just a moment, please."

Cardinals hold the second-highest position after the pope, and there are five priests holding the position of cardinal. Cardinal Creio oversees

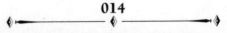

the monks who maintain the Church, the holy knights, and the department for the opposition of darkness.

He is also the supervisor of Out Crusade and the man who decided to dispatch me for this mission.

Before long, I hear the voice of Cardinal Amen Creio. He is very young for a cardinal—probably not even yet thirty. The tone of his voice is gentle, giving you a sense of security when he speaks, but the cleverness required to reach cardinal at his age is not to be underestimated.

"Is everything all right, Ares?"

"Don't give me that crap. What the hell is going on with these party members?!"

The hero himself aside, the levels of the party members are much too low. If this was only about lineage, they'd be first-rate, but you can't defeat a demon lord with your family history.

I'll be honest: Even a priest like me, whose main role is to cast buffs and healing spells, is still much stronger than them.

At this point, these girls are like rough gemstones. If polished, they could shine, but we don't have time for polishing.

"Hmm... Both the School of Sorcery and the School of Swordsmanship said they had sent the highest talents humanity could offer..."

Which isn't necessarily incorrect. I don't know much about elemental magic or swordsmanship, but that's probably the truth. It just feels like we're being cheated. I adopt as calm a tone as I am able and give my report.

"First, the mage is the daughter of Friedia."

"Hmm, Limis Friedia... Even the prince is taking drastic measures..."

"And she's only level...ten..."

"The only daughter of a prince... She has lived a sheltered life, so it follows that her level is low. He's quite the doting father. Every time I meet him, he brags shamelessly about her to me. It is certainly a virtue for a parent to love his children, but..."

Wha...? If she's lived a sheltered life, then just leave her in the shelter!!

If a priest must be able to heal, then a mage must be able to attack. To

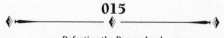

defeat a demon with such an astoundingly powerful life force requires a strong attack. Make no mistake that it is an extremely important role in defeating the Demon Lord.

"That is…a bit unexpected indeed… That he would send his only daughter off to fight the Demon Lord is, well…"

"No. No matter how well you equip her or back her up, to bring that little tadpole along… We'd put the hero in danger!"

Limis, Aria, and I are all expendable, but there is no replacement for the hero. The hero summoning is a sacred technique used to change the fate of this world. I was told that just to summon Toudou, an enormous amount of magical power had to be used. There might not be a second chance at that.

I'm not claiming to be a noble, peace-loving person, concerned for the fate of the world. The fact is that if the hero dies, the blame goes on the party's healer—me. Of course, I plan to avoid that, but I also want to reduce the risk as much as possible.

Cardinal Creio responds in a calm, admonishing sort of tone.

"Sorry, but it isn't the Church that chooses the other party members. If one of them is a burden, provide additional support yourself."

No way. That won't work! It's not like there's *one* burden; there are *only* burdens.

"How about the swordmaster? The grand swordmaster said he would send a swordmaster of first-rate genius…"

"It's Norton's daughter…"

When I say it, I hear a sound like a coughing fit on the other end of the line.

There's no way this guy is *laughing* about this, right?

"A-ahem… Excu…excuse me. D-did he, now? Well…"

"Yeah, she's level twenty, and…her boobs are huge."

I was focused on her chest to the point that I don't even remember what kind of person she was.

"Is that so…? No, actually, I knew that. I've met her before."

"Have you? I'd like a little more detailed information about her, if you could."

"The overdone sense of justice is a crime."

"...Rightly so. It can be problematic to get caught up in assumptions about a person, but having no information at all is also problematic, I suppose. Aria Rizas is...to sum her up in a word...a tomboy, it seems..."

A tomboy?! She didn't look like one at all, but...that's not the kind of information I need...

"It seems Norton is also at a loss for what to do with her... Apparently, she dislikes the traditional swordsmanship of the Pramia school and recently changed to the Mixirion school."

When she introduced herself, she didn't explain any of that... How bizarre.

The traditional Pramia school and the Mixirion school have completely different approaches to swordsmanship. To put it simply, one is defensive and the other is offensive. In the Pramia school, a sword and shield are of about equal importance, but in the Mixirion school, shields are not used at all. That sole distinction translates to totally different footwork.

I'm not necessarily saying that the Mixirion school is inferior to the Pramia school. But—hold on—did he just say she changed schools *recently*?! That's what he said, right?! What were they thinking, sending a woman like that to join the hero's party? And I mean, if she were stronger, then I could understand, but level 20? *Level 20?* She's just a beginner!

I really have no clue what the School of Sorcery and School of Swordsmanship are thinking. Many people live in the Kingdom of Ruxe. There's no need to send out the amateurs. There should be many excellent martial artists with years of experience. We're going to *battle the Demon Lord*, not have a goddamn picnic!

The lack of ability in every role of the party is all going to come down to the healer. Looking at who our party members are makes it even worse—a hero, a prince's daughter, and a swordmaster's daughter.

If even one person dies, it could be a huge issue. What do you do when you can see a problem coming from a mile away?

"So...what should I do?"

"...Well, your burden has only increased from one person to two people, so there isn't a great difference there. I will try to influence them,

but the Church, the School of Sorcery, and the School of Swordsmanship are all separate organizations. Don't expect much to come of it."

"What? Are you serious?! I have no choice but to go like this?! Even though I don't feel like we can succeed?!"

I mean, if we come across a group of orcs while they're at this level, won't we just be annihilated?

The transmission cuts out. I give the earring a tap, but Creio doesn't come back on the line.

I take a deep breath and rub my temples to try and relax. It doesn't help much.

At any rate, when you're given orders, your only option is to follow them to the best of your ability.

The kingdom gives heroes a complete support package.

For example, any powerful weapons obtained by the previous hero. If one of those is a rare magical tool, the hero receives instruction on its use by a first-rate warrior.

As the hero, Toudou also received several valuable pieces of equipment:

The feather-light holy armor Fried, highly resistant to both physical and magical attacks.

The holy sword Ex, the sword of exorcism, which is particularly powerful against demons and can cut through stone like butter.

These are the kinds of treasures an ordinary person could never get their hands on. If you sold just one, you could live free and easy for the rest of your life.

However, the most important thing one needs when fighting demons is a reliable, exceptional party.

Regardless of how strong any individual is, fighting many demons at the same time is difficult, and if you are paralyzed or poisoned, you won't have anyone to help you. So above all, fighting alone is the greatest mental burden.

It is generally recommended to assemble a party of four to six members when confronting demons and monsters.

"The overdone sense of justice is a crime."

There are a few roles required at minimum for any party, which are consistent with the three party members chosen for our mission:

Our magic user, Limis Al Friedia, casting magic attacks for the party's offense.

Our swordmaster, Aria Rizas of the Mixirion school, maintaining our front line through close combat.

Myself, priest Ares Crown, using the holy arts for support during battle and healing thereafter.

And lastly—our Holy Warrior Naotsugu Toudou. He who is under the protection of the Three Deities and Eight Spirit Kings—and one of the rare few who can play all roles on the battlefield.

With the divine support of the spirits, he is able to use offensive magic, and his physical abilities are increased. He may even be able to use holy techniques eventually. He has the potential to be the greatest warrior in this world.

The previous hero also was a magic user and fought at the front line—this was commonly called a *magical swordmaster*. Toudou is following that same path, and it would probably be best for him to take charge of the front line using both swordsmanship and magic.

"—So I think our best plan for battle formation is to have Aria and Toudou at the front line, myself in the center, and Limis in the rear. I have a lot of stamina, so if anyone sustains a serious injury in the front line, I can take their place. Well, in that situation, I won't have time to use healing magic, so you'll have to make use of medicine or other items to heal…"

We're at an inn discussing our combat formation and plans moving forward.

For some reason, Toudou is sort of frowning while I talk. He has his feet up and is fiddling with a ring on his finger, but he doesn't try to put a word in.

It's very clear that I'm the most experienced person in the party. Limis and Aria have no battle experience to speak of. They most likely know that. They are simply listening to my explanations in silence.

When I finish speaking, the hero gives a little nod.

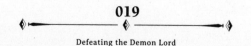

"I understand what you're saying. I was trained by a knight, so I do think the front line is a suitable position for me. But, you know—"

"But what?"

"Parties can typically have up to six members, right? Isn't it a better idea for us to first find two more members?"

Toudou stares in my direction. His eyes are black—a rare color for this region.

I wasn't expecting the first thing he said to be that we need more party members…

They say that great power breeds arrogance—not to mention that Toudou has never been in a battle, and the divine power bestowed on him by the gods and spirits who summoned him to this world must be overwhelmingly great. To the extent that he may feel a strange sense of omnipotence.

No… Maybe that isn't it. This man isn't a warrior. Perhaps it is precisely because he has never experienced combat that he wants to approach with caution the threat of battle with monsters and demons. In either case, it's not a bad idea.

But since Toudou is probably still not familiar with the common practices of this world, I continue to explain.

"Additional party members are something we can keep in mind, but for the time being, I would like to move forward with just us four."

"Huh? Why? It's not like the thought of adding another guy to the group bothers you, does it?"

What the hell is this guy talking about? Naturally, I would want a man with superior physical strength for a swordmaster. It's almost to the point that I wish we could switch out Aria for a muscle-covered war veteran.

He's grinning, but there's no hint of a smile in his eyes. Is he on his guard against me?

"Of course not."

"Then, why not?"

"To make leveling up more efficient."

This is one of the reasons why recommended party size is from four to six.

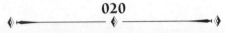

"The overdone sense of justice is a crime."

I swish a little water around my mouth and am about to continue explaining, but Toudou indicates that he understands.

"Ahhh, got it... So *that's* the reason."

"Hmm? I haven't explained yet. Did you get it just from that?"

I was told that the hero knew nothing about this world, but...

He turns to me triumphantly as he answers.

"When you defeat a monster, the experience points are divided by the number of people. So the more people you have, the less efficient it is for leveling up, right?"

He appears confident that this is correct. Limis glances back and forth between the two of us with a puzzled look.

"...Experience...points? What are those?"

"...What?"

Experience points. *Experience* points, huh? That's a phrase I've never heard before, but I can at least get the idea.

Aria also wears a serious expression and has her arms crossed in front of her. No, maybe it isn't a serious expression. It's this kind of expression:

"I haven't heard of that, either..."

"What?! Your level increases based on how many experience points you've earned, right? It's always like that in games."

I heard that in Toudou's world there is no such thing as leveling up, but it seems they must have something like it. It appears conceptually similar, which makes my explanation simpler.

"It's a bit different. When you defeat a monster, you acquire their spirit, or life force, and the amount your level increases is dependent on that. There is no such thing as *experience points* here. Well, one way or another, the nuance comes across, but..."

"Life force...?"

"Right. After killing a monster, a portion of their energy is absorbed by the being who killed them. That energy is the *life force*. After absorbing a certain amount of life force, a level up occurs, giving a substantial increase to all your physical abilities. Since you're level fifteen, you must have already experienced this, I think..."

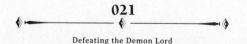

The difference of a level up is big enough that you can feel it from just one level change.

It is possible to increase muscular strength through physical training, but ability increases from leveling up are not really on the same plane. The power of *life* is certainly on a higher plane. Consequently, this energy is called life force.

"Yeah, my agility definitely increased... But this is the same kind of thing as experience points, isn't it?"

"From what you said, it seems similar in theory. But there is one major difference."

"A major difference...? What?"

His head leans to one side with curiosity.

"Life force... is not divided among party members," I explain. "Only the person who kills the monster receives it."

In other words, the more party members you have, the more difficult it is to level up evenly.

Toudou appears to understand, so I move to the next topic.

What we need is a way to increase Toudou's level as quickly as possible.

Fortunately, I have experience with this. We're going to go somewhere I have been to before.

"...The Great Forest of the Vale?" Toudou mumbles to himself, a serious expression on his face.

I chose this as our first destination because it's the best place for leveling up in the Ruxe Kingdom. There really is no better place in the country to get up to level 30.

The Great Forest spreads out hundreds of kilometers in all directions, and the monsters that inhabit it are beast and plant types that use mainly physical attacks. The battles are very easy, and it's also a good place to gain basic survival skills.

The area is appropriate for level 15 and up, so it's on the dangerous side for our group. They'll just have to work hard.

At one point in my explanation, Aria cuts in.

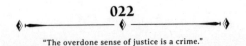

"The overdone sense of justice is a crime."

"The Great Forest of the Vale... Isn't it dangerous for someone at Sir Toudou's level?"

Toudou is level 15. I want to say, *That's hardly different from you!* But I don't, of course.

This girl's impression of me must be awful. The way I stared at her chest was pretty shameless.

"It might be a little dangerous," I say, trying to respond gently. "But I think we can manage it with this group. We can't really afford to take our time."

This isn't the first time a hero has been summoned from another world.

The Church calculated that in the past it has taken a month for the Demon Lord's forces to become aware that a hero was summoned. You can also think of that as the time limit before the Demon Lord sends out his assassins. It's important for us to level up as much as possible before then.

The hero doesn't seem to understand the danger of demons. "Are demons really that strong?"

"If we ran into a high-level demon right now, we'd be dinner in five minutes flat."

"*Five minutes?!* N-no way... I mean, I learned to fight from the Knight Commander—"

"Demon attributes are hundreds to thousands of times higher than human attributes. Just knowing a little swordsmanship and magic won't make you a match for them."

If a group of first-rate mercenaries were to challenge one of the really high-level demons, it's hard to say who would win. There are a variety of demons out there, but that's the kind I'm talking about. Even as a hero, at this stage, that is a battle he needs to avoid.

Toudou looks taken aback, but after a little thought, he nods quietly. He appears to be easily teachable.

"Five minutes, huh? In that case...even if it is dangerous, we need to level up quickly."

"You want to get your body accustomed to its new power little by

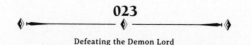

little so as not to cause strain, while still leveling up rapidly. Our goal is level thirty—if we can start by getting you to there, then at least if a demon appears, you should be able to escape."

Conversely, that means until then, we'll be constantly on our guard.

If you also take leveling up Limis and Aria into consideration, we're going to have to hunt quite a lot. One might ask, *If you defeated a high-level monster, wouldn't your level go up in one go?* Not exactly, because there is a limit on how much life force a person can take in at one time.

There's no easy way to raise your level, and a hero must also learn combat skills.

I start talking while still working out a plan in my head.

"Our top priority is to get Toudou up to level thirty. Worst-case scenario, I have replacements for Aria and Limis."

"…*What?*" says Toudou in a low voice.

I didn't mean any offense by it. Although I have my complaints about Aria and Limis as party members, I have no intention of abandoning them.

It's purely an issue of priorities. Even if you're the daughter of a grand swordmaster or a prince, as a priest from the Church of Ahz Gried, I must think first and foremost of the safety of the hero.

But I suppose Toudou himself may not have expected me to use those words.

Suddenly, at the sound of Toudou's low voice, a chill enters the room. The hairs on my body stand slightly on end.

I touched a nerve. By the time I realize it, it's too late.

This is a little something called *murderous intent*. Toudou's expression is sharp and severe as he bites down on his lip. His graceful appearance has turned unbelievably threatening, and a visible darkness clouds over his eyes.

A low-level person would be overcome by an uncomfortable sensation to run away in fear. It's a technique any high-level mercenary can use—but absolutely not someone at level 15.

A technique to sublimate and strike a person's will.

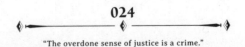

"The overdone sense of justice is a crime."

"?!"

"Ah…urgh…"

Aria's and Limis's voices catch in their throats at this bizarre and sudden occurrence. They look wide-eyed at Toudou and me. I stare at Toudou in silence.

This is legitimate genius. Or no, this…this is surely a result of the hero's divine blessing.

At what level was it that I became capable of binding people's movements with murderous intent?

We stare at each other for a while, but since he looks like he's about to attack me, I clap my hands together to break the silence.

"Sorry. I didn't mean to insult Aria and Limis."

"You owe them both…an *apology*," he growls. His once husky voice seems now to be wrung out from the back of his throat like a corpse crawling out of the depths of hell itself.

Best not to go looking for trouble. I am a disciple of God and gave up my pride to Him long ago. If the way to end this is to bow my head, I will bow it as low as needed. I would even kneel on the ground.

Before things progress further, I turn to Limis and Aria and bow low.

"I was wrong to say what I said. Forgive me."

"Ah…sure…"

"Um…okay."

At their responses, the hero calms slightly. Aria and Limis breathe sighs of relief.

While slowly raising my head, I think on the meaning of this change.

The emotional shift was much too sudden. He is gifted, but is he unstable? Does he have an excessive sense of justice? Or did he experience some sort of childhood trauma? Whatever it was, I'll have to be careful what I say and do around him.

When you think about it, he was abruptly called away from the world where he was born and raised to come to this world. It's natural that he might be a little on edge. I clear my throat and make direct eye contact with him.

"Sorry about that."

Even at my apology, his expression is stern, and his gaze does not waver.

"…Yes, I'm sorry, too. But I don't want to hear you talk about Limis and Aria in that…*condescending* way ever again. It's unpleasant. And extremely offensive."

"I apologize for the offense. And I apologize for saying something that could so easily be misunderstood. But…what you're asking is not possible."

"…*What?*"

Toudou's expression changes dramatically. The table where his hand rests makes a small creaking noise.

I can't help it if he hates me, but it must be said. It's not like I'm saying it because I want to.

"The reason is that our mission first and foremost…is to defeat the Demon Lord."

"What? That's—"

"And the one called here to defeat him was *you*, Naotsugu Toudou. Limis, Aria, and I—our only role is to support you in your quest. Just that."

If you'd told me a month ago that I'd be a member of a hero's party, I wouldn't have believed it.

A person who supports the hero in bravely defeating the Demon Lord will receive status and honor and fortune, but it really isn't worth the risk of facing a high-level demon. Even worse if your opponent is the greatest demon, Lord Kranos. Rumor has it the general public calls him the King of Despair, a true monster.

The party of level-80 mercenaries who challenged the Demon Lord and were destroyed is fresh in my memory. What's our party's average level—20? You've got to be shitting me. It's like asking infants to do the work of adults.

I'm not a member of this group because I want to defeat the Demon Lord. I'm in it because I had no choice. It was an order from the cardinal, and I had to leave my regular duties to take part in this.

"The overdone sense of justice is a crime."

But I will do my job properly. It's my work, and it must be done.

"Do you understand? Without you, the Demon Lord can't be defeated. Haven't you heard this from the king?"

To be totally accurate, as long as they have divine protection, other people besides Toudou can injure the Demon Lord. But that information doesn't need to be shared just now.

"Well…yes…," he affirms, his voice a little strained.

"Then you understand, right? The hero-summoning ritual isn't something that can be done frequently. Toudou, if you die, the world will perish. Are we clear?"

He is shaken by the intensity of the words. But when you put it that way, it sounds like the most terrifying thing. If I were in Toudou's place, being summoned without warning to defeat a demon lord, I would have boycotted.

"Aria and Limis will get stronger, too. It would be reckless to face the Demon Lord on your own. That's why we all need to raise our levels. But at the same time, in a worst-case scenario, Aria and Limis have a duty to give their lives to protect you. Of course, they should have been told this when they were chosen to be members of this party…"

By the way, I wasn't told. I joined because I was given a divine order to do so. But when you consider the purpose of this fellowship, it goes without saying that death is a possibility. Of course, I'm not planning on dying, though.

"I-is that true? Limis, Aria…?"

Toudou looks as if he's going to embrace them.

Grand swordmasters and princes are important people in the kingdom, but at the same time, they're still parents. It's unclear why they chose to send their daughters for this mission, but there's no way they didn't understand the possible outcomes.

Aria and Limis exchange glances and then nod nervously.

"It's true…," says Aria. "My father commanded me to protect you even if it means losing my own life—"

"My—my father said the same—"

027

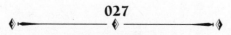

Before they even finish speaking, a change comes over Toudou. His eyes widen, and he puts his head in his hands and cries out in anguish.

I can't see his expression, but his cry is a mix of emotions I can't describe.

This is certainly not the image of the hero, humanity's glimmer of hope, but I decide to pretend I don't see it. To be frank, I don't really care if Toudou is the hero or isn't.

Due to the nature of my work in the Church, I know that the hero summoning isn't a technique that calls forth a hero who is guaranteed victory.

The future cannot be foreseen, even by an exceptional mage. My role is to get him as far as possible and keep him alive using every method and technique I know.

Cry all you want. Get angry all you want. The trials you are going to face are nothing compared to this…

I sigh as the hero's lamenting goes on in the background and proceed to point out the obvious as if it was wisdom.

"Toudou, all you need to do is get stronger yourself so you can protect them. You have the divine power of the Three Deities and Eight Spirit Kings—the potential to become stronger than anyone. Become as strong as you can and defeat the Demon Lord. If you don't want your companions to get killed, then protect them with all your strength."

With those words, it's like a switch has flipped. Toudou's groaning stops, and he slowly raises his head. Drool trickles from the corner of his mouth, and his swollen, bloodshot eyes shine blearily.

…Whoa! I had only a slight hunch before, but maybe this guy actually is out of his goddamn mind?

The look in his eyes is strange. He's staring in my direction but not really at me. It's almost like he's in a trance, as if he's witnessing something not of this world.

He suddenly coughs and starts to speak, his body trembling slightly. "O-oh…I see! That's true," he says, speaking as if to himself. "I have to win… All I need to do is win."

"The overdone sense of justice is a crime."

"Yes...that's right... All you have to do is win. That's all I'm saying here. Isn't that right? Limis? Aria?"

I immediately request backup. Limis's and Aria's faces once again stiffen at the hero's unexpected countenance.

"Y-yes...that's it!"

"A-ah...of course! You were chosen by the gods, Sir Toudou—you should win easily!"

Seriously, though—is this hero gonna be okay?

§ § §

When I wake up, I'm looking at an unfamiliar ceiling. It's before dawn, and the dim, lightless room comes vaguely into focus. My biological clock is right on target.

I sit up in the soft bed—the kind exclusive to luxury inns—and press down on my head from the resulting dizziness.

Once we start leveling up in the forest, we'll be longing for even a hard bed at a cheap hotel. That's the kind of life waiting for us. Last night we decided that—while usually it's best to be frugal—just for the first night of the journey, we would stay at the best inn in the capital.

We rented two double rooms...but the second bed in my room is empty.

Reason being, Toudou said he didn't want to sleep in the same room as me and withdrew to bunk with Aria and Limis.

"That bastard hero... What a perv..."

If he defeats the Demon Lord, I don't care what he does, but starting with this from day one? Come on.

That guy's sense of urgency and ability to read a room are lacking. Same goes for those two who took him in.

Considering the mental instability we caught a glimpse of yesterday, I shouldn't complain about him, but...it's true that people are often different than they appear.

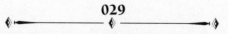

I stand up and get dressed. I put on my priest's robes, which are black with a white stripe, and fix my hair in front of the mirror.

The same determined face that has been there for eighteen years stares back at me from the glass. The evenly trimmed silver hair and green eyes came from my mother, who was from the Ahress region. In the past, people used to underestimate me, since I seemed so calm and gentle in appearance, but as my stare gets harder the more I work, these days I barely give that impression at all.

Lastly, I put my black ring on the ring finger of my left hand and affix the cross-shaped earring, which serves as a communication device, to my ear.

A bit of time remains before departure. The room next door is still, and when I focus my hearing, I can faintly pick up the sleepers' breathing.

I leave my room, trying to make as little noise as possible. A sleepy-looking employee stands idly at the reception desk.

Under the indigo sky before daybreak, I head to the church to worship.

The season is early spring. The air is cold, but little by little, the early risers of the town are getting up and about. Occasionally, a passerby notices my appearance and greets me.

"Good morning, Father."

"Ah, good morning. May the god Ahz Gried bless you today." It's just a standard phrase you spit out with a smile. It's meaningless—like saying *abracadabra*.

Priests… Thought of as an embodiment of the miracle of the holy religion of Ahz Gried.

Field of expertise, the holy arts. Healing, prisms, buffs, and lastly—exorcism.

The effectiveness of holy techniques increases with faith. Morning worship is the priests' most well-known custom.

Leisurely taking in the town as I walk down Main Street isn't such a bad feeling at all.

As I head toward the church, a brawny man who looks like a swordmaster catches my eye.

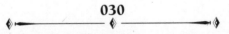

"The overdone sense of justice is a crime."

He's almost two meters tall. A longsword hangs from his waist, and his armor is covered in dents that show where it has protected him. But what draws my eye most of all is the bandage wrapped around his right hand. I consider for a moment, then stop walking and call out to him.

"Hey, you there, with the sword."

He doesn't notice when I call the first time, but finally, after a few more attempts, he turns to me.

"Huh? ...Are you talking to me?"

For a moment, the man's expression seems to indicate he wants to kill me for having shouted at him out of nowhere, but when he sees my clothes and the cross-shaped silver earring, the hostility vanishes.

"...A priest, huh? What do you want?"

"Let me heal that wound for you." Disregarding his dubiousness, I touch my index finger to the crudely bandaged arm. Then I say a prayer.

"Ex Heal."

As I speak the words, my fingertip lights up with the bluish-white glow unique to healing magic. In an instant, the light permeates his arm before immediately vanishing.

"Is the pain gone?" I ask the man, who is taken aback.

"Ah, oh... It...it *is* gone!"

The man tears off the filthy bandage. It smells of iron from the dried blood.

But there is no wound on the arm. By the look of the bandage, it seems like it wasn't such a big wound in the first place...

"It isn't good to just let a wound be."

An indescribable expression appears on the man's face. He begins stammering wordlessly, but once he calms down, he quickly turns his head down into a deep bow.

"Thanks. What a relief!"

"No need to thank me. I just did what is expected of a follower of God," I respond, surprised to hear my own words. It's not like I'm doing it out of charity.

It's good to work on your reputation when you have the opportunity.

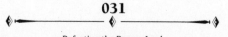

Priests are human, too, and there are some rotten ones out there, but a priest with a bad reputation stands out in the worst way.

I don't lose anything by doing it, so I try to help when I can.

The man seems like he's itching to walk away, and I ask him, half-jokingly, "Did I just steal the job of your party's priest?"

"No way! Our priest just joined the party, and he can't even really use healing magic yet. Right now, he's still laid up in bed because he used all his holy energy in yesterday's hunting."

Due to the nature of the role, priests' levels tend to be comparatively lower than other classes. I smile at the man as he rambles on.

"Is that so? That's too bad. But if he just builds up his faith, he'll end up an excellent priest. I'm sure it causes some inconvenience now, but do try to help him along."

"Ah...right. Of course."

I continue my self-indulgent explanation, and the man nods as I talk.

"While I'm here, let me just cast a few buffs on you. Do you have enough life force stored up? Here—let's level you up, too."

"Uh, all right..."

Holy techniques use a type of energy called *holy energy*, but this shouldn't use up much at all.

I reach out and touch the man's head, then, one by one, his forehead, cheeks, shoulders, ribs, and stomach.

"Ex Strength, Ex Agility, Ex Vitality..."

The elemental magic used by mages and the holy techniques used by priests when activated both emit light, which is called *magical light*. Passersby keep glancing over at the colored lights flashing red, blue, yellow, and green.

When I'm finished casting the buffs, I clap my hands together.

"You don't have enough life force to level up yet. You need two hundred and nine more to get to your next level."

The man bows again, as if overcome with emotion.

"Th-thank you so much!"

"Those buffs should last for ten hours. I think you know this, but

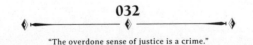

when they're about to run out, it's probably best not to go hunting any unfamiliar monsters."

"G-got it... I understand. Ah, as a thank-you—"

He rushes to pull his wallet from his pocket, but I put out my hand to stop him. If he gave me a stack of gold coins that would be one thing, but I don't really need the loose change from his pocket. And my purse is full anyway.

"I don't need a thank-you. Give that to the priest in your party, okay? Help him out."

The world would really benefit from more capable priests.

If an ordinary person were to do this kind of thing, you'd wonder if there's a catch, but when a priest does it, you can trust him as a faithful servant of God.

"Huh? Oh... Well, then, at least tell me your name—"

"—Oh, I didn't do enough for that..."

I look at the pleading man, then steal a glance at my surroundings to check if I'm being observed.

This is a business opportunity. Bad deeds are easily broadcast; good deeds less so.

I breathe a sigh and give my name as if I could do nothing else.

"Ares Crown... I am just a humble servant of God. May you receive the blessings of Ahz Gried."

"Hey, Ares! Where have you been all this time?!"

"Sorry. Morning worship...and guiding little stray lambs."

By the time I finished my morning worship and returned to the inn, the day had already begun. I finished my preparations and met with the rest of the group in the dining hall where they were getting something to eat.

Limis looks surprised by what I said.

"...So you really *are* a proper priest, Ares..."

"What's that supposed to mean?"

"No, it's just that...the way you talk is kind of crude compared to the clergymen I know."

It's true my manner of speaking is pretty rough around the edges, so I understand why she says it. Originally, my job was primarily the extermination of darkness, and those kinds of priests are different. If you smile, you'll be caught by the underlings of darkness.

Of course, I can't be too honest about that kind of thing. I think for a moment and give a short answer.

"This is just—how I normally talk."

"…Isn't that more of a problem?" Toudou points out.

Where's the craziness from last night? I wonder. He seems like he's completely back to normal. I respond with a forced smile.

"Of course, I am perfectly capable of polite speech… If this is preferable to you, I will adjust my manner of speaking, Sir Toudou, Miss Limis."

"…Uh, no. That creeped me out just now."

The two of them look at me like I'm weirding them out. So what the hell do you guys want me to do?!

Aria seems to be on Limis's side.

"Although…I had also been wondering about the way Ares speaks to Sir Toudou…"

"R-right! Isn't he rude to him?!"

Holy Warrior is a high title, and respect for the hero is deeply rooted in the people. Aria and Limis are proof of that. However, my purpose is to *lead* the hero. I can't be subservient to him.

As I'm wondering how to respond, I notice Toudou has a sour expression on his face.

"Politeness isn't necessary," he says. "Not just Ares. That goes for you, too, Limis and Aria. I'm almost embarrassed to be called *sir*. I'm not that kind of person."

"So I'm told, but…?"

He doesn't seem to have that attitude of superiority. The abomination I witnessed yesterday seems like a lie.

What was it that they said about him…? Oh, that's it—they said that Toudou was a student in his world. Not an aristocrat or anything, just a commoner. That explains the humility in his speech.

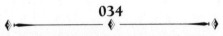

"The overdone sense of justice is a crime."

"But…you're the legendary Holy Warrior, and—"

"Limis, it's fine. I'd be much happier if you'd call me by my name instead of using the formal titles."

Limis is baffled. Toudou looks at her with an expression of total seriousness, reflected clearly in his perfectly symmetrical features. If someday they write about Toudou's deeds in the scriptures, he'll probably be described as "the most handsome man in the world." Although I think "most in the world" is a little excessive.

Toudou and Limis are still gazing at each other. I deliberately ignore the feeling that I shouldn't interrupt.

"Well, in that case, thanks, Toudou!" I say, giving him a slap on the shoulder.

"EEP?!" he yelps. I didn't hit him that hard, but it made him jump in his seat.

"HEY!" shouts Limis, slamming her hand on the table. The look in her eyes now is totally different from a few moments ago. "Forget politeness; you don't even show the hero any *respect*!"

"Ha! I am a faithful servant of Ahz Gried, and you say I don't have any respect for the Holy Warrior?"

"Uh…w-well…"

Ridiculous. There is no one I respect more than the hero. If I didn't, I'd have abandoned this mission a long time ago.

After I mention God's name, Limis hesitates. Being the daughter of a prince, she must have had a good education.

I have never thought once of mocking God. I am willing to die daily for my faith.

"Limis, don't argue with him," says Aria, looking at me reproachfully before turning back to Toudou. "Sir Toudou, since all the party members are assembled, shall we head out soon? I've been told that by carriage it takes five or six hours at a steady pace to get to the village near the Forest of the Vale."

"Yeah…you're right… There's no time to waste."

The way to the Forest of the Vale is on the main roads for the most

part, but that doesn't mean you are completely protected from monsters. It's just relatively safer than other roads. When they appear, they appear.

At this point, I announce in a decisive tone the goal I have privately set.

"To start with, we'll get Toudou's level up to thirty in two weeks."

"…What?! *Two…weeks?!* That's just—," says Aria, shocked. Toudou and Limis don't seem to understand.

One day, one level. The kind of goal that would make a mercenary ridicule you for your recklessness.

But if I support with holy buffs and Toudou throws all the finishing blows to the monsters, it isn't an impossible number.

"That's absurd! No, there's no way! Are we really in such a hurry?!"

"At level thirty, there's a higher possibility that he'll be able to run away from a demon if attacked. I want to get his level up before the demons become aware of him."

Ignoring Aria's outburst and the severe expression on her face, I turn to the hero in question. I'm starting to understand his personality.

"That said, we'll certainly be on a very strict schedule. If you think it's impossible, Toudou, I'll reconsider, but—"

"I'll do it."

I don't know if maybe he remembered our conversation from yesterday, but despite his face turning somewhat pale, he replied immediately.

I recall the previous night for a moment and wonder how I should report it to Creio.

"I'll get stronger. I will. I'll get strong enough to protect Limis and Aria."

The jet-black irises of his wide-open eyes burn brightly. Is that fear or resolution?

Either way, he seems determined. All that's left is to fine-tune that determination and make sure it doesn't turn into recklessness.

What will we do about transportation? is the one question that had been on my mind, and it was resolved by the magical item Aria brought along from her home.

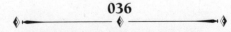

"The overdone sense of justice is a crime."

Grassland Wind, it's called. A magical carriage built by sprites. Normally small enough to fit in the palm of your hand, this legendary magical item transforms into a full-size carriage when charged with magic.

Being the only person in the party who knows how to drive a carriage, I sit alone on the driver's bench. How many years ago was it that I learned to drive? The carriage accelerates quickly, and the refreshing spring breeze brushes against my face and sweeps around behind me.

The driver's bench has room for two, but no one sits next to me.

Preferably, I'd have had someone sitting beside me and learning how to drive, but as they all seemed somewhat tired, I put that on hold for the moment. The horse golems that pull the magical carriage are very easy to handle. In these circumstances, it would probably be easy even for an amateur to learn.

In the area around the capital, it's mostly wide-open fields with few hills. To the east are grasslands with nothing obstructing the horizon, and one can see far.

The magical carriage has the smoothest, most comfortable ride of any I have ever ridden. Steering it while gazing out over the beautiful grasslands, for a moment, I'm able to forget all my obligations.

I drive briskly for an hour.

As I do, I chase away the monsters that occasionally appear using murderous intent. Suddenly, the curtain behind me is thrown open.

"Yeah, what's up?"

"Ugh…"

Out pops Toudou's face from the carriage. He's completely pale, and his eyes are clouded over. It isn't like the madness from before—he just looks like he's not feeling so good.

He clutches his mouth with his right hand as he looks up at me in desperation.

"Guh… I j-just need some…fresh air…"

I look down at Toudou in astonishment. Did he actually get nauseous from this level of movement?

Behind the hero are the concerned faces of Aria and Limis. The two

of them don't look sick at all, which makes sense, because this carriage makes for a pretty comfortable ride.

"D-don't look—at me—like that—!"

"The carriage is well ventilated. The air outside probably isn't much different from the air inside."

Toudou refuses to back down, so I jab my index finger at his cold, clammy forehead.

"Mini Recovery."

Who would have guessed my first use of magic on this journey would be healing motion sickness?

Pale-green light glows at my fingertip, then slowly spreads out across Toudou's entire body. It's instantly effective. With his hand still covering his mouth, Toudou looks at me, stunned.

"How do you feel?"

"Uh...um..."

Toudou gingerly releases his hand from his mouth. The blood has come back to his cheeks, and his complexion is entirely different from what it was moments earlier.

"Wha...what did you do...?"

"I'm a healer."

We don't have the time for disputes or rest. If we stop every time someone gets sick, the sun will be setting before we know it.

Toudou looks baffled for a moment but withdraws without a word back into the carriage.

I wait for a short while, watching the cabin, and when I'm sure Toudou isn't going to come back out, I face forward.

"...Looks like we've got a lot of difficulties in store for us."

Will he get used to it? Maybe as his level increases, he won't get so sick? It'll probably be fine, but I'm worried.

Eventually, the hero ends up coming out for air three times before we even reach the village near the Forest of the Vale.

§ § §

"The overdone sense of justice is a crime."

The village is simply called Vale Village.

It was established as a gathering place for the mercenaries who would come to level up at the Forest of the Vale and the merchants who would come to do business with those mercenaries.

Because it's near the Great Forest, it's surrounded by sturdier walls than an ordinary village and is always crowded with people, although few of them actually live here. If anything, it feels more like a town than a village.

As we pass through the gate, we come upon a bustling scene different from that of the capital. Mercenaries' wagons rattle as they pass by, loaded with the enormous bodies of the monsters they've hunted, and the air stinks of blood and sweat. It's almost like a battlefield.

Word of our journey must have spread throughout the kingdom. When I show our travel certificate, we are guided to the home of the village headman.

The Vale Village headman is a short, bearded man in his prime. He smiles broadly as he bows to Toudou.

"We heard from the capital and have been waiting for your arrival, our hero."

Perhaps Toudou isn't used to being bowed to by someone his senior, because he's blushing furiously.

"Ah, no…there's no need to bow. You call me hero, but I haven't even accomplished anything yet…"

"No, that's not—"

Toudou takes on a humble attitude, and I avert my gaze from him in embarrassment and notice that Limis is looking curiously around the room.

In battle, the mage is an essential element. I can stand in for Aria on the front line if necessary, but I can't use elemental magic. The efficiency of our leveling up depends considerably on what magic Limis can use.

She probably hasn't been out of the capital much before. Being in a new village seems to have put her in good spirits.

"Hey, Limis."

"Hmm? What?" she responds moodily. She clutches her metal staff

with its enormous red stone tightly as she turns to me. She's distant toward me, but we can let that resolve itself with time.

"What type of magic are you best at?"

Star of the battlefield—the *mage*.

The tremendous power of the offensive magic used by mages is unmatched by any of the other classes, and on top of that, it can be used long-range. The mage class is so remarkable that some say in battle everything is decided by the number and skill level of your mages.

The House of Friedia is known for its *elementalists*, who are masters of elemental magic.

As the name indicates, elemental magic borrows energy from the various spirits living in the world to perform miracles. Compared to the level of magical energy it consumes, elemental magic exhibits a high level of power. Those well versed in magic will say that if you're going to put a mage in your party, you can't go wrong with an elementalist.

Limis stands there silently, giving no response to my question. I suddenly get a bad feeling.

"…Don't tell me that you're like Aria, and even though you're from a family of elementalists, you can only use necromancy?"

"H-hey! What do you mean by that?!" Aria, who's standing next to Toudou, whips around. I guess she heard me.

What a pain in the ass! You're the one who made the decision to leave your family's school. Before telling us your level, use some common sense and share all the facts!

"D-don't go making fun of me!" Limis shouts back, red-faced. "*Obviously*, I can use elemental spells!"

"All right, I hear you… Sorry for the comment, then."

"Hey! *Ares!* What did you mean by that?!"

I completely blow off Aria, who looks about ready to whip out her sword, and turn my attention to Limis's staff. The rare gemstone it's decorated with is a highly transparent red lotus crystal. I'm certain it's one of the flare rubies, a high-grade gemstone preferred by fire spirits.

Elementalists collect weapons to optimize their skills depending on

the spirits they contract with. Since Limis has a flare ruby, her strongest attribute is probably fire—the most powerful type of elemental magic.

If she doesn't want to talk about her magic, that's fine, but I have one thing to say.

"Don't use fire-type magic in the forest."

"?!"

Limis is obviously startled by this. Her cheek twitches as she stares at me. Seems like I hit the bull's-eye.

The strength and range of magic is wide, so it's important that mages consider their environment and exercise self-control.

You need to pay careful attention if you use fire magic in an area where there's a danger it could catch and spread. In the heat of battle, there is no time for hesitation, and you have to keep in mind that you could actually kill your own team members if you use fire instead of choosing a safe alternative like water or wind magic.

Her staff is intended for fire magic, so other types won't be as powerful, but I guess that can't be helped.

I was just giving reasonable advice, but Limis shoots daggers at me.

"Hmm? What's the problem?"

"......rit."

"Huh? What was that?"

And just as I'm feeling relieved to hear that she can use elemental magic, Limis says something I can't believe.

"H-how am I supposed to fight without a spirit?!" Her angry outburst is so loud that the room shakes, and Toudou and the village headman suddenly stop their discussion and turn around to face us.

And here I am, with no idea what she's talking about or why she's angry.

"What do you mean *how*...? You just need to use energy from another type of spirit."

When elementalists are young, they make contracts with spirits of various types so they can use all the elements.

Spirits and magic users have varying compatibility, so it's natural for

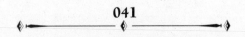

a mage to have strengths and weaknesses, but to say that you won't fight because you can't use fire is just stubborn and childish.

As I recall the other elementalists I have met before her, Limis answers with tears in her eyes.

"I can't."

"…Huh?"

I tilt my head to one side as I take this in. Aria, Toudou, and the village headman all hold their breath and watch us intently.

"What are you talking about? All I'm saying is that you should just use any type of magic other than fire—"

"I *can't*."

…What the hell is she talking about?

I let out a forced laugh as I look down at this level-10 mage. Somehow, I find myself in a cold sweat.

"Ah-ha—ah-ha-ha-ha-ha-ha! What are you talking about? Friedia is in the top three houses for elementalists. That blood has been passed down through generations, and the present head of the family is supposed to have made contracts with two great spirits—isn't that right?"

"That's…my *dad*!"

"Hey, I'm not fucking kidding around here!"

Without realizing it, I had grabbed hold of her fragile arm and was berating her from a distance of centimeters. In her blue eyes, I can see my reflection, and my own eyes look as they did the last time I faced a follower of darkness.

"So you're telling me that the direct descendant of His Excellency the Prince, he who has the divine blessings of the spirit kings, can't use any magic other than fire? *Seriously?!*"

It's absurd. Unbelievable. She doesn't even meet the minimum standards for a mage. Well, I'm not going to make it my job to protect her!

Aria and Toudou try to separate us, but I pay them no mind and stare right down into Limis's face.

"This isn't even fucking funny. Limis Al Friedia, how the *hell* do you intend to fight?"

"The overdone sense of justice is a crime."

"Th-that's what I'm saying! *How am I supposed to fight?!*"

"Hell if I know! Come back and join us once you've got a contract with another spirit—then you might be halfway useful!!"

Unbelievable… An elementalist who can use only fire magic… That's extraordinary in its own way.

After a short while, the burning anger subsides in a wave, as if it were never there at all.

My grip on Limis's arm loosens, and Aria and Toudou quickly pull me away and hold my arms back from behind.

"Hey, Ares, stop it! Relax!"

…*All right, all right. I'm calm.*

I mull over the implications of Limis's revelation again and again.

It's fine. It's just that a bad situation has gotten a little worse. It'll be all right. No problem.

If I had to put it into percentages, I'd say we had a 5 percent chance of success before, and now we're down to 0. If we have to get it up to 100 anyway, then 5 percent isn't that big a difference.

"…Yeah, I'm fine now." When I catch my breath, I look back at the two holding my arms, and they finally release me.

Still under watch, I turn to a startled Limis and make my apology.

"I'm sorry, Limis. I lost my composure."

"Um… Right…"

"I'm gonna go cool down a bit. I'll be right back…so wait for me."

My head is still spinning, maybe from the shock.

I quietly cast a spell to stabilize my mind, and with everyone's eyes on me, I leave the room.

As I try to get my breathing back to normal, I exit the front gate of the village headman's residence. I confirm no one is around and use magic to activate my earring.

It's all right. This isn't at the level yet where you should lose your cool.

As soon as the line connects, I say, "This is Ares. Connect me to Cardinal Creio."

"You seem upset, Ares. I will connect you."

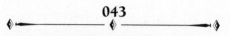

The operator's emotionless inflection is somehow comforting. Then I am immediately greeted by the familiar, informal voice.

"Has something happened, Ares?"

"Yeah. It's about Limis Al Friedia."

I try to present the information without getting agitated. Certainly, there must be a way for us to replace an elementalist who can use only fire magic. If not, then the people in charge must be insane. I explain the situation.

What? Are you telling me to look for a spirit to contract with the elementalist while I level up the hero?

Ridiculous. My role is supposed to be only to take down the Demon Lord. I'm willing to help raise my companions' levels, but I don't intend to do any more than that.

"Hmm... Well, I understand what you're saying. But the bottom line is—"

"The bottom line?"

I wait for him to finish as he takes a breath.

"You must continue with things as they are."

"As they...are...?!"

And just how are they, exactly?

"Ares, those in charge have their own considerations that, for the sake of confidentiality, I cannot explain to you. The point is there are no substitutes."

"No...substitutes..."

No...substitutes?! Hold on—what does that even mean? Do the rivers of Ruxe Kingdom run dry?! That's not possible.

"Our average level is only fifteen...," I say, almost pleadingly.

"Do the best you can. You're on a trip with a couple of pretty girls—try to enjoy it. You like girls, don't you?"

What the hell is he saying right now?

I take a deep breath. "I am...being *serious* here," I say in a clear voice.

"So am I." I know from the cardinal's resolute tone that there is no room for discussion.

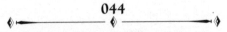

"The overdone sense of justice is a crime."

This isn't something I can overrule. Even if I explain things, I won't make any progress with him. *Damn it all.*

At some point, I must have unconsciously pressed hard on the top of the gate, as my fingers are now sunk into the wood. I pick off the broken pieces and grind them between my fingers as I pose a final question.

"...Cardinal, I want to ask just one more thing... Is this truly the will of Ahz Gried?"

"It is, indeed, Ares Crown. May he guide you on your journey."

"To hell with him, then!" I spit out childishly, cutting the transmission.

The sky is clear. Not understanding my turmoil, the sunlight shines cheerfully down on the earth.

I rub on my temples and close my eyes to contemplate—to straighten out my thoughts.

Rather than agonize over it...I just need to deal.

By nature, a mage's offensive magic is highly powerful. If we're focusing on leveling up Toudou, then Limis's strategic use of magic is important. It's just that we've gone from *strategic* use of magic to *no* use of magic.

The problem is, once we've finished raising Toudou's level, how will we raise Limis's? That, and...the issue of contracting with another spirit.

While racking my brain on how we should proceed, I return to the room, where the atmosphere from before already seems completely changed.

The village headman has tears in his eyes, and somehow Toudou's face is brimming with confidence. When he notices me, he calls out.

"Ares! It seems recently some high-level monsters have been appearing in this area and causing trouble. I've decided we're going to take them out," Toudou declares, his tone strong-willed.

"Thank you so much! The way you immediately took up the task truly shows you are a Holy Warrior of legend!"

I wonder if this is an unlucky year.

I stare at Toudou, my head filled with emotions I cannot put into words.

I frantically try to process what is going through the mind of this

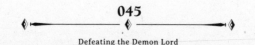

guy who can't seem to understand that this may not be a monster he can defeat.

And it's likely that these are not low-level monsters.

I mean, if the headman of a village filled with specialized monster exterminators calls them *high level*, that should mean something to you. Just what is going on in Toudou's head?

...Whatever, let's just be calm. I glare at the village headman.

"What's the monster?" I ask shortly.

"It's something called a glacial plant... Since it's called a plant, it should be a plant type, right? If Limis uses fire-type magic on it..."

I've heard of these. Glacial plants...are not plants at all.

They're *dragons*. To be precise, they are a plant dragon—hence the name.

More than five meters tall, it uses its roots to move and its countless thorny brambles to bind its opponents and then freeze them with its breath.

It's technically a dark-dragon type, which is easier to defeat than a dragon type, but that isn't much of a consolation.

The recommended level to battle these is 50, and that's for a party with six members. This is an area where people come to level up to 30, so there certainly can't be many mercenaries around here who could defeat this thing.

Toudou...

I glance at the village headman. He already appears fully confident that his request will be fulfilled.

As a member of the Church, it's not a good idea to undermine the authority of the hero. To those who believe in the Holy Warrior, from the moment he is summoned, he is considered a superhuman poised to defeat the Demon Lord. I'm sure the village headman has no ill intent, but...

"I'm against it."

"Huh? ...Why?"

"We don't have time to waste fighting a small fry like that."

I certainly can't lower the hero's reputation.

The village headman glances at my earring, and an unmistakable frown crosses his face.

I'll fucking end you.

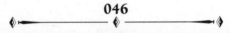

I can't put Toudou in direct conflict with a glacial plant. At level 15, it would take nothing less than a miracle for him to win. It's true that fire is its weak point, but Limis's level-10 magic probably isn't enough.

Toudou, not understanding my reasoning, takes a deep breath, as if taken aback.

"Ares, I'm the hero. I can't just abandon those who are being harmed at the hands of the Demon Lord."

The dedication is admirable—it's like a line from a heroic tale. Where the hell does he get all this conviction from?

As we glare at each other and the atmosphere between us grows tense, the village headman intervenes.

"Well, now… As you say, the hero shouldn't have to bother with monsters like dark dragons, I suppose."

"…Dragons?" says Limis.

Unsurprisingly, she didn't know it was a dragon. Toudou stares wide-eyed.

The village headman pays them no mind and continues. I really wanna punch this guy.

"However…to us, this is a serious matter. Already the mercenaries have labeled this as a danger zone, and there are those even now abandoning the area. For the time being, there have been no major injuries, but rumors can spread quickly. My only course of action in this situation is to ask powerful warriors to defeat the glacial plant."

"Ares, I'm the hero. That's why I was summoned. I have a responsibility to fight for the people of this world."

No, your responsibility is to defeat the Demon Lord. That's it. Don't waste time on foolish things.

I just barely swallow my words. *Stay calm, Ares Crown.*

The hero has no replacement—if he dies, we will be forced to abandon all hope.

Toudou isn't a fool. Surely, as we continue on our journey to defeat the Demon Lord, he will realize where his responsibility lies. *You have to believe that, Ares!*

I grab Toudou's shoulders and shake them.

"No, Toudou, listen to me," I say deliberately. "I'm not telling you to just abandon this village."

"?!"

I let go of him and then turn to the village headman.

This guy, causing us all this trouble... Well—maybe not. This might actually be a good thing. If the village headman hadn't said anything, we might have unknowingly walked into the forest and encountered a glacial plant.

"Hey, you just want to get rid of the glacial plant, right?"

"Um... Yes... Yes, I suppose so..."

"There's no need for us to be the ones to defeat it. You don't have any issue with other mercenaries from the town defeating it instead, do you?"

"Of course, that thought has already occurred to me. But right now, there isn't anyone that powerful here—"

So it's okay to force it on the hero?

I take one long, resentful sigh and glare at him. *Fuck you, asshole!*

"I'll talk with the mercenaries. Then we'll have nothing more to discuss here. Toudou, you're fine with that, right?"

The hero has gone slightly pale, but as he slowly nods, I feel a little relieved.

It's fine. I'll do it. I'll crush all the obstacles in our way.

§ § §

"Hey! Which of you here is the highest-level hunter?"

They turn in the direction of my loud query. I'm suddenly struck with the feeling that I have entered the den of a beast.

The tavern where monster hunters gather for a rest and a drink, known as Tuller's, reeks with the smells of beer and tobacco, of blood and iron, and of people. There are a few patrons already passed out on tables from a full day of drinking.

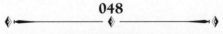

"The overdone sense of justice is a crime."

Among mercenaries, there are those who specialize in defeating monsters as their trade, dubbed *monster hunters*.

They are professionals who hunt monsters for both the experience and the reward, and their levels are far above average.

After what happened at the village headman's residence, I've come to the Vale Village watering hole in order to do some negotiating.

The mace that I've used for many years is in my hand. I grasp it tightly as I repeat:

"I'm looking for the highest-level hunters in this village."

"...Whaddaya want, priest?"

A woman with dirty rust-colored hair sitting right in front of me staggers to her feet.

She's about my height, with a large build. She seems to be a local worker—her arms are twice the size of mine, her chest is broad and muscular, and she wears clothing made of thick, heavy cloth. Next to her is a crude battle-ax the size of a grown man. With each step she takes, the floor creaks, and she comes close and looks down at me.

Her breath smells strongly of alcohol. Her ash-colored eyes are cloudy, which might be from the booze, but her pupils shine with a robust, glaring energy. She's built like a troll—this is promising.

"There is a monster I want taken out—and soon. Today, if possible."

"...What kinda monster?"

"A glacial plant."

The atmosphere in the tavern tenses at the monster's name.

"Take yer business elsewhere. There ain't nobody here who could take that on," says a redheaded mercenary curtly over his shoulder, without so much as a glance in my direction.

The woman stoops down to peer at my expression as if there's something funny about it. She roars with laughter.

But I have no intention of giving up so quickly after being told *no*. I silently clap my hands together and pray.

"Exa Area Recovery."

"Wha—?"

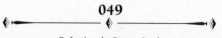

Bright-green light bursts from my fingertips and floods the entire building.

I ensure that it spreads through the bodies of a silver-haired young man lying down at a table, another absorbed in a card game, a man with reddish-brown hair drinking liquor straight from a bottle, and the woman standing in front of me. Then the light disappears.

Well, they shouldn't be drunk now.

The woman's eyes go wide with astonishment, and she howls like a hound. Her expression has completely changed.

"Area of effect magic... No way, you're...you're a high priest?! Why'd you come to a village like this?!"

High-level priests who can use area of effect recovery magic are rare. There certainly aren't any here.

I repeat myself one more time, patiently, like a parent instructing a disobedient child.

"I'm looking for someone who can defeat a glacial plant."

"...What's the reward?"

This reaction is different from before—more interested.

"The glory of defeating a dragon," I say, maintaining my serious demeanor.

"...So you're saying there's no reward?"

"You can do what you want with the remains of the glacial plant. I don't need a share."

Although it's a dark dragon, it's still a type of dragon. Its hide can be used for armor, its fangs and bones for swords, and its organs for medicine. If you can defeat it, all of that becomes your property. There is also the glory of defeating a dragon in battle, which is a status symbol for monster hunters.

Normally, a job without reward wouldn't be worth considering. But the hunters raise their eyebrows and huddle together at their tables in discussion.

What I need are the strongest hunters in this place.

"You fool, a dark dragon is still a dragon. The risk is too high."

"The overdone sense of justice is a crime."

"But we've got a high priest here. If we pass this up, when will we have another chance to take down a dragon...?"

"Shit, why is it always at times like this that I don't have my weapons? I thought I'd take a few days off and sent them in for repairs."

"Just think about our average level. It's impossible!"

Around the room, opinions are exchanged here and there, and appetites flit about.

Monster hunting is an extremely high-risk line of business. Most lose their lives in battle before achieving any kind of glory. In order to be successful, you need great ability, but you also need a lot of luck.

The buffs used by high-level priests are a game changer—to the extent that they can make up for a level that's a bit too low.

And the mercenaries know that, which is exactly why I came here to negotiate myself.

"Can I just ask...? You'll be in the battle, too, right?"

"I won't. But before you engage, I'll give you all the buffs I can use. They last for ten hours, so they won't run out mid-battle."

If I wanted to make absolutely sure, I would accompany them, but I can't just forget about Toudou and the others.

The tide of the discussion among the hunters changes once again—many of them had thought I would be accompanying them.

The presence of a high-level priest would directly affect the outcome of a conflict. They might be uneasy about going in just with buffs.

I don't have any use for the hunters who hesitate. I need people who will deliver results.

One by one, the hunters fall silent until, finally, only one party is left discussing.

It's a party of five, including the troll-like woman. Three members are front-line warriors, one is a mage, and one is a priest.

Average level 40. That's notably higher than most parties leveling up in these woods.

The one who appears to be the leader—a bearded giant who looks to me like he would win in a fight with a troll—extends his hand.

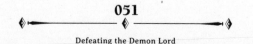

"I'm Thomas Gregory, the leader of this party," he says in a deeply masculine voice. "This is our swordmaster, Gustaf; our mage, Damien; and our priest, Eric. The one who got up in your face before is our smasher, Marina."

He stands leaning on a massive bastard sword. The mage is a younger guy, reclining lazily in his chair, and next to him is a timid priest who seems like just a boy. I look them over and then turn back to Thomas.

"I'm Ares Crown, a servant of God."

"Why've you come here?"

"The only reason for a faithful servant of God to be here is that God wills him to be."

While I could say that I came with the intention of leveling up, this place is too remedial for me. I've been through here once and had no plans to return. So my only explanation for my presence is that it is the will of God.

"Well, I'm thinking of retiring from service before long."

"Hmph... But you've reached the point of being able to use area of effect spells. Why quit?"

"Because God's servants get pretty rough treatment."

If this ordeal is a trial from God, then God must be an awful sadist.

Marina—her gentle name completely contrary to her troll-like exterior—looks at me with interest.

"You're a funny guy."

"Glad I can entertain you. Now, let's get down to business. The day is wasting away."

My negotiations with Thomas proceed without a hitch. When people are profiting from a situation, things tend to move along smoothly.

We wrap things up, and lastly, I cast the buffs on Thomas and his party.

I'm not trying to rush things, but I want to move quickly so I can get back to Toudou and the others.

Responding to my prayer, a bright light shines from my fingertips, wraps around Thomas, and suffuses into him.

The color of the light emitted by a buff depends on its type. The various shades look like the stained glass windows of a church, and it is sufficient to make a person grasp the power of the God of Order.

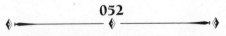

"The overdone sense of justice is a crime."

Thomas's strong face stiffens slightly. As if in a daze, he opens and shuts his hand a few times. "Wow...incredible..."

"Not bad, right?"

It looks like this is his first experience with high-level buffs.

Thomas gives a silent nod. I smile, relieved.

I have to hurry and finish up here before Toudou gets tired of waiting and starts into the forest.

After I finish the buffs, I make the basic preparations for the next day and return to the inn, where Toudou and the others are discussing our plans moving forward.

"...Did you get it figured out?"

"Yeah, fortunately... It should be dealt with by tomorrow."

I did my part.

Even though their opponent is a dark dragon, they should be able to defeat it as long as nothing out of the ordinary happens.

Toudou probably has questions, but he doesn't say anything.

Limis, on the other hand, makes no effort to hide her dissatisfaction.

"...Nao said we would defeat the monster...but you went and got another party to do it..."

"...Nao?" I say, thrown off by the unfamiliar name. Aria sits beside her, sighing.

I get the feeling that things went downhill when I flared up at Limis. If I hadn't been preoccupied with that, I might have been able to stop the village headman the moment that he brought up his request.

"She means Sir Naotsugu Toudou. It seems that in Sir Naotsugu's world, Toudou is his family name and Naotsugu is his first name."

"I see. The *Nao* came from Naotsugu. Should I call you by that, too?"

It seems like somehow while I was gone they all became friends. Toudou glances at me with a tired expression.

"...Sure. Do whatever you like."

"Hey! Don't just ignore what I said!" says Limis. Her expression is

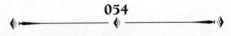

"The overdone sense of justice is a crime."

stern, like something rubbed her the wrong way. Dealing with her is aggravating.

I breathe a sigh, toss the cloth bag I've brought with me onto the table, and remove my priest's tunic.

Nao looks from the bag to me.

"Ares, what's this?"

"It's a weapon for the princess over there. It's not like she can go hitting people with her staff."

I sit in an open chair and remove it from the cloth bag. Nao looks at it.

"A gun…?" he murmurs.

"…Oh, you're familiar? It's just a minor weapon, though."

"I mean, I know it…but…"

I hold the revolver I've just purchased at a weapons shop by the grip and lift it to show him.

The weight of the metal and the black barrel of the gun give a sinister impression. I go through the unfamiliar movements of shaking open the cylinder and carefully loading the bullets.

Limis watches warily, as if she's never seen this before.

"…What is that thing?"

"It's a weapon called a revolver. You load the metal bullets like this, and when you pull the trigger, it uses the force of gunpowder to shoot. Even someone as helpless as you should be able to use it."

It isn't a very powerful weapon, so it's really only useful for delivering a finishing blow, but it's more legitimate than striking with a staff.

However, Limis must have doubts about my intentions, because her face starts to turn red, and she shouts at me.

"Huh? Why do I have to?! No way! I'm a *mage*!! An *elementalist*!!"

A mage who has a contract with only one spirit is in no position to complain, you faker!

I refrain from voicing my frustration and glare at Limis.

"So how do you plan on fighting in the forest, then?" I ask, trying to appear as calm as possible. "You're not planning on using fire magic, are you?"

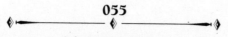

"Um… W-well, I—"

Probably having put no thought into it, Limis hastily turns to Nao and Aria.

"Setting fire to the Forest of the Vale would definitely be problematic. Do you want to burden the renowned hero with the crime of arson? Hmm? Miss Limis, what are your thoughts on that?"

"U-um… Hold on! A contract—I just need to make a contract with another spirit! If I do that—"

"All right then, go and make that contract."

"……"

A daughter of the House of Friedia, one of the great elementalist houses, who has a contract with only one spirit…

It sounds absurd, but if you think about it, there must be a logical reason. All the money and power of the prince of the Kingdom of Ruxe may not be sufficient to learn what that reason is, but it probably exists.

I fold my arms and look down quietly. Limis glares at me, biting her lip, saying nothing.

At this point, Nao takes a deep breath in and puts an end to the discussion.

"Ares, you're too harsh. And, Limis, it's dangerous to face monsters without a weapon. Whether you actually use it or not is one thing, but since Ares went through the trouble of buying it, at least keep it for the time being."

"…If you say so, Nao…"

At least it seems she'll listen to him.

Now that she's calm, I continue.

"We'll start off in the shallow layer of the Forest of the Vale. Even if Limis is useless, we should be able to fight with just Aria and Toudou—I mean, Nao. If someone gets hurt, I should be able to heal most injuries."

Our armor is first-rate. As long as we don't go too far into the woods, the possibility of sustaining major injuries is low.

Nao's combat strength is still an unknown, but I can guess Aria's from her swordsmanship background. It's just Limis who will be totally useless in the first skirmishes.

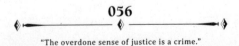

"The overdone sense of justice is a crime."

"HEY!" barks Limis. "Did you call me *useless*?! So rude!"

"Well, do you have any means of being useful?"

Typically, mages have very low physical strength and stamina. But with her, I'm concerned she won't even be able to walk through the forest without getting hurt.

Limis scowls at me, teary-eyed. I can hear her mumble, "I can use fire, y'know," but I wonder if she's realizing that just isn't enough as an elementalist. She doesn't give me a clear answer.

She turns her gaze to Nao.

"Did you stock the supplies?" I ask.

"…No."

What were they all even doing while I was talking to the monster hunters?

…Well, whatever. I also didn't *tell* them to do it.

"All right, then the first thing is to stock up on supplies. There are some things you can find in the forest, but it's essential to be prepared with food and water. Right now, we already have enough, so no need to get more. But we should get a variety of recovery medicine to make sure we have what we need. I can heal and cure poison using holy techniques, but you never know what's going to happen on the battlefield, so it's best to be prepared with some of each kind of the essential medicines."

At that point in my explanation of demon-hunting fundamentals, Nao interjects.

"Holy techniques…"

We make eye contact. I suddenly recall that in certain kingdoms, clear black eyes are a symbol of holiness.

"Can I also learn holy techniques?"

"You can."

Elemental magic requires a natural aptitude, but the holy arts are different. The essence of holy techniques is prayer. Through prayer, priests ask God to perform miracles. It's only logical that Nao, who has been given so much divine protection, can do this as well.

"Are you interested?"

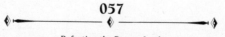

Nao closes his eyes. His loose, heavy clothes rise and fall slightly with his breathing, and finally he opens his eyes again.

"…I am… Can you teach me?"

"I guess I have no reason to refuse."

Versatility in battle is the hero's privilege. If the hero himself can use holy techniques, that will be to our advantage in the confrontation with the Demon Lord.

The range for holy techniques is fundamentally low. If there are more party members who can use it, the security of the party greatly increases.

When Nao hears my response, the corners of his mouth raise just a little.

This might be the first time this hero has directed a smile at me. In contrast to it, a strange feeling of dread or guilt stirs in my chest that I cannot quite pin down.

I feel compelled to look away from Nao and turn instead to the other two, who are quietly observing us.

"Nao is still new to this world. It's best for him to learn everything he can. We are…all in this together."

Either we succeed in defeating the Demon Lord or we falter along the way. We can only go down one of those two paths.

Thankfully, there isn't a cloud in the sky the day of our departure. We quickly finish up our breakfast and head for the edge of town.

We travel light because we're making use of a magical tool from my kingdom that stores items away in another dimension. The tool is in the shape of a ring, and it is a precious, one-of-a-kind item. As our leader, Nao is the one to wear it.

It's still early in the morning, and there aren't many people outside. As we walk, I check with the group.

"Nao, have you ever defeated a monster?"

"…I haven't," Nao responds sleepily. He slept in Limis and Aria's room again last night.

"I have."

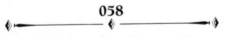

"The overdone sense of justice is a crime."

"I have, too. It was only a monster that my father had weakened for me, but still…"

Limis and Aria chime in with their answers.

There aren't many people in this kingdom who have never delivered a killing blow to a monster. In order to establish their basic abilities, most people reach level 5 by no later than the age of ten. Just the fact that Nao has never defeated a monster demonstrates that he was summoned here from another world.

It's a mystery to me how someone who has never defeated a monster has reached level 15, but Holy Warriors will never cease to surprise you. There are similar things written in the records of past heroes.

"Have you ever *encountered* a monster?"

"I've seen a doglike monster that was in a cage."

"Are you confident you can defeat them?"

"…Yes."

I wonder if he really is. I don't sense any anxiety in his definitive response.

At that moment, the ground shakes slightly—a sign of something coming this way. Nao looks in the direction of the woods.

A sturdy wooden cart trundles down the center of the road, the remains of an enormous monster resting on it.

The beast's body is a deep-blue color. It has many thin layers of skin, and there's a slash straight across its torso from which deep-blue blood is flowing. The lower half of its body is covered in countless creepy little legs.

"…What is that? …It's huge… There are monsters like that?"

"That's a pretty big one. They don't live in the shallow part of the forest where we're going."

The group of mercenaries and merchants is a hunter's party. They carry their game proudly.

The man leading the group notices us and opens his mouth to say something, but when I make a point to look away, he laughs instead. Hearing his sudden outburst, the rest of the group eyes him curiously.

It's best this way. You have completed your task, and we have no further business with each other.

We stand aside to give them room on the road, and the remains of the glacial plant pass us by.

Nao waits for them to pass completely.

"Wow…I have to be able to defeat monsters like that," he mumbles. "I wonder if I can do it."

He seems to be talking only to himself. Surely, he must understand that, in his current state, he could not defeat such a beast.

It's not actually a question of if he can defeat it or not—eventually he *must* be able to defeat it. And not just glacial plants but other things well beyond them.

It is for that reason you were summoned to this world, Naotsugu Toudou.

Although we call it a neighboring village, Vale Village is several kilometers from the Great Forest.

I sit in my usual spot on the driver's bench of the carriage, and to my surprise, Limis comes out to join me.

"I—I…I'll drive."

"…Do you know *how* to drive a carriage?" I ask, considering her skeptically. This is a bit unexpected.

The Friedia House is the most distinguished family in Ruxe Kingdom. She's probably never driven a carriage before, and it does require a certain amount of physical strength.

Once we get to the forest, we'll be fighting battles. The mage is important, and I don't see any reason to exhaust her unnecessarily with this task.

"S-so…I will permit you to sit next to me and teach me how," she says, obviously reluctant.

This really isn't something she *needs* to do… So where did the sudden sense of duty come from?

"I won't waste time complaining about how you phrased that, but anyway, if I'm going to teach anyone to drive the carriage, I would prefer it to be Aria or Nao."

"The overdone sense of justice is a crime."

"Huh? What do you mean by that?"

It's not that I hate her—I just have come to see her as a selfish, helpless, useless person. I choose my words carefully so as not to make her angry.

"Mages don't have much physical strength, and it's a bad idea to waste it on driving a carriage. Even if you can't be of any use in these woods, it's still best to stick to the principle."

"…You—you are seriously so rude!"

"In the teachings of the Church, lying is a vice. Not many people actually follow that, but as a faithful servant of God, I am honest."

Incidentally, alcohol, tobacco, and women are all vices, too. Could anyone really abstain from all of them…?

Limis frowns at my joke but quickly responds.

"We can't have Aria or Nao do it."

"…Why's that?"

They all seem to have bonded—I think they'd do it if she asked. They're all aware that they're beginners at this.

To my surprise, Limis has quite a logical explanation.

"First, for Aria, it's physically impossible. Apparently, she…doesn't have any magical power."

"…Wait, what? Hold on—"

It's true you need magical power to be able to use magical tools, but for starters, magical tools were created specifically for people with low magical power and unable to use spells. This carriage is a pretty pricey item, and I would guess from the design that it was made specifically for use by humans. Even though my magic power isn't very high, I'm able to drive it just fine.

A close-combat specialist like a swordmaster tends to have lower magical power than a mage, but powerful sword techniques still require magic. There's no reason why a level-20 swordmaster like Aria should be unable to use it.

I frown and ask again, praying that I misheard the first time.

"Did you say…she has *no* magical power?"

"Yeah."

"As in…absolutely none?"

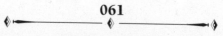

"Yep."

Seriously...?

I discreetly glance back at Aria. A swordmaster with zero magical power. Zero, huh? How is she planning to fight?

Maybe if we hadn't had the revelation that Limis can use only fire magic just yesterday, I would give Aria an earful now. But the second time, the shock factor isn't as bad, and I manage to assimilate this information with just a frown.

I've heard it said that in rare cases people are born with magical power of absolute zero, but it's supposed to be something like one in a hundred thousand or one in a million. If you're one of those people, though, that means you can't use any magical tools or close-combat techniques that require magic.

No matter how you look at it, she isn't suited to be a magic-based warrior. I imagine her life in general is more inconvenient, too.

Daughter or not, why would the grand swordmaster put forth someone in this position for the mission to defeat the Demon Lord? This isn't some fucking game!

I exert pressure on my temples to relieve the dull, throbbing pain and limit myself to saying the most constructive thing possible.

"There is a type of support tool for people who have zero magical power that enables them to use magical tools. It's a crystal that functions as a storage container for magical power. You just have to replenish it when it runs out. When we go back into town, let's request one from the kingdom. So what about Nao?"

"...You're so calm," says Limis, looking a little surprised.

I'm not calm at all! I really would like to tell her off for withholding that information for so long. But it can't be changed, so it's pointless to even mention.

"So *what about Nao?*"

"......"

Limis lowers her eyes and hesitates for a moment before immediately looking back up at me. "I think it might be better not to tell you, for the sake of your...mental health."

"The overdone sense of justice is a crime."

"Too late now—my mental health is in bad shape after the last few days. I don't think it can get any worse. Just tell me."

If you don't deal with problems head-on, you'll pay for them later. Might as well get everything out in the open at the start. If she tells me now that our hero can't use magic, either, that might be the last straw, but I doubt that's it.

"…No, I think it's best not to say. Nao isn't an option—let's leave it at that."

"…I mean, just for the sake of knowing, I'd like to hear it. Does he have a physical disfigurement or something? Or is his magical power so low that he can only use it for magical tools?"

A physical disfigurement… That's probably not it, but at this point, nothing surprises me anymore.

Noting my increasing anxiety, Limis quickly shakes her head.

"No, it's nothing like that… There are just reasons."

"Uh, okay…"

What *kinds* of reasons…? I really would like to know, but I say nothing and scoot over. Limis sits down next to me in an awkward motion.

She asked me to teach her, but the actual operation of a carriage is simple, and the driver just needs to get a feel for it.

The carriage starts moving slowly. Limis smiles a little at the swaying of the landscape.

It's been thirteen days since the hero was summoned.

We have only seventeen more days until the predicted day the demons will realize he's arrived.

I quietly make the sign of the cross and pray that, in the journey ahead, no trials will stand in our way.

§ § §

Ex. That is the name by which the holy sword that holds the power of light is known.

The sword, thought to have been forged by God himself, has the ability to exorcise darkness, and its power is said to increase in response to the spiritual strength of the holder. Using that sword, a previous hero supposedly battled a high-level demon with a devil sword and cut him down.

Who knows if the rumors are true, but seeing the weapon wielded right in front of you, you can sense its power.

The bluish-white blade reflects the sunlight pouring through the gaps in the trees and draws a line of light on the ground.

Letting out a battle cry as he strikes the olive-brown bud torrent, Nao easily slices through the hard trunk and cuts it in half. As the monster's screech of agony echoes through the woods, Limis makes a face and covers her ears.

Our first battle in the Forest of the Vale went better than expected.

We encountered just one monster, and even though Aria had her sword ready, the battle was over before she could use it.

Nao looks down at the body of the bud torrent and deftly drops his sword into its sheath—an impressive display.

Aside from defeating a monster, Nao also got a little battle practice and executed a clear, unwavering slash attack.

However, the most unusual thing was that in his first battle with a monster, Nao didn't seem afraid. Most people in their first battle are so terrified that their movements become rigid and jerky.

When I was expecting to have to jump in and help, this is like a bolt out of the blue.

"Well done, Nao," says Limis, running over to him.

But even after so easily defeating a monster in his first battle, there is no joy in Nao's eyes.

"No, no... Of course I should be able to do this. I'm the hero."

"No, your swordsmanship was magnificent," says Aria. "Do you have training in sword techniques?"

Limis and Aria show their admiration. There's no doubt that his swordsmanship was excellent.

Looking down at the remains of the monster he has killed, Nao smiles just a little.

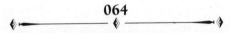

"The overdone sense of justice is a crime."

"No, really... This is the first time I've been summoned. Before this, I've only done kendo at school."

"I see... To wield a sword without any hesitation is no easy feat. I feel you have considerable talent," says Aria.

"Ah...thank you."

Nao not so happily thanks Aria in spite of her praise. "This monster that I just killed... Do we just leave it like this?"

I step forward and examine the creature's remains.

The cut from the sword is perfectly clean. Surely that can't be from the strength of the blade alone.

"The bodies of torrent-type monsters make excellent kindling. There are those who cut out the eyes—the most valuable part—and leave the rest in order to lighten their load, but since we have a magical storage tool, we can take all of it."

"I see... Got it."

The hero leans over the body of the torrent and touches it, using the magical tool. In an instant, the torrent's color changes to black, and it disappears into thin air. The power of the magical tool has stored it within another dimension.

Nao takes a deep breath, standing up slowly.

"Tired?"

"No, I'm all right. Actually, that was easier than expected."

"From what I saw, you didn't seem to have any trouble. Now, let's see if we can raise your level."

"Ah... Right... Do you have to actually touch me to do that?" he asks evasively.

Your level increases when you receive the life force of a defeated monster, but it doesn't happen instantaneously.

If you leave it be, the body will start evolving on its own, but one of the roles of a priest is to accelerate this process. Being level 15, Nao should have experienced this several times before.

"It's easier if I am in direct contact with you, but I can still do it without."

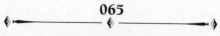

"...Got it. So you can do it without touching... Okay, let's do it that way."

Come to think of it, he does seem irritated every time I touch him.

"Nao...do you have some kind of issue with physical contact?"

"Um... Yeah, a bit."

"You know, the buffs and healing spells used in holy techniques are based on physical contact..."

"......"

Nao says nothing, an uncomfortable expression on his face. I sigh back at him.

Thinking again about the situation thus far, it seems like he's not going to die just from being touched. If I have to cast something on him, I'd better just cast it and touch him whether he likes it or not. This problem doesn't compare to the importance of his life.

I raise my right hand high and hold it as far as I can above Nao's head.

"Breath of Ahz Gried."

As I speak the prayer, a glittering, golden light radiates from the palm of my hand and covers the hero's body.

As the beam touches his body, it disappears like melting snowflakes, and after a moment, his entire body glows with a bright-white luminescence.

"Looks like you accumulated enough life force to level up."

The glowing light is evidence that the vessel is filled with life force—proof that a level up is possible.

Aria's eyes open wide. She looks impressed.

"Ares, you can perform the level-up ritual?"

"I can."

"...But I heard that even among priests, only those who are mid level or higher are able to perform it..."

"...There's no way the Church would dispatch a priest who can't perform the level-up ritual to join the hero's party."

Aria nods in understanding, but her expression is somewhat skepti-

"The overdone sense of justice is a crime."

cal. This certainly isn't a ritual that a level-3 priest can perform. That's a hole in my story for sure.

Moving on, I grasp my right arm as I lower it, then make a small cross in front of the hero's body.

Nao lets out a tiny sigh. In a few seconds, the light that had covered him is gone. His physical appearance hasn't changed, but Nao is now level 16. His ability points should have increased as well.

"Urgh… No matter how many times I do that, I just…can't get used to that weird sensation. Feels like it's crawling up from deep inside my body."

"That can't be helped. Think of it as your existence moving up by a degree—there is a sensation reflecting that change. By the way, until you reach the point where your level increases naturally without the use of the level-up ritual, a less intense version of that sensation will continue for a few days after."

"…It will? That sounds…unpleasant," says the hero, looking deeply unhappy.

Lastly, I say the words that conclude the level-up ritual:

"Nao has now reached level sixteen. Two thousand five hundred and eighty life force units are required to reach the next level."

"…When the sister performed the ritual for me at the castle, she used that gamelike wording, too. Is there a reason for it?"

"It is established in our creed that at the time of a level up, we must announce the experience needed to achieve the next."

"…Why does this world feel like a half-assed RPG…?" he mumbles.

I can't make sense of what he's saying, but he's got a perturbed expression on his face.

I take a few steps back to give him his personal space. He suddenly looks up at me.

"Oh! That level-up ritual—I can learn it, too, right?"

Usually, it's enough for just one person in the party to know the level-up ritual. But…

"…Yes. I'll teach it to you after you have gotten comfortable defeating

monsters and have learned the more critical holy spells. For now, it's enough that I can do the level ups, and there is bound to be at least one priest who can do it in every town."

"...I defeated a monster just now, though, didn't I?"

"That was a plant type. Fighting an animal-type monster is different. There are a lot of people who have a difficult time with animal types."

Well, someone like that wouldn't really qualify as a hunter, but there are plenty of people who dislike animal types.

Nao looks at me in disbelief, his eyes narrowing seemingly in contempt.

"But...why?" he asks.

"Because of the smell. Sometimes you get covered in blood and innards."

"...Ohhh..."

Some people even vomit if they aren't used to the smell of blood. It ought to be called something like *the hunter's baptism*.

Nao responds in grim acknowledgment. Aria and Limis nod in the same bleak manner.

Actually, the way I see it, there's no reason for concern.

Nao can defeat any animal-type monsters that we encounter in exactly the same way he defeated the plant type: slaughter without a moment's hesitation. Seeing his strength of will and incredible raw nerve, his mercilessness and value of justice, I understand for the first time since joining this party that the hero isn't just an ordinary human being.

He cut down life without any elation or sadness, as if it was just a job.

There's something that feels inhuman about a hero who doesn't even blink at the splatter of blood.

After finishing our battles for the day and getting what we could from them, we set up camp on the riverside while there is still daylight.

In the three hours that we spent in the woods, we encountered around fifty monsters.

That being said, Nao wiped out the majority in a single stroke. Even though most of the beasts were high level, Nao was able to defeat them because the blessings of the Three Deities and the Eight Spirit Kings greatly increase his strength.

As the daughter of a grand swordmaster, Aria showed considerable strength as well. Limis and I basically just tagged along behind the two of them as they cut down all the monsters in their path.

After defeating fifty or so monsters, Nao increased two levels and is currently at level 18. As your level gets higher, it becomes more and more difficult to level up, but I would say we made good progress for the first day.

Once it becomes completely dark, the movement in the woods is revived and creatures that respond to darkness—different from those we encountered during the day—begin to appear.

Hunters typically have to set up camp in tents, but we have our carriage. If you close up the hood, it keeps wind and rain out completely, and it's much more spacious than an ordinary tent.

Aria is on first watch, Limis is gathering tinder for the fire, and I'm at the river filling my canteen with water to cast a prism that will keep monsters away. I notice that Nao is observing me.

"…You use water, huh?" he says.

"Not just regular water. This is holy water."

I continue my work while I explain, as he is showing interest in holy techniques.

"I'm going to cast a prism that will keep away the weaker monsters. Holy water is the simplest medium to use for a prism."

Nao looks confused. "You say *holy water*, but didn't you just take water from the… Wait, is that river made of holy water?"

"No, actually, I'm blessing the water. Making holy water is one of the clergyman's skills, so naturally a priest can do it, too."

There are other positions besides *priest* in the priesthood, but blessing water is a basic skill that people of any position should be able to perform.

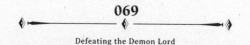

Nao looks on with curiosity as I bless the water. I hold the canteen so he can see and make a cross over it.

"Blessing of Water."

The water emits a bright light for just a moment. The light goes out, but the water hasn't lost its holiness.

Nao observes with unwavering attention. I show him the canteen.

"That completes the blessing. It has gone from ordinary water to water with one hundred lux per canteenful."

"…It's fairly simple, isn't it?"

"Priests in training will often make holy water as part-time work."

Holy water has various other uses besides creating boundaries, and these days, there is never enough of it.

"…So you can cast the blessing just by making the cross symbol?"

"Not *just* that—the important part is the prayer."

"…In my world, nothing happens when you pray." Nao looks down dispiritedly and sighs. "Each time I see that kind of magic, it's a reminder that I really am in a different world, you know?"

"Holy techniques aren't technically *magic*… Did you say that in your world magic doesn't exist, Nao?"

"…Yeah… Well, actually, until I came here, I didn't know it existed at all."

An emotion that I cannot describe comes over Nao's face. Could it be that he misses his home? Or maybe regrets having been summoned here?

I can't even imagine a world without magic. Being born into this world, to me, magic is something that was always there. I think for a moment, then tip the canteen and dump out the holy water I just made.

I fill up the canteen with water from the river again and toss it to Nao, who stares at me wide-eyed.

He hurries to catch it, uncertainty on his face.

"Try to make some holy water."

"…Huh?"

He looks down at the canteen in his hands and then back up at me, unsure what to do with it. "I…don't know how."

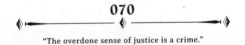

"The overdone sense of justice is a crime."

"You just watched me do it. Make the cross over it and pray."

The most important part isn't really your faith or the way you make the cross—it's your spiritual power. I explain it again more clearly.

"Make the cross and repeat after me. 'Lord, please help us. With your power, through the Holy Spirits, give us your blessing. Blessing of Water.'"

"But that isn't what you said before," he says.

"That was an abbreviated version. Would you really want to say that whole wordy thing out loud every time? I said it all in my head."

"Ares...are you actually a priest? You don't seem to have even a fraction of the religious devotion of the sister at the castle." Nao is raising his eyebrows at me in rebuke. He lets the subject drop when I prompt him again to try the spell and returns his attention to the canteen.

He focuses intently on the water and says the prayer, looking even more nervous than the first time he swung his sword.

"Lord, please help us. With your power, through the Holy Spirits, give us your blessing. **Blessing of Water.**"

In an amateurish gesture, he makes the shape of the cross, and at the same moment, the water emits a faint glow—evidence that he was successful.

His blessing isn't as strong as mine, as it is my profession, but it's unmistakably a blessing and proves that Nao receives divine power from the gods.

"That is a blessing," I say, wanting to make it clear to Nao what he has accomplished. "That in itself is proof that you are loved by the gods of this world."

"Proof...that I'm loved by the gods," he repeats.

As Nao stares down at the holy water, dumbfounded, he looks almost too helpless to be a hero.

But we can't let him back down.

Of all the Holy Warriors summoned before him, there isn't a single record of a hero who returned to their own world.

Heroes are granted protection from the gods, but in the end, that isn't worth much to someone who doesn't want the job.

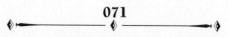

It would be good if the gods could provide the hero with at least a little mental support, too.

I watch Nao as he looks down at the holy water, unmoving.

"Ahhh... What a pain in the ass," I say, the words slipping out of my mouth.

"What is?"

Well, anything and everything.

I got the short end of the stick here. I understand that if I take on this task, then someone else doesn't have to, but I don't have that kind of selfless spirit. Which means I'm not really in a position to say anything to the hero about dedication.

I take a breath and am careful to respond so that Nao doesn't sense what I'm thinking.

"Putting up the boundary."

"The boundary... You said you use the holy water to put it up, right?"

"Correct."

Perhaps he wants to learn this technique, too. He hesitates for a moment, wondering how to pass the holy water back to me from far away. Rather than bothering with it, I go to where I poured out the holy water on the ground earlier and stamp on it.

"Hexa Holy Field."

A wave of light spreads out from the earth soaked with holy water. It makes no sound, and the light is faint, but a perceptive person would be able to pick up on the change in the environment even with their eyes closed.

Monsters tend to appear in stagnant places. In this moment, the power of the gods has purified the area around the camp. For a period of time, monsters will instinctively avoid it.

I wonder if he can feel the change. Nao blinks in amazement and looks back and forth between me and the holy water.

"Huh? ...What was that?"

"That was the boundary technique."

"...But you didn't use any holy water."

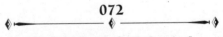

"The overdone sense of justice is a crime."

"I did."

I just made use of the water that I tossed earlier.

"...It looked like you just stomped on the ground, though."

"I said the proper prayer."

"...You're joking, right?"

"The gods don't like jokes. Well, probably."

If this situation was some kind of joke, I might have stepped down as a servant of God. A joke you can't laugh at.

But there's no use lingering over these things. I don't know about Limis, but Aria has fought pretty well so far, and Nao is stronger than I expected, which has made me more optimistic.

He still looks like he doesn't understand, so I wave it off.

"Prisms are the most difficult type of boundary technique. It's one of the last things that you'll learn."

"...All you did was stomp your foot on the ground where you spilled the holy water... I don't get it."

"I told you, *I prayed*. Now I say, 'Please forgive me for stomping my foot.'"

By the way, God may not like jokes, but I kind of enjoy them.

Nao clicks his tongue loudly. Maybe I messed with him a little too much. I move past it and give him his next task.

"Okay, Nao. I've laid the boundary, so this area is safe for the time being. Go with Aria and find something for us to eat. No monkeys or wolves—something that tastes a bit better."

We do have some food stored away, but procuring food is a survival skill I'd like them to learn through practice. That's one of the reasons I chose these woods for our hunting grounds.

Nao takes a long, hard look at me. In a voice like a whisper, he asks, "Are we actually going to eat monsters?"

"If there's an animal that isn't a monster in these woods, we can eat that, but I'm doubtful you'll find anything."

"But the sister told me that, according to the doctrine of the Church, you're supposed to avoid eating meat from monsters...?"

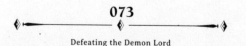

"Don't worry. I'll eat it."

Of course, I wouldn't eat a demon, but the monsters in these woods are essentially just animals that have grown extra hair.

Nao looks up at me like he thinks I'm beyond help.

"...Ares, you *are* a priest, aren't you? Don't you intend to stick to your creed?"

"I do. The boundary technique I just performed is proof of that."

"It looks to me like you do nothing but break the commandments of your religion."

"I get that a lot."

I'm just stating the facts, but Nao stares at me indignantly. I wasn't trying to taunt him, but not wanting to end up as rust on the holy sword, I explain myself.

"I understand that the act of eating a monster doesn't look good from an outsider's point of view, but it isn't actually prohibited by the Church."

"...Is that so?" Nao doesn't seem entirely convinced by my differentiation of *prohibited* and *to be avoided.*

"These woods have a village nearby, so food is accessible. As your level increases, though, we'll have to defeat monsters that live in more remote locations. When that happens, our only option will be to eat whatever lives there."

"...I see your point."

People can't live if they don't eat. The Church understands that, which is why they label this as *to be avoided* and not specifically *prohibited.*

He seems to have understood to an extent, but Nao doesn't look totally satisfied by my explanation. He walks over to Aria.

He says a few words to her, and she looks at me in shock.

Aria is just as straitlaced as he is... This is really no big deal.

Anyway, we're going to have to do it no matter what.

Once I see that Nao and Aria have left to find food, I sit down next to Limis, who has gathered a lot of branches and is preparing the fire. It's a clumsy pile of tinder but enough to get a fire started.

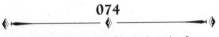

"The overdone sense of justice is a crime."

"Do you have a fire starter?"

"…I don't need one."

As I reach to take out my own magical fire-starter tool, she grumbles, annoyed. I notice the sleeve of her loose robe move unnaturally.

A shiny red lizard leaps out of her sleeve and lands soundlessly on the ground.

No, it isn't shiny—it's actually giving off light. About ten centimeters long, it has smooth crimson skin and dark-red eyes that shine like gemstones. It has the aura of a creature that transcends both animals and monsters.

"This is your fire spirit?!"

"Garnet."

My eyes widen with surprise. She doesn't answer my question, only saying that single word.

As if in response, the lizard's little tongue flits out to lick one of the branches.

In the blink of an eye, the branches are engulfed in colorless flames. The transparent flames create a dreamy haze, warming the breeze. It's a small fire, but it produces tremendous heat that warms my whole body.

I am quiet for a moment and look away from the fire to Limis, who appears to be a bit proud of herself.

"The fire is too strong. We don't want to burn all that up right away."

"Huh—?! …Garnet!"

A fleeting glimmer passes through the lizard's eyes. The blazing transparent flames turn red, and the fire grows dimmer.

Most of the wood was reduced to ashes, so I gather another bundle of branches and leaves from the forest and add it to the pile.

As I quietly watch the burning and crackling of the fire, I take a moment to think.

The technique used to manifest a spirit as one of the life-forms of the physical world is extremely high level. I didn't think someone at level 10 would be able to do it. An ordinary elementalist is only able to manifest a spirit's energy as magical spells.

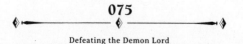

075

Defeating the Demon Lord

That being said, how is it she's able to manifest spirits but has made a contract with only *one spirit*? She's too far to the extremes!

After thinking it through, I end up being direct with her.

"Can you call your fire spirit?"

"It's *Garnet*."

That appears to be its name. The lizard's eyes do indeed shine like garnets.

The fire spirit raises its head slightly to look at me.

"A salamander, huh?"

The strength of an elementalist is proportionate to the strength of the spirit it contracts.

Fire spirits are the most popular spirits to contract with. They tend to have above-average strength, and often mid-level elementalists make contracts with them. But usually mid-level elementalists aren't able to manifest them, so they can't take a physical form.

In response, Limis glances up at me and mumbles something that shocks me.

"...Garnet can change shape, y'know."

At Limis's signal, the glimmering lizard swells, changing into a large ball of light—and explodes.

The blast is so bright that it blinds me for a moment.

When I can see again, in front of me is an enormous light, about two meters tall. Its silhouette is blurry, but I can make out that it's mimicking a humanoid shape. The energy swirling around the half-transparent body isn't something one can ordinarily see. The strength and density of the spirit's magical power materializes around it like burning flames.

I feel the heat radiating from it, and unconsciously, my breathing becomes strained.

I can't take my eyes off it even for a second. The voice that emerges from my lips is dry as bone.

"No way... *Ifrit?!* How does a level-ten elementalist have one of the most powerful spirits?!"

"...Ares, you're...surprisingly knowledgeable."

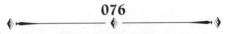

"The overdone sense of justice is a crime."

It is said that high-level spirits can change their form at will. If that's true, then this must be its natural form.

It hasn't completely manifested. A completely manifested spirit looks like its previous salamander form, with a clearly defined shape.

Even though it isn't complete, just being able to manifest a spirit of this class is clearly natural talent. But somehow...she's still at level 10.

"To put it your way... 'There's no way the Prince of Friedia would send an elementalist who can't manifest to join the hero's party,'" she says with satisfaction. Retaliation for my earlier comments. "Does that sound about right?"

Surely the kingdom didn't send Limis as a joke. Her actual fighting ability aside, in terms of aptitude, I don't think I've ever seen anyone better.

Seemingly content with my reaction, Limis snaps her fingers, but it doesn't make any sound. Garnet, having understood his master's intent, shrinks down and returns to salamander form.

Limis blushes with embarrassment, but I can't even bring myself to make fun of her.

"Why...?"

"...?"

"Why the hell can you do *that*, but you still haven't made contracts with any other spirit types?!"

"Huh?!"

That is seriously strange. An elementalist who can manifest Ifrit is extremely rare! It's weird... It's too weird. It's so weird that I feel like I'm having a terrifying nightmare.

"...I-it's really none of your business!" Limis barks back, her face twitching.

It's true that I am a complete stranger. I don't have connections to anyone in the Friedia House, and I don't have any intentions of meddling in other people's affairs. The point is that we need to win. If we win, then none of this matters, and if we don't, all is lost anyway.

"You're right, it really isn't my business. It isn't, but *damn*... Nothing makes sense in this world!"

That headache that I finally got under control comes back at half force.

Between a mage who can handle Ifrit but use no other magic types and a mage who can use all magic types equally, I would choose the latter. It would be nice if I had that option. It's important to be able to choose your magic type to suit your opponent, and what's more, there is a possibility that even Ifrit in his optimal condition may not be a match for the Demon Lord.

Enduring the persistent throbbing in my head, I regard Limis seriously.

"Limis, I'm not doubting your abilities... You're obviously a prodigy."

"...Huh? What's this sudden change of tune?"

I'd much rather make fun of you, but I don't have a good reason to!!

I lower my head at Limis, who looks uncomfortable.

"Please, for the sake of the world, just make a contract with another spirit and learn to use other elemental spells."

"...What? I can't."

"What do you mean, *you can't*?! Don't fucking toy with me!!"

"Wait a min—"

The sounds of my wailing and Limis's shrieking cut through the air and echo through the night into the Great Forest of the Vale.

§　§　§

Ten days have passed since our plunge into the forest.

Although there was some anxiousness at the beginning, as we're leveling up, things are moving along really smoothly.

Our hero, Naotsugu Toudou, is strong.

I sensed in his first battle that he has talent. As a warrior, as a monster hunter, and as a hero, he is naturally talented. That mercilessness that he showed in the first battle is not the kind of thing that can be learned overnight.

"The overdone sense of justice is a crime."

That is certainly not only due to his blessings from the gods—he must have been that kind of person even before the summoning.

In this ten-day march, his ability has already increased to a level that rivals mid-level mercenaries. If he continues to gain experience at this pace, I have no doubt he will acquire a level of strength befitting a hero.

I guess my only complaint at this point is that the three of them sleep in the carriage at night while I sleep outside alone. Apparently, his dislike of physical contact is limited only to men. Or maybe it's limited to just me, but either way, I decided to just accept it rather than deal with the hassle. It's an issue that will likely resolve itself in time.

Nao's strength far exceeds my expectations, and Limis and Aria aren't too bad, either.

For Aria, there were two major points of concern—her change in swordsmanship schools and her lack of magic—but neither of those has presented any major problems in battle so far. To the untrained eye, her swordsmanship looks excellent, and she should be able to continue fighting without magic for a while.

There is the question of how far she can go without any magic, but that's not for me to decide. She's a sincere, dedicated warrior, and I have confidence that she will come to that decision on her own.

About Limis, I have nothing noteworthy to say for the time being.

Although she may actually be the strongest of the group, since she can use only fire, her role is limited to lighting campfires and the like for now.

She undoubtedly understands the danger of using fire in the forest. During battle, she stands by me, looking a little dejected but dutifully supporting Nao and Aria and refraining from using her magic.

She hasn't really participated in a battle yet, so it's hard to say what her weak points are, but if I had to guess, I would say that her pride as a mage and an aristocrat might be one.

In the first few days, for example, when we ate monster meat, she was the one who showed the most aversion to it, and she also gave no indication that she wanted to practice with the gun. Eventually, she did

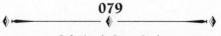

eat the meat (albeit reluctantly) and did use the gun a few times to finish off monsters, but she clearly wasn't happy about any of it.

Leaving it alone might result in more trouble later, but since the issue is rooted in her way of thinking, it's difficult to immediately resolve. Whether it's having a conversation about it or checking her pride more directly, I intend to observe the situation and take action accordingly.

My primary role as the senior member in a party of my juniors has become teaching Nao holy techniques and instructing the party in survival skills. Originally, I had planned to participate in battle, but as Nao and Aria have done well on their own, I've resigned myself to watching from the sidelines and keeping an eye on Limis.

Nao is also making good progress learning holy techniques. As the one chosen by Ahz Gried, his divine protection is strong.

He has already mastered most of the low-rank spells, and omitting offensive holy techniques—since Nao already possesses an abundance of physical attacks—the only thing left is prisms. He has also learned the level-up ritual, which is not a low-level technique, and although his holy energy is still low, it won't be long before he can manage the work of a priest pretty well.

Currently, Nao is level 27, Aria is 25, Limis is 17, and mine has not changed.

Nao's level is first priority, but as Limis has the lowest level at present, I would like her to reach at least level 20 by the time we leave these woods. The plan is to continue leveling up as we have been until Nao reaches level 30, at which point we can move on to the next location.

Lastly—there are no signs that the Demon Lord's assassins are nearby. The Church could be right that they have not yet noticed the summoning of the hero. That's all I have to report.

I finish my report and breathe a sigh. Cardinal Creio speaks to me over the transmission, chuckling softly to himself.

"Heh-heh-heh... You seem to be enjoying yourself over there."

"...I'm not. I'm just...doing my job to the best of my ability."

While it's true that things are going better than I expected, I still don't have peace of mind.

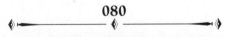

"The overdone sense of justice is a crime."

I don't want him to misunderstand. I frown and look over at the carriage where the group is sleeping.

"If I could quit right now, I would be *running* back to my old job."

"Unfortunately, I don't know of anyone who is more qualified for this than you. Please keep moving forward and contact me if anything comes up."

"…Understood."

I confirm that the transmission has ended and click my tongue.

My attention is drawn to the woods, where I can hear a strange, distant howling.

Our journey to defeat the Demon Lord has only just begun.

Then, on the night of the eleventh day in the woods, the hero suddenly says, "I think I'd like to briefly return to the village."

Nao's current level is 27. He's continuing to evolve at the moment, and by tomorrow morning, he should be level 28.

Our initial goal was to get Nao to level 30 in two weeks, give or take a few days. Basically, we just need to get him to level 30 within the one month period before the Demon Lord's forces become able to sense his presence.

I stare at Nao, caught off guard by this idea that has never come up before.

We sit on opposite sides of the fire. The orange glow of the flames is reflected in his ever-serious eyes.

"I'd like to stay in the woods and level you up until you reach thirty. If we return to the village, we lose all the time it takes to travel there."

"But we have time, don't we?"

"…True, we do. If we stayed just one night in the village, we should still reach our goal."

I look over at Limis and Aria, who are sitting quietly. Maybe they're exhausted. I can heal stamina with holy techniques, but I can't do anything for the mental strain. Limis may also be increasingly stressed by her inability to fight.

We will reach the target level in two or three more days. This isn't the best timing, but I can't neglect their needs…right?

I don't know what made Nao bring it up all of a sudden, but this is his party.

"We'll do whatever the leader thinks best."

"…All right, thanks. And I finally learned all the holy techniques up through the prism, too."

The hero slowly surveys the camp. Today Nao was the one to cast the prism. It isn't as strong as mine, but that will come with practice. I think it's sufficient for any of the monsters that would come out of these woods.

"Well, I can't do it quite like you can, with just a stamp of your foot…"

"I do it in a particular way for efficiency. The original method is to set a boundary with holy water."

The most common method is to pour holy water in a line around the area, and that line becomes the boundary of the prism.

"Right now, your maximum holy energy amount is low. But if you use the techniques every day, that will gradually increase."

Typically, priests will spend a lot of time practicing one technique, and as their holy energy increases, one by one, they learn new techniques. Nao went an entirely different route, so his holy energy is low.

That being said, his primary role is to attack. It shouldn't be a problem if he can use only small amounts of holy energy.

Nao listens attentively to the explanation.

"Once you get comfortable with the spells, you should take the exam at the church. If you pass, they give you a magical tool that aids in the use of spells."

"A magical tool for spells?"

"This thing."

I show him the silver cross and moon earring on my left ear.

The earring is proof of priesthood and that you can use holy techniques above a certain level.

Nao is interested in the earring. "…What do you have to do for this test?" he asks, staring at it.

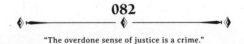

"The overdone sense of justice is a crime."

"You perform the designated holy spells one at a time in front of an examiner. If you can use the spells I taught you, you should be fine."

The exam isn't that difficult, but they do have a requirement for your pool of holy energy. It might be tough for Nao to pass in his current state.

Nao stares for a moment, thinking. Having nothing else to say about it, he tosses a few branches on the fire and changes the topic.

"If we go back, a good plan would be to leave in the morning, rest for the day, spend the night in the village, and head back here the following morning.

"...And I should sell the remains of the monsters we defeated," he adds.

"Near the hunter's tavern, there's a marketplace specifically for this kind of thing," I explain. "Or you can trade directly with the merchants. Typically, the hunters are easier to trade with, but the merchants will pay more."

This reminds me—I've taught them about survival and battle techniques but not about how to act in a village. Aria and Limis are both princesses. They probably don't know much about these things.

All of a sudden, Garnet, who was darting around near the fire, stops and looks up at me. The shimmer of the flames in his dark-red eyes feels like an ill omen, and I avert my gaze.

I have more concerns than I can handle, but presently, things are fine. If we continue at this pace, things should progress well.

The Three Deities and Eight Spirit Kings—the major spirits in this world and the three gods who are its pillars—are smiling down on this hero.

"I'm sorry, Ares, but...could you leave the party?"

And with that, back at the village, I am cut from Naotsugu Toudou's party.

Fuck you, Nao!

On the Path of the Hero and the Organization of the Party

"FUUUUUUCK YOOOOOOOU!"

I wake up in the cheap bed at the inn to the sound of myself shouting.

Then the dim, lonely room comes into view. My whole body is damp with sweat. I get out of bed, my breathing ragged.

I don't think I dreamed last night. Or if I did, the cold sweat covering my body tells me it must have been a bad dream.

"Hey, shut the hell up! You know what time it is?!" comes a boorish, wild voice from the next room. It roars through the wall like it wants to kill me.

This is a nightmare. I feel completely awful—my body is unbelievably heavy, and my head throbs with pain.

In the darkness of the room, I sigh loudly. Outside, rain pours down furiously, and big drops strike against the windowpane.

I press on my temples, glare vengefully into the blank space in front of me, and cast status ailment recovery magic on myself.

My headache and nausea dissipate, but my mood doesn't improve in the slightest.

"It's all right. I'm still calm," I mumble again and again, as if trying to carve the thought into my mind.

After a few minutes, it feels like my head has cooled down, and I decide to take a shower.

Maybe the anger will wash off with the sweat.

"I'm sorry, Ares, but…could you leave the party?"

After a few hours in the carriage, we arrived back at Vale Village, and Nao said he wanted to talk to me about something.

We went back to the same inn. As soon as we arrived, Limis and Aria headed straight for one room, and it was just Nao and me in the other.

I had an uncomfortable feeling about the whole thing. As soon as Nao opened his mouth, I understood why—that was the first time since we met that Nao and I were without Limis and Aria. The first time we were one-on-one. His words took me completely by surprise, and for a moment, I didn't understand what he meant.

I was the priest selected by the Church, after all. Of course, I have the utmost respect for the will of the Holy Warrior, but only under extreme circumstances would the Holy Warrior dismiss the priest chosen by the Church.

Nao's expression was as serious as always, and his jet-black eyes burned with determination.

I hadn't seen it coming. In that moment, I wasn't angry—I was genuinely confused.

"Why?"

"Because you've become unnecessary. Limis can drive the carriage, and now I'm able to use holy techniques."

His voice was calm and unwavering as he answered my stupid question.

I can't comprehend it. He's able to use only the most basic techniques, so how effective can he be in battle with the Demon Lord? The strength of Nao's divine power is undeniable, but he shouldn't assume that he can somehow manage to defeat the Demon Lord based on that alone.

"Thank you for your help, Ares. Our personalities didn't really match, but nevertheless, you did your part well. When we first met, I didn't think you would be willing to teach me your holy techniques."

He said this with such indifference. My head turned awfully cold, and it wasn't the coolness of calm. It was more like my brain had frozen because of how shockingly opposite his reasoning was to mine.

Although I was still struggling to understand the situation, my mouth opened of its own accord.

"It's a matter of course that I would teach you what I know. Nao, my

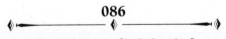

"The overdone sense of justice is a crime."

mission is to support the hero in defeating the Demon Lord. I would do anything to raise our chances of winning."

"I don't like your apathy."

"Being liked by you isn't part of my job."

There was no emotion in his words. I felt like I was talking to a bratty child.

My brain automatically began thinking through the next steps. After fighting so many battles, it was trained to be efficient under pressure.

"Do you really think you can be both a healer and an attacker?"

"I can. I'm the hero."

"That's just arrogant. It's considerably difficult to manage both those functions, and it isn't the hero's role."

Holy power and magical power are in contention with each other. You can't use holy techniques and magical spells at the same time.

As your level gets higher, you become increasingly less able to attack without magic, which means you can't afford to use holy techniques.

The hero curled his lip at my matter-of-fact statement.

"...I can at least do the necessary minimum."

No, it's impossible. At Nao's current state, it's impossible. In the future, he might reach a point where he could handle it, but not now.

Guessing something from my expression, Nao continued to justify himself.

"For the most part, you've hardly used any holy techniques in battle. And I can handle the basic healing techniques just fine."

"No, that won't work. If you're trying to be both attacker and healer, you'll completely exhaust yourself. Your speed in battle and the pace at which you level up will decrease. You'll be giving the demons a weak point to take advantage of."

Nao closed his eyes as if verifying my statement and slowly opened them again. "...I'm prepared for all of that."

Prepared for it. His voice held the same conviction as his words. A steely conviction, determined to insist on his own way.

Hearing that, I became indifferent to all of it.

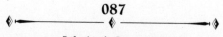

This was not something I could change.

I don't know the details of how he came to that decision. But Nao's personality, his courage and recklessness, everything he had been summoned for, was encapsulated in that statement. His jet-black eyes stared back at me. How or why he'd become so foolhardy, I have no idea. But at that point, I didn't really care.

I may have the right to disagree with the Holy Warrior, but I still have a responsibility to follow his orders. That much is decided by my creed.

The hero's lips bent into a smile, but there was no smile in his eyes.

"This is just between you and me, but originally...I had requested only female party members."

"Is that so?"

"And yet, for some reason, you were the priest. If you were a devout believer, I thought it might work out. But in the end, although you were an excellent priest, you weren't a good fit. The issue isn't your ability, it's just that I prefer women."

What an idiotic reason. Whether or not that kind of requirement is really worthy of consideration when the fate of the world is at stake, that's not my call to make.

"I have two conditions," I said, holding up two fingers. I was calm, but I knew my eyes must look like they do when I face a follower of darkness.

Not that I'll be facing any more of them on this mission. Asshole.

"Conditions...?" he inquired skeptically.

"Yes."

I responded to him in the clearest way I could. This was the minimum responsibility that I could fulfill. "Number one. First thing tomorrow morning, you will find a new priest to join the party."

"...That's—"

He hesitated to respond. This in itself showed that he only had the knowledge equivalent to an amateur mercenary. If he knew more, he'd have been quick to say, "Of course."

"Healers are indispensable to a party. Without a healer, you'll be annihilated."

"The overdone sense of justice is a crime."

Nao looked at me hard, considering it.

"...Ares, you're giving me advice as I throw you out of the party."

Bullshit. Bullshit. This is all bullshit.

My head and my chest are cold as ice. At this rate, it feels like my heart might stop.

But even if it did, I might keep on moving, unnoticing. That's how efficiently my mind and body are operating at this moment.

"Don't misunderstand me," I said without missing a beat. "I'm not doing this out of goodwill. I'm doing it because of my creed." My voice was calm, and my tone was flat, rid of any emotion.

"Your...creed."

"Unfortunately, I happen to be a devout follower of the God of Order, Ahz Gried."

I got out of my chair and went to pick up my battle mace, a deadly weapon used to crush demon skulls, which rested in the corner of the room.

The colorless eyes of Holy Warrior Naotsugu Toudou followed me around the room.

Nao wasn't wearing any armor, and he didn't have his shield or sword. I could have killed him in one blow had I wanted to. But to do such a thing would be meaningless.

Mace in hand, I shouldered my bag and headed for the door. He apologized as I passed in front of him.

"I really am sorry about this. And about that money the kingdom provided us with, let's split it up by four."

A quarter of that should be quite a bit of money.

I turned just enough to look back at him over my shoulder. "I don't need it. Consider it an investment in your victory. You'll need to buy equipment for the next priest anyway."

"Oh... All right then."

My head was so light that it felt like my spirit might fly out of my body at any moment. I suppose you could call it a feeling of emptiness.

Just before I walked out the door, Nao said one last thing.

"...Wait, Ares. You...still haven't told me the second condition."

Why does he care about that?

I turned to face him, grinning, and said the one thing that didn't need to be said.

"You have to defeat the Demon Lord."

I have no memory of where I went from there.

I ended up in a room at some cheap inn. When I got there, I placed a transmission to the operator and requested to have a message sent to Creio explaining that I had been driven out of the hero's party. Before the transmission was even cut, I tore off the magical tool, flung it at the table, and collapsed onto the bed.

Sleep was like mud, catching hold of my ankles and dragging me down toward death, but when I woke up, I was calm.

Yes—right now, I am calm. Now I see things clearly.

That feeling I had when I was talking to Nao—I mean, Toudou—wasn't calmness or resignation. It was an unbearable anger and despair at the collapse of all good sense.

It's probably a good thing I'd been calm when we talked. Had I understood my feelings then as I understand them now, I might have smashed his skull in.

The hot water washes over my body. Although the mirror is cloudy with steam and water droplets obstruct my vision, I can still make out my warped expression in the reflection. The look in my eyes has gone from bad to villainous. I see the eyes of a man who would thoughtlessly commit murder if you caught him on the wrong day.

The resentment I feel doesn't go away. There's no way it can.

I did my best, so I don't see my performance as the issue. What did he say it was? Ah, yes—he said that he had planned for an *all-female party*.

At this moment, as I recognize that the resentment won't completely abate, I also understand that it will lessen with time. Why? Because it doesn't serve any purpose. It wouldn't be *efficient* to dwell on this.

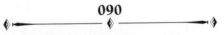

"The overdone sense of justice is a crime."

Within the Church, the command of the Holy Warrior outranks that of Cardinal Creio. If Toudou tells me to leave, all I can do is leave. Even if that means abandoning my mission.

"That bastard… It's been a long time since someone made such a fool out of me."

There are no gods. Even if there were, I wouldn't care. It's been more than a decade since I realized that.

So why not eat monsters and carry a blade? Why not kill and smoke and drink and sleep with women? Honestly, who gives a shit about the creed?

I followed Amen Creio's orders because it was business and I have pride. To be brutally honest, I wouldn't have cared if my orders were to ignore the hero's command and refuse to leave the party. Were it necessary, I could even carry out orders to kill the hero. I wouldn't hesitate.

I turn off the shower. Taking a deep breath to calm my mind, I massage the bridge of my nose.

The hot water has washed away my emotions, and all that's left now is a specialized priest, a member of Out Crusade, the Church for the Eradication of Heresy.

I need to get in contact with Creio directly. What I provided yesterday can't be called a report.

I move to the dining hall and order myself a drink and a light meal.

While I was in the hero's party, I refrained from alcohol. When I considered the huge impact it could have on my clarity of thought, I didn't feel much like drinking.

When the drink is served, I bring the glass to my lips. I gulp down the amber liquid and feel the burn of it.

I down the whole glass in one go and order another, then take the transmission earring out of my pocket and put it on my ear.

The moment I activate it, a transmission comes in. It's from the Church.

"This is Ares."

"‼"

Although I can't see her, I can sense a change in her usual composure.

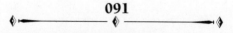

"Ah… You are all right, then?"

"Not really, but I'm getting along, I guess. Sorry for the abrupt message last night."

"Your physical condition appears to have recovered. I'm relieved that there are no problems," she says in her typical level tone, though she's a bit more talkative than usual. Perhaps she had been concerned.

Another drink arrives, and I take a sip. Fuel for thought.

No problems? There are lots of problems. Even though I'm out of the party, the problems are there just the same.

"I will connect you to the cardinal."

I sense the change on the line when the transmission is transferred. The dining hall around me is noisy, but it doesn't distract me.

"Is that you, Ares? It seems you're all right." Although my being cut from the party is a significant turn of events, Creio's voice doesn't sound out of the ordinary.

"I am, but the situation isn't looking good. I think you heard from the operator, but I was dismissed from the hero's party."

"Yes, I heard. How inconvenient for you… Heh-heh-heh, this is unprecedented."

He chuckles, but I can't make out his feelings from the laughter. I wait for him to continue.

He poses a question. "Ares, do you think Naotsugu Toudou can defeat the Demon Lord in his current state?"

"You're joking, right? He hasn't even reached level thirty. His level is absolutely too low to take on demons."

The monsters that the party defeated in these last ten days were all beast types. Demons are not beasts. They are devils with intelligence equal to or greater than humans. That is an entirely different level of combat.

We're still in the opening act of this race against time.

"Currently, there's no priest in the hero's party. I told them not to go out leveling up until they've found one, but it's unlikely they'll be able to find someone right away. You'll need to dispatch a replacement as quickly as possible."

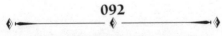

"The overdone sense of justice is a crime."

A mage using offensive magic could be replaced by another offensive class, and there are countless swordmasters in the kingdoms. But priests are scarce, and their absence in a party can be fatal. Toudou's own holy techniques still aren't up to the task.

Creio's response is not what I expect.

"Ares, your mission is not over yet."

"...Huh?" I respond, stupefied. Though there's no hint of jest in his voice, what he says can only be a joke.

"This is a trial. There will be no replacement. The Church has no intention of dispatching anyone else."

"...Is this some kind of a joke? I was discharged from the party on Toudou's orders."

"To put it another way, you've only been discharged from the party. Do you remember your orders?"

I can't understand the point he's trying to make. The number of priests is small, and among mercenaries, they're even rarer. The longer the party goes without one, the more it will be like searching for a grain of sand in the desert. They probably won't find one at Tuller's, and given that the majority of priests outside of mercenaries are employed by the Church, the Church itself would need to act as an intermediary.

Can Toudou defeat the Demon Lord in his current state without a priest? Not a chance. That's like sending him off to his own death.

As I desperately try to work out Creio's meaning, he repeats himself.

"Ares, recite your orders."

"...To provide support for the Holy Warrior Naotsugu Toudou and defeat the Demon Lord Kranos."

Simple and clear-cut. As I recite them, a bad feeling stabs through me.

Defeat the Demon Lord. Defeat Demon Lord Kranos. Support Naotsugu Toudou to defeat the Demon Lord Kranos.

"Precisely, Ares. To use your vernacular, defeating the Demon Lord is a matter of...business."

The last word echoes in my mind. Any devout priest would be shocked to hear a cardinal employ it in that way.

"At the request of the Ruxe Kingdom, the Church summoned the Holy Warrior Naotsugu Toudou and furthermore invested in you, Ares Crown, as the priest most suitable for the mission to defeat the Demon Lord. Think of this as a transaction. The circumstances in Ruxe Kingdom are of no real concern to us."

If the hero heard how matter-of-factly Creio said this, I wonder how outraged he would be.

He's right, though—the Church is not tied to any particular kingdom. There is a division of the Church in Ruxe with a multitude of believers, but that is only a minor concern to the Church headquarters.

Because Ruxe is just one kingdom.

"We are the disciples of God. The point is that you need to win in the end, Ares. Don't concern yourself with minor losses. The Church has already done all it can, and thus, if problems arise, they are trials put upon the warrior by God."

"……"

"Of course, you should not simply observe the defeats of the party in silence. Please do intercede at appropriate times. Not to worry, Ares—if the destruction of mankind is imminent, another country will probably want to summon a hero."

"……"

Creio notices my silence and poses the same question again.

"Ares, you understand the meaning of your orders, don't you?"

The chilling question kills the heat from the alcohol. I already understood.

My orders were "to provide support for the Holy Warrior Naotsugu Toudou and defeat the Demon Lord Kranos."

I bite my lip. "So what you're telling me is…my part in this isn't over yet," I say, my voice stifled.

The sound of dry applause echoes over the transmission. I gulp down the entire contents of my glass. I won't be able to do this without a drink.

"That's exactly what I'm saying, Ares. Your comprehension is the

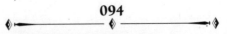

"The overdone sense of justice is a crime."

best in all the Church. I almost wish I could take the head of one of these senile old men at headquarters and trade it for yours."

He's obviously messing with me. He said himself that this wasn't over yet.

"Creio, you bastard... You knew I'd be cut from the party, didn't you?"

"Naotsugu Toudou wanted a female priest. That's all I knew. There is a reason for everything. There is a reason why Toudou asked for female party members, why the schools of magic and swordsmanship submitted novice warriors, and why we chose you, Ares."

This isn't efficient at all. It's completely counterproductive. I don't need all the false pretenses of this useless conversation. Just give me the hard facts.

"This is your job. If you hadn't been thrown out, the situation might have been simpler. But this is business, and we are overruling the hero's order. You know well that the only thing that matters in business is results, don't you, Ares?"

I know in this moment that I misjudged the difficulty of my mission. The glass in my hand cracks under the strain of my grip.

"Support Naotsugu Toudou and defeat the Demon Lord. We can't afford to invest in another priest because of the foolish self-interest of the hero. Ares, this is what you're good at. It's your field of expertise."

"...Damn... I'm shorthanded here."

Creio responds promptly, as if he knew what I would say. "We are investing in you, Ares. May you be a faithful priest. And may God bless you."

"Go to hell!"

The transmission cuts out, and the noise of the dining hall comes back.

I understand—this is a trial. The greatest obstacle I have encountered so far. I need to carry this business through to the end, no matter what it takes.

I catch a glimpse of ferocity in my reflection in the window.

"The overdone sense of justice is a crime."

I have to support Toudou from outside the party and make sure he defeats the Demon Lord.

I mobilize immediately. I leave the inn and head for the church.

The first thing I need to do is follow Toudou's trail and figure out where he's headed.

If I'm going to support him from the shadows, I'll need to stay one step ahead.

Fortunately, I can guess what he'll do next. Toudou doesn't really have common knowledge of our world, and he may not have liked me, but he still listened to my advice. It's likely he'll heed my final warnings.

He's looking for a priest. Where will he go to do that?

If a mercenary party was looking for a priest, they might go to the tavern. But Toudou is the Holy Warrior, and for him, there's an easier option.

On my way, I stop at a clothing shop and purchase a hooded brown coat to hide myself. I also find a shop selling masks. There's a mask with crescent-shaped cutouts for the eyes and mouth. It would look highly suspicious, but right after being expelled from the party, showing my face to Toudou would be a bad idea. I hesitate a minute and then purchase it and put it away in my pocket. It's always best to be prepared.

The church is located in a crowded area on the main street of the village.

Its walls are painted white, and on top of the steeple, there is a monument—a cross resembling a scale, the symbol of the God of Order.

The church is a home to priests and a lifeline to ordinary townspeople. There is at least one in every town and village, and a high-level priest is dispatched by the Church headquarters to watch over each house of God.

The role of that priest is to heal the wounded and sick, to assist with level ups, to certify new priests, to remove curses, and to proselytize. In some places, the role of the resident priest includes assisting other priests who want to increase their faith.

The time for morning prayer has long passed, but the church is crowded with people.

I check that Toudou and the others aren't nearby. Then I call out to the sister sweeping in front of the church.

"Sister, there's something I'd like to ask you."

"Yes... Ah!" The young sister turns to me and jumps with a start. Our eyes meet, and she looks like she's about to cry.

I suppose the look in my eyes might be a bit frightening... I point to the earring on my left ear.

"I was born with these eyes, sister. I'm not gonna bite you."

"Ah... P-pardon me!" She hurries to bow her head after seeing the evidence that I am also of the Church. In front of the church, there are many watchful eyes, which makes things a little troublesome for me.

"If you could please lift your head. There's something I'd like to ask you."

"Um, all right...," she says, slowly lifting her head. "What is it?" She examines me with interest, but I ignore it.

"I'm looking for someone. I heard he was headed for the church. Have you seen a man with unusually dark hair and eyes?"

At that point, the sister's expression changes. She fumbles with the handle of the broom and looks downward.

"Ah... Yes... I saw him just an hour ago. It seems he came here to speak with the father."

"An hour ago, huh? I just missed him..."

Well, maybe it's my good luck that I did. It's not like I wanted to come in direct contact with him.

"Did he say anything to you?"

"Um... Well, yes. He invited me to join his party," she says, blushing a little. The wind blows her wavy brown hair over her face.

Toudou isn't a bad-looking guy, so a girl like her, probably an amateur priest, might take a liking to him and get swept up in it.

"Did you accept?"

"N-no, no! I couldn't! I'm still very new to the faith..."

The lowest-level earring hangs from her ear. This sister probably can't even perform the level-up ritual yet.

But she should have completed her studies of the basic healing spells

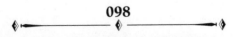

"The overdone sense of justice is a crime."

and buffs. And her face isn't half-bad, either. If this sister joined the party, it would be relatively stable. On the other hand, the burden of leveling up would increase, and there is still the fundamental risk that when female priests lose their virginity, they are no longer able to perform miracles...

I debate whether I should advise her to join the party—

"I see. Is the father here?"

"Ah, yes... He's inside."

—and decide to leave it up to fate. I would feel badly for the girl, but I'm prepared to sacrifice a lot of lambs.

If she did lose her ability to perform miracles, it might at least make Toudou reflect on the situation he has put himself in.

I head inside. The church warden is kneeling silently in the chapel.

He has blond hair and wears jet-black priest's robes. He appears to be five or six years older than me. I catch a glimpse of his cleric's earring. As I come closer, the man quietly gets to his feet.

"Do you require something of this church?" he asks without turning. His voice carries through the chapel.

"I'm looking for someone."

"...So I've been told." He turns around.

His features are exposed in the sunlight pouring through the stained glass windows. His eyes are the same golden color as his hair, and there's a deep scar on his cheek. Perhaps he used to be a mercenary.

He examines me with a narrowed gaze. He finds the proof of my priesthood on my left ear, then notices the ring on my left ring finger.

"My name is Ares Crown."

"It's an honor to meet you, Sir Ares. I've heard your story. My name is Helios Endell."

Creio was clear that the Church has no plans to intercede...but does this mean that he has taken steps to help find another priest?

Helios smiles softly. Behind his gentle voice, I sense something suspicious.

This may be my personal bias, but I have the impression that many of the high-level priests in the priesthood are good-for-nothings—more so among priests than among mercenaries.

099

"Sir Toudou came to us not long ago."

"Looking for a priest?"

"Yes...though I politely refused." Helios shakes his head as if it amuses him. His golden eyes look almost transparent, and he gives an impression of unpredictability.

His refusal doesn't surprise me. While it is one of the Church's roles to mediate on behalf of priests, there are certain standards that must be met. If the party composition, ability level, and character of the members do not meet those standards, a priest's services will not be offered.

If a man comes along with two women looking for a female priest for his party, no matter how he asks, that is unlikely to be granted. These kinds of ill-conceived groups turn up on occasion, and I doubt they have ever been passed.

Though I wonder how much this guy knows about Toudou. Does he know that he's the Holy Warrior?

"I see. How did he respond?"

"He was quite indignant...but he intends to return tomorrow to take the priest's exam."

I see... Once Toudou realized he wouldn't be able to get a priest for his party, he decided to take the exam. It's a logical step.

Anyway, I'm glad for the extra time it gives me.

Even if I'm going to be supporting them from outside the party, there isn't much I can do for the moment. At the very least, I need to think of a way to track their movements from a distance. I'd rather die than wear that shady mask around.

"...Is everything all right?" asks Helios, looking at me curiously.

The fact that he's a cleric means he must be at least level 50. If I could get this man to join Toudou's party, I might feel reassured, but that probably isn't an option.

"...Do you think Toudou will pass?"

"...Hmmm."

Helios puts a hand to his chin and contemplates for a moment.

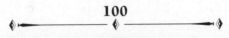

"The overdone sense of justice is a crime."

"…Well, it may be difficult for him. Although he can perform the techniques, his holy energy is low."

"I'm of the same opinion."

While Toudou does know the minimum necessary holy techniques for the exam, his total amount of holy energy is also a factor. His current level is certainly not enough to withstand consecutive casting.

Helios gives a superficial smile at my reply. "My goodness…what an honor."

"If he's taking the exam tomorrow, it's unlikely he'll leave the village today, don't you think?"

"Yes, indeed… That gives you a little time."

"…Thanks for the help."

The priest's exam can be taken at essentially any time. I'm grateful for the extra day.

Helios continues, smile unchanged, after my short thank-you. "It was an order from the Church authorities to delay it by a day… I have also received a message for you, Ares."

"A message? …What is it?"

"It is, 'Someone has been dispatched.'"

I recall my conversation with Creio that morning. Was he being serious or not?

"Understood. Did they tell you the meeting place?"

"The inn from this morning, I was told."

"What kind of person am I looking for?"

"You'll know when you see them, they said."

I'll know… I want to voice my criticisms of that vague statement, but Helios couldn't do anything about it anyway.

"Got it. Thanks for your help."

"No trouble at all… May God bless you, Ares."

"I may ask for your help again in the future."

Helios opens his arms wide in an exaggerated gesture. "Ask anything of me that you require, honored crusader. As a servant of God, it is my great privilege to be of help to you."

*   *   *

I consider what the hero may have decided to do after Helios refused him. Did he return to the inn? Is he replenishing supplies? Or is he selling the raw materials from monster hunting?

I must be putting more thought into what the hero is doing than anyone else in the world at this moment. How is it that I'm the one who has to think about the guy who just sent me packing, like I'm a young girl with a crush?

I set Toudou aside temporarily and head back to the inn to meet Creio's contact.

I check at the front desk to see if anyone has come asking for me, and I'm told someone is waiting for me in the dining hall.

If they can dispatch someone this quickly, I wish they'd send a priest for the hero's party.

It's in between mealtimes, so there is hardly anyone in the dining hall. I peek inside, searching for this person I'm supposed to know on sight.

There's a group of four and a group of three that have been drinking since morning, as well as a pair in the middle of a heated argument, spit flying between them. The person I'm looking for should be alone, so it isn't any of them.

There is a girl with indigo-blue hair sitting by herself. She wears a light-gray dress-like garment, but as she lacks a priest's earring, it can't be her, either. From her delicate figure, I can guess she isn't a mercenary, so what on earth is she doing at a cheap inn like this?

I survey the dining hall for a few more seconds, and finally, my eyes are drawn to a priest sitting alone.

No—it isn't a priest.

He's a bald middle-aged man, body as muscled as Thomas's, the mercenary who destroyed the glacial plant. His dark eyes and tanned skin give off an aura of toughness, and the hardness of his face suits his large, masculine build. You can feel the ferocity in his gaze. The silver cross of a low-level priest hangs from his left ear, but next to it is a narrow gold rectangle. This shows that he isn't just an ordinary priest but a monk, who trains his physical body for his faith in God.

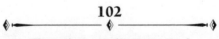

A monk, huh… Not bad at all. I nod to myself. This man seems like he will be a reliable resource.

He's strong, and he's got a tough exterior that mercenaries will take seriously. Toudou and the others would respect him as well. You heed the advice of a man who looks like this.

On the other hand, monks tend to have less advanced holy techniques than the average priest. But since I'm well versed in them, as long as he can use the fundamentals, it shouldn't be any problem.

I wondered who they would send, but to lend us a monk… I guess Creio wasn't lying when he said he was "investing" in me.

"You'll know when you see them." Yeah, he was sure right about that.

Just to be certain, I look around the room once more, but there isn't anyone else it could be. I wait for the right moment and then walk up next to the man.

He notices my appearance at his side and looks at me. His eyes are clear and gray. The pale scars on his face are evidence of his experience in battle. He eyes go first to my earring and then to the black ring on my left hand.

"My name is Ares Crown. Sorry to be so abrupt, but you're the person who's waiting for me, right?"

"…You're a crusader…?" He has a deep, husky voice that matches his exterior. He casts his vision upward again and glances at my face. "Dallas Blank—monk."

"I see, you're Dallas. I know it's sudden, but can we get right to the point?"

It seems that luck is finally on my side in this mission.

As I go to sit down across from Dallas, he frowns.

"…Sorry, but I think you've got the wrong guy. I'm not waiting for anyone."

"…What?"

My eyes widen. I wasn't expecting this response. How could he be the wrong guy? He's the only priest here.

As I stand there confused, a voice calls out from behind me. A voice very different from Dallas's.

"Mr. Ares, I'm the one you're meeting."

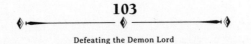

"...Huh?"

I don't want to turn around, but at the same time, I know I have to. I finally give in, and who's standing in front of me but the blue-haired girl I saw when I entered.

She looks nothing like a mercenary, her body so delicate that she might snap in half if you squeezed her too tightly. She appears to be a year or two younger than me. She wears a dress and has perfectly straight dark-blue hair that matches her eyes.

But most importantly, she doesn't wear a priest's earring or a ring that shows her marriage to God.

She seems self-assured and determined, and she looks at me with an emotionless gaze.

I reflexively look back and forth between Dallas and the girl.

What is happening here?

As I look imploringly at Dallas, he sighs.

"Looks like you found who you were looking for."

"Really...?"

"Really," confirms the girl, pushing her hair off her face in a terse gesture.

..."*You'll know when you see them*"?

I turn back to the girl. She faces me with a cold, almost disdainful look. Okay, I get it. She's strong-willed. Now...what do I do with her?

"...Mind if I send a message and come right back?"

"Go ahead."

My optimism was short-lived indeed. The difference between the two of them is...extreme.

The hero is looking for a priest. Why did they send this girl?

I decide to make my objections to Creio.

I head to a corner of the dining hall and start the transmission. Normally it connects right away, but this time, it takes a few seconds.

The person on the line isn't the usual operator, and she seems flustered.

I can hear a lot of noise in the background—has something happened at headquarters?

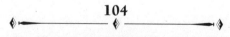

"The overdone sense of justice is a crime."

"Ah… Uh… H-hello! You've reached the Church headquarters!"

"This is Ares. Connect me to Cardinal Creio."

"Yes, certainly, Mr. Ares! I'm, um, I'm the n-new operator. My name is S-Stephenne Veronide. Pleased to make your a-acquaintance!"

Who is this girl, and what the hell happened to the regular operator?

She's frustrating me already, but that's the nature of new employees. Right now, I just need to get in contact with Creio.

"Stephenne, I'm Ares Crown. Nice to meet you. Can you connect me to Creio, please?"

"Y-yes, of course! C-certainly!"

"Just connect me to Creio."

"Ah, y-yes! Understood!"

So unproductive…

I wait for about a minute, listening to the flurry of noise in the background, and finally, Creio comes on the line. Why did it take so long just to link the transmission?

"Ares, has something happened again? This is…not a good time."

"It's about the person you sent. This chick isn't even a priest."

No matter how you look at it, I've been cheated here. She isn't a priest, isn't strongly built, and the only thing I can think to use her for is as a lure to catch monsters.

After first seeing the monk, it's even more aggravating. But, well, that was my mistake…

Creio's response surprises me.

"Hmm? She isn't wearing the earring? Well, she must have just taken it off. She is absolutely a priest, as you well know."

Must have taken it off? The rule is supposed to be that priests remove the earring only when sleeping and bathing…

I glance at the girl sitting stick straight in her chair. Well, even if she is a priest—

"Didn't you decide not to invest in a female priest? And by the way, I don't know this chick."

"…Hmm? That's strange… She said that she's met you…"

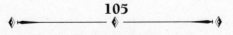

She's as attractive as Limis and Aria—the type that stands out in a crowd—and she has the look of a nobleman's daughter. I'm confident I would remember if I'd met her before. Not to mention that I hardly ever visit the Church headquarters.

My head swells with questions, but I ignore all of them except one.

"Can she...*endure* this kind of journey?"

It won't be easy to support the mission to defeat the Demon Lord. You can expect a physical and mental burden.

Creio responded, sounding irritated.

"Ask her that yourself. Ares, you come to me with too many complaints. I am, first and foremost, a cardinal..."

"Well, I'm not just complaining for the sake of complaining."

"Hmm..."

Creio pauses for a moment. "I am placing my trust in you. If you requested a different person, it's not like I wouldn't consider it," he says thoughtfully.

"...Who've you got?"

"A sister named Stephenne Veronide. She possesses both high magical power and high holy energy, and she's the youngest person we've ever had as an operator... She's something of a prodigy. She's still inexperienced, but you could help with that, couldn't you?"

That's the name of that hyper sister from before. *Fuck.*

I get the feeling our personalities wouldn't mesh well. To the point that I don't even want to interact with her as an operator.

"...She seems like she'd be more of a burden than a help. Or maybe I should say I just don't think we'd get along."

"There's one more person available. I didn't mention it because I'm fairly certain you'll refuse, but..."

There's someone worse than Stephenne, huh? What the hell is going on with the Church...?

I wait silently for Creio to continue.

"He's also a member of Out Crusade. His nickname is Matsudo Eater, the Exterminator—"

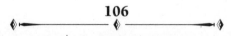

"FUCK!" I shout involuntarily, then hurriedly glance around me. Thankfully, no one is paying me any mind.

I know this guy. I know his real name, and I know his face. I've even been on a mission with him.

Gregorio Legins—the crusader who goes by the nickname Matsudo Eater and is so obsessed with eradication techniques that he's no longer capable of other holy rites. He's thrown all his faith into offense and is absurdly strong. He's the only priest I know with a stronger offense than me.

"He's not the kind of man to work under someone. And I've always thought he should be banished from Out Crusade."

"Is that so?"

That's the kind of guy who'll get you killed. He's been out of his mind since the day he got the nickname Matsudo Eater.

I sigh loudly enough that it can be heard on the other end of the transmission and look over at the girl Creio sent. Compared to the other two candidates, she may actually be preferable.

"Well, try to make do with who we dispatched. If more personnel open up, I'll send them your way, but we're shorthanded right now."

"…Got it."

There's no point pestering him if they have no one else to offer. Anyway, I initially didn't think they'd send anyone at all.

Just before I cut the transmission, I ask something that's been on my mind.

"By the way, about the change in personnel—what happened to the usual operator?"

"…Hmm?"

The operator before Stephenne was far better suited for the job. If it takes Stephenne a full minute to connect a transmission under normal circumstances, how would she even manage in an emergency?

"What happened to her?" he repeats flatly, as if it was a foolish question. "*I sent her to you, didn't I?*"

Sent…her…?

"…No way."

Well, that explains it. The blue-haired girl is the operator.

107

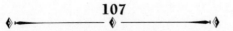

We've been associating for so long through the transmissions, and I thought that her voice sounded familiar... How could I be so stupid?!

"...But why did you send me someone from the *office*?"

Without answering my question, Creio cuts the transmission. *Piece of shit.*

I stare at the wall for a moment, dumbfounded. I quietly cast a status ailment recovery spell to calm the churning pain in my stomach.

I can't help but feel like lately I've been using holy techniques for all the wrong purposes.

Taking no notice of me, the operator sits with her eyes closed, her posture so perfect she almost looks like a doll. She appears totally sedate, unbothered by the noise of the dining hall. It matches the impression I had of her over the transmissions.

People have aptitudes for different things. To be calm, unemotional, and able to exchange only the minimum conversation might be excellent qualities for an operator, but I doubt they'll be useful on this mission.

Besides, she comes from administrative work. Although the fact that she worked in the office at the Church headquarters means she did well, I don't know how long she can last in the field. Intelligence is useless if you can't keep your body moving.

Before sitting down at her table, I observe her intently. It's unlikely she volunteered for this thankless job. She was probably forced to come here under Creio's orders. From her perspective, this mission probably feels like a demotion. When I think about it that way, I feel a sense of kinship with her as a comrade who has also had to accept his superior's unreasonable demands.

Of course, just because I say I feel a kinship with her doesn't mean I'll be soft on her...

Facing her, I clear my throat, and her eyes slowly open. She looks at me, motionless.

"I'm Ares Crown."

"I know."

She responds flatly, barely smiling. Regrettably, she seems to like me even less than Limis and Aria. I wonder if we'll be able to work well together.

"The overdone sense of justice is a crime."

"…Right. I suppose you would know. We've been associated for a few years through the transmissions. Thanks for your assistance there, by the way. But this is the first time we've met in person, isn't it?"

She frowns so faintly that you'd miss it if you weren't paying attention.

"…It isn't. We've met…once before."

"…Have we?"

I have no memory of it. I openly study her face.

She has soft features and long eyelashes. Her eyes and shoulder-length hair are such a deep blue that they look almost black. She has an average-size chest, but the daintiness of the rest of her body makes it look larger. She's tall for a girl and probably a little younger than me. She is a level of beautiful one doesn't see often in an area like this.

She fidgets a little under my scrutiny. I don't recognize her, and I don't even know her name.

I stare for ten more seconds, searching for her face in my memory before raising both hands in surrender.

"I give up. Sorry, I can't seem to remember."

"Is that so…?" she mumbles, her voice sounding the slightest bit disappointed. I may not have noticed these things if this had been our first conversation.

I wonder what she'll think if she discovers I don't even know her name. I vaguely remember her introducing herself over the first transmission, but never having had occasion to use her name, I can't recall it.

I think for a moment, then sit up straight and extend my right hand.

"Let's introduce ourselves again. I'm Ares Crown, and as you know, I was a crusader."

She looks reproachfully at my outstretched hand. Perhaps she expresses more emotion than I thought.

She stares for a minute and then finally puts out her hand. Perhaps from the office work, it's white, like it has hardly seen the sun.

"Operator at the Magical Coordination Department in the Church of Ahz Gried…Amelia Nohman. As you know, I was your operator. By order of my superiors, as of today, I am to support you on your mission."

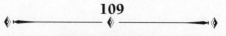

"Thanks for coming, Amelia. Look forward to working with you," I say, pretending not to notice that she seems upset.

Incidentally, hearing her name didn't ring any bells. It could be that whenever we met I didn't have the mental space to remember it.

The Magical Coordination Department—the department that brings together the divine miracles of the Church and the miracles of magic. It's a specialized division within the Church, but rather than priests, those who work there are called *holy casters*.

Magical power and holy power. Those who can use those two conflicting energies are the elite of the elite within the Church.

I reexamine my unexpected companion.

I hadn't realized that the transmission operator is under the jurisdiction of the Magical Coordination Department. It could be beneficial to have a holy caster.

I start to envision a path forward. I may have also figured out the reason Amelia was dispatched.

"What level are you?"

"I'm level fifty-five."

That's considerably high for someone who worked in an office. I involuntarily gasp in amazement.

Generally, priests over level 50 can use the more powerful holy techniques, and from that point, they are called *high priests*.

Not bad. Not bad *at all*. Even without any attack power, with her level of holy power, she could stand in for me.

"Where is your priest's earring?"

"I have it."

She produces a white cloth bag and shows me a priest's earring and a white ring.

The earring isn't the one that low-level priests wear. It's a silver cross and a smaller gold cross combined—a cleric's earring, like the one Helios wore. Helios was cooperative but not the kind of person who would be useful to me. This girl is different. I can't help but have high expectations for her.

I stiffen my expression and ask, "Why weren't you wearing it?"

"The overdone sense of justice is a crime."

"…I wanted to see if you would know it was me."

"That so? Well…sorry I didn't."

"No, no… It doesn't matter."

She took off her earring for *that* pointless reason? I want to ask her what she thinks a rule is, but anyway, since I failed her test, I can't really complain.

Her response was indifferent, like it didn't bother her at all. She pushes her hair just out of the way and affixes the earring to her left ear in a practiced motion.

The glimpse of the delicate nape of her neck and the faint sensuality of the deft, nonchalant way she moves her hair catches me off guard, and I involuntarily take a deep breath.

This will work. This one will work. We have no reason to sacrifice one of the novice sisters.

This girl, already familiar with our situation, will be the perfect replacement priest for Toudou's party—and the perfect spy.

The higher-ups have done pretty well. Sending someone like this after saying they had no plans to send another priest… They must have meant they have no *public* plans, and in reality, they sent her.

I really thought they might have intended to leave the hero without a priest, but it was just a bluff… Damn, that guy is cruel!

You could say that someone like her—purely in battle for support with no combat ability—provides comparatively less stability to the party, but on the other hand, with her taking my place, I'm able to move about freely. I can become a special support force, eliminating obstacles to the party.

I drum my hands on the table in celebration of my good fortune, and Amelia looks at me strangely.

Finally, luck has turned in my favor. Even without tracking every one of Toudou's movements, I should still be able to function as backup.

We're talking about a guy who thoughtlessly accepted a mission to defeat a dragon. That's a path that leads straight to death. With her here, I'll be able to provide the proper support.

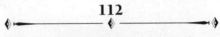

I attempt to contain my joy, biting my tongue and trying to keep a straight face, but I slip into a smile.

I clear my throat exaggeratedly and face Amelia.

"Amelia, I've considered our situation and thought of a system."

"A system?" she says, opening her eyes wide and inclining her head slightly.

I'd like her to go to Toudou's inn at once, because I have no idea what his next move will be.

"Yes. The Church has said that they'll send more people as they become available, but at present, we can't count on that. There's no knowing when Toudou might be killed. We need to be practical."

She hasn't understood my meaning yet, so I explain my instructions bluntly.

"Amelia, I want you to join Toudou's party as their priest and aid the party while also surveying their movements."

"What? No, I'd rather not."

And then, I died.

§   §   §

I doubt Naotsugu Toudou will ever forget the feeling of complete power he received in that moment.

His body was filled to the brim with energy, and his ability of perception was sharpened. This was the divine protection of the Three Deities and Eight Spirit Kings. In this world, we call this *divine blessing*, and it is so tremendous that even Toudou, coming from a world where it doesn't exist, was able to experience its power.

The whirling wind, the rushing water, the shining sunlight—all the world bestowed its strength on Toudou.

His body had become lighter than ever before, and when he picked up his sword to test it, it was light as a feather. He felt the immense gratification that comes with this kind of power.

Gods, spirits, swords, magic, a demon lord, and finally…a hero.

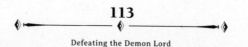

113

This group of words that exists only in fiction in modern-day Japan became terrifically real and completely changed Naotsugu Toudou's world.

However, the thing that impacted him most was just one word, spoken to him by a summoner in the Ruxe Kingdom royal castle; it was the first word he heard upon arriving in this world.

The summoner wore a white robe with a pattern in gold thread and held a pale crystal in her right hand. She was a saint in the Church of Ahz Gried and an incredibly beautiful girl.

Welcome, great hero, she said. *We have called you here to save our world. Hero.*

An ordinary person might have been overwhelmed by it, but the moment Toudou heard that word, he accepted this world completely.

Heroism. Honor. Justice.

These are things that Toudou wanted desperately but could not acquire in Japan. He wanted them so badly that he was willing to travel to another world and battle a monster called the Demon Lord.

What's going on here? Why won't they cooperate with me?

Toudou is in his room at the inn, feeling irritated, and puts his feet up on a chair.

Only fools show anger on their face.

He knows this from experience, and though he's able to remain calm on the surface, he is not yet capable of concealing the anger that seeps out through his eyes.

He has known from the beginning that the journey to defeat the Demon Lord won't be an easy one. This is an enemy so powerful that the kingdom had given up trying to defeat him and summoned a hero from another world to help. But at the same time, Toudou is confident he can accomplish this task.

However, the journey that had been going favorably has now ground to a halt because of a trivial problem.

"I'm the *hero*. Why don't they cooperate with me?"

Toudou bites his lip and glares at the ceiling, struggling to understand it. If the root of this problem were an inadequacy in his own abili-

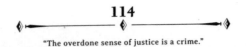

ties, he would accept the failure. But the problem is that the people here will not cooperate with him, and that is what has him so frustrated.

The hero was summoned to this world to defeat Kranos, the Demon Lord who despises humanity and has destroyed many kingdoms. The hero is humanity's last ray of hope. These people should do everything in their power to assist him.

Toudou visited the village church to search for a priest, and he couldn't understand the father's refusal.

I'm the hero. Toudou had exerted so much effort to stop himself from blurting out those three words that instantly began bubbling up inside him.

Because Limis and Aria were with him and he'd left his sword at the inn, he somehow managed to swallow the disgrace. But if he'd been alone and his sword had been handy, he might have drawn it.

The father's pointed stare, almost looking down on him, is burned into his mind. He can't let it go.

Seeing Toudou's serious expression, Aria interjects.

"...I have heard that the majority of the priests who are demon exterminators are men. We may not be able to avoid it."

"...Yeah, I understand the reasoning. I understand it, but...I just can't accept it..."

He takes a deep breath and tries to suppress the smoldering impatience in his mind.

Toudou is a virtuous man. Or at the very least, he aims to be.

Although he has obtained power, Toudou has no intention of deviating from his mission or wasting his time on other things. His goal is to defeat the Demon Lord as quickly as possible, and consequently, he opted to follow Ares's reasonable suggestions. As Ares was born and raised in this world, he has more insight and experience.

Ares Crown, the silver-haired, green-eyed priest. His gaze was sharp as a knife, and he was coolheaded and ruthless in both word and deed.

Though he didn't look at all like the kind of person who would pray to a god, he did fulfill his role as a priest. They had conflicting personalities, but Ares was a capable man, and Toudou took his advice to heart.

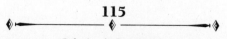

Before dismissing Ares from the party, Toudou discussed it with Aria and Limis.

While he was sorry to expel a party member who'd committed no errors, to Toudou, who had requested all female party members from the start, Ares was always the one he'd eventually have to let go. He had no regrets about it.

This news is met with silence until Limis suddenly speaks.

"…Of course, it might have been better to wait until we'd found a replacement to dismiss Ares—"

"Limis!!" interrupts Aria. Flustered by this rebuke, Limis turns to Toudou to apologize.

"Oh… I-I'm sorry, Nao… I hadn't m-meant to criticize your decision—"

"…No, that's all right," he responds, shaking his head at her apology. "I was…acting out of my own convenience."

Limis's observation was reasonable. However, if they'd decided to wait for a replacement, there was no telling how long it would take. They'd have felt worse about ridding themselves of Ares after receiving his help in battle for a long time.

So Toudou had decided to learn the basic techniques and knowledge of the holy arts from Ares before ejecting him from the party.

"This timing minimizes the damage to both Ares and me," Toudou states firmly. "I know it's somewhat inconvenient for everyone, but there's nothing to be done about that."

"…Yes," agrees Limis with a small nod.

"The only thing I can do is what I promised Ares—defeat the Demon Lord as soon as possible."

Toudou didn't like Ares, but he didn't dislike him so much that he wanted him dead, which is why he contacted the kingdom regarding Ares's dismissal and informed them that it wasn't due to any wrongdoing on his part.

"That's—that's right… Let's get to the Demon Lord as soon as possible and take him by surprise!"

"Yes… That's what we'll do." He smiles weakly at Limis's enthusiasm.

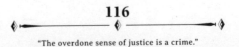

"The overdone sense of justice is a crime."

Seeing that Toudou has settled down somewhat, Aria shares her thoughts.

"However, to continue the journey without a priest would be too dangerous. At a certain point, it will be impossible."

"Yes... I understand that."

While Toudou has learned basic holy techniques, he doesn't intend to ignore this warning.

In the end, without Ares, the number of party members simply decreases. Healing after battle would be no problem, but Toudou understands how difficult it is to cast healing spells in the heat of combat.

"...I sent a letter to my father just in case, but priests aren't under our jurisdiction...," says Limis.

"...I will send one as well, but a priest may be...hard to come by," admits Aria.

The Church of Ahz Gried is an organization independent of the kingdoms, and as such, Ruxe Kingdom has no authority there.

Even if the Church were to send a replacement priest, that would take time.

"There's no time...," Toudou mumbles, a distressed look on his face.

It would have been ideal if the village church could have provided a replacement, but they refused.

The one-month limit until the hero's presence is perceived by the demons draws nearer every day.

"It is somewhat reckless, but it may be better to set the priest aside for the moment and prioritize leveling up," suggests Aria.

"...Right, that's true."

Ares's words swim through his thoughts: *If you can get to level 30, you should be able to escape a demon.*

Toudou's level has increased a fair amount, but Aria—and especially Limis—are still too low.

Toudou closes his eyes and thinks. *Lacking a party member. Levels are too low. Time is wasting.*

A heavy atmosphere, like that of a funeral, hangs in the air. Finally, Toudou slowly opens his eyes.

"Our next moves are clear. If I pass the exam tomorrow, I'll be able to do the work of a priest in battle. Then, rather than adding a priest to the party, we can add someone to the front line, and I can switch to the role of healer as needed."

It will be more work for Toudou, and he'll level up more slowly, but that is the only available course of action at present.

"Finding an attacker shouldn't be hard, right? And besides, parties aren't limited to just four members, so if we find a priest later, then we'll just continue with five."

"...For a front-line warrior, we could certainly bring in someone from my house, or we could request the services of a mercenary at the tavern," suggests Aria.

There's no time to just sit around indoors. Toudou shakes his head as if to wake himself up and gets to his feet. It seems that being confined to the inn is affecting his mood.

"Just in case, let's bring as much restorative medicine with us as possible. My holy techniques might not compare to those of a priest."

"A priest... Ares was level three, right? It seems impossible that at level twenty-seven, you wouldn't be a match for him..."

"...Apparently, the effectiveness of holy techniques is dependent on faith, and mine is still low. In any case, it's best to be prepared."

Of course, this doesn't mean that Toudou lacks confidence in his holy techniques. If he did, he probably wouldn't have dismissed Ares. Actually, he practiced the skills he'd picked up in front of Ares, who'd given them passing marks.

But at the same time, one has to take into consideration that priests deal with life and death.

He has confidence, he has talent, and he has determination. However, Toudou is painfully aware that those things alone aren't always enough.

That's precisely why he came to this world as the hero.

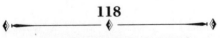

"The overdone sense of justice is a crime."

On the Difficulties Surrounding the Holy Warrior and How They Were Handled

I can feel the muscles in my face stiffen. My mind flooded with thoughts, I ask her again.

"...You'd rather not?"

"Yes. I'd rather not." The look she's wearing almost dares me to ask why. It pisses me off.

She doesn't want to do it, huh? All right, I get that... If I were in her place, I might not want to, either.

But this isn't the time or place to be demanding what we want! We're dealing with the fate of humankind here.

"Why?"

She answers my question with a question. "...Ares, have you thought about why Miss Limis and Miss Aria were chosen to be members of the hero's party?"

Naturally, I've thought about it. Not a day has passed that I haven't thought about it.

Why would the leaders of Ruxe assign their own daughters to join the Holy Warrior? Even if those daughters had natural talent, there should have been a great number of other women who were suitable candidates.

It's clearly an impractical choice, and a major power like the Kingdom of Ruxe is bound to have noticed.

When I contacted Creio about exchanging party members and he refused due to *unexplained circumstances*, I started forming my own theory.

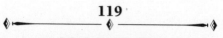

So this girl is smart—an elite indeed. She seems to have put some thought into this.

"I *have*."

"Tell me, then."

"...It's only a theory."

"So tell me, then."

I give in completely to her cold stare. Surely, she's already realized the reason. She doesn't need me to say it.

I glance at our surroundings and check that no one is observing us. Or maybe I'm just stalling. Amelia's gaze has me nailed to my chair.

If I hadn't realized it just now, I would have figured it out eventually, of course.

I prepare myself and face Amelia. Licking my dry lips, I answer in a word.

"Blood."

"..."

"They want the Holy Warrior's blood. For one thing, there is the possibility that the divine blessing can be passed down genetically. On top of that, being the relative of a hero would grant you an extremely high level of influence. The Ruxe royal family themselves assimilated the blood of a Holy Warrior into their family several generations ago."

Which also explains why the holy sword Ex and other strong weapons and armor had been stored in the Ruxe royal family's vault.

Amelia remains silent. I don't notice any change in her composure.

Love and lust are the easiest ways to control a man, but presently, there are no princesses in the Ruxe royal family. It follows, then, that the two leading noble families in Ruxe, both extremely loyal to the royal family, would be chosen instead. Toudou is essentially the property of the Ruxe Kingdom, summoned here at great risk. He is their asset not only for defeating the Demon Lord but for various matters of national interest thereafter.

Thinking back on it, I should have figured this out much earlier. Why would Limis, born into a family of aristocrats and raised like a

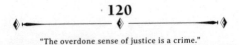

princess, and Aria, raised in a strict, militaristic family, allow a man they just met to sleep in the same room with them?

Naturally, this isn't something they'd have wanted to discuss at our first meeting, but it is possible they received orders of this nature from their parents.

Then Cardinal Creio (that bastard), most definitely aware of these intentions, pushes me into this matchmaking party under the pretext that the sole objective is to defeat the Demon Lord.

Amelia listens to my explanation in silence but eventually heaves an exasperated sigh. "Ares, you are an awful person."

"All right, I concede."

"You think in terms of efficiency. Of practicality. And you assume that, because you think that way, so does everyone around you."

"I said I concede, didn't I?"

I underestimated her. At this point, I won't be able to convince her with any religious dogma or logical explanations.

"I'll ask you again—"

She leans halfway over the table and continues to upbraid me.

Her gaze is almost sharp enough to cut through me. She speaks quietly with her expression unchanged, but I know she's angry.

"I am a *bride of God*. What did you just order me to do?"

"You've got some work to do on that personality of yours."

"Not as much as you do. Ares Crown, do you actually intend to sacrifice me to the Holy Warrior?"

Sacrifice—that's well put. She's gotten to the heart of it.

I'm kind of backed into a corner now… How am I supposed to justify that?

It's not that I *planned* to sacrifice her, but I was aware that things could work out that way. There were no indications of anything happening within the party while I was a part of it, but it's safe to assume things are moving in a certain direction.

"At level fifty-five, even if he makes a move on you, you can refuse him. Toudou is still only level twenty-seven."

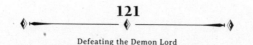

"But that's just *for now*, isn't it? How long do you think feeble little me can keep a Holy Warrior like him at bay?"

I don't know how this girl can call herself feeble, but I keep my mouth shut.

She's won this argument. It's only natural for her to oppose something that puts her in danger. Besides the fact that fornication is labeled a vice by the Church, she can't be forced into that. I think of proposing to her that if she explains to Toudou that losing her virginity means losing her ability to perform holy techniques, he would probably leave her alone...but at this stage in the conversation, it feels pointless. She obviously has a clear understanding of the situation.

Can I really ask her to violate the creed?

Understanding that I have completely conceded, she gives a satisfied sniff and sits back in her chair.

"So you understand why I don't want to do it?"

"...Okay, you win this one."

"By the way...," she continues, clearing her throat. "My orders from Creio were only to function as your support."

"Meaning that...joining Toudou's party was never on the table."

"Yes, that is how I understood it."

I can't understand that. Can't understand it at all.

Creio dispatches a sister but then eliminates the option of sending her to Toudou's party. It might not be the most virtuous thing to throw her into, but she would undeniably be useful there. Why didn't he tell me that wasn't on the table in the first place?

Is it that he values a priest from the Church more than the Holy Warrior? No, he's not that kind of guy... He's more ruthless than me and would stop at nothing to accomplish his goals. My own overly practical way of operating is due considerably to his influence. Taking into account his character, there's no way he's actually thinking of this as a trial from God.

Dammit, all this speculation is starting to muddle my brain... I don't know what to think anymore.

I pause my musings for a moment—the only thing I can do right

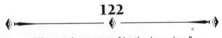

"The overdone sense of justice is a crime."

now is follow the instructions I've been given. Even if there are constraints I don't understand, I still need to keep moving forward.

"Let's get down to business. Amelia, what can you do?"

If she can't join the hero's party, she is considerably less useful to me. As for her holy magic skill, I'm more advanced than her, so that isn't much of an asset. Even so, I'll take all the help I can get right now. I'd rather have her than not.

"Let's see…," she says, her expression overly serious. "Cleaning, laundry, cooking—"

"Wha—?!"

"—I don't do any of that."

…Is this chick taunting me? I can't tell if she doesn't realize she's pissing me off or if she's doing it deliberately. I'd like to spit some kind of retort back at her, but she continues without a trace of anger. I'm not sure if she's deliberately being dense or not. She's got a lot of nerve… Nerves of steel, maybe?

"I've completed my studies of holy magic up through roughly mid level. The only thing I can really do in battle is swing a mace. I've never studied any combat techniques…"

"Okay, that's all fine." I didn't have any plans to have her fighting monsters. If I were looking for front-line support, I would probably hire mercenaries.

"You scared of monsters?"

"Do I look like I am?" She raises her eyebrows slightly and responds as if trying to get a reaction out of me.

…This girl has some serious nerve. Was this always her persona? …No, I suppose I wouldn't have noticed it before, since our exchanges were only the minimal. Anyway, I guess I'd rather have a person with a little nerve than with none at all.

"If anything, I'm more afraid of people than monsters," she says jokingly, the littlest smile on her face.

"What a coincidence, so am I! You can't join the hero's party, but you can trail them, right?"

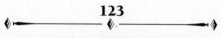

"If anything, I'm more afraid of people than monsters."

...Will I really be okay with this chick...?

I feel the hopes I had for her start to deflate. All these highs and lows are driving me crazy.

She's even more of a mess than I thought... Or, rather, she's a pile of junk. I wonder if hitting her on the head would fix her. Almost as if she'd read my thoughts, at that moment, Amelia bows deeply. "I am whole-heartedly at your service, Ares."

"If you feel like you can't handle this, Stephenne can take your place. So let me know."

I can feel the mental image I had of Amelia as the operator crumbling to the ground. Dealing with Stephenne might be less trouble than Amelia and all her sarcasm. I made the suggestion in relative seriousness, but Amelia promptly strikes it down.

"No, I'm sufficiently motivated... After all, I volunteered for this."

"...Volunteered...?"

She wasn't demoted; she willingly accepted this mission... *What the hell...?*

At that moment, I know I've acquired a partner who could be an unbearable nuisance.

If her practical abilities are outstanding, she could be all right...but if not, I'm gonna be miserable.

My eyes stare off into space, and hers wander here and there around the room.

Will we... Will we really be okay...? Her actions at least show that she's highly motivated, don't they?! Remember, she's an elite. This girl is an elite.

I clench my fists under the table, desperately repeating these things to myself. But it doesn't make me feel any better at all.

I wake up feeling lousy. I haven't woken up feeling good since the day I was put on this mission.

"Good morning."

"…Yeah, whatever," I grumble, not having heard the words for some time. I slowly sit up in bed.

Standing by my side is Amelia, dressed in a deep-blue priest's robe different from the one she wore the day before, looking all ready to go. It's still early morning, but I don't see any sign of sleepiness in her face.

Her attitude yesterday seems like a joke compared to the sight of her now. Like it was some kind of trick.

Either she's faking it now, or yesterday was some kind of deviation from her normal self. I want to believe it's the latter, but thinking back on it…it's definitely the former.

"This is a shitty joke."

I take a breath and survey the room. The double room we rented is much more spacious than the single room I was staying in before.

Amelia was supposed to have slept in the bed next to mine, but it's already made up so perfectly that it looks like she didn't use it at all.

This new companion is pretty brave—or rather than brave, you might say she's foolish. Camping while you're on the road might be a different story, but under normal circumstances, it's not a good idea to sleep in the same room with someone the first day you meet them.

Naturally, I tried to rent two single rooms, but we ended up in a double because Amelia made a fuss that it would save money. It is cheaper, but it's not like we're hard up for cash. Her insistence showed the difference between her own personality and the quiet reservation of most sisters.

Amelia hands me my robe, carefully folded, as if it's the natural thing to do.

I can hear the wind rattling the window. Yesterday, we had bad weather, and today doesn't appear any better.

I quickly get dressed and then turn to Amelia. Having filled her in on the hero's current situation the day before, now it's time to get to work.

"We'll wait for Toudou to show up at the church. His next move could change based on the outcome of the exam."

"Understood."

"One way or another, we need to be aware of Toudou's movements.

125

My face is already compromised, so you'll have to be the one in contact with him."

Amelia nods, her face void, with no sign of confidence or lack thereof. "...If he asks me to join the party, I can refuse, correct?"

"Yes, of course you can. You can also accept, if you are so inclined."

"I will *refuse*."

She narrows her eyes at my half-hearted joke. I turn away from her stare melodramatically.

The holy arts are divine miracles. Magic produces similar results, but the theory behind the two is different. Consequently, the Church wanted to differentiate the holy arts from magic—and thus uses the terms *holy arts* or *holy techniques*.

The word *magic* is more commonly understood, so it's easy to group the two together, but there are priests who cringe when they hear the holy arts referred to as *magic*. Anyway, I digress.

Helios and Toudou stand facing each other in front of the altar. Somewhere in the background, an anxious Limis and steadfast Aria are waiting, and Amelia stands behind Helios under the pretense of being his assistant.

I observe this from my seat among the dozens of attendees, hidden in the crowd, a hood pulled far over my head.

I can see shadows under Toudou's eyes, perhaps from fatigue, but there is no apprehension in his face.

"We will now conduct your ability certification, Naotsugu Toudou," says Helios.

"...Yes, sir."

"God will grant you miracles corresponding to your faith. I will now state the miracles you are to perform in the order in which you should perform them. If the miracles you are granted are deemed satisfactory, you will pass."

"...Understood."

"The overdone sense of justice is a crime."

Toudou listens to the ceremonial explanation with complete seriousness.

Then the exam begins.

Toudou is a reasonably intelligent guy. His chanting, his technique, and his gestures are all just as I taught him—flawless. He's even able to perform the level-up ritual, which isn't a requirement for the rudimentary qualification exam.

Toudou performs the blessings, healings, and buffs with no mistakes and no hesitation. Watching his focused, serious expression and fluid movements, I catch Limis breathing a sigh of relief.

After Toudou finishes all the basic techniques, Helios suddenly stops speaking and claps his hands.

"You are a magnificent talent, Sir Toudou," he praises with superficial politeness. "How much time has passed since you learned your holy techniques?"

"About…ten days, I think."

"Although it is the lowest level, to be granted miracles in just ten days shows that Ahz Gried is surely, *undoubtedly* smiling down upon you. I have no issues with the efficacy of your miracles thus far."

"…Well, then—"

Toudou's stiff expression relaxes a little. Almost as if he was waiting for this, Helios continues.

"Now, perform all the holy techniques you have just performed once more."

"…What do you mean?"

"Let us complete your certification as a class-five priest," says a smiling Helios, ignoring Toudou's question. What a wicked man.

Bewildered, Toudou starts performing the holy techniques again in the same order.

The change comes over him immediately. When he performs the class-five healing technique for the second time, his face contorts.

Although he has completed the task, he gives no indication of starting the next one.

"What's wrong, Nao?" asks Limis.

"...It's nothing." He grimaces as he begins the next technique.

But the exam is already over.

Toudou casts a physical strength buff and an agility buff, and at that point, the discomfort he was surely experiencing begins to show. Even from a distance, I can see that something's wrong.

His posture changes. His legs begin shaking. There's a visible tremble in the hand making the cross, and his voice begins losing its composure.

Helios is stone-faced. His placid smile seems plastered on.

Meanwhile, Toudou must finally have become aware of his condition. His eyes turn toward his trembling fingertips in blank amazement.

Holy energy is the evidence of a person's faith, of their divine protection. All people have holy energy at birth and receive the protection of the God of Order. It's different from magic in that it's impossible for a human to have a holy energy level of zero.

The divine protection that a person unconsciously receives at birth is actually very powerful, and under normal circumstances, it should never run out.

So what does it take to use it all up?

"My body is...so heavy...," Toudou murmurs, his lip quivering. He looks like his knees might give out at any moment, and Aria rushes to hold him up.

Here's your answer. *This* is what happens when your holy energy runs dry, when you lose the divine protection you've always enjoyed.

At this moment, the weight of Toudou's frame must have felt unbearable. Without holy energy, there is an abnormal decline in your physical ability. This is something that every priest has experienced at least once.

The cost of asking for a miracle from God is great. As your level increases, your divine protection becomes stronger as well, so when your holy energy runs out, you feel an even greater disparity.

With a little rest, your holy energy will be restored, and your divine protection will return to you. But running out of holy energy during battle must be avoided at all costs.

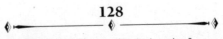

"The overdone sense of justice is a crime."

"Sir Toudou," says Helios in a gentle voice. "This is the cost of holy techniques. This is the evidence that you have exhausted your holy energy."

"My holy energy is...gone?"

"Yes..."

Amelia steps out from behind Toudou and touches his head to conduct a *holy energy transfer*.

The palm of Amelia's hand glitters an amber color, and moments later, Toudou manages to stagger to his feet. He opens and closes his hands, making sure that his power has returned to him.

"Although your holy techniques are powerful and demonstrate the strength of your divine blessing from the God of Order," continues Helios, "this alone is not sufficient."

"Not sufficient...?" Toudou's face twitches as he looks at Helios's fixed smile.

"The number of times that you were able to perform the miracles was exceptionally low. To become a class-five priest—that is to say, to be recognized by the Church as a priest—you must be able to perform all the basic techniques twice consecutively, at the very least."

"Hold on... You're saying he failed the examination?" asks Aria, glaring at Helios. She may not have been expecting him to fail.

Helios, unbothered in the least by Aria's cutting glare, starts a slow clap.

"Correct. Well, there were no problems with the results of the miracles themselves. They were brilliantly done. I award him the Prize for Fighting Spirit."

Sure enough, at the blatant ridicule by this outsider, Limis lashes out furiously at Helios. "What the heck?! Are you mocking him?!"

"No, not at all, my dear mage. It is undoubtedly a great achievement to have learned the miracles of the Church in only ten days."

What Helios says is true. The speed at which Toudou learned is excellent, his divine blessing is strong, and his natural ability is outstanding.

What he lacks simply comes down to time and effort. Those techniques are usually learned little by little over time.

"The overdone sense of justice is a crime."

"So…there's no way…I can pass today…?" murmurs Toudou dejectedly, almost imploringly.

"Indeed. Please accept my sincerest apologies, *great hero*. A human life can be saved or lost by virtue of the holy arts, and the exhaustion of holy energy can endanger the life of the priest himself. It is impossible for me to compromise on this point," says Helios, adding a logical explanation after the ridicule.

It's unlikely that Toudou will insist now that Helios has brought human life into the conversation. His own sense of righteousness is both his strength and his weakness here.

Limis's face reddens, but she says nothing and trembles in anger.

Helios reaches out to touch Toudou's shoulder, as if to console him. Toudou reflexively takes a step away. Helios withdraws his hand and continues, still smiling, as if it never happened.

"…Sir Toudou, do not lose heart. What you lack can be gained with time. If you practice your techniques in repetition and increase your holy energy, you should be able to pass the exam very soon."

"Time is…running out… We don't have time to just…stand still."

His voice is frail, but I can sense that his will is absolute. A touch of doubt appears on his face.

So then, why did he kick me out of the party? It's bizarre. It's truly bizarre. He's a principled person with a sense of duty, and although he's impulsive, he isn't stupid. Our relationship wasn't so bad, and there weren't any signs that he intended to get rid of me. And that's why I insisted on prioritizing leveling up.

Is he just the type of person who discards a party member solely because of gender?

I strain my eyes to examine Toudou's profile but discern nothing from it.

Suddenly, Toudou looks behind Helios to Amelia. He takes a step toward her.

"H-hey… You there—will you join my party?"

"…Me?"

It won't work. It won't work. It didn't work even when it came as an order from her superior.

But I desperately want her to agree to it.

Even at this abrupt scouting, Amelia's expression doesn't waver. She looks at him, straight-faced as always. It's not the kind of expression that gives a favorable impression, but Toudou doesn't seem to mind.

"Yes," he continues earnestly. "Due to some unavoidable circumstances, my party is without a priest. If you would be willing to join—"

Say yes, Amelia! I'll report it to Creio! Go save the hero!

For the first time ever, Toudou and I want the same thing.

Amelia tilts her head slightly and just barely moves her lips to answer.

"No."

A one-word rejection. Toudou, Aria, Limis, and even Helios are taken aback by the shortness of the reply.

Who cares if it's a lie—for God's sake, give them a reason!

"There were no shortcomings in the techniques themselves… He certainly possesses a powerful divine blessing," says Helios, putting a hand to his chin.

Toudou has left the church. Helios speaks of him as if truly impressed.

"If he focuses on his offensive strength…it may be within his reach to become a *holy knight*."

Holy knights are specialized warrior monks of which there are only a very small number in the world. I give Helios a meaningful look and take a deep breath.

"He can use magic, too."

"Oh dear, what a hero *indeed*…"

Holy energy and magical energy are oppositional forces, and to develop both simultaneously is very difficult.

I've said it before, but in terms of potential, there probably isn't anyone superior to Naotsugu Toudou.

"The overdone sense of justice is a crime."

But that isn't what I came here to talk about. There is something I wanted to confirm.

"How did you find out about the hero? The presence of the Holy Warrior is supposed to be secret."

"Who can hold people's tongues? The circumstances of the war are unfavorable, and furthermore…the movements of the saints who perform the summoning are easily tracked."

"…Tsk."

He disregards my glare and answers me readily. A shrewd man.

It can't be helped that he found out about the hero. I may as well make use of it.

"Any demons sighted in this area recently?"

"No. For the time being, we are at peace."

We're at peace for now, but the Demon Lord is cunning. As time passes, the traces of the summoning will most definitely be discovered.

Just for the sake of it, I ask Helios a question.

"Helios, can you fight demons?"

He laughs softly. "I can handle the lower-level ones."

Helios pulls his lips into a wide grin. In his eyes, I catch glimpses of a craving for violence. That first impression of him has solidified into a certainty. As I thought, this man is no ordinary priest.

"…Were you an exorcist?"

"…I have retired, and now I am just myself. But I could defend against a demon if the situation called for it."

Defend, huh…? That works. If a demon appears, I need to consider above all how I'll get Toudou out of harm's way.

"If you happen to sense the presence of any demons, could you report it to me?"

"I certainly will. What will you do now, Ares?"

I look to the exit through which the hero recently departed.

"It's a lot of work, but I intend to put all my efforts into this."

§　§　§

133

Amelia is outstanding.

She's high level, she has guts—not to mention her looks. But above all, her most valuable characteristic is that she's a holy caster.

She's an operator and a mage, and she's even able to send transmissions to distant locations without a tool.

It appears that magical tools used to send transmissions were created based on the transmission technique itself, and the unique magic Amelia uses doesn't require a tool for herself or for the recipient.

I had been puzzling over a secure means of conveying information, so to me, this was a turn of good fortune.

Just as I leave the church, I get a transmission from Amelia. She's been following Toudou and investigating his comings and goings.

"Ares, I have information on Toudou's party."

"You do? Nicely done." I already have a general idea of their next move, but I wait to hear her report.

"They intend to go to the tavern in search of a new party member and then return to the forest to continue leveling up."

As I expected.

This must have been Aria's suggestion. They are most likely looking for someone for the front line. The easier it is for them to defeat monsters, the less they'll need to heal themselves. At the very least, it's more sensible than just the three of them going out to level up. But there's one problem with this plan.

To begin with, it will be fairly difficult to introduce a new party member while still concealing that Toudou is the hero.

It's been two days since I was dismissed from the group. I think Toudou is probably realizing all the problems that are coming up as a result.

I look at the sky. The wind is strong, and there is a heavy gray cloud cover as far as the eye can see. It may rain again tonight. Not that I believe in these kinds of superstitions, but it's almost like an ill omen of what's in store for Toudou.

"It seems like the time has come for Toudou's fate to be tested…"

"Fate…?"

There are several taverns in the village, but if they're looking for someone really strong, they'll end up at the tavern where I recruited the party to defeat the glacial plant. That tavern also isn't far from their inn.

I head in that direction at a leisurely pace.

The road is crowded with hunters and merchants. People with food stalls, people buying and selling monster parts, people shilling charms of questionable effectiveness, and people who'll sing your praises if you cast buffs on them for cheap.

Toudou—

How many of the people here do you think will accept your black-and-white morality?

The sword Ex becomes more or less powerful depending on the strength of the wielder's willpower. So when you grasped the harsh reality of this world, when you realized that things don't always go as you want them to, did your sword lose some of its strength?

It's not all smooth sailing, even for champions. Or perhaps I should say, one becomes worthy of being called a champion only after experiencing suffering and overcoming hardship.

The first owner of that sword also faced countless hardships. And he overcame them.

The trials you've faced since we went our separate ways are only the prologue.

When I arrive at the tavern, it's in total chaos.

Red and black fill my field of vision, and the floor is covered in a pool of blood. A man whose face is deathly pale hunches over a table, and another who has lost an arm writhes around on the floor. The man bent over the table convulses intermittently, and his eyes roll back in his head. Groans of pain and angry cries echo throughout the room.

The place is filled with the wounded.

Some without legs. Some bleeding from their feet. Warriors lying on the ground with their steel armor ripped open. The wounds take a variety of shapes—but all were clearly made from slash attacks.

135

Defeating the Demon Lord

There are priests kneeling in front of the injured, hurrying to heal as many as they can. But the priests in this village don't have the abilities to recover lost limbs, and if they attempt to heal every injured person here, they'll exhaust their holy energy.

There is terror and despair in the wails of the wounded. I check around the room for Toudou and the others, just in case, but they aren't here.

"*Pant, pant, pant*... Ugh... The blood... Ugh..."

"...So that's how it went," I mumble to myself.

Toudou certainly is causing a lot of trouble. This is the guy we're stuck with as the hero?

...On the other hand, I suppose this particular issue isn't such a big problem. Toudou's role is to defeat the Demon Lord, and mine is to support him.

I walk through the pool of blood and lean down next to the white-faced man bent over the table.

The lower half of his arm is gone. I examine the wound. It's been severed in one clean strike, but I don't get the impression this was done intentionally.

Not much time has passed since it was lopped off. I was right to come directly here.

I quickly survey the room, and it appears no one was killed. For all this, Toudou may as well have just killed them and taken their life force to level up... but I suppose if he went that far, he couldn't really be called a hero anymore, could he?

I didn't hear even a single person call out the name of the man responsible for this terrible spectacle, but I'm convinced.

You owe me one, Naotsugu Toudou.

I throw off my hood. As I breathe in, the metallic smell of blood fills my nose. Then I pray.

The tavern fills with light, and the cries of misery throughout the room suddenly cease.

This is the class-one holy technique *full area heal*.

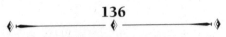

"The overdone sense of justice is a crime."

My prayer invokes a miracle, and all wounds are healed. Limbs that had been severed are regrown, and all scars vanish.

The eyes of all the mercenaries gather on the source of the light—me.

"Can anyone tell me what happened here?"

The man who'd lost an arm, now restored, expresses his gratitude. He weakly embraces me, his face soaked with tears.

What I want right now isn't gratitude.

His words are interrupted by sobs, but I manage to gather some information from him.

He explains that a black-haired man accompanied by two women came through about ten minutes ago looking for another companion to add to his party.

He asked for a woman around level 30 who could fight on the front line. This unfamiliar party comes in looking for a mercenary, and not only are they looking for a woman (which is hard to find in the first place) but have additional conditions to boot.

Mercenaries are unusually sensitive to risk. Highly advanced warriors will deeply understand the importance of a priest in a party.

The mercenaries have no obligation to him, he has no authority over them, he offers no money, and there is no priest in his contingent. There's no reason anyone would want to join a party like that.

Toudou, not understanding a mercenary's good sense, probably thought they would be able to pick up anyone looking for work.

When he was laughed at, Toudou's face turned red, but he seems to have resisted reacting angrily at that point.

And that's where the problem came in. One of the mercenaries, teasing the ignorant newcomer, grabbed Toudou by the shoulder. In an instant, Toudou had cut the man's arm clean off. The other swords for hire tried to stop the violence but were unsuccessful.

At this point in his explanation, the man's tone changes from angry to fearful, and his voice gets shaky.

"That son of a bitch… He just drew his sword without any warning. If I ever see that bastard again, I'll kill him."

137

Defeating the Demon Lord

Meanwhile, listening to him, I feel relieved.

No one died, and those who sustained serious injuries were mercenaries. Had he attacked ordinary citizens, it would have been tough to keep it quiet. It doesn't take long for word to spread in a small village like this one.

I take a breath and say to the poor guy in front of me, "So what you're saying is, you lost."

"…What?"

I can't allow this to damage the hero's reputation. I need these guys to keep quiet about it.

But I'm not concerned. I'm sure they'll be reasonable.

The man's eyes widen with surprise as I press him.

"You taunted him, grabbed his shoulder, and he cut off your arm. That's what happened, right?"

"Uh… No, no—"

"You were careless, and you lost to an amateur. You let him cut off your arm. And on top of that—"

I look around at our surroundings.

A broad-shouldered man who looks like a swordmaster is wrapped in bandages, and a thin man, looking up at me, rubs a leg that has just regrown.

The blame here is entirely on Toudou. These guys were just messing around, like they would normally, with no intention of causing him harm. But the point here isn't who's at fault.

I need Toudou to defeat the Demon Lord, and I need these guys to hold their tongues. Right now, they're an obstacle to be dealt with.

"—even though you had him totally surrounded, you still ended up like this? Are the mercenaries of this village really so pathetic?"

Dumbstruck by the unexpected criticism from the priest who just saved them, the men exchange confused glances.

"…Huh? Wh-what are you—?"

"It's pretty shameful that you'd be done in by a level-twenty-seven swordmaster."

The mercenaries here are probably higher level than Toudou. But the outcome was what it was.

"The overdone sense of justice is a crime."

No one in this place could have stopped him. He isn't just a level-27 warrior—he's a level-27 *hero*.

The men look astounded. "Did you say…level twenty-seven? W-wait—how do you even know that…?"

"Nothing happened here."

"…Huh?"

I ignore the dumbfounded man before me, narrowing my eyes and looking around the room.

"There was a scuffle, but hey, these things happen all the time. A newcomer caused a little trouble, and you veterans let it go. There were a few injuries, which the church sent a priest to attend to."

I pat the shoulders of the man in front of me.

In these situations, it can be useful to have an intimidating face. Your opponent will willingly concede without much convincing.

"It's simple, right?"

"Uh… Y-yeah…," says the man before me, nodding slightly. His face has turned pale. Perhaps he understands that this isn't something he should challenge.

The others wear similar expressions, and all nod in agreement.

I pull my hood back over my head and cast a glance about, meeting their eyes.

"You had some bad luck today. Might want to head back to the inn early and get some rest."

"…Yeah…"

"Remember—nothing out of the ordinary happened here. You didn't see or hear anything. Don't cross me. I won't go easy on you like that guy did."

"…Yeah… G-got it…," someone says hoarsely.

If I push them this far, they'll have put the whole thing behind them by tomorrow. I throw the door open and look back over my shoulder one last time.

I always take care to settle my affairs and destroy any evidence.

They say word gets around quickly, but these guys are smart—they know that *dead men tell no tales*. They won't go looking for trouble.

As I close the door, I can hear a person behind me gulp and say, "Is that guy...actually a priest...?"

Mind your own business.

Outside the tavern, I find a familiar figure peeking in through the window. A petite girl holding a staff with a large gemstone—not someone I would easily forget. I walk up to her and grab her arm.

"Hey, what—what are you doing?!" she demands.

"...What are *you* doing?"

"...Th-that's...not important!"

I drag Limis by the arm and move away from the window before the guys inside notice us.

Why the hell would she be snooping around outside? And what would she do if they found her? One of the companions of the guy who'd just gone in there lopping off limbs...and what's more, a dainty little girl. That undoubtedly would not have gone well.

I walk far enough that the tavern is no longer in view, and Limis shakes her arm to escape my grip.

"...Let—me—go!"

"Fine."

"?!"

When I release her, she teeters backward and falls to the ground with a cry of surprise.

I notice that Limis looks tired, and her skin is pale. It gives me an idea of what might be going on in her head.

"Urgh... Wh-what's up with you? Why are you even here?!"

"I healed all the wounded. No one died."

"O-oh...really?" Limis lets out a sigh of relief.

At this rate, Toudou is going to end up proclaiming to the entire world that he's the hero. We can control the information spread about him to an extent, but if he doesn't exercise some common sense, there won't be anything we can do to help him.

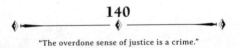

"The overdone sense of justice is a crime."

"I did you all a favor. They told me what Toudou did. If I hadn't just happened by the tavern, people might have died."

"R-right…"

Limis looks down as if to hide her feelings at my emphasis on the word *died*.

It occurs to me that it would be a pain if Toudou and Aria witnessed this scene, so I get straight to the point.

"Limis, I just want to know—why'd you come back to the tavern? Did Toudou tell you to?"

"Wha…? N-no—"

"Never mind."

Regardless of whose idea it was, it was a bad one. But what's done is done. Limis starts to stutter a reply, but I cut her off.

"Just tell Toudou to make sure this kind of thing doesn't happen again. This time, I was able to cure the injured and prevent any casualties, but those mercenaries will be holding a grudge. These things make the Holy Warrior lose face."

"…B-but…but it's not like Nao did it on purpose—," she blurts out in his defense, then shoots me a cold look.

Not on purpose? He butchered a bunch of mercenaries, but not on purpose?

Anyway, it doesn't really matter whether he did it intentionally or not. In the end, he's still a wild, dangerous person. I have to wonder why the summoning chose him.

Then again, there have been other heroes in the past who had similar issues. If he can defeat the Demon Lord, all will be forgiven.

"I have only two things to say: First, don't let it happen again. Second, if it does, make sure the witnesses keep their mouths shut."

"…What? Keep their mouths shut…?"

This certainly isn't something she'll receive well, but it needs to be said. Limis and Aria should be prepared in case this kind of thing happens again. They should also be able to restrain Toudou.

141

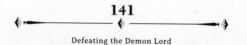

"What is the point of your status, Limis, daughter of the Prince of Friedia? At least within the Kingdom of Ruxe, your father's name holds weight, doesn't it?"

It's not something they can do again and again, but if they use the names of the Prince of Friedia and the grand swordmaster, they should be able to exert some influence. It's bad news for the mercenaries, but sometimes sacrifices have to be made for the greater good.

Registering my meaning, Limis's face starts turning red. "Y-you're telling me to—to dishonor my father's name?!"

"I'm saying it's something you can use. When someone's arm is cut off, walking away isn't an acceptable way to handle it."

A mercenary makes his living using his physical strength—he wouldn't just keep quiet about that. If you don't deal with the issue now, it will come back and haunt you later.

"If you don't want to play that card, all you have to do is stop Toudou before it becomes necessary. Your job isn't just to follow Toudou around."

"I don't need you to tell me that...," she says feebly.

To be fair, this incident was totally unexpected for me, for Limis, and possibly even for Toudou.

I can get a situation on this scale under control, but anything worse, and they'll need to completely destroy the evidence. There could be times when they have to terminate everyone involved. I want to avoid any needless killing, and naturally, it would be a problem if the hero himself were killed.

Limis finally recovers her composure and looks at me. "...What have you been up to?" she asks disappointedly.

"Straying from the priesthood."

"...I see."

She once again goes silent, as if she has nothing more to say.

I consider Limis. She couldn't be a spy, could she? She probably doesn't have the right personality for it, but if I say it's a request from the Church, she might go along with it. The Church isn't Toudou's enemy.

I put the thought aside and say instead, "While you're here, let me

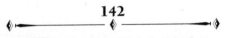

ask you—can you tell Toudou to periodically notify the Church of his whereabouts?"

"His whereabouts…?"

I checked with Amelia, and apparently, her transmission skill isn't something she can use at any time.

"Yes. I was doing it before, but the Church needs to stay informed of the progress of the mission to defeat the Demon Lord. Your current circumstances, your levels, your future plans, any problems you're having—things like that. If you keep the Church up to date, there may be things they can do to help."

"…Oh… Right, I understand. I'll tell him," agrees Limis seriously, nodding. My explanation must have been believable enough.

And then suddenly, as if she just realized something, Limis turns her face to me.

"Oh, that's right! Ares, we can't find a new priest—do you know of anyone?" I'm taken aback by her lack of empathy for my situation.

How can she look me in the eye and ask me that? I suppose that kind of egocentrism isn't entirely a bad thing. It's a talent, in its own way.

"I asked around but couldn't find anyone. Sorry. The Church is short-handed, and there are very few female priests with combat skills."

"…Yeah. Yeah, that's true." She sighs deeply, puzzling over it.

That's when it occurs to me. They need a healer for the party, but there may be another way besides finding a new priest.

"Limis, if the party still hasn't found a priest, you could temporarily fill the role."

"Me…?"

Priests are essential to a party, but there are mages who can take their place.

As a priest, I don't understand the finer details, but I've heard there's a type of magic called *sprite magic*, which can be used to heal wounds and create something similar to a prism. I explain this to Limis, who frowns.

"But I'm not a druid…"

"It's not like there's a rule that says elementalists can't use druid magic."

There are mages capable of using several types of magic. They're different fields but similar in that they both use magical energy. If they're going to fight the Demon Lord with a small party, it's essential that the party members be versatile.

Even if a priest eventually joins them, Limis's efforts won't be for nothing. It's good to have a lot of options.

Though resistant at first, Limis eventually starts coming around. She sighs, then mumbles timidly.

"...All right... I'll try it. I don't know if I'll be able to do it, but..."

"I've never seen another mage manifest a spirit at level ten. I think you'll be up to it."

Limis looks a little surprised. I said it because it was true and not necessarily because I wanted to cheer her on, but she fidgets with her fingers and sheepishly mumbles, "Th-thank you."

"Don't thank me, just hurry up and defeat the Demon Lord."

We'd ended up talking for a while. Toudou and Aria must be worried about her.

"All right, I'll be going, then. Please tell Toudou what I said about reporting to the Church." I turn away and take a few steps before Limis calls after me.

"Ares!"

I look back over my shoulder. It's hard to see her face clearly in the bright sunlight, but she seems overcome with emotion.

"Thank you! Don't worry, we *will* defeat the Demon Lord... You just get yourself to church and pray!!"

"...Will do. It's all up to you now." I watch her as she turns and runs off, her small, quick steps reminding me of a cat.

The journey to defeat the Demon Lord. It will probably span at least a few years.

The thing that makes me an asset to them right now is my high level. My actual abilities aren't anything special, which is why my help will benefit them for only so long.

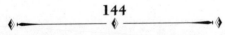

In the latter part of the quest, I could even have become a burden, as I lack the divine blessing of the hero. Without it, you can't battle the Demon Lord.

Limis slowly disappears out of sight.

If I could help them with just prayer, I'd spend all my time praying. But right now, there are still concrete things that I can do. I can help to make their journey progress as smoothly as possible.

I think about the future and take another deep breath. Just then, a voice reverberates through my head.

"Ares, I have a report."

It's Amelia, a sense of urgency in her usually calm voice. Suddenly, I get a sinking feeling.

"What is it?"

"It appears the village headman has made a request of Toudou."

...What?

An image of the bearded village headman flashes through my mind. The nerve of this guy, coming around and causing problem after problem.

"...Tell me."

"Apparently, a monster called a glacial plant has appeared."

When I hear this, I can feel something snap inside my head.

This again?!

Of course, I can't blame Toudou for being asked, but why does he commit to these things without properly thinking them through?

I'm not saying he shouldn't accept any requests. I'm saying he should choose battles where the odds are in his favor. Throwing yourself into a skirmish where you're not confident of the outcome isn't courage. It's recklessness.

I hurry over to the village headman's home, and he comes out to meet me, his face beaming.

"Well, well, if it isn't Ares! How can I help you?"

"Don't give me that crap."

I take a deep breath and get my thoughts in order. When I look at the man's good-natured expression, I get so enraged that I could kill him.

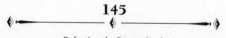

"I heard you made a request to Toudou."

"…Ah, yes. Is that what you've come about?" He sighs worriedly while scratching his beard. "These things don't usually happen often, but it seems another glacial plant has come out of the depths of the forest…"

I suppress my rising irritation as I listen to his explanation.

The issue itself isn't complicated.

To summarize, for whatever reason, another glacial plant turned up, and since Toudou happened to be in the village, the headman asked him if he could defeat it. Toudou accepted the task gladly.

There was a reason why I refused him the first time, so what is this man thinking asking the same thing again?

Glacial plants live in the deepest parts of the Forest of the Vale, and it is certainly a rarity for them to venture near the forest perimeter. After the appearance of a second one, I can understand his concern. But in the end, this is his problem, and his solution shouldn't be to push it off on someone else.

I should have warned Toudou about this kind of thing the first time it happened. This is my mistake.

"That being the case, why didn't you dispatch the royal knights?"

"Well…"

The Kingdom of Ruxe has its own set of rules. Usually when these kinds of extraordinary situations arise, the next logical step is to request that the capital dispatch the royal knights.

The first incident could have just been a random occurrence, but when it happens twice in a short period of time, it can be considered extraordinary. Coming up with a strategy to solve these problems is one of the responsibilities of the village headman—and not something he should foist off on the hero.

"Did you inform the royal capital?"

"Y-yes, of course," he says, his shifty gaze giving him away. I take a step forward and press him further.

"This isn't the first glacial plant; it's the second. Isn't that right?"

A little of the color goes out of his face. After a moment, he finally admits, "W-well, I…haven't informed them quite yet."

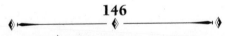

"The overdone sense of justice is a crime."

"Why not? After a second instance, you should have requested a team to investigate the source of the problem."

The village headman reflects on it. "...You are exactly right. Do you think I could ask that of the hero as well—?"

You've got to be shitting me!!

I had reflexively thrown my hand in the air, and I bring it down to touch my forehead, casting the technique *tranquility* to calm myself.

Dammit, why is everyone around me such a pain in the ass?

"Quit screwing around. You should know that the hero doesn't have time for that."

"...If you say so, Ares."

As I desperately attempt to maintain my composure, a dry smile comes over the headman's face. "But you're not a member of the Holy Warrior's party anymore, are you?"

...All right—that's the last straw. Is this asshole toying with me? I can't take it anymore. What happens now, he brought on himself.

I take a deep breath and clench my fists. Giving him no warning, I hurl my fist toward his house a few meters in front of me.

A shock passes down my arm and shoots through the air, hitting the wall and causing the building to shake violently. There's a thunderous roar like the sound of an explosion. Shelves and decorations within fall from the walls and crash to the ground.

"Wha—?!"

The headman crouches down and presses his hands over his ears.

When the building finally stops shaking, the wall that I struck with the shock wave has entirely collapsed, revealing a hallway filled with debris.

Kicking pieces of the crumbled roof out of my way, I approach the village headman, who is curled up futilely on the ground. I grab his arm and force him to his feet.

"Just like you said, I'm not a member of Toudou's party anymore." I wish I could have dealt with this guy like this from the beginning. If you're going to do something, then do it thoroughly. Monsters and

demons are neither the hero's only adversaries in this world, nor are they mine. Meeting the headman's trembling gaze, I continue matter-of-factly. "But as a priest of the Church, it's my duty to use any means necessary to aid the Holy Warrior in his mission. I'll eliminate any road blocks in his path. It makes no difference whether you're a human or a monster—anyone who obstructs the will of God is an enemy of God."

In the Church, there are those called *exorcists*. They're the priests who cleanse the world of the followers of darkness—the devils and the undead.

So what's the difference between them and crusaders like me? One simple thing.

A crusader's enemies are not limited to the followers of darkness.

I stare venomously into his eyes. I try to soothe my thoughts, suppress my anger, manage my impulses. "The second time. This is the second time. And this is *the last time* that I tolerate this."

If a village leader could resolve this kind of problem without having to enlist the help of the kingdom, that would of course be a notable achievement. But this—this way of handling things is unacceptable. And I won't let it slide next time. I sure as hell won't.

His self-serving behavior is a threat to God's will, and it can't be allowed to continue.

I catch sight of my face reflected in the village headman's eyes. There's no anger; it's emotionless.

Yes, I am calm.

"So tell me…," I say soberly. "Are you an enemy of God?"

The village headman says nothing, his face pale, and like a poorly made puppet, he shakes his head side to side.

§　§　§

It can't go on like this. As things are now, Toudou is throwing himself headlong toward certain death.

When I return to my room at the inn, I set down my bag and remove

"The overdone sense of justice is a crime."

my cloak. I wore the cloak only for the purpose of concealing myself, and it has no defensive power. Now I need to change into proper battle attire.

"What do you intend to do…?" asks Amelia over the transmission.

"I'm going to let Toudou get a taste of what a tough battle is like."

I check that there is no break in the blessing applied to my mace. In place of my mythril knife, which has the power to cleanse darkness, I arm myself with an orichalcum knife with high physical-attack power.

I hang five glass bottles filled with highly potent holy water and five with restorative medicine onto my belt, so I can access them any time I need them. I put on my specially made gloves.

"No matter how much I do to make things easy for Toudou, his current way of operating isn't going to work."

I'll let them come close to defeat in this battle.

Up until now, Toudou has been butchering monsters with hardly an effort at all. While that is admirable, he also needs to understand that there are much more powerful creatures in the world, and he needs to know his place among them.

Toudou is still no match for a glacial plant, but even so, there may be a way to accomplish it.

"Let's think positively. This is an enemy with high offensive-attack power that is far beyond Toudou's level. It's the perfect way to break his aggressive spirit."

Also, if Toudou is able to throw the final blow, he will level up. And if it seems like he might lose, I can just cast buffs on him.

"I'll weaken the glacial plant to a level where Toudou can just barely manage to defeat it, after a bit of struggle."

I have to do whatever is necessary. The fate of the world is resting on this guy's shoulders.

I quickly finish up my preparations and throw my bag over my shoulder.

"Ares, I'm going to go, too," says Amelia decisively.

"…Where are you now?"

"I'm at the church. Toudou came with a letter of referral from the

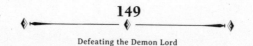

village headman saying he wanted to temporarily borrow a priest. He's talking with Helios now."

I see... I guess that means the village headman isn't so stupid that he would send them out to kill a dragon without a priest.

I can feel things falling into place. There's a chance this could work...

"There's no need for you to come with me. For now, all I'd like you to do is stall Toudou. Keep an eye on him."

I walk quickly toward the village gate. Amelia hesitates in silence for a while.

"...Understood. How long should I delay them?"

"A day... Or at least a half day would be good. I have to find this dragon before I can fight it."

That being said, dragon types have an enormous amount of life force. When I get close to it, I'll undoubtedly be able to sense it.

"...You intend to fight it alone?" Unexpectedly, Amelia's tone is almost reproachful.

"It won't be a problem. At my level, I should be able to weaken it without difficulty."

Thomas and his party were able to defeat one, which means there's no reason why I shouldn't be able to handle it.

Over the transmission, I can sense Amelia's skepticism, but at last, she says simply, "Good luck."

"Thanks."

If you're going to be wishing people good luck, say it to the guy who actually needs it, I think, but it'd probably be inelegant to point that out to her.

When I get to the gate, I find a few familiar faces. It's Thomas and his party, going through the entrance procedures. Thomas wears a grim, serious expression on his face, and Marina stands next to him with her arms crossed in front of her testily. Their equipment looks battered.

"...What happened?"

"Well... Oh! If it isn't Ares!!" Thomas looks up at me, and his expression changes completely.

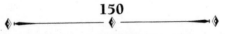

"The overdone sense of justice is a crime."

§   §   §

The sun has set, and there are no signs of life around.

The entrance to the woods that I've passed through so many times before, now enveloped in darkness, looks like a giant creature's open maw.

Humans aren't meant to be traipsing around at night. Most monsters (not to mention the followers of darkness) are nocturnal.

When I listen closely, all I can hear is the wind. The usual sounds of insects and of bird- and beast-type monsters are absent. Monsters rely on instinct, and their senses are sharp. Monster hunters can even learn a thing or two from them.

I think back on the unexpected tidbit of new information I received from Thomas and his group:

"Stay away from the quiet places."

Apparently, this glacial plant is stronger than the last one they fought.

They ran into it by chance while they were hunting in the woods. He said they had leveled up and purchased new weapons and armor after their last battle, so they thought they could handle this one. But they were defeated.

Fortunately, they were able to get away with their lives, but some of their new weapons and armor were destroyed. I recall Marina's over-whelming resentment as she explained this.

The eyewitness report was extremely useful to me as I headed to the forest in search of my target.

My opponent is a flightless dark dragon that is several meters tall. It shouldn't be too difficult to track.

I enter the woods. The chill air doesn't bother me, but the forest's dim fog could make things difficult.

I feel the pre-battle nerves. As I breathe deeply into my lungs, all my senses become sharper. For just this moment, I'm able to get Toudou completely out of my head. I move forward through the fog in silence. Even as I go deeper into the woods, I hardly hear any noise at all.

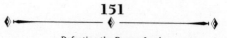

I didn't see Thomas's party battle the first glacial plant—I saw only its carcass. But it didn't seem to have been weak. Which means this second specimen must be particularly strong.

Of course, the strength of a young dragon and a full-grown dragon will differ, and among full-grown dragons, each individual is unique.

Glacial plants were an advanced enemy for Thomas and his party to begin with, so it's not entirely surprising that they lost to one when they challenged it without buffs. But would veteran monster hunters like them misjudge their own ability to win a battle?

About an hour has passed since I entered the woods. The fog is thick, and though there is no moonlight, I can see clearly in the dark.

I feel a presence. Something so huge that it gives me goose bumps over my whole body. It's close, without a doubt.

I try to breathe without making a sound. I lick my dry lips.

I walk toward the presence, heading off the road. My surroundings are surprisingly quiet, and there are no signs of any other monsters, which isn't uncommon.

I grasp my mace tightly in my hand. After a while, I arrive at a clearing.

Or no…it isn't a clearing. The trees here have been crushed.

Countless trunks have been smashed by sheer brute force and trampled into the ground. There are large indentations in the earth from the giant thing that passed through, and scattered branches and leaves are all covered in an icy frost.

A bitter cold rises off the frost, and I pull the collar of my coat in tightly around my neck as I step into the path left by the monster.

"…It's tiny."

I survey the monster's damage. The path it left is only about three meters wide. If this is a glacial plant, it's smaller than the remains of its predecessor.

Generally, the larger a monster is, the stronger it is.

I feel uneasy but try not to worry too much about it and resume tracking the monster. Once I find it, this will all make sense.

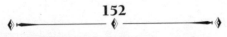

"The overdone sense of justice is a crime."

★　　★　　★

After another ten minutes, I finally find it.

The glacial plant is about ten meters away from me. The first thing I see is its enormous tail scraping against the ground.

Concealing myself in the trees, I examine my target.

In the darkness, I can just barely make out its dark-teal color. It has a long, flexible tail, and gnarled branches protrude from its back. The leaves falling down from the trees freeze in midair around it and shatter into tiny fragments before vanishing. Just being near the creature, you can feel the destruction it is capable of.

This one looks far more threatening than the one Thomas dragged back. It's clear to me why it bested Thomas—even from a distance, I can feel the dragon's vast amount of life force and magical energy.

As soon as I see it, I understand.

This one is different—it's no ordinary glacial plant. This is an evolved form.

Toudou really has a talent for trouble, doesn't he?

Glacial plants are dark dragons, which are entirely different from other dragons. The glacial plant that Thomas brought back was enormous, but really, it was more like a wild boar than a dragon.

The one in front of me is clearly more of a dragon.

"This one was stronger than the first one." I frown as I recall what Thomas said.

This one isn't just stronger—it's clearly at least twice as dangerous as the first.

There's actually a wide spectrum of creatures called *dark dragons*, but essentially, the closer they are in physical form to a dragon, the more power they possess.

Why hadn't Thomas said more about its appearance?

…Well, maybe it isn't that he *chose* not to say. He's an experienced hunter and not the type to conceal information for the sake of his pride. It could be that when Thomas encountered it, this was just a normal glacial plant.

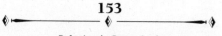

Humans aren't the only ones who can enhance their abilities by increasing their life force. Every species can change form after amassing a set amount of energy, and some species are capable of evolving to a superior form.

"...Has it molted, too?"

This timing is really bad. Dark dragon evolutions are rare.

Taking into account his divine blessing, his armor, and his combat experience, I estimated Toudou's ability to be about a third of a glacial plant's. If you add in the fact that he's level 27, that's actually pretty exceptional.

But the beast in front of me is...different. When a monster evolves to a superior form, there's usually a huge spike in its abilities.

However, it's possible that if it just leveled up, it's not used to its new power quite yet. That might be a weak point.

Even so, this isn't a good situation. Without voicing the words, I move my fingers and self-cast several holy spells.

Full Regen.

Full Cold Resist.

Full Vitality.

Full Concentration.

I finish casting, set down my bag, and quietly step halfway out of the trees.

The temperature is already below freezing, and as I emerge, the wind that whips around me is colder than any winter gale.

Dragons usually have a keen sense of perception, but the glacial plant shows no sign of turning its attention to me. Maybe it doesn't see me as a threat?

I take a step closer on the frozen ground. I dash toward the glacial plant and, without losing my momentum, use my mace to strike with all my might at the side of its towerlike trunk.

Then time slows down, and everything seems to happen at half speed. My mythril mace bends against the dragon's body, the thorns digging into its stonelike flesh. The dragon convulses from the impact of the hit.

And then—the energy is released.

"The overdone sense of justice is a crime."

I feel the shock of the hit move through my hand, my arm, my body.

The dragon's huge bulk flies into the trees and mows them down. The frozen ground makes loud cracks as it fragments.

The wind blows away the fog. In front of me stretches a new path of demolished trees, a wide-open space. The dragon was thrown so far that I can't see it.

I put down my mace and rotate my arm a few times. A sticky brown liquid clings to the mace's thorns—the dark dragon's thick blood.

The dragon wasn't in a defensive position, so it was definitely a critical hit. But I don't get the sense that the battle is over. It certainly took some damage but not a fatal wound.

With my heel, I flatten the cracked ground underfoot as I stare into the darkness.

This dragon might be too strong.

"Even if I weaken it, Toudou still might not be able to finish it off…"

As I stand there in amazement, suddenly the dragon's cold breath, littered with icicles, comes at me out of the darkness.

Level 60—after a few minutes of combat with this target, that's where I estimate you need to be to defeat it.

I use my mace to repel the daggerlike thorns it rains down on me and then send my own dagger flying back at its throat.

The dragon's roar, a cry of rage, echoes through the darkness.

My first strike was hard, and I could feel that its skin, flesh, and bones were remarkably tough. Its icy breath is mostly an annoyance, but the trickiest part of fighting a glacial plant is the chill that envelops you when you're near it. When you go in for close combat, it can sap your strength and severely limit your mobility.

This enemy isn't such a big deal for me, but Toudou, Aria, and Limis might have a pretty hard time.

Just from the one hit, my mace is coated with ice. I swing it through the air a few times. If I was using a sword, the ice would dull the blade, but a mace is a blunt-force weapon—a little ice won't weaken it.

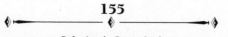

Defeating the Demon Lord

A strong wind blows out from the darkness in front of me. A sign that its breath is coming.

I step into it, unconcerned. I gather my coat to shield myself and bend down, pulling my body into a bullet. I don't look away. The wind, cold enough to freeze you to the bone, is filled with icicles that I bat away with my mace. One icicle scrapes my cheek, and the regenerative spell I cast before the battle heals it almost instantly.

It's like walking through an ice storm. I head toward the emerald eyes glittering in the darkness.

Not losing my resolve, I jump toward the dragon and swing up at its chin, throwing its head back. Then I drive a kick into its exposed chest.

The dragon flies backward again, and I chase after it, continuing with a series of attacks. Its bark-like skin peels away in places, and brown blood scatters.

The dragon screeches, and the hide on its back makes a strange, crackling noise.

It has wings.

Wings that look like they're made of bark, small compared to the rest of the dragon's body. They open and shudder.

I plant my feet into the icy ground and brace myself against a fierce blast of wind. While I'm rooted for that moment, the dragon swings one of its front legs at me.

I react quickly and meet the blow with my mace. Its thorns pierce the leg, but the dragon shows no signs of slowing down.

At this close distance, my eyes meet the dragon's. I can see the relentless fighting spirit in those twinkling emeralds.

Having taken a number of hits, the dragon surely understands the difference in our levels and abilities, but for some reason, it doesn't try to flee. Maybe it's pride? Anyway, it's convenient for me—it would be a pain to have to chase it.

As the dragon leans into its clawed foreleg with all its weight, I channel strength into my arm and push back.

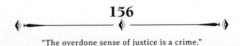

"The overdone sense of justice is a crime."

This is a head-to-head battle of strength. What I lack in size and weight, I make up for in strategy and the merits of my higher level.

I shake my mace free, throwing the foreleg out of the way, then take a hard swing at its jaw.

The dragon's thunderous roar rips through the shrouded silence, and the strange black birds that had been hiding in the trees suddenly flap their wings and disappear into the night sky.

During the battle, I turn some things over in my mind.

The dragon's hide is sturdy, but a holy sword shouldn't have any trouble cutting through it. Then the only question is, will Toudou be able to get close enough to hit it? The dragon might freeze him before he gets there.

I suppose this may not be the best time to be thinking about this.

Without warning, white flakes start floating down from the sky. The wave of cold brought on by the dragon must have caused it to snow.

The falling flakes look just like cherry blossom petals. I close my fingers around one that lands in my palm and start walking toward the dragon.

It lies still on the ground, catching its breath and releasing a cry that echoes in the pit of your stomach. I stand in front of it, and from up close, I can see the rage in the dragon's cloudy eyes.

The wind throws itself at my side. The dragon swings a claw toward my neck, and this time I have to stop the blow with my bare hands.

My mace is out of reach, and the pointed claw makes a sound like a shriek.

At that moment, that burning desire to kill in the dragon's eyes falters for the first time. Maybe from surprise or maybe from fear.

"SKREEEEEE—"

It must understand that it can't win this battle. My intention was just to weaken it, but for an opponent this strong, that may not be enough.

The glacial plant opens its jaw wide. What comes out isn't a roar or its icy breath—it's a hoarse cry, almost like language.

"SKREEE…GRAAAH…"

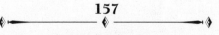

I can't make out words, but there is certainly meaning in the sounds.

I was aware that there are some dragons that can understand human speech, but for a dark dragon, it's completely unheard of.

I don't concern myself with that. So the dragon can talk? Then I'll have to cut its throat, because it might communicate something of this to Toudou.

I smash its legs, its wings, and its throat. That's as far as I go.

After my first battle in a long time, there's a lot of adrenaline running through my veins. I realize my heart is beating furiously.

Sometimes violence can give you a sense of satisfaction. It's important to exercise restraint.

I feel my pulse beating in my temple, and taking my blood-soaked mace, I swing it through the air a few times.

Silence has fallen again in the forest.

"Hey, I'm finished. I'm waiting nearby."

"Understood."

Leaning against an ancient tree, I catch up with Amelia.

I've already taken care of things. After crushing the dragon's wings, legs, and throat, I pierced it with a halberd I found in the woods.

The glacial plant has lost stamina, and the cold it brings with it has weakened. If he has Amelia's support magic to assist him, Toudou should be able to handle it.

Now I just need to wait for Amelia to lead Toudou's party to it. It's half-dead already, so this won't exactly be a struggle, but just coming in contact with a monster so overwhelmingly beyond him should be enough of a wake-up call for Toudou.

"Ares, are you going to take a rest?"

"No, I don't need it."

The battle didn't exhaust me or leave me injured. Although it's an evolved form, it's still a dark dragon, so it didn't present any unexpected difficulties.

"The overdone sense of justice is a crime."

What I do need to do is cool myself down. I'm so worked up from the battle that I might not sleep well tonight. Through my transmission earring, Amelia speaks to me in an unusually forceful tone.

"…You need to rest. If you don't do it now, you may not have the energy when you need it later."

"…I'm not so tired that I'm less capable of doing my job. Plus, I can use holy techniques to recover from the fatigue."

"But you can't use them to recover the *mental* fatigue."

My impulse is to come back with an excuse, but I manage to stop myself.

I close my eyes and slowly take a deep breath. A chilly, murderous intent swirls around in my head, and I have trouble finding my center.

Amelia's probably right. There will be another battle soon enough, and it's best to take a breather when you can.

"Please leave the rest to me. It would be good for you to get some sleep."

"Yeah. Yeah, you're probably right…"

"After all…you're not working alone anymore."

There is truth in that. I slowly lower myself, leaning back against the tree trunk.

Right—I'm not working alone anymore. That…hadn't really occurred to me. There are benefits to having multiple people sharing the responsibility of a mission.

"Got it—I'll take a quick break. I'm leaving the rest to you. If anything comes up, contact me."

"I will."

"And also, let me know when you're about to enter the forest. Before Toudou reaches it, I'll go back and check on the glacial plant."

She responds, seemingly surprised at my insistence. "Understood… I see you're the type who worries about everything, Ares."

"…Maybe so."

Honestly, for the first time, I am actually worried. But I suppose there's no point in that.

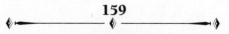

Toudou completely betrayed me, and now he's like an insect flying into the fire. And he isn't just flying into a fire that was already burning—he lit it himself.

Anyway, I've done everything I can for now. All that's left is prayer. For now, I need to rest.

"I'm going to sleep."

"Good night."

I might be overthinking things. Am I really so fainthearted?

No matter how much I dwell on it, I don't have an answer for myself.

§ § §

And then—the worst possible thing happens.

From my vantage point hidden among the high branches of the trees, I wait with bated breath as Toudou rushes over to the half-dead dragon. He crouches down next to it and mumbles something, but I can't quite hear him.

"How cruel... Amelia, could you heal it...?"

At this stage in the game, I'm not even surprised. I'm almost impressed. *Ah, so this is another way to handle this situation.*

Sure, sure, I see... *Huh?*

"The overdone sense of justice is a crime."

Fourth Report

Current Status of the Hero's Support Team

Quick and effective decision-making is essential on the battlefield. In my life, I have engaged in many fierce battles with darkness and always emerged victorious. I have confidence in my judgment. Or should I say, I *had* confidence. But that confidence is now being smashed to pieces.

The half-dead dragon lies on the ground.

I can't believe that this flightless, impaled creature is still alive. And the hero, heartbroken by the sight of it, kneels sympathetically at its side. A scene from a fairy tale.

Does Toudou even remember what he came here to do? Did he come here to *heal* a monster?

After Toudou asks her to heal the monster, Amelia is speechless.

She appears calm, but I can see the slight change in her expression. It's a look of disapproval and agitation. She's so flustered that she doesn't even think to talk to me via transmission and has unconsciously started looking around for me.

Seeing Amelia vexed actually reassures me. Once she gets over the shock, I can see the sense of helplessness that overcomes her.

I still can't believe what Toudou asked her to do. I understand the words, of course, but not the intention. He must be able to sense how strong the half-dead dragon before him is—how much stronger *than him*. I can't help but wonder what meaning there was in my fighting it first.

Toudou stands up and looks to Amelia. "Its injuries are severe... What kind of person would do this...? Amelia, please heal it—"

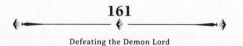

"What are you saying?" Amelia interrupts, her voice cold. Somehow Toudou doesn't seem to pay her any mind.

"Heal it, quickly... Or else it might already be too late—"

"...Why do you think we should heal it?" It's a logical question, but Toudou appears shocked by it. I wish I understood how this guy's brain works.

"Amelia... Are you actually saying...that I should kill it like this?"

"Yes. This is our target, the glacial plant. I don't know who it fought before us, but we should consider ourselves lucky that we found it in this weakened state. Now we should be able to kill it just by severing its head."

At the bluntness of Amelia's explanation, Toudou shakes his head vigorously, his lips trembling. "I can't believe what you're saying... You would kill something that's been crippled like this? Where is your humanity?"

I'm so shocked by this response that my foot slips from the branch, and I nearly fall. Flustered, I right myself and get my footing.

Humanity...?! How much humanity does he think there is in a beast?

This is an evolved dark dragon—it's a monster. If you let it live, there's no telling how many people will fall victim to it.

Has he forgotten that the reason he came here in the first place was to fulfill the village headman's request and kill that thing?!

Amelia blinks in surprise. She couldn't have been expecting that response, either. I find it kind of cute.

"I...I didn't become the hero so that I could torment the weak," Toudou declares emphatically.

Torment the weak! This guy is a riot.

Then it occurs to me—maybe I weakened the dragon too much?

But if I didn't go as far as I did, Toudou would have had no chance of defeating it. Maybe I should have forgotten about trying to strengthen Toudou's position against it and just killed it myself?

...Well, live and learn.

"Even though it's half-dead, I can feel how strong this creature is.

Somewhere nearby is something that was able to do this much damage to it. Rather than killing this monster, isn't it more important that we find what attacked it?"

...This is starting to move in a strange direction.

Amelia is dumbfounded. At that moment, I realize Aria has approached the dragon. She is closely examining the silver halberd thrust into its torso and the deep wounds left by my mace.

You dumbass, don't just thoughtlessly approach a dragon! That's so reckless!

It's then that the dragon stirs.

I immediately strike the glacial plant with murderous intent. It shrieks in pain, and its huge body collapses inward, now motionless again. Murderous intent is always effective against monsters you've damaged yourself.

Aria gasps and takes a step back. "Sir Nao, these wounds...," she says in a trembling voice. "They appear to have been inflicted by a blunt-force weapon."

"Blunt...force?!"

Giving up on convincing Amelia, Toudou goes over to Aria.

"Please examine the body. Its legs are unscathed, but there are marks on its back."

"...Hmm? And that means...?"

"It's a sign that it has been hit with a blunt-force weapon. It was sent flying backward, and its back scraped against the ground. Also, on our way here, there were a great number of trees that had been leveled, which could also have been from the recent battle."

...True, I didn't tidy up the battlefield. But I'm a priest—it's not like I can burn down the forest.

"The marks on its body aren't the type that can be made by a human. These kinds of injuries aren't left by slash attacks or magic."

"What about the spear?"

"The spear—or halberd, actually—is not usually used that way. It would take a great amount of strength to do that."

Yeah, it did. It took all my might. Sorry. A blunt object was all I had.

It should be noted that Aria is showing surprisingly strong analytical ability. She has skills in unexpected places.

"These injuries are not typical. They're not made by a spear or a sword… It's almost like they were made by a strike from some kind of spherical weapon…"

I sense in Aria's tone that she has drawn a conclusion.

…Hang on. This could be bad.

They know what my weapon looks like. I hadn't expected Aria to be able to conduct such an in-depth analysis of battle wounds.

I focus in on Aria's speech. Toudou is standing next to her, his stare fixed on the twitching body of the dragon.

"…I'd like to hear your conclusion."

"…Yes."

Amelia, finally realizing that the situation has taken a bad turn, tries to stop Aria but misses her opportunity. She licks her lips once and begins to speak.

"Wai—"

"It's highly unlikely that a human caused this much damage to the glacial plant."

…*What?*

My mind is blank for a moment.

Aria continues. "Monster hunters generally only move in parties. For one thing, this was not a battle with a large number of combatants. And even if there was a warrior who could overpower this glacial plant in one-on-one battle, there is no reason he would leave it alive when he could obtain its life force by killing it."

"…I already knew this wasn't the work of a human. These wounds are much too violent, too grotesque. Only a psychopath could do something like this."

That's a bit harsh…

Amelia draws back the hand she had extended to stop Aria and quietly rescinds into the background.

"The overdone sense of justice is a crime."

"My guess is it's a type of subhuman monster, perhaps more than three meters in height, with thorns covering the backs of its hands."

"Thorns…on the backs of its hands?"

"Yes. There are a number of puncture wounds in the dragon's hide that appear to have been caused by some kind of thorns or spikes. It's the mark of a strike, so it's possible it could be from a fist. Moreover, it appears the glacial plant was struck many times over." Her body starts shaking at the sound of her own words. Perhaps she has never been injured in battle before and the thought of this imagined enemy frightens her.

As if the response is contagious, Toudou's shoulders also begin quivering, and he looks restlessly at his surroundings.

What kind of goblin are they even imagining? I thought Aria had it, but she ended up nowhere close. Not that I'm complaining…

"…In any case, seeing as there is a possibility of a new threat in the forest, we need to notify the village chief."

"Why do we keep having one problem after another…?" grumbles Limis. For once, Limis and I are on the same page.

Toudou sighs deeply and then turns to Amelia, the outsider of the group. "You understand, don't you, Amelia? We're no longer concerned with the glacial plant."

"…What on earth are you saying?"

Seriously, just what is this guy saying?

Toudou reacts with shock and frustration. "Don't you get it?!" he shouts. "There must be a reason the glacial plant was attacked. If we just kill it now, there could be more problems later. It needs to be healed."

"Problems…? …What kinds of problems, exactly?"

Toudou frowns, looking confused for a few seconds. "For example… If glacial plants are the guardians of the forest and a new kind of monster invades, they would need to chase it away," he answers, his voice lacking conviction.

He's got quite the imagination.

Amelia sighs heavily, amazed by his response. Then she says everything I wish I could say in this moment.

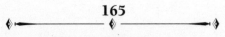

"For one thing, I've never heard of anything like that, and also, there aren't any monsters living in this region that could defeat a glacial plant. I think it's much more likely that a capable mercenary happened upon it while passing through and battled it just for amusement."

"...Huh. That makes sense." He sighs in disappointment, casually walking over to the fallen beast. "I suppose you're not a member of my party, Amelia, so you can do as you please. I'll heal the monster myself."

WHA—?!

For a moment, my brain ceases to function. Before I can stop him, Toudou extends his arm toward the glacial plant.

"Mini Heal."

A faint green light flickers at the palm of his hand and heals the injured dark dragon. The rudimentary spell does nothing for the dragon's torn wings and broken legs, only closing a few of the open wounds.

What it *does* do is bring the dark dragon back from the brink of death and give it enough energy to move.

The glacial plant roars. The sounds don't have meaning, but it is a cry that could burn life to the ground.

It struggles to move its broken front legs and manages to raise them overhead. The halberd piercing its torso keeps it stuck in place. Cracking sounds reverberate from its wounds as it struggles, but it doesn't stop struggling.

The dragon aims the sharp ends of its broken front claws at Toudou. My thoughts are frozen. I impulsively cry out.

"WWWWWWWHHHHHHHOOOOOOOOOOAAAAAAAA!!"

The trees shake, and the wind dies down. I can't believe the animalistic sound that just came from my own mouth.

At the same time, I once again deploy my murderous intent. This time, I don't have enough time to aim, so rather than affecting only the dragon, it targets the entirety of the surrounding area. Limis falls to the ground as if her knees have been broken, and Toudou is thrown backward.

The dragon's claws just barely miss Toudou, swiping through the air in front of him and cutting a few strands of his hair.

"The overdone sense of justice is a crime."

The glacial plant's body convulses, and it collapses to the ground. A chill runs down my spine.

I was almost too slow—that was a close one. It's a good thing I so thoroughly weakened the monster before, because if I hadn't, I might be digging graves right now.

"Wh-what was that?!" Toudou shouts, not realizing that he just barely escaped with his life. He involuntarily drew his holy sword and now grips it tightly in his hand. His face has turned pale, and sweat rolls down his cheeks.

"This is foolish...!" says Aria, her voice shaking. "That murderous intent... Sir Nao, it's...not safe here!!"

"Urgh... Agh..."

Perhaps being too low level to bear the hit, Limis sits motionless on the ground, showing no signs of moving.

I couldn't afford to hold back on that one.

Toudou shuts his eyes and desperately tries to steel his nerve.

Amelia, the only one who knows the truth of what happened just now, rushes over to Toudou. "We should withdraw immediately. If the owner of that cry finds us, at your current level, you will certainly not be able to win."

"Guh... N-no, I can't do that. I'm not gonna...run away." Toudou grits his teeth and opens his eyes.

Does he really still intend to stay after being hit by that murderous intent?!

In agreement with Amelia at last, Aria touches Toudou's shoulder. "Sir Nao... This is too much for us. There is even the possibility that it's a demon."

Even so, Toudou wants to fight to the bitter end. "A demon... N-no, if it is a demon, I definitely—"

"Sir Nao!" Aria shouts. Her expression is stern, filled with regret, anger, and grief. Having never seen her this way before, he falters.

Aria attempts to speak calmly, but there is a waver in her voice. "If you die, who will defeat the Demon Lord? If you feel we absolutely must

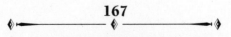

167

fight this battle in which we don't stand a chance…at least leave it to Limis and myself. We cannot allow you to die here."

Hearing this, still sitting on the ground, Limis looks up at Toudou with tears in her eyes. There is fear and despair in her gaze, but I see no anger toward Toudou. Aria and Limis have both come to this task prepared to do what they must.

Looking back and forth between Aria and Limis, Toudou's eyes are lifeless. His movements are so slow that he looks like a mechanical doll that has run out of oil.

"You're…sure I can't win?" he asks, his voice shaky.

Aria and Limis don't reply. They don't have to; their expressions say it all.

Aria comes from a military family, and Limis is the lowest-level member of the group. Their sense of hopelessness is surely greater than Toudou's.

"You mustn't misunderstand, Toudou. You just can't win *yet*," adds Amelia. Her timing is excellent.

"Not…yet…?"

"Your level is still quite low for a hero."

That is true, and it's good that she's taking the focus off his good qualities. Toudou needs to be more self-aware. He needs to understand his own weaknesses, his recklessness, and the weight of his own existence.

"No matter how great your merits as a hero, if your level is low, you cannot rival a demon. To say that another way, if you just increase your level, you may be capable of defeating demons."

"If I just increase my level…" Toudou turns the idea over in his mind. Limis and Aria watch him with concern. Finally, he closes his eyes and takes a deep breath in and out.

When he opens his eyes, they're hazy. He looks like he's half in a trance. Looking at each of them individually, at last he says, "…I will withdraw."

"Understood," says Aria. "Limis, let's go."

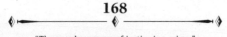

"The overdone sense of justice is a crime."

"I—I don't know if I...can stand..." Her legs may be temporarily paralyzed.

Aria looks concerned. She lifts Limis with ease and carries her on her back. Amelia furrows her brow.

"Toudou, you would like to leave the glacial plant as it is, then?"

"Oh, right..."

Toudou looks over at the glacial plant as it twitches on the ground. After staring at it for a few seconds, he looks back to Amelia. "...Amelia, I know it's an unreasonable thing to ask...but could you heal it for me?" he asks in a weak voice.

What makes him keep asking that?

It's a monster... Even if you feel bad for it at first, in the end, you should understand what it is. I wonder if this way of thinking has some connection to Toudou's upbringing.

I get a transmission from Amelia, asking what she should do. I think on it and conclude it may be better to go ahead and heal it. Going back and forth on this point is a waste of time.

In any case, I'm going to kill it as soon as they're gone.

Amelia approaches the dragon. I gather my energy and use murderous intent to bind its body. Toudou stands next to Amelia, as if he wants to see for himself that the deed is done.

Imagining a worst-case scenario where the dragon escapes, I channel more energy into binding it.

My head gets so hot that I feel like I might burn out. But I'm all right—just a little more.

Amelia chants, "**Heal.**" The green light emitted by her hand is far brighter than Toudou's and envelops the creature's entire body.

Then, when the light fades...the dragon suddenly transforms into a little girl.

I'm going to file a complaint with Creio about this.

§　§　§

"Wow. So the dark dragon transformed into a human?"

Although I myself am drowning in a pool of despair, I don't sense even the slightest change in Creio's tone.

Toudou's courage goes without mentioning, but his mental abilities in this situation also seem to transcend those of ordinary people.

I'm back at the village inn. After a hot shower, I've managed to calm down, but I'm still in a terrible mood.

It's been a few hours since the incident. Just thinking about all that has happened gets me agitated.

Just when I thought it was over, the instant I finally started to relax—that's where it took a turn. I nearly fell out of that tree.

Amelia is still with the party, and according to her, the dragon girl has been cooperative so far. I'd like to think that she wouldn't go berserk in this town full of mercenaries, but…is it really safe to bring a dragon here?

"Stay with Toudou for now. The dragon is docile for the moment, but if something changes, I want to know."

I was aware of demons capable of changing into humans, but I don't ever remember hearing about a dragon doing so.

Because she's an unidentified creature, I wanted to get her away from Toudou. Unfortunately, he's been leading her everywhere by the hand, so it's tough to separate them. We might be screwed on this one.

This is a pretty risky situation, but no matter how we decide to handle it, we need a plan of action. For the moment, I just want information.

Creio thinks about it for a while. "…I *have* heard about dragons that can transform into humans."

Seriously? …Well, I suppose it would be stranger if he *hadn't*. After all, it unquestionably happened right in front of me today.

"Ares, are you aware of the dragon knights from Lemwraith Empire?"

"…I am."

Most kingdoms have a group of royal knights, but none are more famous than the Dragon Knights of Lemwraith.

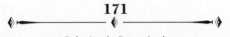

As their name indicates, their defining characteristic is that they ride dragons.

Dragons won't ordinarily submit to humans, but the dragon knights have established command over them and are able to wander the skies as they wish. Using their unique battle strategies, the dragon knights are the strongest of all royal knights.

I wait quietly as Creio continues.

"I've heard that the dragons of Lemwraith have a habit of taking human form. But as you know, Lemwraith is not under our jurisdiction."

The method of taming dragons is kept secret in Lemwraith, and no other country has ever been able to accomplish it. The frustrating part of this is that the official religion of Lemwraith is not the Church of Ahz Gried.

Not that there's any quarrel between us. It's just that the followers of their church are different from the followers of Ahz Gried, so it may be difficult to circulate information. I see what Creio is getting at. I chew my lip in agitation.

"The fact that he was able to recognize something unusual in the dragon could be considered proof of his divine blessing. You yourself, lacking understanding of the Three Deities, couldn't accomplish such a thing."

"Why are the gods such a damn hassle...?"

"...Oh, come now. You should have a little more respect for the gods."

Then, finally revealing his true intentions, Creio's voice shakes with strained laughter. *"If we can win over Lemwraith, we may gain an advantage there. It may be dangerous to keep the dragon girl around, but taking risks is a necessary part of the battle to defeat the Demon Lord."*

"...I see your point."

I need to change the way I'm thinking about this. Having a dragon in the party could be an excellent form of security.

The dragon knights' home ground is in the sky, and the girl most likely can return to her dragon form.

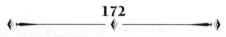

"What do you think of keeping her with the party?"

"…I think that if they're going to have a dragon, it would be ideal having one that can fly."

After all, we're talking about a glacial plant, which is a type of dark dragon. It hasn't necessarily been decided that the dragon girl will stay with the party, but if she does, one ought to consider that she may end up out of her depth. Can she even level up?

Creio suppresses a laugh at my comment. "Heh-heh. These kinds of things are partly why I chose you."

"Is that so?"

"May Zion protect you. I'll see if I can get any more information, but don't get your hopes up."

The transmission cuts out. I stand there for a little while.

Another hassle to deal with.

This certainly isn't in my wheelhouse. Now, what should I do…?

The primary attribute of the god worshipped in Lemwraith is love. He is one of the three supreme deities, the god who bestows love onto every living thing, human or monster.

The God of Love, Zion Gusion.

This is the god the Lemwraith Empire serves and one of the three gods who bestowed diving blessings on Toudou. He's also the god worshipped by fools who try to tame monsters.

§ § §

If I'm being completely honest, my thought when Creio first told me about Toudou was that he might actually be able to overcome the Demon Lord.

That judgment was based on the divine blessing he received when he was summoned.

There are many gods and spirits in this world, but the blessings he received from the Three Deities and Eight Spirit Kings are especially powerful.

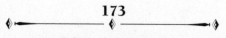

On rare occasions, there are those who receive protection from more than one god, but it is unheard of to receive it from all the Three Deities, the most powerful gods in this world.

Namely—

He who has the most followers in this world and governs the holy arts, Ahz Gried, God of Order.

He who promises certain victory to warriors and is worshipped by many mercenaries and monster hunters, Pruflas Wrath, God of War.

And lastly, Zion Gusion, God of Love.

As the God of Order, Ahz Gried bestows the power to exorcise darkness and subdue chaos. As the God of War, Pruflas Wrath gives the strength to destroy any obstacle you may face in this world. The power of Ahz Gried has many uses, and the power given by the God of War is necessary to break through the impenetrable prism used by the Demon Lord and his followers.

But I have never known what power Zion bestows on his followers. I guess I assumed he didn't really have anything to offer. Actually, in terms of followers, the God of Love has only a fraction of the number of the other two gods.

Whatever the blessing of Zion is, if it has an effect on Toudou, I had better make sure I know about it.

While eating my first decent breakfast in a whole day, I listen over transmission to Amelia's report.

"—We are currently at the inn. Our plan for the day is to purchase some clothes for Glacia and then report to the village headman."

"Glacia...?"

"Yes. We can't just call her 'the dragon' forever, so we chose that name."

Glacia from *glacial plant*... That's simple enough.

"Is she behaving?"

"For the time being, yes. She is still highly wary of us, however, and doesn't show any sign of speaking. I don't know how long it will take for her to let her guard down..."

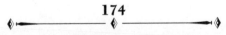

I want to say, *It ain't gonna be so simple*, but I let it go.

"And Toudou?"

"…Toudou doesn't seem too concerned about her. His perspective is that she just needs time to get used to everything. Aria, on the other hand, has been keeping a close eye on her."

I think on this while cutting the meat on my plate with the silver knife.

I don't think Toudou will try to leave Glacia behind. Now that Amelia will be leaving the party, it would make it easier to gather information if we could somehow control Glacia and keep her with them.

The problem is, how do we get Glacia to understand this…?

I mean, I already nearly killed her (?) once. That alone makes this pretty difficult.

Whether she ultimately cooperates or not, I need to talk to her as soon as possible.

"I want to get in contact with her. Can you get Glacia alone?"

"…That may be difficult. We have made it a rule not to leave her alone."

Perhaps that means they understand the danger in a dragon that can transform into a human… Or maybe they're just afraid to leave her alone?

"Later some of us will be going to buy Glacia's clothes, and at that point, there will be fewer people watching her…"

"That's convenient… How many will stay behind at the inn?"

"…How many do you want to stay behind?" Amelia implies that she has some level of control over it. That's promising.

"As few as possible. If you can manage it, I'd like to have Aria and Toudou out of there."

I can handle Limis. It would be ideal if just Amelia and Limis could stay behind. But if I were in Toudou's place, I wouldn't leave a mage and a healer to monitor a dragon.

Anyway, if it doesn't work out the way I want, we can improvise. It wouldn't be the first time I've had to abduct a person or two.

"…Understood."

I finish my breakfast and set down my fork and knife. Just as I'm standing to leave, Amelia asks another question over the transmission.

"...By the way, Ares... Do you know why you were given this mission?"

"Sure I do." The question is a bit unexpected.

I take a small knife out from my bag. The knife is a rare item, its dark-green scabbard ornamented with patterns in gold and silver. At a glance, it may look ceremonial, but in fact, it is one of only a few magical tools that I possess.

After a silence, Amelia continues. "I think what you assume to be the reason...may actually be only one part of the whole."

"...What do you mean?"

She hesitates to reply. Regardless of the reason, what I can and will do on this mission remains the same.

She finally responds just as I'm heading out of the inn. Recently, we've had a lot of bad weather, but today, without a cloud in the sky, the sun shines brightly.

"Ares, the purpose of this mission isn't just for you to support Toudou. It is also...for you to overcome your own weaknesses."

"My...weaknesses?"

I can think of a lot of weaknesses that I have. My magical energy is low, for example. I have very little divine protection. But what Amelia says isn't anything I'd considered.

"That's right. Ares, your shortcoming is—it's that you try to do everything alone. It isn't in your nature to rely on others, so you take on everything yourself. To the leaders of the Church...this is a great weakness."

I don't rely on other people—that much is true. I understand what Amelia is saying but am unable to offer up a response.

No, it's not that... It gets me thinking about how these things Creio views as my weaknesses may influence our current circumstances. I've been reporting back to him, and I've adapted to the people involved in this mission. But I don't think that's the kind of thing she's talking about.

"The overdone sense of justice is a crime."

Amelia continues matter-of-factly. "Fundamentally, you have no expectations of me. Wouldn't you agree, Ares? As an example, even when you learned that I can use magic to send transmissions, you didn't ask me to handle the reports to Creio. You'd rather just do it yourself."

"..."

...*She's paying close attention to these things.*

It is true that I have basically no expectations of her. The important thing on a mission is the results. I can determine my own actions, but I have no control over those of others.

What Amelia does already is sufficient. The rest I can accomplish myself, one way or another.

Amelia continues her analysis in an unwavering voice. "From your perspective, this mission is your responsibility in all respects. I am only an assistant, bearing no responsibilities. You are very specific with your instructions, and you never forget to consider the outcome should I fail. You might think of this as being practical, but in the end, it goes to show that you fundamentally have no confidence in me."

As a matter of fact, all of that is true, and I am perfectly aware of it.

I look down at the black ring on the ring finger of my left hand. The ring is proof of rebellion against God. It is a symbol of those who revoke the teachings of Ahz Gried and strike down the enemies of God as crusaders. Which is why, even if Amelia points these things out, it doesn't bother me in the slightest.

"So what do you want me to do?"

"I ask that you make some adjustments. My assignment is to support you in your mission, and I don't want to do my job halfway."

Make some adjustments, huh? I think about what she says—halfway—and picture her frozen in the middle of a road, when she says:

"This is my business."

There's almost no one around the rear of the inn. I pull my hood over my head and lean my back against the wall.

"Aria and Toudou are gone."

"Got it."

I'm used to stealth operations.

A high level translates to a high amount of life force. A high amount of life force translates to being able to do more than others with lower life force. When I hold my breath and focus my mind, I can sense all movement around me.

I know for certain they're gone. I could sense Toudou's and Aria's presence through any number of walls.

When I look up, I see a small window that has been left open. The party is on the third floor of the three-story inn. I move silently to a spot underneath the window where I can sense Amelia.

The window is large enough for me to fit through. I feel the wall with the palm of my hand—it's almost completely flat. There is no sun on this side of the building, so the wall is pleasantly cool to the touch. I scratch the surface with my fingernails.

"Okay, Ares."

Amelia signals that the coast is clear. I breathe in and kick off from the ground.

Digging my fingernails into the wall, it takes me only a few seconds to climb up to the window. I grab on to the ledge and peer inside. In the room with Amelia are Limis and the dragon girl.

Supporting my body with my right hand, I use my left to withdraw my knife from my pocket. I hold the scabbard between my teeth and unsheathe it. The knife is a magical tool that causes its target to faint. Being only level 17, Limis will have no defense against it.

I want to do it without her seeing me. I have made my presence undetectable and should be able to get it done quickly. I dive into the room.

I already know the arrangement of the furniture. I quickly survey the scene.

The dragon girl is wrapped in a black cloak, lying motionless on the

"The overdone sense of justice is a crime."

sofa. Limis's body is collapsed on the table in much the same way. They appear uninjured. A leather-bound book lies open by Limis's feet.

Amelia, the only one standing upright, watches the door.

I unmask my presence, and at the sound of my footsteps, Amelia whips around. The quick motion is a little amusing.

I go over to Limis. Her breathing is calm. She isn't dead—just sleeping, as is the dragon girl. "What happened here?"

"How...how did you get in...?" Amelia mumbles, looking toward the window in surprise.

"...Well, I never said I was coming through the door."

"You didn't say you'd be coming through the window, either..."

I peruse the room once more and ask Amelia again, "What's going on here?"

"I put them to sleep."

"How?"

"With magic."

Put them to sleep with magic, huh? That isn't as simple as she makes it sound.

Dragons and mages both have high resistance to magic—not just anyone would be capable of putting them both to sleep like this. I wish she'd have told me in advance that this was her plan, because I can't agree to something I don't know about. Still, this method doesn't pose any problems.

Amelia locks the door and turns to face me. "What do you intend to do now?"

How long before Toudou returns, I wonder? We should have at least ten minutes. Maybe twenty? Or thirty? It should be enough.

I go over to Glacia. She shows no signs of waking. She may be in a deep sleep.

"I'm going to interrogate her. Any danger Limis might wake up?"

"No, as long as we keep our voices low, it should be fine... But *interrogate*? Not negotiate?"

Negotiate with a monster? I have plenty of experience with interrogation—but not so much with negotiation.

We don't have a lot of time, and I absolutely want to avoid being discovered by anyone in the hero's party while cross-examining her.

I look down at Glacia. Her straight hair is a deep-green color, and from the little bit that I can see under the hood of the cloak, her skin is so white that it practically shines. With her eyes closed, she looks almost angelic. I would never think she was a dragon if I hadn't witnessed her transformation.

But looking at her now, I know it with certainty. From this close, I can feel her life force. It's not as strong as when she was in her dragon form, but the amount of life force coming from this skinny little girl is way beyond Toudou's. She's dangerous.

Her left arm is folded across her body. I grab hold of it, wondering how much physical strength she has, and sit her up.

The cloak that had been covering her falls to the floor, exposing her dazzling naked body along with the rising and falling of her chest.

"Wait... Ares, what are you—?"

"Wake up!"

Disregarding Amelia's attempt to hold me back, I give Glacia a slap on the cheek. Unsurprisingly, she awakens at this provocation and stirs slightly, her eyelids slowly blinking open. Her gaze wanders around blankly before finally stopping on me.

Her face twitches. Her pale lips open. Her throat expands. Her chest swells as she inhales deeply. Without any hesitation, I drive my right fist into her stomach.

"—Guh?! Wha—?"

There's a brief shriek, followed by the sound of Glacia's arm cracking as I grab it. She doubles over, her eyes wide and face contorted in pain. She coughs up warm spittle that soaks the floor beneath her.

Using the remaining feeling in my right hand, I take note of her current form.

Soft yet strong. A normal human's abdomen would be ruptured and their arm torn off by now.

"The overdone sense of justice is a crime."

In any case...I don't know how her form changes, but at the moment, she's no different to me than a sandbag.

Glacia continues to cough and splutter. I force a finger into her mouth and grab hold of her tongue. Her mouth is cold, unlike a human's. She desperately tries to cry out as I drop my voice down to a whisper in her ear.

"Scream, and I'll kill you. Lash out, and I'll kill you. And if you don't answer my questions, I'll kill you."

Toudou's intentions? Divine protection from the God of Love, Zion Gusion? I don't care about any of that. If she makes so much as a peep, I'll deal with her—I've got no choice.

No longer attempting to cry out, Glacia instead begins convulsing.

I can clearly see the terror in her eyes. She desperately tries to free her tongue, but my grip on it is so strong that it's pointless.

"A-Ares... Isn't that a little...much?"

"It's no problem. I can use holy techniques to heal her."

Sure, I'm about to pummel Glacia's face in and rip off one or two of her arms, but otherwise, she's the same as ever.

"N-no, that's not what I meant—"

We can't let our guard down. Even though she's taken a human form, this kid is still a monster.

I peer wordlessly into Glacia's eyes, into the depths of her deep-green irises, the same color as her hair. An icy chill fills my brain. *Squash the risk. For the sake of this world, just die.*

After waiting a few seconds, once I've registered the terror brimming in her eyes, I begin my interrogation.

"Answer my questions when I ask. Say anything else, and I'll kill you."

She understands human speech. Her lips move slightly in an attempt to speak but then close. So she also understands...threats.

I release Glacia's arm from my grip, and she crumples onto the sofa.

"Tell me why you transformed," I demand, glaring at her.

That's where we need to start. I need to know how she did it, why

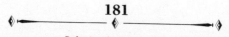

she did it, whether she has any ill will toward us, and why she came out of the depths of the woods in the first place.

Her eyes widen at my question. Her throat moves weakly, but no words come out. Tears in her eyes, Glacia shakes her head.

This isn't defiance. Even if she can't say the words, I understand what she was trying to communicate.

"So you don't know? You're not lying?"

"…"

Furiously shaking her head and her hands side to side, she scoots back into the sofa.

She wouldn't lie under these circumstances, and I'd considered that a possibility. I move on.

"Next question. Do you have any intention of harming Toudou—the black-haired human—or the other humans with him?"

Dragons are destructive animals. Most of them are threats to human life.

I don't mean to get into the controversy of good and evil. Dragons eat humans, and humans slaughter dragons for their life force and the raw materials they can get from their bodies. We're mutual enemies.

The dragon girl's body resembles a human, but what about her mind? How dangerous is she? There's only one way to be absolutely sure.

Glacia looks frightened by my question. But somewhere in the fear, I can sense that she's waiting for an opportunity. She pulls up the corners of her lips, imitating a smile.

Reinforcing my words and gaze with murderous intent, I lightly press my knee into her stomach. She jumps with a start.

"If you put a hand on Toudou, I'll kill you. Anywhere you run, I'll find you. But I promise that if you follow my orders, I'll let you live."

"I—I…," she stammers, speaking for the first time. She has the voice of a young girl, unlike her voice as a dragon. I was prepared to crush her throat if her voice was loud, but it comes out like a whisper.

Her lips tremble, and her breathing is rough. Her complexion is so deathly pale that it looks like there's no blood in her at all. This is no act.

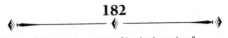

"The overdone sense of justice is a crime."

The trauma and my superiority made an impression on her, so I know I did my job adequately.

"I...promise." The words are understandable but not quite clear—she's not used to speaking yet. But I can tell from her voice that she intends to cooperate.

I slowly let go of her. Her whole body gives a shake, as if releasing tension.

"This is...a contract."

If things had gone any other way, I would have dispatched the girl immediately. She trembles under my gaze.

"Ares...," says Amelia.

"I'll hear your objections later."

I check the clock on the wall. It's already been ten minutes. Before Toudou and Aria come back, I need to get out of here, and Amelia will have to wake up Limis. There isn't much time. But there is one more thing I want to confirm.

This is the big question. I look back at Glacia, collapsed on the couch.

"Glacia, why did you come out of the deep parts of the woods? You were out of your territory."

This was the second report of an appearance of a glacial plant. Just once could be considered happenstance, but a second time indicated cause.

At my question, Glacia makes a sound in her throat like a hiccup. Then, with trembling lips and fearful eyes, she manages to say, "Demon—appeared—in woods."

Her response confirms the bad feeling I had.

Problems tend to breed more problems. You need to dispel disaster before it takes root.

Amelia looks at me, her shoulders shaking slightly in shock. But I'd already predicted this.

No matter what happens, I need to accomplish my mission. I'm prepared to handle anything.

Dark dragons don't often show themselves, and two had turned up

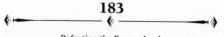

in a short amount of time. Soon we may have one or two demons on our hands.

§ § §

"Yes, that's right. A demon. Its class and type are unclear, but it was powerful enough to drive out the dark dragon, and I think you'd have to be around level fifty to defeat her. On the other hand, apparently the dark dragon felt that if she built up enough strength, she might have been able to defeat the demon, so it could be comparable to her in strength."

Leaving Amelia to handle Toudou's party, I report to Creio while examining the outer wall surrounding Vale Village.

I've collected all the information I need from Glacia.

It appears that she was living modestly in the depths of the forest, when one day, a powerful demon suddenly appeared and forced her out of her territory. In order to take her revenge on it, she went to the shallow part of the forest to increase her strength by devouring other monsters, and it was there that she evolved to her new form. We didn't know anything about the first glacial plant, but it could have been in the same situation.

A demon. One of the many beings that live in darkness.

A natural enemy of humanity, demons have an aptitude for magic in addition to their intelligence and great physical strength. Even low-class demons are so strong that an ordinary human can do little to hurt them.

The wall around the village isn't just a wall. It is also a boundary designed to keep monsters away.

In the holy arts, boundary techniques require a particular level of skill.

The boundary surrounding Vale Village was put in place by a talented priest, and although years have passed, there are no major tears in it. However, this barrier was made with the monsters from the Forest of the Vale in mind, and its ability to defend against the followers of darkness that do not inhabit those woods most likely is not very high.

I take a small pouch out of my breast pocket.

"The overdone sense of justice is a crime."

It contains highly valuable mythril shards. While checking a map, I walk around the perimeter of the village and bury the beads in the ground. Using the mythril as a medium for the boundary will make it strong enough to hold off demons, if only for a little while. The possibility of a demon attacking at this stage in the game should be low, but I want to be absolutely sure the village is prepared.

It's widely known that there are highly powerful demons in service of Demon Lord Kranos. I knew we would have to face them eventually, but this is much sooner than I had anticipated.

Hearing this news, Creio seems soberer than usual. "A demon... Perhaps the hero has been discovered?"

"I don't know, but it seems unlikely. If they'd found out about the hero, you would think they would do something more drastic than setting a dark dragon on him."

Looking at the past, the appearance of the hero has always ignited a fierce struggle with demon kind.

If they believed a hero had appeared and had discovered his whereabouts, there would already be a powerful demon targeting him directly. Plus, assuming the demon first appeared around the same time as the first glacial plant, that would mean that the demons had discovered the hero significantly earlier than the estimated one month.

"Hmm... It could be that they suspect it but are not certain of it yet."

The same thought had occurred to me. I finish up laying the prism, then lean against the wall and catch my breath.

"At any rate, the best thing to do now is capture the demon and interrogate it. Can you dispatch a crusader?"

"What about the hero?"

"You must be joking—he isn't ready for that. He won't be until he reaches at least level sixty."

If Toudou is going to have a go at a demon that drove a glacial plant out of its territory, I'd like him to be at least level 60...although 70 would be better.

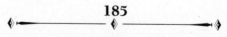

Generally, you can sense a demon's life force as you get closer to it. When I was searching the woods, I didn't sense anything that could have been a demon. If one is still lurking in the Forest of the Vale, it must be considerably far in.

"A demon, a demon... I don't have anyone available for this."

"You said Gregorio is available, didn't you? He would be fine for this."

He has a lot of experience, and he's sufficiently competent. My only concern is that he might finish the demon off before he has a chance to interrogate it.

"...*I thought you didn't like him?*" says Creio, sounding surprised.

"It's not that I don't like him. He's just hard to deal with."

He is by no means a man of the Church, but I can't deny that he's an outstanding solider. It makes me wonder why he chose to become a priest rather than a mercenary in the first place.

Above all, regardless of whether the opponent is a demon or the undead, he'll be able to destroy it without any trouble. If they request Helios's assistance as well, he'll have an even higher chance of success.

"It's settled, then. He happens to be at headquarters on standby right now, so he should arrive there in two or three days."

"I'm going to go on ahead with the hero's party to the next town, so I'll leave the rest to you."

"...You're leaving? What about leveling up?"

"It will be faster and safer to level up in another town, rather than staying here when there's a demon nearby."

Considering that it's possible the hero's whereabouts have been discovered, it's risky to stay in one place.

Not to mention that Golem Valley, where they'll be going next, is much more open than the forest, which will make it easier to follow them.

"They've taken Glacia into their group, so I intend to control their movements through her."

Perhaps lost in his own thoughts, Creio is silent for a while before finally sighing deeply.

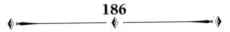

"The overdone sense of justice is a crime."

"…Understood. We'll do something about the demon."

"Got it. If anything else comes up, I'll report back."

Well then, all that's left is to guide Toudou where I need him to go. We have to wrap things up here and move on before we step on any land mines.

§ § §

"…All right. Thank you for your report, Sir Toudou."

"Uh…yeah…"

The Vale Village headman bows at Toudou's report, his expression somehow tired.

The headman's request was that they defeat the glacial plant. Due to unexpected circumstances, they weren't able to achieve that goal.

Having expected that the village headman would voice some complaint, Toudou is surprised by his short reply.

Standing nearby is Glacia, wearing the dress they just bought for her, looking nervously at her surroundings.

Toudou shows Glacia to the headman as proof that the dragon transformed into a human. They had expected him to be suspicious of this explanation, but he doesn't question it.

"Um…we haven't exactly *defeated* the dragon. You don't have any issue with that?"

The headman's eyes wander around the room, as if looking for someone. His eyebrow twitches, and he looks at Toudou with a smile that seems somehow bitter.

"…No, no issue. The problem no longer has any effect on the village, so from my point of view, there is nothing more to say."

"…Sir, are you…all right? …You're kind of pale," says Limis with familial concern for this man around her grandfather's age.

"Y-yes, I'm fine. I'm just—just a bit…tired. Yes, I must be tired."

"…Is it that you've been worrying over the incident with the mercenaries?" asks Toudou, a guilty look on his face. Toudou is referring to

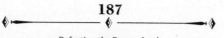

when he impulsively attacked the mercenaries at the tavern. The headman, however, is preoccupied with our last encounter. I still remember the dumbstruck look on his face.

The village headman, flustered, quickly shakes his head from side to side and waves his hands. "No, no, no—most certainly not! It has nothing to do with you, Sir Toudou... It is a personal matter."

"...Well, all right..."

Toudou tilts his head slightly to one side, puzzled by the change in the village headman's demeanor. The old man seems frightened; usually one would expect a village leader to be confident. Despite being his age, he'd previously had an aura of cunning seemingly immune to the hero's party. Now, the village headman regards the Holy Warrior warily, almost like a frog being stared down by a snake.

Disquieted by Toudou's stare, the village headman asks in a high-pitched voice, "W-well then, Sir Toudou, where will you be going next?"

"Actually, I haven't decided yet..."

Because of all that had happened, Toudou hadn't leveled up at all in the past three days.

After the quick change of subject, he looks at the village headman suspiciously. "I'm thinking of spending a little longer in the Forest of the Vale—"

"Actually, Sir Toudou," interrupts the village headman. He puts a hand to his forehead and closes his eyes, choosing his words carefully. "I've decided to close off the forest for a while."

"You're closing it off?!"

The village headman stammers awkwardly in response to Toudou and company's shocked expressions.

"Um—well, actually, there is a dangerous monster in the forest, as you said yourself...and until it is defeated, I have decided to prohibit entry..."

"I've never heard of such a thing...," remarks Aria suspiciously.

Forests are, by nature, home to monsters. You enter at your own risk. When a dangerous monster appears, it's typical to dispatch the royal

"The overdone sense of justice is a crime."

knights to defeat it, but it's not common practice to prohibit entry to the area entirely.

The village headman looks to Aria, straight-faced. "Considering the amount of danger posed by this particular monster, it was decided that special measures need to be taken. Not to mention that the monster has been very active."

"...It did seem to be quite powerful..." Limis's face turns red as she recalls the howl of murderous intent and how it paralyzed her legs.

Toudou cocks his head skeptically. "We only just reported the monster to you now, and you've already decided to close it off?"

"...No, no, the decision wasn't made because of your report, Sir Toudou. I heard from another source..."

"...Another source?"

"Yes... I can't expose this individual here, but I have another source," he responds with finality, closing his mouth. Though they may have questions, he clearly intends to say no more.

Toudou opens his mouth to say something but quickly reconsiders. Maybe he recalls the howl in the forest.

For him to challenge an opponent that he realized only this morning is way beyond him would be an act of suicide. He understands clearly that no matter how prepared he is, he is no match for it.

Aria, who had been watching Toudou apprehensively, breathes a sigh of relief.

"We don't have much time, so that makes things a bit difficult for us...," says Toudou. "How long do you think it will take for it to be defeated?"

"I've been told it will take two or three days for the hunter to reach us. I think you can expect it to be over in a week, all told."

"A week, huh...?"

The one-month marker is coming up fast. It's not like they can sit around doing nothing.

As Toudou mulls it over, the village headman suddenly claps his hands together loudly, almost to snap him out of it. "I'm aware that you

don't have much time, Sir Hero. I would suggest that you head for the next level-up area."

"The...*next* level-up area?"

"That's right." He produces a weathered parchment from his desk drawer.

It's a map of the territory within Ruxe Kingdom. It's covered in markings and notes.

"Our current location is here," he says, putting his finger on a large wooded spot on the right edge of the map. From there, he drags his finger across the map, over the grassland and prairie that extends east of the royal capital, stopping at the foot of the mountains.

"*Golem Valley*," says Limis.

The village headman nods and readily launches into an explanation. "Yes, Golem Valley. In the mountain region, which is inhabited by golem-type monsters that have high life force, the valley is the foremost place to level up in Ruxe Kingdom. It should be much more efficient to level up there instead of in the Great Forest."

"Hold on a minute," Aria jumps in, sternly objecting. She glares at the village headman. "That area is recommended for those level forty and above. The average level of our party is not even thirty."

Toudou is 27, Aria is 25, and Limis is 17—all below the recommended minimum. On top of that, they don't have a priest. Aria stares down at the map, roaming her finger around it.

"For leveling up, we should go somewhere more suitable for our level... Hmmm, let's see... I think the area around the Great Tomb would be a good choice, as it is about the same level as the Forest of the Vale."

Toudou's gaze follows the path of Aria's finger, which stops at an area far at the bottom of the map called Yutith's Tomb. It's a grave site known for being home to many undead-type monsters.

While an undead king is thought to live in the depths of the tomb, the area near the entrance is populated by low-class monsters that can be easily defeated in large numbers. It's for this reason the tomb is famed as a hunting ground.

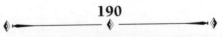

"The overdone sense of justice is a crime."

The village headman explains his opposing viewpoint. "Going into the Great Tomb without a priest is like walking to your death. Its reputation is as a place good for *priests* to level up, you know. Because the undead have so little life force, you need to take out large swaths of them to level up by attacking. And the further you go into the tomb, the more monsters there are that can cause paralysis or poison. What's more, the grave is filled with miasma. Sir Hero should be safe from it with his holy armor, but Miss Aria and Miss Limis—I don't think you'll be able to stand it very long. It will also be difficult for Miss Limis to use her fire magic, as the area is all underground. Overall, I wouldn't say it's your best option."

Aria stares wide-eyed at the bearded man's explanation before speaking.

"...Sir, how is it you know so much about our party...?"

"...O-oh... These are just guesses, only guesses. I would be honored to know so much about the hero."

He averts his eyes and looks down at the map, tapping his finger on Golem Valley. "Compared to all the trouble of the tomb, the golems in Golem Valley are an easy fight. Typically, they will not approach you and attack, and you can obtain a fairly large amount of life force from each of them. Their offensive and defensive power are both high, but their movements are slow. If you attack them at their core, they are easily defeated. Also, because the area is in open air, Miss Limis should be able to burn the golems to ash with her fire."

Limis had been listening quietly, but now she nods emphatically. "Okay, let's go there, then!"

While Aria and the village headman are locked in a stare-down, Toudou thinks it over, his head inclined to one side. "From my point of view...either would be fine," he says.

When it comes down to who Toudou trusts more, it's unquestionably Aria. There is also the consideration that the village headman is acting strangely—he knows all kinds of information about them that they never shared with him.

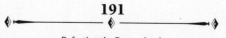

Under Toudou's suspicious gaze, the village headman starts sweating.

After being silent and motionless through the entire exchange, Glacia suddenly chimes in. "*Goh-lem Val-lay!*"

"...Huh?"

This is the first time she's spoken in front of them. They certainly can't ignore it.

Toudou hastily looks around and then directs his gaze down at the dragon girl standing at his side.

Paying Toudou no mind, Glacia repeats herself, her pronunciation still strange. "Go to Goh-lem Val-lay!"

"...What are you saying? I mean—you—you can talk?!"

Ignoring Toudou's confusion, Glacia repeats it again, like a broken toy. "*Goh-lem Val-lay! Goh-lem Val-lay!*"

At first, Limis is completely shocked by the unexpected support, but she quickly reevaluates. "Oh, see—see, Glacia agrees! *Golem Valley! Golem Valley!*"

The two of them start chanting it together.

Aria looks exasperated. "No matter how you look at it, that's a dangerous—"

"...It appears that a decision has already been made, hasn't it!"

"?!"

The village headman's interjection cuts Aria off.

He turns to Toudou and speaks quickly, trying to end the discussion as soon as possible. "If you're going to leave the village, it's better to go sooner rather than later. When the hunt for the monster in the woods begins, we will be prohibiting departure from the village."

"Wha...? So soon?!" says Toudou.

"*Goh-lem Val-lay! Goh-lem Val-lay!*" shouts Glacia persistently, as though it's her duty.

"*Golem Valley! Golem Valley!*" continues Limis.

"What in the world...?" says Aria, her lip quivering in frustration. Aria and Toudou watch in confusion as this unexpected turn of events continues to unfold.

"The overdone sense of justice is a crime."

Then the village headman takes three large bags out from behind his desk and sets them at Toudou's feet.

"I've put together supplies for you. Everything from food and potions to things like spare bullets."

"...What?!"

"You can take this map with you, too. I have prepared all these things for you, Sir Hero. Please do not hesitate to accept them." He thrusts the map toward Toudou, practically forcing him to take it.

"N-no, really, I haven't even decided what I want to do yet—"

"Come now, please hurry, Sir Toudou. Your time is limited. I am so grateful for all of your help. So sad to see you go, but that is the nature of those who journey. After you've defeated the Demon Lord, please do me the honor of visiting Vale Village again. You'll receive a grand reception!"

"Wait, hold on—"

The headman puts the three bags in his hands and pushes him out the door before he can ask any questions. The man is so aggressive that, even as the hero, Toudou can't manage to get a word in.

Once he's pushed them all the way out of the house, the village headman stops Toudou. Raising his eyebrows, he says in a low voice, "Sir Hero...I think you need to get yourself a priest."

"Huh...? Uh, wh-what?"

Toudou is lost. As he frantically tries to wrap his head around all of it, the village headman closes the door in his face.

Everyone is quiet except for Glacia, who continues chanting the same thing again and again. *"Goh-lem Val-lay! Goh-lem Val-lay!"*

"What just happened...?" asks Aria.

"Uh, yeah, that's what I want to know...," says Toudou.

§　§　§

The sun has completely set, and only a small sliver of moonlight filters through the window. Amelia's expressionless face is reflected in the glass.

She ends the transmission with Glacia and looks over to Ares, who sits sharpening his knife.

"Ares, I have Glacia's report. It seems the party has decided to head to Golem Valley."

"Have they? That's good news. What's their schedule?"

"They plan to leave tomorrow morning."

Their decision is as expected. Ares puts away his knife and breathes a sigh. "All right. Somehow things seem to be going according to plan so far."

"Indeed. Our method was a bit heavy-handed… I wondered if it would work."

They'd convinced the village headman to cooperate and had coached Glacia on what to say as well. The execution was clumsy enough to make anyone suspicious. Ares stands up straight at Amelia's reproachful tone.

"Don't overthink it. As long as we achieve our goals, who cares about the methods?"

The transformation of the glacial plant into human form had certainly been a shock. There'd been no warning it would happen—the most unexpected of unexpected circumstances. Witnessing it happen right before her eyes, Amelia had felt as if she was having a bad dream.

After spending an entire night preparing Glacia and the village headman for that meeting, Amelia doesn't understand how Ares can be so flippant. "…Ares, don't you take this seriously?"

"Do I look like I'm not taking it seriously?" The crusader responds by turning up the corners of his mouth slightly into a sarcastic smile. He looks like he isn't taking anything seriously at all, but Amelia forgoes pointing it out. If that mind-set lightens the load on his shoulders, she can let it be.

"…Well, would you say we've done all we can for now?"

"Yeah, I'd say so. We asked Helios to assist with the demon, so that's done… Now we have a little free time until tomorrow morning." In spite of his casual tone, Ares's expression is grim. He doesn't seem relaxed.

Amelia and Ares have known each other for a long time.

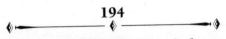

They first met more than five years ago, when Amelia started as an operator, but they have hardly spent any time face-to-face. Amelia herself is still shy around Ares, as if he were a stranger.

Ares sits facing away from her, his arms crossed, looking deep in thought. As Amelia hazily observes him, it suddenly occurs to her to invite him for a meal. But as soon as she opens her mouth to ask, she hears him thinking out loud.

"Right now, Toudou lacks fundamental knowledge... I wonder if there's someone I could ask to join up with him, teach him a few things..." Then he takes out a bundle of paper and unrolls it on the table.

"Um...Ares?"

"Hmm... Yeah, what is it?" he asks without looking away from the pile.

In a pitch slightly higher than her usual, Amelia asks, "Um... How about getting some dinner? Neither of us has eaten anything today, right?"

"Hmm... Yeah, feel free to go get yourself something. I've still got a few things to do."

"...Are those things you need to get done *today*?"

"No, not really." Ares takes out a pen and starts writing a letter.

Amelia takes him by the shoulders and looks at him. "We've done all we need to do for now, haven't we?"

"Yes, I guess we have."

"...So will you come to eat? A lot has happened the past few days, and it's good to give yourself a rest every once in a while."

"I still have things to do. It's perfectly fine with me if you go."

"...But are those things you need to get done *today*?"

"...No?" He remains focused on the letter.

Amelia frowns, saying nothing for a while. Then she asks cautiously, "Ares...are you really this much of a workaholic?"

"No, I'm not really...," he says, his pen not stopping for even a second. Watching him, Amelia remembers something the cardinal told her.

Amelia, he's excellent at what he does, but if left alone, he never stops

195

working. He casts holy techniques on himself to keep going, which doesn't always have good results. Try to get him to rest when you can.

…He's worked this hard and still feels he hasn't done enough?

Looking at Ares's face, Amelia can see the weariness in his eyes. It makes sense that he would be tired. As far as Amelia is aware, the only time Ares has rested in the past several days was that few hours in the woods. Looking at him now, she's not even convinced he rested then.

Making up her mind, Amelia reaches around Ares from behind and covers his eyes with her hands. "Ares! Can you please stop working and rest for a while? You're going to work yourself to death."

"No…I'm fine."

"?!"

To Amelia's surprise, she can still hear the pen scratching the paper. She peeks down and observes that he's writing properly, not just scribbling. Even with his vision completely obscured, he doesn't stop.

Then Amelia can hear him whisper, "You can't stop me from working just by covering my eyes."

"You're—you're focusing on the wrong thing, here!" she shouts, reaching out and snatching away the unfinished letter. Ares looks up at her, surprised, as she protests firmly, waving the paper in the air.

"Ares!! *This* is not something you need to do right now, is it?"

"Oh, right. If there's something else you think should be prioritized, I'll take care of that first," Ares responds, oblivious to her point.

Amelia glares at him icily. *This guy is a lost cause… If left to his own devices, he really would never stop.*

She regains her composure and chooses her words carefully. "…Actually, there is something I would like to discuss with you."

"Discuss? …What is it?"

"It's a little difficult to explain here… Can we talk while we eat?"

"…Yeah, sure." He finally puts down his pen and heaves a quiet sigh.

Later, during their meal, Ares still can't seem to think of anything but work. It only reinforces what the cardinal told her.

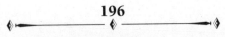

"The overdone sense of justice is a crime."

§ § §

Although it is called Vale Village, from Toudou's point of view, the hustle and bustle feels more like that of a *town* than a *village*.

The look of the streets and houses is very Western, and although it isn't modern, having just graduated high school and not knowing much about Western history, Toudou thinks it is sophisticated in its own way.

This world is entirely different from his world. The culture is different. There are beings with intelligence equal to or greater than humans, and there are spirits, magic, and all kinds of mysteries that could only exist in daydreams in Japan.

The first time Toudou witnessed the use of magic, he was dumbstruck. Even now, there are still times when he feels like he's in a dream.

Somehow, the other world already feels so far in the past. Toudou sighs. "I guess the only thing that doesn't change is human emotion..."

Joy, sadness, anger—these are the only things that remain the same in both worlds.

The Vale is far from where the war is raging. Looking at the peaceful landscape, you wouldn't think the Demon Lord had invaded. But that doesn't change the fact that he continues to take more and more victims.

Toudou feels an ache in his arm. His chest feels tight, and his heart pounds loudly.

Naotsugu Toudou's purpose in life has always been carrying out justice—even before he was summoned to this world as the hero.

But before, he had no power. Now, he does. The question is, does he have the determination to follow through?

As Toudou stands there in a daze, he hears Aria's familiar voice from behind him.

"Sorry to have kept you waiting, Sir Nao."

"Ah, no... Not at all." As he turns around, his expression changes, and a gentle smile comes over his face.

He looks at his two companions—the two he must protect.

"I think we should go while the sun is high," says Aria. "We need

197

to cross the prairie. If possible, I would like to reach our destination by this evening."

"We need to start leveling up as soon as possible," Toudou says.

"Yes," Aria agrees, nodding soberly. Her fortitude and dignity remind Toudou of the knights of legend. "We might have trouble with the monsters of the prairie, as most of them travel in large groups. I think it best to pass through as quickly as we can."

"But…Garnet could scorch the entire prairie," says Limis.

"Yes, but it's best not to underestimate monsters that travel in packs," counters Aria. "If they sense the presence of magic, they will undoubtedly target it. Of course, I would do my best to protect you, but if we end up surrounded by dozens of monsters, the battle may become extremely difficult. Not to mention—"

Aria pauses, glancing behind her. Glacia is looking here and there around the room, examining everything with childlike interest. Even smaller in stature than Limis, Glacia has a fragile figure and long green hair, looking almost like a sprite.

It's still uncertain why she changed into this human form, but as she has no intention of returning to the forest, they felt they had no choice but to take her along.

Toudou reaches his hand out and smooths her long green hair. Glacia looks up at him sadly and mumbles, "I'm…hungry…"

Aria sighs. "…It seems our food expenses are going to increase substantially."

Although her physical body is much smaller, somehow there is no great change in Glacia's appetite—she seems to eat as much as a dragon. Their bill at the inn was more than twice what they expected.

Toudou smiles wryly and takes his hand off Glacia's head. "Ah-ha-ha… We're going to need to prepare a lot of food."

"Well… If she's going to eat so much, I wonder if she can at least help us in battle…?" muses Aria.

"But can she even fight? She's so little…," asks Limis, staring down at the only party member smaller than herself.

"The overdone sense of justice is a crime."

"…We'll find out soon. Seeing as she *is* a dragon, I don't think she's incapable of fighting…," says Toudou.

Even Aria, who comes from a highly educated family, had never heard of a monster that could take human form.

Limis eventually loses interest in staring down at Glacia and looks up. "Anyway, let's leave for Golem Valley right away! I want to show you guys what I can do."

"Yes, I'm looking forward to that," says Toudou. "Let's head out… after we've put in the report to the Church, I suppose?"

"Ah, right. I forgot about that," says Limis.

Then Toudou's party starts out toward the church to fulfill Ares's request.

The father who governs the church is in the farthest room in the back.

When Toudou enters, he is arranging some sort of tools on his desk. He turns to face Toudou, and a thin smile comes to his lips.

"I say, if it isn't Sir Toudou…" Helios still has his usual taunting smile. He slowly gets to his feet.

"I came to report… I think Ares will have told you I'd be coming."

"Yes…naturally, I have been informed." His smile broadens as he claps his hands together.

Limis looks casually at the table, and her eyes widen when she sees the variety of tools all lined up.

There's a silver cross and several silver stakes ten-odd centimeters in length. There's a bottle filled with a glittering, transparent liquid and a silver staff with a rounded tip. There are also several other strange tools, their respective uses difficult to guess.

"What are these…?"

"Ah, these… They are tools I will use to defeat the demon, Miss Friedia." He casually picks up one of the stakes and, holding it between his fingers, gives a flick of his wrist. The stake makes a soft sound as it shallowly pierces the wall.

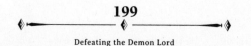

Ignoring the surprised looks on their faces, Helios pats the stakes with his hand, as if they are precious.

"These stakes are not actually very sturdy, so they may not be useful against an ordinary monster. However, demons are weak to silver that has been blessed."

"You're going to fight a demon?" asks Toudou, suddenly looking up from the tools on the table. "Is it the demon in the woods?"

"Ah, you know of it?" he says, narrowing his eyes. "Demons are an enemy of the Church... I intend to cooperate with the Church and fight it to the best of my ability."

"A priest going to fight a demon...?"

"Indeed... We possess techniques for the eradication of evil spirits."

Toudou's eyebrow twitches at the mention of these techniques—the only ones he hadn't learned, thinking they were unnecessary.

"Naturally, eradication techniques would be effective against demons... Sir Helios, will you fight it alone?" asks Aria.

Seeing her serious expression, Helios waves his hands in an exaggerated gesture. "No, no... I am only going along to support. We have called in an expert."

"You have requested the royal knights...?" Aria asks.

"No, a specialized priest from the Church."

"This expert is...also a priest?"

"Yes. We should have this foolish demon terminated within a few days."

"...Isn't it dangerous to fight a demon with only priests?"

Helios chuckles, not at all concerned. "Heh-heh-heh... We are well aware of the danger. One cannot overthrow an enemy of God without taking some risks."

Smiling, Helios goes to the wall and removes the silver stake.

After purchasing the necessary supplies, Toudou's party confirms that they haven't overlooked anything and heads for the village exit.

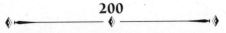

On their way, they pass by the mercenaries who were involved in the *incident*, though Toudou doesn't realize. The mercenaries, on the other hand, do notice Toudou and jump back in surprise at the sight of him. Saying nothing at all, they quickly hurry out of sight.

When they nearly reach the gate, Toudou calls out to Aria. Since they left the church, she seems to have been lost in thought.

"Did something happen earlier?"

"No… Nothing really happened. It's just…," Aria mumbles and glances back in the direction of the church, now out of view.

"Was it something in that conversation about the demon in the woods?"

"No…it isn't that… Well, yes." She tries denying it at first but gives up under the pressure of Toudou's stare and relents.

There are more people than usual crowding around the village gate. It seems it will take time for them to be let out.

Glacia is still looking around restlessly, and Limis holds on to one of her sleeves, supervising her. Toudou glances at them, then looks back to Aria.

"…Is there something that concerns you?" he asks quietly enough that the others can't overhear.

"…Yes," Aria answers in a low voice.

Aria had been contemplating whether or not she should say it. She remembers Toudou's reckless actions in the forest—if she hadn't been able to stop him from fighting, what would have happened?

But Toudou is the hero. They'll be together for a long time on this journey, and she shouldn't start keeping secrets from the leader of the party.

Honesty is a principle of the House of Rizas. Aria may have changed swordsmanship schools but has no intention of casting away her family's principles.

She examines Toudou as she reaches her conclusion. He's the Holy Warrior. She's supposed to trust him. He's the one who will save the world.

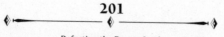

"...Sir Nao... Do you remember the cry of murderous intent that assailed us in the forest?"

"...Yes... That isn't something I would forget."

"The owner of that cry...was not a follower of darkness. Not a demon."

"...What?!"

Being from a family of warriors, Aria has a certain amount of learning about monsters.

"The presence of a follower of darkness brings with it a unique sensation. A certain fear that is hard to express in words, a feeling that the darkness is seeping into your body, down into your gut. But when we were in the woods...I didn't sense that."

Aria's expression turns more serious. "To begin with, followers of darkness do not inhabit the Forest of the Vale. That cry we heard must have been a plant-type or beast-type monster."

"...A plant- or beast-type... Does that pose some kind of problem?"

Aria stares silently at Toudou and breathes a heavy sigh. "Eradication techniques are only effective against followers of darkness. Sir Nao, those priests who go to fight it will surely be—defeated."

"...Defeated?" repeats Toudou, his voice dry. It takes him a moment to fully understand.

Then Toudou's pupils dilate, and his gaze pierces Aria.

"You're saying they're going to lose?"

Hearing the emotion in Toudou's voice, Aria feels a pang of regret. But in the end, she is the one who decided to join him on this journey. Her role is to follow him where he chooses to go and support him until he defeats the Demon Lord.

"But they said they've called in an expert."

"That will be an expert in *demon* hunting. In this kingdom, *monster* hunting is handled by the royal knights, who are under the jurisdiction of the School of Swordsmanship."

In fact, the powerful monsters that invade the kingdom are defeated

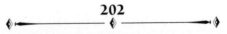

"The overdone sense of justice is a crime."

primarily by the royal knights. Of course, priests are also dispatched from the Church, but their primary role is to heal and cast buffs.

Toudou whips his head around, looking back toward the church. He doesn't have much good will toward Helios, but he certainly doesn't hate him so much that he would be glad to hear of his death. That would be contrary to Toudou's ideals.

Then, Toudou realizes something. "Wait...," he says, looking back at Aria. "Why didn't you say that to Helios? If you had told him—"

"Because...it wouldn't change anything."

"What? What do you mean...?"

They are nearing the front of the exit line. The mercenaries queued up behind them inch forward, pressing them onward.

"When the Church dispatches a priest on a mission, that is considered an order directly from God. To them, completing their mission is top priority. Even if he didn't stand a chance, I don't think that priest at the church would withdraw from a battle."

Toudou is taken aback by this information. Aria continues.

"This also applies to a specialist dispatched from the Church. Sir Nao, don't you remember when Ares proposed we consume monster flesh? He would break his creed as a priest in order to defeat the Demon Lord, to accomplish his mission from God. That...is how many priests are."

Listening to Aria, Toudou recalls Ares, a severe man who would sacrifice anything to defeat the Demon Lord. If what Aria says is true, it explains Ares's actions as well.

Aria remains silent for a while, observing Toudou's expression and his shallow breaths.

This is how she expected him to react. As the hero, of course he doesn't want to let that happen. He is in pursuit of higher ideals and doing what is right, so he cannot choose to ignore this. He is the type of person who readily makes the choice that an ordinary person could not.

"Sir Nao, I...didn't want to say it, but...I think we have two options."

Toudou listens to Aria with a grim expression, biting his lower lip.

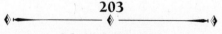

§ · § · §

"Ares, that was Toudou's party confirming that they have exited the village," Amelia reports, just returning from outside.

"Oh, they have?"

Instead of her normal priest's robe, Amelia is wearing a more comfortable white jacket and pants. The only remaining evidence that she is a priest are her earring and her ring. If she didn't have them on, you wouldn't think her a sister. She is a bit of a...free spirit. Perhaps a little too free.

Amelia notices me looking at her and makes a little twirl. "Does it suit me?"

"...It does." Although my response is mild, a slight smile comes to Amelia's face.

It isn't clearly defined in the creed, but normally priests always wear their robes. I try to wear mine pretty much all the time. But I suppose things could be different for holy casters.

This job can be such a burden. They should at least let us wear what we want—it's not like our clothes affect our work.

"Let's leave here around the same time that Toudou arrives in the village at the halfway point. I'd like to avoid running into each other."

We've already made all our preparations. That being said, there isn't much prep needed for the road to Golem Valley.

We'll be crossing the prairie, which is quite a distance, but the monsters there aren't strong, and we have a means of transportation.

I flip through my bag, confirming that I haven't overlooked anything. Amelia observes me while fiddling with her bangs.

"Amelia, today we'll be traveling through the night," I tell her. "You should get some sleep while you can."

"...I could say the same to you," she says, her tone almost admonishing.

"I can fight without sleeping for three straight days."

One of us needs to stay awake in case something happens.

No matter how coolheaded Amelia is, she's still a woman. Human

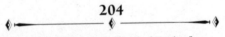

men are biologically predisposed to being physically stronger than human women, and on top of that, my level is much higher than hers.

Amelia sighs uncharacteristically. Maybe she doesn't believe me?

"I actually *have* done that. One time, there were three towns overrun with the undead, and I handled all of them alone."

"...Are you some kind of tireless golem?"

"I mean, that was an urgent situation. Naturally, I'd prefer not to work under those circumstances, but I could do it again if I had to."

That was about three years ago. If it had been only undead, I could have wiped them all out pretty quickly, but demons were also involved in that incident.

"I'm just going to say it," pronounces Amelia indignantly. "If you don't rest, neither do I."

What's the point of saying a thing like that? Our personalities are just too different.

I stare into Amelia's face and consider how to dissuade her, but eventually, I give up. It's a waste of time.

Anyway, although we're traveling at night, I'm really the only one who needs to stay awake. It would be fine for her to sleep.

Maybe feeling a little awkward because of my silence, Amelia claps her hands together and changes the subject. "Now then, until nightfall we have spare time."

"Don't forget about the periodic reports."

At seven AM, seven PM, and noon, Amelia checks in with Glacia. It's a job only she can do.

"I know," Amelia says curtly, no change in her expression. "*You* don't have any more work tonight, Ares."

"There's nothing I *need* to do, but there are things that I *can* do."

"Right... There's something I want to discuss with you."

...Yesterday she also said she had something to discuss, but in the end, there wasn't anything at all.

She pays my suspicious look no mind and says coolly, "Let's have a drink first. Helios sent over a nice bottle."

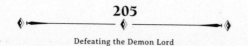

"...Are you *actually* a priest?"

Alcohol isn't specifically prohibited by the creed, but it should be consumed in moderation. There are many devout believers who don't drink at all.

Actually, neither of my parents were fond of alcohol. What a strange girl.

"You're aware it's still the middle of the day, right? You want to start drinking now?"

I point to the window. It's just past noon. There probably aren't even that many mercenaries who would start drinking this early.

Not at all concerned by my comment, Amelia pulls a bottle of alcohol out of nowhere and shows it to me.

"Can I pour you a glass?"

It's no use—she isn't getting the message at all. Looking as disagreeable as I can, I ask her, "Can you even drink?"

"Of course. I'm no lightweight."

"...Is that so?"

...Maybe she's just really stressed out?

What an absurd situation. It's not that I'm opposed to drinking during the day, but is it really part of my job to keep people company?

I sigh and concede to Amelia. "All right, after we check our preparations one last time."

"Got it."

...Who is this person in front of me? I thought Amelia said she's not a lightweight.

"Areeeees, are you liiistenin'?"

"I'm listening, I'm listening!"

Talking to her when she's sober, I couldn't have imagined her being so inarticulate.

She plops her glass down on the table. There's a little red in her white cheeks, and her indigo-blue-colored eyes are hazy.

Observing her, I take a swig from my glass. The strong, sharply fla-

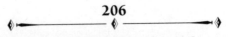

"The overdone sense of justice is a crime."

vored alcohol makes its way down my throat. Amelia might feel like she can hold her liquor, but all it took for her to come this far was a few sips.

Once she's sobered up, I'd like to ask what makes her think she's a strong drinker.

Paying no attention to my stare, Amelia lifts her nearly full glass to down it in one go.

A few drops dribble out of her mouth and roll down her neck, and some spills on the table. When we started drinking, she took off her jacket right away and tossed it on the floor. Now she's down to a thin light-blue shirt. Some alcohol spills on that, too, and the bra beneath it is visible in places. Some "bride of God" this chick is.

"...You're drunk already?"

"I toldja, I'm not drunken!" Amelia says, frustrated, shaking her head side to side.

Not drunken! No sober person would say something like that.

I extend my hand to use a holy technique on her, but she dodges it with surprising agility.

Holding the bottle in her left arm, she jabs her right index finger at me. "Occashonally, it's fine, right? Ares, ya gotta lighten uuup!"

It's hard to lighten up when a person is transforming before your eyes!

"Are you...stressed out by the job or something?"

"Nooot reeeeallyyy? I mean, I wanted dis job, ya know?"

Then what the hell prompted this shameful display? I've drunk with a lot of people before, but this is the first time I've seen anyone this far gone.

Amelia looks at me with cloudy eyes, clinging to the bottle with both hands, childishly, like she thinks someone might take it from her. Her current state is so completely opposite her normal self... Alcohol's some scary stuff.

"I mean, we're not on da job, riiiiight? Like, offishally?"

"...All right, I get it. It's fine. Drink to your heart's content."

When it comes time for the evening report, I'll be able to return her to normal anyway.

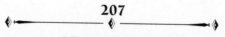

I can't tell if she's aware of this or not, but she breaks into a big smile at my reply. "Yaaaay! Yer da beeeest, Ares!"

She carefully sets the bottle on the table, and then throwing her arms open, she dives at me in a tackle. I quickly alight from my seat and dodge her. There's a clatter as Amelia falls to the floor, knocking over her chair in the process.

Is she really *this* kind of drunk? What a pain in the ass.

Amelia rolls over on the floor and looks up at me resentfully. "…Dat was ruuuude."

You're the rude one here! I'm sure Creio has never seen her in this condition.

I frown and raise my voice to scold her in an effort to sober her up. "Sisters shouldn't be going around jumping at men in the first place!"

Seeing a sister, expected to be modest and pure, getting drunk like this is a little jarring.

I'm not sure if she understood what I said or not, but Amelia starts to get up and then plops into a seated position on the floor. She says only, "…It's…it's hawt in here."

She sighs loudly and pulls at the buttons of her shirt with unsteady fingers.

I stare at her in shock. She looks up at me, red-faced, swaying side to side.

…Thank God. Thank God she didn't join the hero's party. If she had, she would have lost her holy techniques in no time.

I wonder if she'll remember any of this foolishness when she sobers up.

As I begin to stand, Amelia starts undoing her buttons so forcefully it looks like she might tear them off. This is really too much.

"This is the last time I let you drink," I announce while glaring down at her, aware that she may not remember it when she's sober.

I check the clock again. There's still time before she has to collect the report, but I think this needs to be taken care of now. If I let things continue, she might end up naked before long.

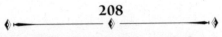

208

"The overdone sense of justice is a crime."

She's thrown off her shirt and is now just in a white undershirt. I've never seen this much of her before, but for some reason, I feel no desire for her.

Amelia looks up at me in a daze. I crack my knuckles and take a step toward her.

"I'm gonna show you just what I can do."

"If ya lay yer hands on me, will ya take responsibility for it?"

"…What the hell kind of a person do you think I am?"

I understand that being a lightweight isn't her fault, but I decide to complain to Creio about this later.

No, it goes without saying: This sucks.

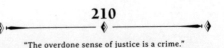

"The overdone sense of justice is a crime."

A Full Account of the Strange Incident in the Forest of the Vale

"You're sure about this?" Limis asks a little nervously.

"...I am," says Toudou, nodding.

A cloudless blue sky hangs over the endless grasslands. Behind them is the outer wall of Vale Village.

Toudou faces the direction opposite the way they'd planned to go. There is no enthusiasm in his face.

"Sir Nao...," says Aria, her voice tinged with regret.

Nao mumbles to himself. It's his choice—not Aria's, not Limis's.

"I—am the hero," he says, as if to remind himself. His words blow away with the breeze, and his feet take him once more toward the forest.

He must always try to fulfill his role as the hero. Naotsugu Toudou's code of conduct is as steadfast as his will to succeed.

§ § §

Dammit, just one more pain in my ass. I'd rather battle a monster to the death than deal with this.

Still cloudy-eyed, unsteady on her feet, and convinced that she isn't drunk, Amelia demonstrates surprising evasive skills.

I'm good at chasing monsters but not so good at chasing people.

Even so, after she deftly dodges me for a while, I manage to corner Amelia by the wall and catch hold of her arm.

Finally got her. This lightweight...

211

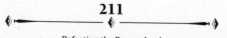

Defeating the Demon Lord

Just as I stretch out my hand toward her head to cast a holy technique, suddenly Amelia jumps with a start.

I stop. She turns her face to me, a pointed look in her eyes.

Her cheeks are still red, but she doesn't appear drunk anymore. Then, in her normal, flat voice, she says, "...Ares, it seems that Toudou... has gone back to the Forest of the Vale."

The only thing more shocking than this drastic change in Amelia is what's coming out of her mouth.

Toudou is...going into the forest? No, no, no, no.

It doesn't make any sense. We went to the trouble of coaching the village headman and Glacia to convince the party to go to Golem Valley, and they reported to Helios that they intended to make that their next destination.

There's no reason why Toudou would lie to the Church, and even if he changed his mind, he doesn't have any reason to go into the Forest of the Vale.

I try to act calm but can't help my voice from lowering. *"Why?"*

"...I'm receiving the transmission from Glacia now. She's...just saying nonsense. She isn't giving a reason."

"...Shit."

Why can't they just do what they're supposed to for once? *I told you the forest was dangerous, you dumbasses!*

I try to think this through clearly. Amelia says they've already gone back into the forest, so even if we leave now, it'll take us an hour to get there.

Amelia is sitting soberly in the chair across from me. "I'm sorry... If only I had contacted Glacia earlier..."

I check the time. It's still several hours before the update we'd decided on.

"No, I'm glad you caught it when you did."

"I was just a little uneasy..."

Of course, it would have been even better if she'd realized when they first started heading toward the forest, but that's in the past.

Now, hold on a second—is this the Amelia who was completely drunk a moment ago?

"The overdone sense of justice is a crime."

I stare at her. She seems entirely back to normal. Does she have an *on* and *off* switch or something?!

I want to pursue that, but for the time being, I set it aside. Right now, it's time to work.

The first thing we need to do is gather information and review the safety concerns of the situation.

I steered Toudou away from the forest because it's highly dangerous. But that isn't the *only* reason.

"The area of the forest Glacia was chased out of—the area inhabited by the glacial plants—is the very deepest point in the forest. That woodland is enormous. It's highly unlikely the party will encounter the demon right away."

"But what we haven't established yet is *why* the demon drove Glacia so far out toward the edge of the forest."

That's exactly right. *That* is the reason I wanted to keep Toudou away. We don't have a solid understanding of the situation.

It actually doesn't matter if this demon is a servant of the Demon Lord or not. If Toudou encounters any demon at this stage, he has no chance of winning.

"I want to know why Toudou went back there."

If he just wants to level up in the forest, that shouldn't be a problem. They wouldn't wander into the deeper, more dangerous parts of the woods.

Although it seems unlikely, if he intends to fight that demon, this is a much riskier situation. Even the usual monsters that live in the deep parts of the woods would be dangerous for Toudou's party at their current level.

Amelia sighs loudly. "…The only thing Glacia is saying is that she's hungry."

"That's useless to us."

Did I really not scare Toudou enough in the forest? Maybe I should've broken one of his arms.

I take a deep breath and try to organize my thoughts. No point dwelling on the past.

Although my position here is limited, I need to handle this as calmly as possible and do what I can.

"I'm going to go into the woods assuming the worst. I'll kill the demon before it gets to them if that's what it comes down to."

"Understood."

A clear, concise response. How could she have been drunk a few minutes ago?

I clear my throat. "...I think you're aware, but I want you to stay here on standby."

"...Why is that?"

She doesn't get it? I...don't want her holding me up.

My fighting style is simple. I enter the battle alone, make use of a lot of buffs and heals, and strike the enemy using my mace. There really is no place for Amelia.

"I specialize in solo fighting."

"So you're saying I'd just be in the way."

...*Yes, that's exactly what I'm saying.*

Priests are most useful in the context of a party. There isn't really anything she can do to contribute when it's just me.

Amelia fixes a stare at me, her expression unchanging. "Answer me this, Ares. How do you plan to find Toudou's party in that enormous forest in the first place?"

"If I concentrate enough, I'll be able to pick up on their presence."

"Yes, but you have limited range. Using my magic, I would be able to search a much wider area than you could."

There is truth in that. I'm not an expert at life-force tracking—I'm sure with her magic she could do much better than me.

I lick my lips and narrow my eyes at Amelia.

It's a given that if I want to be absolutely sure of finding Toudou's party, I should bring Amelia with me. The thing is, that comes with its own set of risks. If I lose her in the woods now, she won't be around when I need her later.

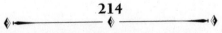

"The overdone sense of justice is a crime."

Also, if Amelia is there with me in battle, I'll have to protect her. An intelligent opponent would recognize that as a vulnerability.

Sensing my hesitation, Amelia sighs and looks up at me. "Ares...I volunteered for this position with full knowledge that I could die."

...*So what you're saying is, "Don't worry about my life."* I stare hard at her, but Amelia maintains her composure.

"...Fine. But if you feel your life is in danger, you are to flee immediately. And you have to follow my orders."

"Got it."

Her quick replies make me uneasy. Does she really understand what she's agreeing to?

The hero's life is important, but so is hers.

I'm not a great warrior, and I don't have a lot of different skills. The only things I can do are pray and smash things with my mace.

"Amelia, contact Helios. He should have prepared a runner lizard for our travels—tell him we're coming to get it a little early. I'll report the situation to the cardinal. We depart in ten minutes. Let's get ourselves ready."

"Understood."

Since we had planned to leave in the evening, our belongings are already prepared for departure.

As I use a little magic to start the transmission, my head throbs with pain. No matter how much trouble Toudou causes, he always seems to come out feeling just fine...

Just once, I'd like to kick his ass.

Of course, I don't think the Church would let me do that, though.

Mercenaries are gathered in front of the church in a wide circle. In the center is a rare creature.

It's a lizard about the size of a horse called a "runner lizard." I asked the church to provide us with one of these creatures as our means of transportation.

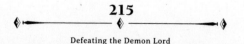

These lizards were crossbred so they can be mounted, and although they are more difficult to handle than horses, they're also a lot tougher.

Helios stands next to the wild-tempered creature, holding the bridle to restrain it.

"Looks like you've got it all set," I call out to him.

He smiles slightly in his usual way, shrugging. "Being so close to the forest, where there are many monsters, we are prepared for these situations. This is, however, the first time I have handled one of these creatures."

The lizard becomes aware of my presence, and its body shudders. It growls, perceiving me as a threat.

"Do you have experience riding lizards?" Helios asks.

"I do. No problem at all."

I take the reins from Helios's hands. The moment I take hold of them, the lizard's eyes open wide, and it cries out. Without me saying anything at all, the lizard shudders and immediately lies down on the spot.

It takes a while to get these lizards used to humans, but they will fall in line with their superiors. If you're level 60 or above, they'll cooperate.

Amelia loads our bags onto the back of the pacified lizard.

"If anything comes up, Amelia will contact you," I tell Helios.

"Certainly... What of the crusader who was originally tasked with defeating the demon?"

"He may not be needed. Our plan is to follow the hero, observe his movements, and make further decisions from there. The crusader should be arriving in three days—or actually, two days now. We should be able to decide how to proceed by then."

If it seems possible to get Toudou out of the forest right away, then I intend to pursue him and leave the demon alone.

I touch the lizard's cool, scaly head with the palm of my hand and say a prayer. The lizard is wrapped in the light of a buff.

If we didn't make it in time just because I was trying to conserve all my holy energy, our efforts would be wasted. I intend to do this job properly.

"The overdone sense of justice is a crime."

I lightly jump off from the ground and mount the saddle.

My line of sight is higher from the lizard's back. Runner lizards have more strength in their legs than horses. They move at a considerable speed, but it isn't as smooth a ride.

After Amelia finishes loading the bags, I extend a hand to help her up.

"Use holy techniques on yourself before you get completely sick. If you think you're going to vomit, say so before it happens, and I'll let you off."

"Who do you think I am, Ares? I don't mean to brag, but I'm a strong rider."

You also said you're a strong drinker, *didn't you?*

I grab Amelia's hand and get her up in one pull. I check that she's seated behind me, then turn back to Helios.

I can't decide what to say for a moment but finally go with, "I owe you one."

"Not at all. I have learned much from you."

The first time we met, I thought he was kind of a shady character, but people don't always turn out the way they seem.

"May Ahz Gried protect you."

"…Thanks."

The runner lizard they found for us is a fast mover.

Its body shakes as its feet thud against the ground. The scenery flies past us at a terrific speed.

Probably her first time on a runner lizard, Amelia grasps my torso firmly, but she doesn't make a peep. She's got a lot of grit to be able to handle this.

"Do you know where they are now?" I ask her.

"Y-yes. They—appear—to be—on the main—forest road."

…Is she really *okay?*

I have a feeling she might be talking up her riding prowess like she talked up her drinking. She doesn't seem to be doing well, so I wordlessly cast a holy technique on her.

"…I'm not lying," Amelia complains. "I can hold my liquor, *and* I am a good rider."

"Is that so?"

"This is just…a bit worse than I expected… It feels like my insides are being churned…"

The constant jostling up and down is a little intense. I remember that feeling of discomfort. I'm not trying to pick on her or anything.

"Can you speak with Glacia?"

"…Moving at this speed, it would be impossible. I can't identify her location."

Transmission magic is still in the early stages of development. It can't be helped that it has limitations.

I work through some thoughts out loud. "Glacia was chased out of her home in the forest during the night, and most demons are nocturnal. So it's unlikely that it would be roaming around during the day."

"…You sound like you're trying to convince yourself of that."

"I mean…it does give me some peace of mind, but it's my honest assessment. Anyway, in the end, this will just come down to Toudou's own luck."

You never know what's going to happen when it comes to Toudou. Nothing surprises me anymore.

Although it's unlikely he'll encounter the demon, it is still a possibility—especially if he's looking for it. They say that heroes have the power to direct the course of fate… How troublesome for their supporters.

"Even if the worst happens, we just need to make sure Toudou gets out of this alive. I don't know if we can count on Glacia, but Limis and Aria have given their word that they'll protect him. Their levels are low, but they could at least draw the demon away from him."

"But wouldn't that cause trouble with the kingdom?"

I don't give a crap about that. I've already been thrown out of the party anyway.

After a little less than an hour traveling on the lizard's back, the forest entrance comes into view.

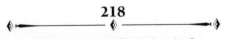

"The overdone sense of justice is a crime."

The closing of the village gate and blocking entry to the forest were lies intended to drive Toudou away from the Vale, but the local mercenaries have been notified of the appearance of a dangerous monster in the woods. There's no one to be seen at the forest's edge.

The main road is wide, but with all the tree overgrowth, it's impossible to enter with the lizard.

Amelia dismounts the lizard's back and throws the largest bag over her shoulder. "I can carry this one," she insists stubbornly.

"Have you walked through the forest before?"

"…I haven't really. My first time was with Toudou a few days ago."

It would be a lot of trouble for me if she collapsed somewhere along the way. I point to a smaller bag.

"Take that one instead."

"Won't you lose agility if you carry all the heavy ones?"

"What I need isn't agility—it's strength and stamina."

"Ares, I think you're a little overprotective."

"If you think you can carry so much, at some point when we have the luxury of spare time, I'll give you plenty to carry."

I'm not being protective, and I'm not doing her a kindness. This is about practicality. I appreciate the sentiment, but everyone has their strengths and weaknesses.

Amelia gives in and takes the smaller bag.

"If you could give me regular updates on Toudou's whereabouts, that would be helpful. I'd like to stay one step ahead of them."

"Got it," she says, nodding.

I look out from the forest entrance. We still have a few hours of daylight. If possible, I'd like to resolve this situation before dark.

We move down the forest road at a quick pace, Amelia using her detection magic from time to time to confirm Toudou's location.

At present, it appears Toudou's party is still traveling the main road.

This gives me a bad feeling. The path of the main road is carefully planned, and there are few monsters near it. If you want to level up, you need to get off it and into the woods.

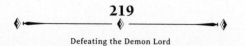

As I turn this over in my mind, a torrent appears along our path. I smash it with my mace. This is a monster I could have defeated when I was ten years old.

I knock it away with one hit and then swing my mace a few times in front of me out of habit.

"...You wouldn't think a priest would be so good at killing things."

"Amelia, even you should be able to keep up with monsters of this level. Although they might not be enough to level you up."

I'm no good at talking, but killing is where I excel. I've spent a lot of time leveling up. A lot of time wiping out the followers of darkness.

Whether my opponent is a demon, a dragon, or even a human, I destroy them without mercy.

Toudou is moving pretty quickly, but he's spending more time in battle. We're rapidly closing the distance.

I first start to feel uneasy after about our tenth encounter in the forest. After killing a low-level wolf monster, I wipe the blood off my mace and look to Amelia.

"...There are too many monsters," I say.

"Too many?"

"We've already fought ten or so battles since we entered the forest. That's unusually high for the main road."

It's not like we've taken any special measures to avoid the monsters, but they typically don't like to be near the road, as hunters frequently pass through on it. It could be that these were chased out of their normal territory, just like the glacial plant.

I close my eyes as I focus my mind and sharpen my senses. I don't perceive any followers of darkness around us—none at all.

Could it just be a coincidence...? While certainly a possibility, there have been a lot of monsters in a short distance. It might be best for us to try to get ahead of Toudou as quickly as we can.

"We're turning off the road. Let's get in front of them."

"Okay."

"We need to move a little faster. Are you tired?"

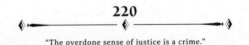

"I'm fine."

I don't know how true that is…but I'll have to take her word on it.

Amelia is no fool. If she couldn't move any faster, she would say so. Worst-case scenario is that she collapses, and then I can just carry her.

"Can you keep tracking them as we walk?"

"Yes, for about an hour. I also brought medicine to restore my magical energy, so if we need to continue tracking, that will give us a little more time."

An hour isn't very long, and we should be reserving magic for when we really need it. Maybe it isn't realistic to be tracking them continuously.

"Forget about the constant tracking. Just check periodically to make sure there aren't any major developments."

"Okay."

I take a step off the road. Then something occurs to me—there are a lot of old trees with thick trunks and thick branches in the Forest of the Vale.

I ask Amelia just for the hell of it. "It'd be faster to run through the treetops than walk on the ground. Do you think you could do it?"

"…Ares, what do you think I am?"

I guess that might be asking a little too much…

We walk through the thickly growing trees in silence, trampling grass and snapping branches as we go. The only signs of life are the footprints of beasts.

The sun is getting lower in the sky. It should set completely in about two hours.

I wonder if Toudou will stop and set up camp. Hopefully, he isn't foolish enough to march through the night.

As we head deeper into the woods pursuing Toudou, I notice something.

Compared to the main road, there are actually fewer monsters the farther into the forest we go. Speaking from experience, this is usually not a good thing.

I stop walking and grind my heel into the ground in frustration.

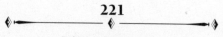

I consider sending out murderous intent in a wide area around us—could that lure the target in our direction? Maybe, but the risk is too high.

Rash decisions can result in mistakes. I shouldn't forget about our more reliable methods.

"Amelia, where is Toudou now?"

"About three kilometers ahead."

"Three kilometers... We should be able to catch up with them."

Picking up the pace was worth it.

Amelia's face is flushed, but from her voice, I get the impression she can keep going.

"So, Ares—"

At that moment, a bat-type monster about a meter long swoops down at me from behind. I manage to smash it with my mace.

I can feel I hit it hard enough to crush its flesh and its bones. The creature lies dead on the ground, and I step on it with the heel of my shoe as I catch my breath.

"Were you going to say something?"

"...No... It's nothing."

"Do you sense any large presences in the woods?"

Amelia shuts her eyes and uses her detection magic. She opens them again, shaking her head.

"...I can sense the presence of several entities deeper in the woods, but as for whether they are our target..."

"Do you sense a demon?"

"No demons... I would know the presence of a follower of darkness."

There are several types of monsters that could rival a glacial plant living in the deepest part of the woods. It's hard to make the distinction between them from this distance.

We can't really know for sure whether our target is still in the woods.

After a moment's consideration, I decide to prioritize following Toudou. All I can do right now is act based on the information I have.

"The overdone sense of justice is a crime."

"There's also the possibility that our target is not a follower of darkness," I point out. "There are others who serve the Demon Lord."

"Is it possible that another monster living in the woods happened to evolve, like Glacia did, and then drove her out?"

"…That could be. But I think if that were the case, Glacia would have mentioned it."

Could this be a coincidence? I suppose there's a chance we're just having some really terrible luck.

Personally, I *wish* that was the case, but there's no point discussing hypotheticals.

I continue swatting away the creatures we encounter as we move deeper into the woods. I occasionally check the map, and Amelia periodically uses her magic to confirm Toudou's location.

Toudou's own ability of detection is still low. We decided to walk approximately one kilometer ahead of the party, from which distance we can still roughly sense their presence without using Amelia's magic.

Perhaps growing tired from their first march in some time, Toudou's party starts moving increasingly slowly. They all have low stamina, Limis especially.

Before long, their progress stops completely, and we stop with them.

Amelia leans against a tree and settles her rough breathing. I toss her the canteen, and although she's a bit flustered, she catches it deftly.

Taking off the cap, Amelia looks a little discouraged. "Ares…aren't you tired?"

"I'm pretty sturdily built, and I'm used to this."

I sense no movement from Toudou's party. They must have finally exhausted themselves.

I open the map of the woods. There's water in the direction Toudou is heading.

Before long, it grows dark. If they don't intend to continue walking through the night, they'll probably camp where they are now.

"Anything from Glacia?"

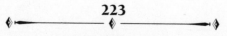

"...Apparently, she's hungry again..." It's the same response she's gotten for a while now.

That dragon girl is useless. I need to have another talk with her.

As expected, Toudou and the others seem to have set up camp. Once they stop moving entirely, we set up our own sleeping quarters.

We camp in somewhat of a clearing, a little more than a kilometer from Toudou's camp. Unlike Toudou's group, who can use the carriage to sleep in, we have to set up a campground ourselves. Fortunately, we have clear weather, and sleeping on the ground shouldn't be any problem.

I can sense Toudou and Aria going into the woods, possibly to retrieve some food. Limis and Glacia stay back at the campsite.

They head out without casting a prism, which is a careless move. I quietly take out a bottle of holy water from my bag, spill the contents on the ground, and cast a prism large enough to cover both camps.

I look over at Amelia, who is moving rocks and fallen branches, clearing herself a space on the ground.

"I'll be taking the night watch," I say.

"Oh... No, I—"

"I don't need you to worry about me," I say firmly. "I'll need you to use your detection magic again tomorrow, so I want you to get some rest."

"..."

"At this distance from their camp, I have a pretty clear sense of things. Try to rest and restore your magical energy as much as possible."

She attempts to appear attentive, but it's clear from the change in her demeanor that she's tired.

A person's level is a good reference point, but there are other factors to consider as well. Amelia has satisfactorily met all my demands, but compared to a veteran hunter, she's still very delicate. She's probably aware of that.

Amelia resigns herself with a nod. "All right... If anything happens, please wake me."

"The overdone sense of justice is a crime."

"Will do."

Even if she hadn't said it, it's not like I would have left her sleeping.

Night arrives.

The woods are covered in an opaque darkness, and I can sense the increased activity of monsters.

I satisfy my hunger with the tough biscuits we brought for travel. Thanks to the prism, I don't sense any threats in our immediate vicinity.

It would be good if Amelia and Toudou's group could recover a bit of their stamina...

I can hear Amelia's short breaths as she sleeps, and I don't think any of Toudou's party has strayed from the campground in the night.

In the end, today was uneventful. The woods seemed a little different than usual, but there wasn't anything particularly strange.

As I stretch my stiff body and try to relax, I suddenly sense a strong presence.

I look up, staring through the trees and into the darkness. I focus my mind and sharpen all five senses.

I open my eyes and stand slowly, not making a sound.

Something is out there. It's still far, but it's definitely there. It isn't my imagination.

The presence isn't a follower of darkness, but it doesn't feel like any of the smaller monsters that live in this area, either.

When I strain my ears, I can't hear any kind of cry or call. But the forest is a little quieter than usual tonight.

The presence appeared just on the edge of my range of perception. From this distance, I can't tell very much about it.

The good news is that it seems to be in the deeper part of the woods, closer to me, so there's no concern about it attacking Toudou first.

I look at Amelia. She's sleeping soundly.

I have little information about this enemy, but its presence is smaller than I'd expected. I should be able to take it down on my own.

I wake Amelia as quietly as I can.

"…Mmm…" She groans, opening her eyes halfway and sitting up.

While I can kill this thing alone, if I consider the worst-case scenario, it's not a good idea to leave her here sleeping.

"There's something big out there. I'm gonna go take it down. Stay with me on the transmission—I'll report the situation to you as I go."

"…Huh?! …Okay. I understand."

Eradication techniques are only effective on followers of darkness. I can't be sure if this presence is our target, but it occurs to me that if it had been up to Helios to deal with this alone, he could have ended up in a tough situation.

For me, it doesn't matter whether this enemy is a demon or something else.

Still waking up, Amelia starts to get unsteadily to her feet. I stop her.

"You don't need to come, Amelia. Stay here on standby in case I need you."

"What…?"

"I can handle this alone. That's an order. And you have other duties. You understand, right?"

If things go south, I'll need her to inform Toudou's party of the situation and help them escape.

Amelia looks frustrated. "Am I just a burden to you?" she asks, her voice shaking slightly.

"No—it's just that fighting isn't your role. You track, I kill. You just need to play your part."

If I knew for sure this was an enemy weak to eradication techniques, it wouldn't be a bad idea to let her try to kill it. But she could be at a pretty big disadvantage with our present opponent.

Amelia bites her lip. "I…I can fight, too."

"…"

It's not a question of whether or not she can fight; it's that there's no need for her to. If I needed her help, I wouldn't hesitate to ask.

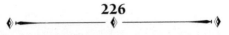

"The overdone sense of justice is a crime."

How do I convince her? As I stare at her, thinking on this, she says, "…But this time, I'll follow your orders. I didn't come here to be a nuisance."

"…Thanks."

If that's how you feel, you could have just said that in the first place, I think, swallowing the words.

It's not coming straight at us, but the presence is slowly moving in our direction.

It makes no sound, and because it's downwind of us, I don't catch any scent. It moves cautiously. I pick up my mace and grip it tightly.

Amelia stretches her arms, then reaches out a hand and touches my head. Her palm emits a bright light that cuts through the darkness.

A holy technique—it's a class-three buff. I can feel my physical abilities substantially increasing.

"So you can conserve your holy energy," she says as she withdraws her hand.

"…Right."

Really, I'd have preferred that she conserve her own holy energy in case something happens to Toudou, but I suppose that wouldn't make for a good response.

"All right, I'll be back soon. Leave the transmission on for me. I'll keep you updated on my status. Questions?"

"None at all."

"If anything happens with Toudou, be sure to let me know. Any questions?"

"No, absolutely none."

I wonder if she was able to replenish a little of her magical energy. Her complexion does look better than before she rested.

Even if the transmission were to cut out while I'm gone, as long as I'm able to defeat this thing, there shouldn't be any problems.

I grip my mace and take stock of my condition. I'm not fatigued. Even if my opponent is a demon, I'll be able to handle it.

"If you don't think you can win, run from the battle and return here. If I let you die, then I'm in trouble," says Amelia, only half-serious. "Got it?"

"…Got it."

I see her point, but it's not like I'm gonna lose. Even though I'm not technically a fighting class, I've been through countless battles. They didn't all go smoothly, but I always came out victorious.

Amelia must know that. She has to be familiar with my background.

I know very well why I, of all priests, was chosen to support Naotsugu Toudou.

My opponent isn't concealing itself, so it takes no time at all to locate.

I find it along a beasts' trail, out in the open, the moonlight shining down on it from the cloudless sky.

When I lay eyes on it, I feel like I'm seeing something from a nightmare.

The beast's body is the color of deep-amber flames, and its crimson hair shines like the sun. It's two meters in height and has shining golden claws and fangs. A wild flame blazes in its fur, setting fire to the grass around it and scorching the earth.

What I'm seeing is a lion. A *flaming lion*. The smell of smoke spreading through the woods confirms it.

I close my eyes and take a deep breath. Then I open them, verifying once more what's in front of me.

I check that the transmission is connected and report to Amelia.

"…It's a flame lion."

"…What?"

I'm not making this stuff up!

Amelia is silent for a moment. "…Did you just say *flame*? There are fire types living in the forest?"

"…There shouldn't be. It's burning everything up."

If it wasn't right in front of my eyes, I wouldn't believe it myself.

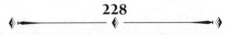

"The overdone sense of justice is a crime."

Beasts like this can't live in forests because they'll burn them to the ground. These types usually live in craters and other places.

I've fought this type of monster before.

Beasts that possess special abilities are generally very powerful. As their name indicates, flame lions are magical beasts that use the power of fire. They are ferocious, intelligent, physically very strong, and able to control flame.

The recommended level to battle one of these is around 60.

As its flaming fur brushes the trees, it sets them ablaze, turning them into torches. A tremendous amount of smoke floats up toward the sky.

"Who would bring something like this here…?"

Regardless of how weak or strong this beast is, the terrific light and heat coming off it make me want to flee for the first time in ages.

…This might be *worse* than a demon. Even if I can kill this monster, I don't have any way of putting out the fires it will leave behind.

"**Full Flame Resist.**" I cast a holy technique that will increase my resistance to fire.

When monsters possess an elemental attribute, only that single element is highly dangerous. If you take steps to protect yourself against it, it isn't so hard to deal with. Having the ability to increase my elemental resistance as needed, I'm fairly well suited to this opponent. What concerns me isn't the enemy itself so much as our surroundings.

There aren't any regions nearby that this type of monster naturally inhabits, so it really shouldn't be here. It's possible that something else brought it…but I don't have time to think about that now.

I click my tongue once and push off from the ground.

Approaching the monster at a high speed, I feel the extreme heat coming off it. I first strike it with my mace, knocking it to the ground. It lets out a cry of rage that shakes the trees. The spikes of my mace tear through its skin, and as I pull the weapon back, blood flies and splatters on the trees and my clothes. The trees burst into flame when touched by the burning-hot liquid, but it doesn't cause me any damage because of my extra fire resistance. The trees have no such protection.

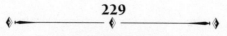

229

"Amelia, can you generate water?"

"…Unfortunately, no."

That's the answer I expected, though I can't help but be disappointed when I hear it.

The lion leaps in the air, coming straight at me. I take a half step back and narrowly avoid the swipe of its claws. I see the crimson color of its mane reflected in those claws as they manage to cut a few strands of my hair.

When I battled this type before in the craters, I had no trouble, but the woods are the worst location to fight this particular enemy.

Its burning tail grows long like a whip, and the beast prepares to attack. As its front leg comes down at me, I catch it with my mace. The mace creaks slightly under the pressure and turns red, but I don't let up.

The lion's mouth opens, and its chest contracts, preparing to breathe fire.

Pulling my mace free from its leg, I drive it into the lion's mouth before it can attack.

There's a bone-crushing shock—a sensation of crumpling flesh. The lion's enormous body flies backward, hitting the ground two or three times before stopping. All the vegetation it touches is scorched. Flames and smoke cloud the air.

At my level, inhaling a little smoke shouldn't give me any trouble, but I try to take shallow breaths to minimize any effects.

I wonder what I should do about the fire. There's nothing I can do, really. I don't have any way of putting it out.

The only way to stop the fire from spreading is to cut down the trees. The entire area will need to be cleared, but that's the best way to handle it.

Still lying on the ground, the lion sends its tail flying toward me, aiming for my head. I catch it with my hand.

"Ares…I have some bad news…"

"Toudou noticed it?"

"…Yes."

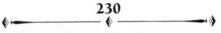

"The overdone sense of justice is a crime."

Of course he did. I would be more worried if he didn't notice this great burning disaster!

I get a firm grip on the tail and yank it in front of me. As the beast comes swinging forward, I aim my mace at its head and knock it down. I can feel its skull cave in as the spikes drive as far as its brain.

The beast's eyes burn with a blinding flame, even brighter than before, as its remaining life burns up. A small amount of life force flows into my body.

I release its tail and strike the body, still emitting a hellish flame, with my mace. The wind and the shock of the blow extinguish the fire. The red of the blood and guts that burst out of the carcass reminds me of the flames, but the body emits much less heat than when it was living. The plants and the trees touched by the blood of the dead beast do not burn.

Now for the tough part—I've got to wrap things up here before Toudou's party arrives.

I take the mask out of my pocket and put it on just in case. I whip my mace back and forth to blow away the smoke. It's only a drop in the bucket, but it improves visibility a little.

"Well, the target is defeated. It's time to clean up. What's Toudou's status?"

"It seems they're heading in your direction… Do you think it was the flame lion that drove Glacia out of the woods?"

"No, I don't."

First off, the basic form of the thing is different—Glacia described a dark humanoid type. On top of that, a flame lion isn't strong enough to chase away a glacial plant.

I calculate where I want the trees to fall and start swinging my mace. A group of trees falls, and the ground shakes tremendously as they land.

With the sounds of crackling fire and falling trees in the background, I gather my thoughts.

In the first place, this is a magical beast that lives beyond the volcanoes and the rocky mountains. The closest edge of the Forest of the

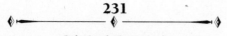

Vale is more than a thousand kilometers from its home ground, and if it traveled that far, a human would surely have seen it along the way. After all, flame lions are hard to miss.

"There's a possibility that whatever it was that went through the effort to bring a flame lion all the way here is still inside the forest."

And that person must have extraordinary abilities—sufficient fighting skills to be capable of handling a magical beast perpetually engulfed in flame and either the ability to fly or to use displacement magic to move over long distances. No matter what it is, it's not the kind of opponent you want to face.

The situation is all the more undesirable under the current circumstances, with Toudou in the middle of the woods.

"I'd rather not confront it, if possible. I'd prefer to leave it for Gregorio. He'll be able to take care of it. He likes this kind of stuff."

"...Oh, does he...?"

"Yes, he does."

As I level the trees, the wind from their fall helps disperse the smoke, and it gradually dissipates. But the situation itself is no better.

The smells of burning wood and scorched earth linger in the air, and the ground is covered with a layer of ash that gives it a different feel as you walk on it. Even so, this is much better than the worst-case scenario I had imagined.

It's a good thing we followed Toudou. Now, if we can just get him out of the forest before the true enemy appears, all will be well.

Just as I sigh in relief, thinking that finally things are looking up, a chill goes through my body. I reflexively raise my arm to guard my face.

"Ares, Toudou's party has started to move. How are things going over there?"

"I've got bad news for you."

"...What?"

I look up to the sky. It turns out my instinct was correct—in my raised left hand, I grasp a beam of jet-black light shaped like an arrow.

"The overdone sense of justice is a crime."

The sinister flickering of the dark beam is strangely visible in the dim light of the dying flames.

I crush the arrow. Ignoring the small sting of pain in my left palm and channeling strength into my right hand, I grip my mace tightly.

That arrow was aimed at my head. If I hadn't been paying attention, I might not have gotten away with my life.

Then I recall that I've seen this magic before.

An arrow of darkness that pollutes and destroys the target's life force. A skill of the evil gods, in direct opposition to the holy arts.

"There's a demon. Battle begins now."

As I speak, a wind starts to blow. Eventually, I can feel the powerful presence of a follower of darkness, putting me on high alert.

The wind is black, and it sucks in everything around it. This obsidian evil is so opaque that it looks as if it has painted over the light, and those who see it are inflicted with a feeling of despair.

A black fog swirls around and gathers in one place, taking the shape of a human.

The figure has pitch-black hair, deathly pale skin, and is clad entirely in black. It resembles a human, but you can be certain by looking at it that it isn't. This is an enemy of humankind. I'm struck by a strong feeling of revulsion.

It's exactly as Glacia described it.

I fix the mask firmly over my face to keep it from falling as I try to quiet the noise in my mind.

I look up into the trees that are still upright and find it there in the darkness, standing on a thick branch. Its eyes are a red more sinister than the flames of the lion's tail, and they indicate this enemy is one of the black-blooded tribe.

It spins its head around in a crazed manner.

Why did it come here, and why now? And how powerful is it really?

Toudou and the others will be here before long. This is the worst possible development. Well, maybe the second worst.

I get a measure of its ability from the evil seeping out of its body. Its lips are so red they look like they've been painted with blood, and they part slightly to let out a breath. It looks to either be sighing or curving its lips into a smile.

I'm the one who wants to sigh here.

I didn't want to fight this thing, but since it showed up at this exact moment, I have no other option.

I'll kill it before it sees Toudou's party. At the very least, I need to make sure Toudou and the others are safe—that's my first priority. I bite my lip and carve that fact into my mind. My heart beats loudly.

I study the figure. It's a male, maybe around fifteen years old. Although his age and his pallid skin give him a frail appearance, I can sense the enormous amount of magical energy in his body.

I absorb this information. He's a black-blood. I've fought them many times before—they're highly intelligent followers of darkness that take the shape of humans.

They have outstanding physical abilities and also possess numerous powerful special abilities. They lurk in the darkness, concealing themselves in secluded places. Some call them vampires because they suck the blood from human bodies.

His hands are wrapped around the tree branch, scratching at the bark with long nails.

We're locked in a stare. I push against him with murderous intent, but he doesn't stir in the slightest.

His mouth opens slightly, and I catch a glimpse of large, sharp teeth.

I immediately take my knife from my belt and throw it at him. I no longer have time to concern myself with the spreading fire. I need to win this battle before this threat reaches Toudou.

From the moment I throw the knife, I dive headlong into battle with all my strength.

The ground shakes violently, and the vampire loses his balance on the tree branch. Arms swinging, he manages to knock away the blessed mythril blade. The knife falls and pierces the ground, exactly as I intended.

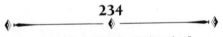

"The overdone sense of justice is a crime."

Black-blood abilities greatly surpass those of humans. Physical strength, speed, visual acuity—all the characteristics of their existence as living beings are above ours. Which is why it's necessary to prepare yourself before a battle with one of them.

As I close in, with a swing of my mace, I gouge out a large chunk of the tree he stands in. Although he isn't in my field of vision, I can sense the movements of the follower of darkness as if he were in the palm of my hand. The tree collapses, but my target has already disappeared from its branches.

"Ares?! Ares?!"

I don't have time to answer the transmission. Taking a quick breath, I raise my arm high in the air and bring my mace down at the vampire.

But it's as if time itself has suddenly frozen. Although I swung forward with all my strength, something stops me.

Right in front of me, almost close enough to touch, are the bloodred eyes of the black-blood. He stares at me devoid of emotion, as if observing me.

His right hand has halted my mace in midair. His hand, so thin and bony it looks like a skeleton's, holds the head of the mace with his fingers in between the spikes. I try channeling more energy into the arm holding my weapon, but I can't move it at all.

The young vampire lets out a little sigh. "When I got this mission, I knew it would be a pain in the ass." He has the voice of an adolescent but a little high-pitched, suiting his appearance.

You and me both.

With my left hand, I take another knife from my belt and hurl it at him. Regardless of the close range or the incredibly high speed of the throw, the devil knocks it away with ease. The knife spins through the air and falls into the bushes—that's number two.

Paying little mind to the silver knives, the vampire continues talking as if we were having a casual conversation. "Why'd they dispatch *me*—a descendant of the Vampire Lord—to this place way out in the middle of nowhere?"

I pull on my mace, but it still won't budge. He's stronger than I am. Left with no other choice, I release my mace and move back.

The vampire seems surprised. Not knowing what to do with the mace, he throws it away.

That's number three.

The strength of this type of monster fluctuates depending on the phase of the moon. Tonight, the moon is full...which makes this the worst possible time to face a vampire.

"You're quite the violent sort, aren't you? Please, be a little more rational. After all...pretty soon, you won't be able to use your brain at all."

"I see you're quite the talkative sort."

Having the time and energy to hold a conversation during battle—that's something to be envious of.

"Ares! Are you okay?!"

"Fine," I answer shortly, my eyes on the vampire who looks like he's about to come at me.

"Do you need help?"

"No."

I seize knives from my belt and ready one in each hand. The vampire looks at me with a bored expression.

"You should already know the difference in our abilities by now. You do pretty well for a human, but you can't beat me. You know—"

Not waiting for him to finish, I jump off from the ground. Aiming at the underside of his jaw, I throw a knife.

His expression changes, distorting wickedly. The knife cuts through the air without touching a hair on his head.

Taking a step closer, I launch more knives at him in succession. Probably predicting their paths by the glimmers from their blades, he dodges them all with minimal movement. He can see them all clearly.

"See, this is why humans are so stupid. Didn't anyone ever teach you to listen when a person is talking to you?"

"You're not a person."

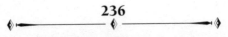

"The overdone sense of justice is a crime."

As he bats away the last of my knives, I catch a glimpse of a smile coming over his face.

Suddenly, a severe pain shoots through my wrist, and I can no longer move my arm. Somehow, without my noticing, he grabbed hold of me.

His skin is as pale as a corpse. His nails dig into my skin, sharp as daggers, and a chill runs through my body.

Not letting this unnerve me, without hesitating, I use my other hand to produce another knife, thrusting it decisively at his heart.

The vampire's face contorts…but I feel no resistance against the blade. It feels like stabbing air.

"I'm telling you, this battle is pointless. Don't you get it?"

The knife in my left hand is piercing straight through his body, but the area around his heart has turned into a black fog that engulfs my arm.

"Have you really never fought a vampire before?" asks the *thing* in a voice feigning surprise.

Ignoring his taunting, I pull my arm back and throw the knife at him. The vampire flinches, but the projectile passes right through him and sticks into the ground behind.

I focus my hearing, but I don't hear anything besides the sounds of wind and fire. I'm at a disadvantage in hand-to-hand combat. From previous battles with vampires, I've learned that there are all sorts of them. This one is by no means lacking in skill, but luckily for me, he's kind of careless.

There's a crooked smile on the vampire's face. I try to shake him off my arm, but I can't move it. I click my tongue and attempt to intimidate him.

"Give your name, vampire."

"Heh-heh-heh… Ah-ha-ha-ha-ha! Now—*now* he asks…" He bursts into high-pitched laughter.

Then a terrible magical power starts to swirl about his body.

The temperature suddenly drops. It's similar to the cold wind near glacial plants, only this is much stronger.

The ground and everything around us cracks and whines as it freezes solid. The smoldering fire is extinguished.

I guess that's one less thing to worry about.

The vampire still has my hand. Despite the overwhelming cold, my wrist burns so intensely that it feels like it's being pressed under a soldering iron.

The laughter abruptly stops, and all emotion vanishes from the vampire's eyes.

"Well, I guess I can tell you. My name is Zarpahn. Zarpahn Drago Fahni. I am a descendent of the great Vampire Lord. I don't normally associate with humans—what an honor for you!"

Fahni... Anyone associated with the Church will have heard this name. It belongs to some of the highest-ranking vampires in existence. I don't exactly feel honored, but if he is who he claims to be, I can see where he gets his confidence.

His fiery eyes shine the color of blood. In them, I can sense madness and an uncontrollable desire to fight.

"Lord of vampires... What is your goal?"

The vampire Zarpahn looks at me quizzically, his eyes narrowing. "...Hmm? What was that? Why would I tell that to *you*?"

...Evidently, he isn't quite *that* stupid.

These strange things have been happening precisely when Toudou is in the forest... The timing is too good to be accidental.

The transmission to Amelia is still connected. If I can figure out his goal, it will be easier for us to decide how to proceed.

I remain silent. Zarpahn stares at me for a while and then finally takes a breath and starts talking.

"...Ah, I guess I could tell you. You probably don't want to die totally in the dark."

Amelia... He is that stupid!

His grip on my wrist is strong. I ignore the pain, not making a sound. I'll be able to heal it with holy energy later.

Zarpahn watches me with a bored expression. He sighs.

"The hero. I'm looking for the hero. Heard of him?"

"..."

Is this guy...serious?

The hero is exposed—this really couldn't be much worse. The only good fortune we have left is that Toudou hasn't encountered the demon himself.

I wait in silence for him to continue. Unaware of my motives, Zarpahn speaks freely.

"Our lord sensed the hero's existence, although his exact location is still unknown. As a future candidate for positions of leadership, I was given the honor of this mission to check the state of affairs in the human world, you see."

"..."

"Now, you might feel completely out of place in all of this. But being of noble blood, I feel a bit out of place myself in these woods filled with low-ranking monsters."

"..."

"He said that he sent me on this mission to allow me to contribute to his cause, but what could he be thinking sending me *here*...? There's no way the Holy Warrior would come to a place with such low-level creatures. Only humans like yourself would spend their time wandering around in here."

"..."

"Are you the one who killed the monsters I brought along? You're not at my level, but you must have considerable fighting ability. Causing me a lot of trouble, though. Forget about the dragon—do you know how much work it was to bring that lion all the way here? I should kill you for that."

Then Zarpahn moves closer to peer into my eyes, scowling at me.

"Why so quiet all of a sudden? Being sent out here to the middle of nowhere, I've got time on my hands. They gave me orders not to make any big public disturbances, but I can take time for a chat. Why don't you keep me company?"

Amelia...this guy is really stupid.

Going on and on in a conversation with your enemy is proof of your

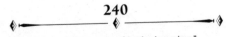

foolishness. If I were in his place, I definitely wouldn't be talking this much. But I guess he might not be thinking of me as an enemy just yet.

"Sure, I get where you're coming from. I just have one question: The *lord* you talk about—is it Kranos?"

"…Huh? You're—"

There is a slight change in the vampire's composure at my question. He doesn't answer, but his reaction is a reply in itself. With my arm still firmly in his grip, it's my turn to talk.

"Zarpahn, you're a powerful vampire. I acknowledge that you are a descendent of the Vampire Lord."

"…What are y—?"

He is powerful—one of the most powerful of all vampires. Toudou is no match for him.

However, he does not exceed my expectations. The only thing I wasn't expecting about this battle is the timing. It would have been better if it could have waited until Gregorio arrived, but there's no use thinking about that now.

"And your king has keen insight, to have dispatched one of his followers to these woods, where it's highly likely that the hero would visit. But you, the one he dispatched, lack awareness. You're negligent. You need to be more devoted to your mission."

"…What the hell are you talking about?"

This is business. Carelessness can't be tolerated. I wouldn't tolerate it even from myself.

With my free hand, I slowly remove my mask, revealing my face to him. My lips bend into a smile as I look down at the vampire in front of me.

"My name is Ares Crown. The hero that your lord is searching for… is *me*."

Right away, I cast a prism, and the forest is flooded with white light. The flash of light hits Zarpahn's face, and he flinches.

It's a good thing this vampire is so stupid. I won't allow him to escape.

He looks away from me and at the shining, pale illumination that cuts through the trees, forming a wall around us.

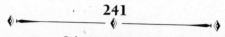

My dropped mace and the thrown knives serve as mediums for the prism. All of them being blessed, they are ideal for constructing a boundary.

I look at the vampire. He still holds tightly to my wrist. "Vampires are different from humans in that it's more difficult for you to level up. We judge your ability by dividing you up into *stages*, and by my estimation, you're about a stage three. An average demon. Could be defeated by a party with levels in the seventies or high sixties."

He faces me once more. The look in his eyes is more like elation than murderous intent.

I don't make conversation mid-battle without good reason. It's important to destroy one's target as quickly as possible. After this amount of time, the prism is now fully formed.

An added effect of the prism is that it will gradually restrict his special abilities. That's why I keep talking—to buy more time.

I face him squarely as I continue. "Besides the usual skills like *Darkness*, your skills are *Form Black Fog*, *Form Animal*, *Blood Manipulation*, and *Energy Drain*. You have various other powers, like sucking blood and manifesting minions, but when opposing your kind in battle, what's important are those four skills. Vampires in the higher stages possess other unique abilities, but you're not quite there yet, are you?"

I notice his eye twitch. He starts to take me more seriously—becomes more cautious.

This guy has information...but I have to make sure I kill him here. I suppose I don't have time for an interrogation.

"The most irritating thing about fighting your kind isn't your strength—it's your mobility. If you transform into a fog and run off, you're difficult to catch. That's why before I go to kill a vampire, I lay a prism to prevent its escape. The prism has the added bonus of limiting the abilities of followers of darkness. The preparation does take time, though, so I was a little on edge until I locked it down just now."

Incidentally, it's possible this vampire may be able to use displacement magic—that might explain why he appeared so suddenly. If you lay

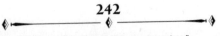

"The overdone sense of justice is a crime."

a barrier, even if your opponent can use displacement magic, they'll only be able to use it within the area of the boundary.

Particularly since Toudou is headed in this direction, although I can't stop him from coming here, I also can't allow him to reach the enemy without at least a prism separating them.

Zarpahn's expression changes from joy to rage. For the first time since we met, he sees me as a threat. The air of the forest around us becomes thick with murderous intent, but the chill from earlier has already dissipated. The boundary is working effectively.

"Zarpahn, from the look of you, you have talent but no real battle experience. Am I right? An experienced vampire wouldn't be so careless with an opponent wielding a mace and wouldn't stand around talking. You should remember that. Although it won't do you much good, because I have no intention of letting you out of here alive."

"?!"

Zarpahn, now on edge, hastily releases my right hand. Then with one hand, he drags his nails across his opposite palm. Black blood, unlike that of humans, oozes from the scratches.

This is *Blood Manipulation*, a type of psychokinesis that uses a person's own blood.

But nothing happens—it doesn't work.

"I said boundaries have the effect of limiting your power, didn't I?"

Although, since I only just set the boundary, he might still have been able to get some use out of it. I don't tell him that, of course. If he knew, there might be a chance for him to escape, which would make more work for me.

I put my mask back on, securing it in place. I can sense Toudou's party approaching—they're only a few minutes away. This isn't a significant enemy, but it still might be tricky to kill him in such a short amount of time.

Without saying a word, Zarpahn's body cracks and starts to expand. His thin arms swell, and his eyes emit a dark light.

He demonstrated before that he has a talent for hand-to-hand combat.

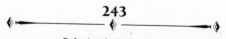

There are some vampires that fight using only their special abilities, but he's not one of them.

Shaking out the hand he had been holding down, I start to overwrite my buffs. I mean no insult to Amelia, but I can cast stronger buffs than she can without using up my holy energy.

"**Full Strength, Full Agility, Full Vitality, Full Sense,**" I cast in succession.

Zarpahn's body vanishes, and the earth cracks as he rushes into it.

But with my senses heightened from the buffs, I can track his movements.

I catch his arm as it comes at me from behind. A shock from the impact goes through my body and into the ground, cracking it again. But I've completely stopped the blow.

The black-blood's breathing is rough, like a beast. For an instant, he doesn't move. Maybe he's surprised I was able to stop him?

It's fortunate for me that this enemy ended up being a follower of darkness—that means I can use eradication techniques on him.

Now I'll let him suffer God's judgment.

"**Photon Order.**"

A dazzling burst pierces the eye. The wave of light, imbued with holy power, envelops the vampire's skeletal body.

Under the pressure of the light, his body is blown away like a scrap of paper, hitting the prism wall and collapsing on the ground.

Normally, this light of judgment would purify and exterminate a demon of his rank in one blow.

I observe Zarpahn, collapsed on the ground. Strangely, he's survived the attack. Black smoke rises from his body, which has somehow retained its shape. Although this isn't the outcome I'd hoped for, I knew it was a possibility.

Hiding my surprise, I approach Zarpahn, saying, "**Photon Bleed.**"

A vague sensation springs from the palm of my hand. What forms is a sword of light—a sword of judgment that is only effective against followers of darkness.

"The overdone sense of justice is a crime."

I take the sword of light, which is particularly effective against vampires, and thrust it into his heart.

The sword disappears.

Zarpahn suddenly jolts to life and takes a swipe at me with his long nails. I move back to avoid it.

"Damn… You have divine protection, huh?" My sword of light had been obstructed by some kind of barrier.

There is a powerful protection barrier that only a handful of demons possess. This shield is the primary reason only a hero and those with the blood of a hero can defeat the Demon Lord and other high-ranking demons.

It is the divine protection of the evil god who opposes the God of Order—the God of Darkness, Lucief Arept. It has the power to nullify the majority of damage received.

Zarpahn slowly gets to his feet. Although his black clothes are frayed and there are small scratches on his body, he has no major wounds. Under ordinary circumstances, that hit would have killed him three times over.

He raises his face to look at mine. Now his expression shows no rage or murderous intent but instead a crooked, joyous smile. He laughs.

"Ah-ha…ha-ha-ha-ha! You—you surprised me… I wasn't expecting to battle the *hero*…"

The protection of an evil God… That's an extremely tough obstacle. I never thought a demon of this level would be granted divine protection.

If I let him go, he'll only become a greater threat. I need to exterminate him while he's still easy to kill.

Perhaps pleased that his divine protection remains intact, Zarpahn seems to have relaxed.

"And how lucky. You…you don't have the protection of the God of War, do you?"

"I wouldn't call yourself lucky." In the moment his guard is down, I throw my fist into his abdomen.

My right fist digs into his exposed stomach, and I feel the shock of the blow in my hand. At the moment of impact, I speak the prayer again.

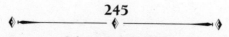

"Photon Order."

"?!"

Once again, light shoots out from my fist. This time, rather than covering a wide range, the hit is concentrated in one spot.

Something makes a popping sound as Zarpahn is thrown back again. His body slides across the ground until it collides with the prism. I hear him coughing violently.

"You know, if you didn't have the protection of Lucief, this would have been over in a moment. Thanks to the prism, I have the time to finish the job."

I'd like to take the battle elsewhere, but it's impossible to move the prism.

I check that my mask is secure and put on my hood to hide my silver hair in case they catch sight of it. There aren't many people with silver hair.

Crushing the ground beneath me with the heel of my shoe, I wave away the dust, waiting for him to stand.

It'll be faster to break his spirit than his body.

Zarpahn gets unsteadily to his feet. Vampires have high regeneration ability, but the prism renders that null. And while he may not take much damage, he should still feel pain. I can still see energy burning in his eyes.

Light-based attacks are hardly effective against opponents with divine protection. I'm using my mace as a medium for the prism, so I can't use it in battle. Instead, I take out a narrow, stake-like dagger from my belt.

It's a short silver blade, blessed and made for throwing like a knife. It's a sub-weapon, but that's better than no weapon at all.

I just need to make sure that Toudou and the party don't get dragged into this.

"Remove your protective barrier, Zarpahn. Make this easier for me."

"Enough with the bullshit. You are strong, but you're a human and I'm a vampire. I'm the stronger of the two of us."

"That's the general consensus."

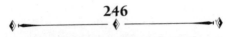

"The overdone sense of justice is a crime."

I swipe the dagger in a quick, slanted motion at my side. A silver slash mark runs across the trunk of the tree next to me, and the tree slides off its stump, collapsing on the ground and sending up a great cloud of dust. I leap into it to conceal myself.

My blood runs hot through my body, and I see my surroundings with clarity. Locating me, Zarpahn swings his arm in my direction.

I slow down to avoid him, putting up an arm to protect myself. With my other arm, I thrust the dagger at him. I hear it scrape against something, but it doesn't pierce him. I must have just grazed his skin. As he recoils, I take his legs out from under him, and he falls to the ground.

I change my grip on the dagger and take out a second. One for each hand.

Aiming for his heart, I come down at him with the daggers using the full weight of my body. There's a flash of light, fierce like lightning, and just as the blade cuts into his flesh, I use the dagger as a medium for my prayer.

"Photon Order."

I had braced myself, but the shock of the strike lifts me off the ground for a moment. As the light burns through the black of night, I'm certain I can see agony in the vampire's face.

He's taking damage, and the prism won't allow him to regenerate.

His arm twitches and then shoots out at me like an arrow. I fall back, but his nails just manage to graze my cheek. I first feel a burn and then a delayed tinge of pain.

I see drops of fresh blood fly into the air. Paying them no mind, I step forward and stomp down on his stomach with all my strength.

He lets out a dull groan as he recoils. Unable to avoid the brunt of the hit, he takes some damage.

I wipe the blood from my cheek with my finger while the vampire looks up at me with vacant eyes.

"I'll keep you company until you're dead," I say, looking down at him.

His lips curl into a defiant smile. "Heh... Eh-heh... We...we'll see—how long—you can last..."

"I'm a healer."

"...What?"

I put a finger to the cut on my cheek and say a prayer. It emits a pale-green light, and in a split second, the cut has vanished entirely.

At the sight of this, the color of Zarpahn's eyes changes. He shakes.

"This is crazy... You're a monster—"

"I'm not the monster here, *vampire*."

He has only a little left in him. I look down at Zarpahn. His arm twitches.

Toudou is almost here. Before he reaches us, I need to weaken Zarpahn as much as possible.

I aim the tips of the daggers at his eyes.

He lets out a stifled scream. Vampires have high endurance to pain, but only because of their formidable regenerative ability, which is currently nullified. His body stiffens at the threat of more pain.

I slash down at Zarpahn from above. Even if the approach lacks precision, my attack power is still a threat.

I only barely graze Zarpahn's right eye, but he holds it and howls like a beast. It echoes through the woods around us.

He slowly rises.

Still holding his right eye, he drags his feet as he walks. Coming at me, running solely on adrenaline at an incredible speed, he takes another swipe at me. I slip to the side to avoid him and catch his swing with my dagger. Having used buffs for strength and endurance, I have the upper hand.

Zarpahn struggles to keep his balance, and I jump at him with a kick. He flies into the boundary and falls to the ground.

Then I kick his head repeatedly as hard as I can. I'm not concerned about the repellent force of his protective barrier—I'm certain that, little by little, the damage is accumulating. I stomp on his body. Kick him. I absolutely have to kill him.

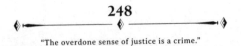

"The overdone sense of justice is a crime."

Zarpahn, collapsed on the ground, starts dragging himself toward my mace.

The mace is the cornerstone. If you look closely, you can tell it's the point of origin for the entire prism.

Crossing my arms, I'm deliberately silent as I watch him.

"This… Without this…," he mutters deliriously. He reaches for the mace, but when he touches it, he's instantly thrown backward with great force.

There is no way for a follower of darkness to safely touch the medium of an active prism. Burned by the blaze of the boundary, Zarpahn groans bitterly. I crouch down next to him.

Is he so weak that he can barely move from this amount of damage? He hardly seems like the descendant of a great bloodline. But I guess if I can kill now what might have become a great demon in the future, that's no bad thing.

"Had enough yet, vampire?"

"Not yet—I haven't lost yet. Not yet. Not yet, not yet, not yet—when my strength, when it returns…" I can't tell if he's looking at me or not, and the sanity has gone out of his eyes.

If he won't dissolve his protective barrier, I'll have to batter him until he's dead.

I pick Zarpahn up by the hair and hit him hard. He spins and slams into the ground, making a crater in the dirt. His eyes widen in pain, and blood runs out of his mouth.

It occurs to me that if I could cast photon order from inside his mouth, it would probably inflict a lot of damage. I force his jaw open, and just as I'm about to put my dagger in—I sense their arrival.

It's been a few days since I've actually seen them.

I stand up and kick Zarpahn in the gut. I check that my mask is on properly and turn to face them.

There amid the burned and broken trees is the hero's party. The sight of them is a little nostalgic somehow.

Toudou stands at the front, having the appearance of someone both

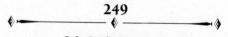

Defeating the Demon Lord

courageous and naive. His smooth black hair is so different from the vampire's wild mane.

Our eyes meet. He doesn't seem to realize who I am.

Seeing him should fill me with anger, but when I look at him now, I don't feel much at all.

His gaze is sharp. He takes ragged breaths and holds the holy sword at his side. He carries no shield.

I can see Limis and Aria behind him. It's likely they took so long to get here because they were preparing for battle. Glacia is nowhere to be seen.

"What—what's...going on...here...?"

Toudou's gaze goes from me to Zarpahn, in a heap on the ground. When the hero sees him, his shoulders start shaking, and his face grows stiff.

This time, it doesn't concern me. Because this is completely different from the situation with Glacia. I'm not worried Toudou will get in the way here.

Toudou should understand. Being under the divine protection of the God of Order, Toudou should know far better than me the evil presence of a black-blood, the power of this follower of darkness that masquerades as a human.

There is a clear difference between Glacia and this follower of darkness—Glacia is only a monster.

It would have been ideal if I could have finished things up before Toudou's arrival, but fortunately, I have a prism set.

For a demon of Zarpahn's power, I'm not concerned about him breaking the barrier from the inside. The worst-case scenario has been avoided, and now this may serve as a learning experience for Toudou, who has never seen a demon before.

I just need to make sure that Toudou and the others stay outside the boundary.

Toudou approaches nervously, his legs shaking as he walks. I try to disguise my voice as I call out to him.

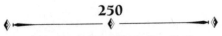

"The overdone sense of justice is a crime."

"Don't move from there. I've laid a prism."

There are various types of prisms, but the type I've set here is a boundary of holy ground, particularly effective against followers of darkness. It is ineffective against anything else, and it creates no physical barrier. It would be quite a lot of trouble if Toudou entered into it.

Hearing my words, Toudou stops and takes a few paces back.

Okay, everything is all right... He understands.

Gripping the dagger tightly in my hand, I walk toward Toudou.

I don't let my guard down around Zarpahn, of course, even as he lies facedown on the ground. You can't afford to be negligent when dealing with a black-blood.

I stop about two meters in front of Toudou. If I get too close, I might put them on their guard.

"This forest is currently on lockdown due to the confirmed appearance of a demon. Why have you come here?"

"Um... Well, we were just...," Toudou stutters, faltering at my demand for an explanation.

Seeing them now, it doesn't look like they came here to level up. It looks like they came to find the demon.

I guess it might not have been a good move to have the village headman warn them about it. But really, what was I supposed to do? I need to know where they're going.

It really is lucky that Amelia got in contact with Glacia before the set time and that we acted as quickly as we did.

I gesture to Zarpahn. He crawls along the ground, observing me and lying in wait for an opportunity.

His will still isn't broken. Given the chance, he would probably throw himself at me. I try to intimidate him with a look, try to constrain him with murderous intent, but it's pointless. That's how vampires are—they are wicked, powerful, cruel, and cunning.

"Never mind. We're in the middle of battle now. It's dangerous here. Leave this place immediately and camp until daybreak. At sunrise, you should leave this forest at once."

I don't know if it's his sense of justice or just stubbornness, but even after my instructions, Toudou persists. He's always such a pain in the ass.

"No, I—"

"Judging by your appearance, you may very well be a good fighter. But I don't need any assistance. This is my—"

I stop, sensing movement behind me.

Could the vampire have seen this conversation as his opportunity?

Even without seeing him, I can tell from the smell, the sound, and the feel of the wind exactly what he's doing.

Toudou's eyes go wide as he shouts, "Look out—!"

I turn around, ducking as I take a step forward. Zarpahn comes at me from above, his sharp nails swinging, but I've moved just out of his reach.

One mistake the vampire made was being so overconfident that he didn't come prepared with a weapon. You should have backup for times when your abilities are blocked. He could kill most ordinary humans with his physical strength alone, but when that fails him, things will inevitably go south. Not only is this a mistake, it's also evidence of his lack of battle experience.

I throw a punch at his stomach, where he's defenseless.

My fist strikes his protective barrier. It's really an unusual feeling to hit someone but feel you haven't damaged their flesh or broken any bones. But I feel the impact.

My arm springs back, and his skeletal figure slams into the ground. I advance and kick him in his head. My senses are a little out of order from the nonstop attacking, but I can feel he isn't taking damage. Also, if he were experienced in battle, he'd be coming right back at me with counterattacks.

Toudou stares at me in shock as I batter Zarpahn. "Demons are tough. Even more so when they have this rare protective boundary. It takes time to defeat them. I don't need any help—this is my job. Please don't get in the way. Don't do anything at all. Do me a favor and leave here quietly. Please."

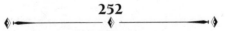

"The overdone sense of justice is a crime."

"Wha—?"

All I need is time to finish this—nothing else.

Don't go causing unnecessary trouble, Toudou. Just think of your own safety. For the love of God.

Toudou is at a loss for words. Aria watches Zarpahn with a grim expression before calling out to Toudou.

"Sir Nao, it appears I made a mistake. I think it's time for us to leave this place. The battle seems nearly over…"

"She's right, Nao," says Limis. "If this guy says we're not needed, then let's go back to the camp."

That's right. Go back. Listen to your companions!

Zarpahn rolls away to put some distance between us. I don't chase him.

His already bloodless, pallid appearance has grown only more haggard. He looks like a ghost.

He totters to his feet, holding his head and wincing in pain. "I—I who have the protection of—of the God of Darkness… How could I lose…to the likes of a human? It's *impossible!*"

A pitch-black light gathers around his tightly clenched fist.

He is invoking the omen of *Darkness*. Casting this borrows the power of the God of Darkness, an evil god equal in rank to the God of Order. Unlike a vampire's other skills, this one is more difficult to obstruct.

The dark light takes the form of one short arrow. It comes flying at me at high speed.

However, the size and the speed of this arrow are greatly reduced compared to the one he shot earlier. Pretty soon, he probably won't be able to produce them at all. He should know by now that he already lost the moment I cast the prism.

I pray silently.

I pray for order in the evil. For the arrow of darkness to be turned to an arrow of light.

In response to my prayer, one by one, countless white lights form around me.

253

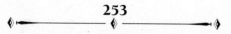

The lights take the shape of arrows, and each is several times the length of Zarpahn's single bolt. Without any signal, the arrows turn to their target and fly. The first collides head-on with Zarpahn's dark arrow and easily dissolves it.

Then the dozens remaining rain down on Zarpahn's body. He doesn't have enough time to avoid or repel them. Just before he is swallowed up completely in the light, I can see the dumbfounded expression on his face.

Arrows of light can't pass through a demon's protective boundary. When the light of the arrows dies out, what's left is a cowering vampire. There is no damage to his body, but there certainly is to his mind. His spirit has been broken.

"Do you understand, Zarpahn? It's time to give in," I say in a tone of rebuke. "I'm not without mercy. Remove your protective barrier."

"No yet...not yet. Ah-ha...ha-ha-ha... I—I can't lose. Ah-ha-ha-ha-ha-ha-ha-ha!" Zarpahn gets to his feet, a crazed smile on his face.

He just doesn't know when to quit.

He pulls his arm back, winding up to throw. He must have picked something up when he was on the ground. The vampire uses all his remaining strength to send a rock the size of a fist flying at me.

I use the dagger in my hand to repel it. The impact makes a dull sound, and the rock is sent flying outside the prism.

"Ah...!" gasps Limis as the stone flies past.

Zarpahn's eyes slowly move to her.

Shit—we slipped up.

"Get out of here immediately!"

"So this prism...is not a physical barrier," says Zarpahn.

I move forward. Wasting no time, I thrust a dagger at Zarpahn's right eye.

He flies backward like a leaf, but I don't really feel like I've done damage. Did he jump backward on his own to reduce the impact?

He is starting to gain confidence—this is not a good development.

Preparing himself to land while he flies backward through the air,

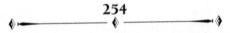

Zarpahn catches himself on his hands and feet. His gaze is not directed at me but instead at the hero's party still standing nearby.

He grabs a clump of dirt.

This is what I mean when I say it's easiest to work alone.

While his physical strength isn't a threat to me, it is to Toudou and the others. Toudou and Aria at least have armor, but Limis could be fatally wounded by a hit from him.

I change my approach. Stepping forward, I put myself directly between Zarpahn and the party.

"Get out of here *now!*"

He pulls his hand back again and prepares. You can dodge a rock, but scattered clumps of flying dirt aren't so easy. In order to reduce his accuracy even a little, I pull off my cloak and throw it into the air to obstruct his vision.

He chuckles. "Heh-heh-heh, it's tough being a hero, isn't it?"

I won't be able to avoid taking the hit. The cloak swells up and is blown away, and to me, what follows happens in slow motion.

The dirt spreads and hits my body like bullets. The impacts are dull. A cloud of dust rises, but I don't close my eyes. It's only dirt—it causes no pain or damage. I maintain my stance.

Looking like he intends to continue his storm of dirt, Zarpahn dives onto the ground. He could still challenge me to close combat, but I wonder if he has the guts? Does he really think that if he just finds the right moment, he could win this thing? That's pretty arrogant.

I meet his eyes. He licks his lips and smiles an awful, crooked smile.

That's fine—I'll be your opponent.

Zarpahn is bent low to the ground. Is he aiming for my jaw?

As he attacks from below with his sharp nails, I bend back to dodge him. He swings at me several more times in succession, and I continue stepping back to avoid him.

His arm is too short—his reach and mine aren't comparable.

Zarpahn's efforts are in vain. I've restricted his abilities, and I'm greater than him in experience and physical ability. Even if he did find

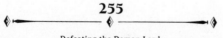

an opportunity to attack, he can't get the upper hand. I wear chain mail under my priest's robes, and attacks of his level won't get through that.

I come at Zarpahn with my dagger in a storm of attacks. The moment the silver blade strikes Zarpahn's arm, it's deflected by his protective barrier. For a brief moment, the protection is interrupted. Not missing the chance, I slash his throat with the blade.

Zarpahn flails as the hit sends him rolling. When he comes to a stop, coughing violently, I hold him down with my foot and turn my palm toward him. He's not getting any more chances to talk. If Toudou and the others won't run, then I need to kill Zarpahn quickly.

"Photon Order."

I direct the light straight down to crush him.

The holy beam cuts through the darkness, and for an instant, the area around us becomes bright as day.

The illumination subsides. I can tell he hasn't taken much damage. What I need is a gap in his protective barrier. In one fluid motion, I switch to an underhand grip on my dagger and press my weight down on him, thrusting the blade into his mouth.

His eyes widen in shock. His bloodred irises constrict. I use the dagger to transmit the holy technique.

"Photon Order."

"?!"

The light explodes in his mouth. A groan of agony rises from the back of his throat.

But it isn't enough. He's taking damage but not enough to kill him. He frantically tries to close his mouth and hits me in the stomach, trying to get me off him.

The silver blade scrapes against the surface of his teeth. With all my strength, I thrust the blade to the back of his throat and cast it again.

"Photon Order."
Photon Order.
Photon Order.
Photon Order.

"The overdone sense of justice is a crime."

Photon Order.

The light explodes in his throat continuously. I can see his soundless scream of pain, and his body convulses with each hit.

Dammit, just die already! Die! Die! I need him to die before he inflicts any damage on the hero!

As a vampire loses its life force, its body starts turning to ash. The fact that he still retains his form is proof he isn't dying yet. I strike with the holy light ten times, but Zarpahn takes only a moderate amount of damage.

"Shit... The dagger doesn't have enough power."

Most demons with divine protection are the highest rank.

Knowing that I'm at a disadvantage in strength and abilities, usually I'll make careful preparations for the battle. I never have random encounters with them, like in this case. Not to mention, this is my first time fighting using only a sub-weapon.

It's not a bad dagger, but it falls short in comparison with my mace, which has a number of blessings that boost its power.

I use my left hand to hit Zarpahn hard in the head. It feels like punching a stone wall. *Dammit, if only I had the divine blessing of the God of War that Toudou has, I could break his protective barrier in one hit.*

Even if he doesn't take much damage from the punches, it should still keep him disoriented. I don't want to give him any opportunities to act.

My fist starts bleeding, but I don't let up. I keep going, and little by little, the damage accumulates. Amelia's voice comes in over the transmission.

"Ares, are you all right?"

"Yeah, I'm fine. This stubborn bastard just won't *die!*"

"...Are you sure you're all right?"

"I'm fine!"

I have no other way of handling this. I knew it wouldn't be quick.

I just keep throwing punches, saying nothing. More and more bruises cover Zarpahn's face. He fights back fiercely, but I somehow manage to hold him down.

I don't even know how many times I've struck him when, suddenly, I hear a voice that turns my stomach.

The one that always spells trouble for me.

"Hey! H-here, take this…!"

Toudou's voice. I knew he was still there. I warned him to leave, but as long as I gave Zarpahn no time to act, I figured it wouldn't really be a problem for Toudou to just loiter there.

I look up and see him standing in a different spot. I can clearly feel my face contort.

He's right next to my mace.

He leans toward it. His fingertips touch it.

"*Don't—!*" I cry.

No, Toudou! I didn't drop it; I put it there on purpose!

But I'm too late.

The moment Toudou lifts the mace, the atmosphere changes.

Once the medium is moved, the prism disappears. It takes time for a prism to form but only a moment for it to dissolve.

Zarpahn's body, pinned under my knee, suddenly starts shaking wildly.

Toudou lifts the mace with two hands, staggering at its weight, and throws it toward me. As it lands at my side, Zarpahn vanishes out from under me.

I told you not to do anything!

I can see Toudou stiffen. He understands his actions changed something. The evil presence swims through the air like smoke and materializes a few meters away from me.

"Form Black Fog."

One of this vampire's abilities is to transfigure himself into a fog. Standing there is a powerful vampire with access to all his abilities.

Other than his torn black clothes and his hair clinging to his face with sweat, he looks just as he did when I first encountered him. All the work I've done on him is erased in a second as he is restored by his natural recovery ability.

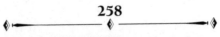

"The overdone sense of justice is a crime."

You've got to be kidding me…

"Ah-ha-ha… Ah-ha-ha-ha-ha-ha-ha-ha!"

The vampire that had been cowering in fear until just a moment ago now bursts into sneering laughter.

I immediately pick up my knife and throw it.

Zarpahn uses the nail of his index finger to make a shallow cut in his palm. Using his psychokinetic ability, he forms the blood from the cut into a thin veil that catches my knife, wrapping around it.

Could I lay another prism? It would take time, and with my weapons used as mediums, I would be defenseless against his skills until it formed.

The blood wriggles through the air, wrapping around another of the knives I'd used for the boundary, pulling it out of the ground.

I needed four mediums to lay that prism. Unfortunately, I no longer have enough to do it again. He's got me backed into a corner.

Zarpahn laughs again, narrowing his eyes at me scornfully. I pick up my mace beside me and slowly lift it. I've recovered my primary weapon, but that isn't much of a consolation.

"I thought for a moment there I might die," admits Zarpahn.

"You *are* going to die," I blurt out.

Shit—I've failed.

Zarpahn's mobility is far superior to mine. He'll be able to escape now.

I turn to look at Toudou. Without the barrier separating them, he now feels the full power of the black-blood, and his eyes widen in fear as he steps back. That coward!

Aria moves to shield Limis and draws her sword, readying herself for combat, but her swordsmanship won't last ten seconds against an opponent like this.

Zarpahn snickers. "Heh-heh-heh… How difficult it must be to have such foolish companions…"

"…Have to give you that one," I say, although they aren't my companions anymore. When even the enemy points it out, I can't argue.

I rethink my approach. Now that things have come this far, the worst possible outcome is for Toudou to be killed. I no longer have any chance

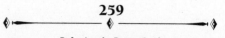

of defeating the vampire. If he uses displacement magic, he'll be able to escape, and there's no way for me to catch him. It's impossible.

The vampire has information now. I wanted to avoid letting him take back any intel, but fortunately, I bluffed and told him I was the hero. With how easily I beat him down on my own, I doubt he suspects I was lying, and it's even less likely he would suspect that the fool who just sabotaged me is the real hero.

I breathe a sigh and press a hand to my forehead, glaring at Zarpahn.

"It can't be helped—I'll allow you to escape. Tuck your tail between your legs and get out of here, vampire."

"…Huh? What the hell are you saying?"

The knife that he held with his blood disappears. Did he use displacement magic to send it somewhere else?

Then the blood swirls around in the air, taking the shape of a narrow blade.

Zarpahn smiles stiffly. He's acting calm, but he's clearly angry.

"I've got my power back. Why don't we go for a second round?"

"…Well…if you want to that badly…I don't really mind…" I take another breath and raise my mace.

I have no motivation to continue this fight. If he's about to lose, he can easily run away using his displacement magic, and I wouldn't be able to stop him. So why is he taking this so seriously all of a sudden?

"…You're surprisingly relaxed, considering that I just regained all my power…"

"Yeah, yeah." I sigh as I jump forward to close the distance between us. At the same time, I cast a holy technique on my mace that will make it more effective against his protective barrier.

Different than the dagger, my mace is the manifestation of my faith itself. Using it to attack him directly with the power of light is much more effective than using photon order.

Zarpahn looks surprised as I come at him but immediately uses the blood knife to fend off my mace.

The blessing of Lucief doesn't seem to apply to the blood itself, and

"The overdone sense of justice is a crime."

the blood doesn't have much power on its own. As I strike with my mace, the evil power in the blood knife is dispelled, returning it to nothing more than a pool of blood.

It's the same for the sword of blood he grips in his hand. How careless.

I drive my mace resolutely into his torso.

His flesh and bones creak in resistance. Now that I'm using my mace, the attacks inflict significantly more damage than before. The spikes dig into his skin, tearing the flesh and spraying blood.

I take a step forward as Zarpahn flies backward. I swing my mace down at the earth, feeling the massive difference in the impact of the mace versus the dagger. Just the blade alone wasn't enough—I needed the power of the mace.

The hit inflicted damage, but that's guaranteed to be undone by the vampire's natural recovery ability.

The scattered drops of blood build themselves into a thin wall. Paying it no mind, I keep attacking with my mace.

My first swing dissolves the wall, the second scrapes the vampire's body and tears his skin, and the third cuts into his flesh. Zarpahn cries out in pain. For some reason, he shows no sign of transforming his body to fog. Is this guy stupid? Or is he just fooling around here?

"Don't want to run away?" I ask, my thoughts slipping out of my mouth.

He raises his hand to strike, but I beat him to it and hit again with my mace.

Even if he has regained his full power, he's still a follower of darkness. He's no match for a crusader specially trained to fight his kind.

The only reason I haven't killed him already is that his protection from the evil god is so strong. His physical abilities certainly are high for a vampire, but they're still inferior to mine—particularly with my class-one buffs—and a vampire's defensive power is somewhat low to begin with. If you add in my attack power, that closes the gap even more.

I keep attacking, using the momentum of one attack to lead into the next. It's chipping away at him little by little.

Regardless of the fact that he could transform into smoke and escape at any time, for some reason, he doesn't even try to dodge.

Maybe his strategy is to use *Form Black Fog* to disappear the moment before I do him in, just to piss me off. If that's what he's doing, he really is a despicable creature.

His once well-groomed appearance is now horribly battered. Light flickers in his crimson eyes, shining with energy.

"**Energy Drain**," he says, using his ability to absorb the life of other living things.

When it reaches my body, it's deflected by the holy light that protects me. It dissolves.

Waves of the deflected attack hit the sparsely growing grass around us and cause it to wither. If an ordinary person or a swordmaster without divine protection were to take a hit from that, it might not be possible to restore their energy. On the other hand, against a high-level priest, skills like *Energy Drain* are ineffective.

I go at him in a storm of attacks, hitting him like a sandbag, and finally throw him back. He lands several meters away, and a stream of black fog comes from his body as it repairs itself.

As Zarpahn kneels on the ground, tears form in his eyes from a fit of violent coughing. His black clothes are covered in holes and stained with blood.

"*Cough, cough…* Wh-what…? What *are* y-you?"

Without answering, I close the distance between us and swing my mace again.

This time, just before I make contact with his body, it turns to fog to avoid the blow.

If you're gonna run away, hurry up and do it. I have a ton of other things to do and no time to mess around.

The fog flies high into the trees and returns to human form atop a branch.

"The overdone sense of justice is a crime."

His breathing is ragged as he suppresses the coughing. I'm certain that his wounds are slowly healing themselves.

"*Pant, pant*... You—you...monster..."

How disrespectful.

Shouldering my mace, I look up toward Zarpahn. *If you're going to run, do it now. I don't have time for this!*

Toudou stands rooted in place as if paralyzed, staring at us. There's a grinding pain in my stomach from the stress of his presence. *Will you please just go somewhere safe?*

When Zarpahn's wounds are about 90 percent healed, his whole body begins to shake. Black fur grows out of his pale skin, and shadows protrude from his back.

This is *Form Animal*, another special ability of vampires that allows them to transform freely into bestial forms.

It's common for them to transform into wolves and bats, and this time, I would guess he's choosing a bat form. Maybe he intends to fly away and escape.

I guess it doesn't matter whether he gets away by magic or by flight—I may be higher level than him, but I don't have wings.

I stand still, waiting for the transformation to complete itself. As I expected, he takes the form of a bat—a gigantic bat that looks like it was cut out of the darkness. About the size of an ox, it cries out in a shrill, high-pitched call. Then it swoops down on me.

Thinking he planned to run away, I stand staring in surprise at this spectacle.

It flies with complicated maneuvers and at a speed far greater than that of a wild bat. When it reaches me, I knock it down with my mace.

A miserable cry echoes through the woods. The vampire was much stronger in human form. Why did he take the much less powerful form of a bat if he intended to attack?

What is this—some kind of bonus stage?

Vampires can't continue to change forms for an extended period of

time. If he isn't able to return to human form, it will be impossible for him to use *Form Black Fog* to escape.

Still unsure of his motives, I stamp a foot down on his wings to stop him from moving and throw my mace into the small skull. It serves to relieve a little of my stress.

I hit him several times over. He attempts to return to human form, but I continue swinging the mace. When he finally regains his proper shape, his head is swollen and indented.

The next time I bring my mace down, I swing straight through the air. *So he transformed into fog...*

Making no attempt at escape in spite of his pain, coming back at me to keep on fighting—is this guy some kind of masochist?

The fog returns to human form a short distance away. The damage to his body hasn't recovered.

For him to stand around making conversation during battle, he has to be an idiot, but I ask him anyway, "...What are you trying to do here?"

"It can't be... It can't, it can't, there is no way that I—Zarpahn Drago Fahni—under the protection of the God of Darkness—no way I could lose to a *human*, a human without a scratch on him..."

I can't tell if he actually heard my question or if he's just talking to himself.

But hold on... Is it possible I might be able to kill him now?

I reevaluate the situation. I think I may be able to manipulate his pride. This guy is a fool—I was sure he would run away, but he didn't. If I can kill him, I should go ahead and do it. Choosing my words carefully, I call out to him.

"...Zarpahn Drago Fahni—come at me with everything you've got. If you have pride in the noble blood that runs through your veins, then let's settle this fairly."

Zarpahn looks at me vacantly. "That's...that's exactly—what I want. Ah-ha—ah-ha-ha-ha-ha-ha... There's no way—no way I could lose..."

There's no energy in his voice. He trembles, from either nervousness

or excitement, and his movements have become unnatural. Even so, he turns to me with resolve.

I can kill him. I'm certain I'll be able to kill him!

This unexpected development gives me a surge of energy. I'll kill him before he changes his mind about it. I don't want to leave any problems for later.

Zarpahn snaps his fingers with a click, and a multitude of dark arrows springs forth into the air around me.

So this is the true nature of his ability?

I offer up a silent prayer, creating arrows of light in the same number as the dark. I still have much more holy energy I can use.

The dark arrows shoot toward me, and the light arrows rush to meet them. This begins the attack, and I lower myself and kick off the ground.

Zarpahn does the same, and producing two new blood swords, he rushes forward.

The arrows of light and darkness collide, and the sounds of their impact echo through the night of the woods.

I study the blood swords. It's likely these are more powerful than the one before, so I doubt I'll be able to destroy them with a swing of my mace. But this isn't a problem. If I can't get rid of them with my mace, there are plenty of other ways to accomplish it.

What the hell is it that makes this vampire think he has a chance of winning, I wonder? Or is it that he's already given up?

As we draw near, he thrusts the blood swords forward, and they stretch out toward me. I predicted he would do this—it's a basic tactic most vampires use. If you've never seen it before, it might catch you off guard. If you're ready for it, it's easy to evade.

I jump forward to dodge the blood swords as they stretch toward me and then kick the vampire in the jaw as I fly past.

I feel the dull thud of contact. Why doesn't he transform into the fog? When I land, I drop my mace and upturn my palms toward his exposed abdomen. Zarpahn's arms grow, just reaching my shoulders, and

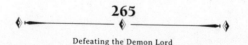

he digs into them with his nails. The strength of his grip presses down on me, but the chain mail under my clothes keeps his nails from reaching my skin.

"Photon Order."

The light that shoots from the palms of my hands blows Zarpahn back. I pick up my mace and follow him.

I swing my weapon around, using centrifugal force to gain momentum, and put my full power into an attack. As I sweep down at him, Zarpahn uses his arms to fortify himself and defend against the attack.

Bad move. His body isn't strong enough to withstand the blow, so he's a fool to try to take the damage.

Zarpahn is forcefully repelled, his body thrown into the trees. I pursue him. Leaning forward, my aim fixed on the vampire's head, I swing my mace.

I ignore the blood that splatters from the hit. Now only half-conscious, Zarpahn is getting sluggish.

Whether you're a human or a black-blood, the brain is your command center. After about ten blows to his head, the vampire transforms into black fog. It seemed like a reflex—he must have acted on survival instinct. That tells me that it won't take much more to kill him.

This is further confirmed when the fog changes back to human form a short distance away. His head is covered with blood, and he looks half-dead. But his consciousness has returned to him.

I swing my mace through the air a few times to shake off the blood. "What's wrong, Zarpahn? You still haven't landed a hit on me. Don't hold back. Show me what you can really do."

The young vampire staggers forward. He suddenly lifts his head, and a glint in his eye catches my attention.

They're the eyes of someone driven by fear, not of a hopeless man on the brink of death. Demons that get this look tend to cause trouble.

I take a fleeting glance at Toudou, who stands watching us in a trance. Why didn't he get out of here when I told him to? I guess it

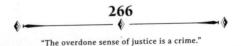

"The overdone sense of justice is a crime."

doesn't matter. Now there's no time to think about Limis and Aria—I just need to make sure to save Toudou.

At that moment, Zarpahn lets out a low groan, like that of a dead man crawling out from the depths of hell. "Ahhh... Ahhh... I...I *lost*..."

For a second, I don't believe my ears. *Did he just admit that he lost? This arrogant demon is acknowledging his defeat? No freaking way.*

I remain on high alert, checking my surroundings. I recall that this opponent has a pattern of acting at unexpected moments. Zarpahn continues grumbling.

"You...monster... Ahhh, ah-ha-ha, ha... This time...I lose. I'll admit it. Ah-ha—ha-ha-ha-ha... Right now, I...I'm no match. No match for you, *hero*...!!"

Is he going to run? As the words come out of his mouth, I notice that he takes a step toward me. He doesn't seem to intend to attack or to run away—I can't figure out what he means to do.

Zarpahn keeps moving toward me, although he looks like he might collapse at any moment.

I take one step forward as well. My opponent's body is covered in wounds, but he's not so far gone that I could kill him in one hit. If I was to go on the offensive once more and hit him ten or twenty times, that would probably do him in.

There's a glimmer in his eyes. A deep, dark, glaring light—I feel somehow repulsed by it. Any member of humanity seeing those eyes would know this creature to be an enemy of God.

Then Zarpahn smiles weakly. "Hero... Next time, I won't lose. I will kill you. I stake my life on that."

"Will there even be a next time?"

"There...will."

Why does he sound so sure of that...?

Something about this doesn't feel right, but I ignore the feeling for now. I strengthen my grip on my mace, and at that moment—the demon in front of me begins to swell up.

267

Or rather, not the demon himself but something *inside* him. The source of his evil power.

"Ah-ha—ah-ha-ha-ha-ha-ha, ha-ha-ha-ha-ha-ha-ha-ha!"

A warning bell goes off in my head.

I move quickly, acting on instinct. I step forward and raise my mace high overhead. Swinging at Zarpahn, still laughing like he's lost his mind, I send him flying and say a prayer.

For an instant, the ground shakes, the air trembles, and the sky is stained with darkness.

My brain is jolted by the tremendous, thundering roar, a sound like the world is being destroyed. My body feels like it might be thrown by the shock, and I just manage to keep my footing. A stormy wind tears off my mask and breaks it in half, and I knock away the tree branches that come flying at me. It's then that I actually understand what happened.

That bastard—he self-destructed!

I regret that last attack now, but it's too late. I grit my teeth and endure the storm. After a minute, it finally subsides. I check the state of things around me.

There is nothing.

No remains of the dead flame lion and none of the trees that were knocked down. The ground is all torn up, and just about everything has vanished from the vicinity.

The tops of the taller trees look like they've been completely shaved off, and Zarpahn...is nowhere to be seen. No sign of him whatsoever. It makes sense—he himself was the origin of the explosion. No matter how strong the protection of the God of Darkness may be, no one can withstand an explosion from the inside.

The semicircular barrier of light that I cast at the last second is spread out over the sky. It faintly blinks and then goes out completely.

It's one of the highest-ranking defensive techniques. Its duration is short, but it's a high-level technique with strong defensive capability.

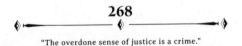

Even so, it wasn't able to withstand the shock of the explosion completely. My blood runs cold when I think what would have happened if it hadn't been there at all.

"Ares?! Ares!" shouts Amelia.

"Yeah… Yeah, I'm alive. I'm okay."

Amelia is…all right? I convulse in a coughing fit but manage to answer her.

Self-destruction magic… I'd heard this sort of technique existed within the dark arts, but this is the first time I've actually seen it. Not many people want to use magic that guarantees their own death.

Zarpahn meant those last words—he wanted to win until his last moment.

I sense no enemies in the area around me. Trying to regulate my breathing, I lightly clench the palm of my hand and move my body to check for damage. I'm unharmed.

I raise my hand to touch my face. The mask is gone. I don't even know where it was blown off to. That can't be helped. I quiet my mind and report to Amelia.

"The threat is gone. Amelia, can you come here?"

"Yes, straightaway… And what about Toudou's party?"

"…They're alive. Toudou is fine, of course, and Limis and Aria are safe."

While I wait for Amelia to arrive, I go and check on them.

Toudou is lying facedown on the ground. I kneel down next to him and check his pulse, just to be sure. His heart is beating. He's unconscious, possibly having fainted from the shock and the noise. His only external wounds are some abrasions. He didn't bring his shield, but it's a good thing he wore his armor. There's a big bump on his head, but that can be easily healed.

Aria and Limis have also fainted from the shock, but they have no major injuries.

Everyone is all right, and the enemy is gone. In the end, everything turned out okay, but I have to say—it's a miracle that it did.

The forest has finally returned to silence. I breathe it in. I feel a sudden onset of fatigue and sit down right there on the forest floor.

Physically, I could keep going, but I'm mentally exhausted.

We can't forget what happened here. This was the party's first level-up field. There's still a long road ahead to making Toudou the strongest hero he can be.

While I sit and wait for Amelia, I wrestle with the unanswerable question of how to best guide Toudou on the path forward.

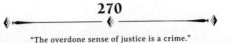

"The overdone sense of justice is a crime."

Epilogue

The Hero's Party Regroups

I'm back in the cheap inn in Vale Village.

I lean back lightly in my chair and put my feet up on the table.

A few hours have passed since the incident in the forest. I take a gulp of water and wet my lips as I continue my report.

"Yes, it was a black-blood. A vampire. Stage three, but his abilities weren't all that advanced. Honestly, he was kind of an idiot. Anyway, it appears the Demon Lord has keen eyes on his side to have discovered the hero already."

"A vampire…," considers Creio. "Has a vampire ever appeared in the Forest of the Vale before?"

"No, this is a first. I checked with Helios, too, and he said there was no sign of a vampire in the days leading up to this."

"A vampire with the protection of an evil god, huh…?"

"If he'd had more combat experience, it could've been a close one."

It was a high-risk situation, and it's fortunate we won. It was lucky I encountered the enemy before Toudou—and that the enemy himself was so careless. We can't expect things to go so well next time.

"He anticipated the hero's arrival, though I didn't get to ask how. Now, once they realize they can't get in contact with Zarpahn, they'll be convinced of the hero's presence and set out in pursuit. We've just passed the one-month marker."

I glance at the calendar on the wall. Our time to warm up has run out.

I stand and walk over to the window and glance outside discreetly.

"What happened to the hero and his party?"

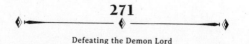

"I put them to sleep and brought them to the church. They didn't sustain any major damage. When they wake up, I'll have the church send them on their way to the next town."

They didn't wake up at all on the way to the church, so they haven't seen my face. Or at least, I don't think they have.

Toudou keeps showing up and playing the hero at all the wrong times. Even though I was the one at the most risk in that battle, he interfered with his nonsense. Why didn't he just listen when I told him not to do anything?

As for Glacia—who has thus far proven to be useless, only ever talking about how hungry she is—I asked Helios to have a word with her. It would be good if she could be a little more helpful.

"Hmm…," says Creio thoughtfully, perhaps understanding my frustration. Then he makes an unexpected proposal.

"Ares, would you rather resign from this mission?"

"I can't resign." Closing the poorly fitting window, I sit back down.

It's a foolish question. I need to follow Toudou and the party on to the next town. I don't have time to think about something stupid like quitting.

"Isn't this a lot of trouble? There are other crusaders who could fill the role."

"None of them is as strong as I am."

This is absolutely an annoying, stressful job. I feel like I'm babysitting children. I have a much easier time in battle, where my head is clear of distraction, swinging my mace at my demon enemies. But the cardinal was right to choose me for this mission.

Among the ten-odd active crusaders, I'm the strongest. I also have the most battle experience and the highest level.

"No need for concern. This is business, and I'm a professional. No matter how stressful or irritating Toudou is, I can use holy energy to heal the headaches. I'm getting used to them anyway. Don't worry. I'm not going to break Toudou's head open. Just today, I carried his defenseless, sleeping body to the church without putting a scratch on him."

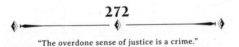

"The overdone sense of justice is a crime."

"...Right, that's all well and good, but..."

He goes silent, hesitating. The transmission stays connected. I wait awhile, and finally he continues.

"Ares, before we dispatched you on this mission, there was actually another candidate we were considering."

This is the first I've heard of this. Crusaders are nearly always on a job—I can't picture there being another available candidate. I know they're not foolish enough to send out Gregorio.

I wait silently. Finally, Creio says it.

"The Saint."

"...What?"

The Saint is an iconic presence in the Church of Ahz Gried. She's a young woman more deeply protected by the God of Order than any other and is the most advanced user of the holy arts. She's the one who performed the hero summoning to call Toudou here from the other world.

"Right up until the hero summoning was performed, we had intended to make the Saint a member of the hero's party. The reason we called you away from your mission was to take her place."

It's true that I was called in on extremely short notice. I'd just finished my preparations for another mission and was about to set out when I was told my orders had changed.

"Why wasn't she dispatched? She would have fit Toudou's... preferences."

The Saint is powerful. She doesn't have much combat power, but her divine protection from the God of Order is on a completely different level than other priests. I don't know much about the Saint personally, but I'm sure Toudou wouldn't have expelled her from his party.

Creio answers my question in a tone one rarely hears from a long-standing leader of the Church—contempt.

"...The hero's disposition was...different than we expected. His *character* itself was different than the heroes recorded in our histories. That was the reason for the change. You understand, don't you, Ares?"

"...I do."

"This is the same reason the low-level Limis Al Friedia and Aria Rizas were chosen. Of course, the School of Swordsmanship and the School of Sorcery have their own motives, but this was the primary motivator."

As Creio explains, I recall the uncomfortable feeling I had time and again when I was a member of the party. His affinity for women aside, there was something in all his actions that resembled...could it be madness? It makes sense to me that the Church would hesitate to trust him with the Saint.

But if that's the case, couldn't it be risky even to allow him to level up?

Well, supposing the Church does see him as a risk, they still need to provide him with support. Which leads me to think that...I was chosen to clean up the mess if things took a wrong turn.

The thought gives me a chill, and I shake my head to dispel it.

At this point, I'm stronger than Toudou, without a doubt. I probably will be for a while longer yet, so there's no reason to overthink this now. But I should at least be mentally prepared for the possibility.

"Ares, don't trouble yourself over it. All I'm really trying to say is that, yes, there is a reason you were chosen. And that you're the only one with the ability to accomplish this mission. Do you understand?"

"...Yes."

I understand. I'm prepared to do what I can—what I must.

My adversary is both the Demon Lord and the hero himself.

I can sense a little smile creeping across Creio's face. "Very well, then. I'm putting my faith in you, Ares Crown, level-ninety-three crusader of the first order of Out Crusade. Continue to fulfill your duty to support Naotsugu Toudou...and defeat Demon Lord Kranos."

"Understood."

The transmission cuts out. I feel mentally strained. I sit there in a daze for a moment, then get to my feet.

I will carry out my orders. It doesn't matter what kind of person the hero is.

The hero has divine blessings, and I have backup from the Church. If we combine those forces, that should be enough to defeat the Demon

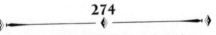

Lord. Anyone could do it, right? I'll raise the hero's level and extinguish any obstacles in our way. It's that simple.

In the hallway, I can hear Amelia's light footsteps. She's just coming back from gathering information on Toudou.

I ready myself for the report and open the map on the table to discuss our next move.

The current level of the Holy Warrior Naotsugu Toudou is—27.

§   §   §

Then Naotsugu Toudou's eyes open.

Still half-asleep, he looks around but doesn't recognize the room he's in. He slowly sits up, and the armor protecting his shoulders, arms, and torso rubs together, clinking as he moves.

His hair sticks to his face from sweat. He brushes it aside, his fingers shaking.

He had a dream—a terrible dream. But he can't remember any of it.

Dropping his feet off the side of the bed, Toudou stands. There is no strength in his legs, and he staggers forward but somehow manages to remain upright without falling. His head throbs. He presses his palm to his forehead to suppress a headache and mumbles softly.

"Where am I...?"

The more time that passes, the more he remembers from the night before.

He realized he needed to go to the forest. He went to fight the demon in order to protect others from harm.

They had little chance of winning, but they still had to stand against the demon. Toudou didn't make the decision to go based on the likelihood of his victory. He didn't this time, and he won't next time. That's what it means to do the right thing.

He remembers the light that sprang forth in the depths of the woods, and the demon—the first he'd ever seen—and the masked man who fought it.

What time is it now? There isn't a clock in the room, but he senses he must have been sleeping for a long time.

Then it occurs to him.

Where are Limis and Aria…?

There is no one else in the room. His memory of the night before ceases at the sudden explosion and the shock wave—he thought the impact would blow him to pieces. Thankfully, he can still move his limbs. He hasn't taken any damage, but he might have his armor to thank for that.

At that moment, Toudou hears the sound of footsteps outside the door. The lock clicks, and the wooden door slowly opens.

"Father Helios…"

"I see you're awake, Sir Toudou." Helios nods as if he knew it already. Toudou remembers his calm expression and cunning smile.

"If you're here, Helios, that must mean…this is the church."

"Yes. You're in a room at the Vale Village Church. Sir Toudou, you were involved in a battle with a follower of darkness."

"I…see… What about the others?"

"All are safe and without injury." Toudou breathes a sigh of relief.

Helios leads Toudou to another room where Limis, Aria, and Glacia have already gathered.

"Sir Nao, are you unharmed?" asks Aria.

"…Yeah. I don't feel so great, but…I'm fine."

"We were really worried, since you were the only one who didn't wake up…," says Limis, walking over to him. Toudou smiles weakly and apologizes.

Helios picks up a pitcher and pours water into a cup, handing it to the hero. Toudou realizes how thirsty he is.

After giving Toudou a moment to settle in, Helios starts to talk.

"Now that Toudou is awake, let me explain the situation. Actually, it's rather simple. You all were caught up in a battle with a demon—a black-blood—and you passed out. Then you were brought here. Do you have any memory of this?"

"The overdone sense of justice is a crime."

"…Yes," says Toudou. He looks to Aria and Limis. They both nod in response. Only Glacia doesn't look up, swinging her legs back and forth from her chair.

Helios nods and continues.

He explains that all the items from the campsite have been stored using the magical tool. They had a few external wounds, but all were treated. Lastly, what caused them to faint was the blast from the demon's self-destruction.

At this, Toudou's eyes grow wide.

"…And the man who was fighting it?"

"He is safe. It was he who carried you all here."

Toudou heaves another relieved sigh.

Helios raises his eyebrows at him. "Now, I have a message for you from that man."

"A message…?" repeats Toudou anxiously. Although he doesn't know exactly how he impacted it, he understands that his interference in the battle was not a good thing.

"Well, he used a lot of…*strong* language, but I suppose I don't need to repeat that. I've already discussed with Aria why you didn't go where you reported to the Church that you were headed. We respect your personal decisions, but it's not as though the Church doesn't make its own plans. It was not necessary for you to interfere in that battle."

"…I see."

When he arrived at the scene and saw the fighting, Toudou was immediately overwhelmed. He knew that every single move they made was far beyond what he could do himself. The reason he got involved in spite of that was because he felt strongly that he had to do his part to help. He knows his intentions were right, but naturally, he feels badly about the way things turned out.

Limis has an irritated expression on her face. Toudou gives her a look.

She probably doesn't understand why they're being scolded for a well-intentioned action. However, that action had unintended

consequences—it's better not to argue the point. "What's done cannot be changed," says Helios. "However, the next time that you intend to take such measures, it would be helpful if you could let us know."

"...Even though you won't dispatch us a priest," Limis grouses under her breath.

Helios smiles at Limis but continues without addressing her comment. "The Church is your ally. Of course, we have no authority to obstruct the will of the Holy Warrior. That is why this is not an obligation... It's simply a request."

"Right... I understand," says Toudou with a nod.

It's true they acted prematurely. They should have reported to the Church before entering the woods. The reason they failed to do so was that Toudou did not entirely trust the Church.

Satisfied with Toudou's reply, Helios moves on to his main question.

"Now, I want to ask you something, Sir Toudou... This was your first experience with a demon... What impression did it leave on you?"

Toudou recalls the events of the night before.

Although the demon looked human, the moment he saw it, he knew for certain it was not.

As soon as it entered his field of vision, the air around him changed. His heart started beating faster, and a feeling of despair entered his mind. He couldn't understand how something like that could be in human form.

He could feel the evil—he could feel it in his bones. He knew this was the natural enemy of humanity.

When he saw it lying facedown on the ground, he didn't feel the slightest bit of compassion. He was constantly on high alert. He didn't even feel peace of mind when the thing was beaten and half-dead.

That was an enemy. He was sure of it. He knew it needed to be killed.

The father, having himself fought many demons, can read Toudou's expression.

"That is a demon, Toudou. What you will have to defeat is at least

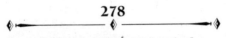

ten times stronger—a demon lord so powerful that no human in this world can defeat it."

"*Ten times* stronger...?" Toudou can't even imagine that.

The demon was strong. He was totally overwhelmed by the sight of the battle. His body went numb, and he couldn't take his eyes off it.

Evil and order. The collision of darkness and light.

Until last night, Toudou had never really considered the possibility of his own defeat. Watching the battle unfold in front of him completely changed his mind-set.

Toudou didn't understand what most of the monster's abilities were, but he could feel their power. And the power of the man with the mask.

"They were strong...*really* strong. Both the demon and the man in the mask."

"Indeed."

"If I fought that demon myself, I'm sure I would lose."

Toudou thought he was strong. And he thought he had become stronger.

The hero possesses the divine blessing of the Three Deities and Eight Spirit Kings that govern this world. During his training at the castle, he was recognized for his talent and even given the equipment of the heroes of past generations.

But Naotsugu Toudou cannot imagine a victory against that demon.

And then there's the man who crushed the demon single-handedly. Just remembering the battle, Toudou feels tense and his heart beats faster.

There is no human in this world who can contend with the Demon Lord. By that logic, Toudou will eventually need to become stronger than that masked man.

Just thinking about this, Toudou's hands start shaking.

"Will I be able to win...?" he asks, voicing his misgivings.

"Sir Toudou," says Helios, looking at him intently. "Do you still have the will to do so?"

The will. Toudou looks startled by the question.

His strength, his knowledge, and his experience are all insufficient.

He is lacking in every area—except for willpower. He hasn't lost his will and his purpose.

He wouldn't even think of abandoning his mission now. This isn't the first time he's faced an impossible enemy.

"Helios... Even before I was summoned here, I wanted to change the world...but before, I didn't have the power."

Toudou takes a deep breath and retrieves his weapon from the storage ring.

In his hand is a long, shining sword—the holy sword Ex. The sharpness of the blade reflects the will of its wielder.

By now, Toudou's hand has stopped shaking. The brilliant shine of the holy sword is proof in itself that Toudou is still the hero.

"But I have power now. I may not be strong enough yet, but I will win. No matter who my opponent is—even if they are far more powerful than I am. I...I am here to save this world."

"I see. Then it seems there is no reason for me to be concerned."

There aren't many people who would stick to their will after an encounter with a demon.

"Come to think of it, Toudou, are you aware of the human level limit?"

"Level limit?" Toudou looks over to Aria and Limis. They shake their heads.

"It appears you are not aware. One theory held by the church is that the maximum level a human can attain is one hundred."

Toudou's current level is 27. He can't begin to imagine how long it would take to reach level 100.

Helios continues. "As far as the Church is aware, the number of people to have reached that level is just *three*. And those three did not achieve it by leveling up in the ordinary way."

"The ordinary way...?"

Helios nods. Then he laughs.

"First of all, it would be good for you to set level one hundred as your goal. If you, already possessing great divine blessing, were to reach

that level, you would certainly be the most powerful warrior in the world. You absolutely must defeat the Demon Lord, Sir Toudou."

Helios holds his hand high in the air, and from his palm, a white light shines down on Toudou.

"Your current level is twenty-seven. You require thirty-two thousand six hundred and fifty-seven more life force units to reach your next level. I pray for your good fortune in the war with the Demon Lord."

They return to the inn. Toudou takes a hot shower to wash away his fatigue, and then they all gather around the table. Everyone is still tired, but they need to plan their next move as soon as possible.

"Thank you all for your support in the forest. I'm sorry my actions caused so much trouble."

"No, we all share the responsibility," says Aria. "It was me who jumped to the wrong conclusion to begin with…"

Toudou smiles wearily at her and shakes his head. He was the one to make the final call.

He looks at Aria and Limis. Spreading the map open on the table, he thinks about something Helios told them.

"I've been thinking our next destination should be…Yutith's Tomb. Not Golem Valley."

Limis and Aria exchange glances.

"Why?" asks Aria with surprise. The village headman already rejected that idea.

"In order to find a priest for the party."

"In order to *find* a priest?"

"Right." Toudou taps his finger on the map. He still looks tired, but his eyes are calm and have some energy left in them.

The encounter with the demon and the priest who defeated it was a shock to Toudou.

"Seeing a demon with my own eyes, I understood how badly we need a priest. Even if we can get by without one for the time being, once we have to start fighting demons, that will be our weakness."

"Ah—I see your point... I suppose that's right."

"At first, I thought I would be able to cover that role myself. I can heal and make prisms..."

"And if necessary, we could just stock up on healing potions..."

This is what they discussed before.

They would prioritize leveling up. They tried to find a priest, but there was no knowing when they would get one to join the party. Instead, they gathered a large quantity of high-potency healing medicine.

"So...what's different now?" asks Limis, raising an eyebrow. "You said yourself that we should put off finding a priest until later."

"But that won't *work*! I see it now... I know what I'm lacking."

Limis looks puzzled.

"Eradication techniques!" exclaims Toudou, nodding for emphasis.

The image of the masked man shooting out countless arrows of light is burned into Toudou's memory. They came down like meteors, destroying all the demon's dark arrows. Arrows of light to cleanse the darkness.

That sight was Toudou's only ray of hope as he despaired at the great difference between the demon's power and his own.

"That power will undoubtedly be important in future battles. The sooner we have it, the better," he says excitedly.

"Well," says Aria. "It certainly would benefit us to have those techniques..."

Having witnessed the sight as well, Aria begins to understand the reason for his proposal.

"The Great Tomb is where priests go to level up, right? I think it would be a good place to look for someone to join the party."

Limis and Aria consider this.

"We may not be able to gain as much experience points there as in Golem Valley, but once we get a priest in our party, we can head over to Golem Valley right away."

"Surely, there should be a large number of priests at the Great Tomb...," says Aria. "We might be able to find someone."

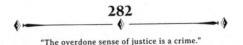

"The overdone sense of justice is a crime."

The tomb is a place where solo priests go to level up and also where mercenary parties accompany their priests to help them level up.

Aria continues. "However…there are a few issues."

Toudou looks confused.

"First, even if we go to the Great Tomb, it might not be possible for you to learn the eradication techniques that you saw yesterday."

"…Why?"

"Because most priests won't have learned such advanced techniques. The man yesterday must have been an eradication specialist."

Aria had heard talk of priests who specialize in demon exorcism, and besides, she could tell he wasn't just a normal priest.

"But any priest should at least have the ability to use those techniques, right?"

"Priests are a support class. Most can probably use some degree of eradication techniques, but it isn't a vital skill. The priest's role is to cast buffs and to heal, and typically, other party members handle the offense."

Toudou recalls that Ares said the same sort of thing. But he wouldn't need to learn *all* the techniques.

"As long as they're able to use *some* eradication techniques, they should be able to teach me—"

"There's a second problem. As a rule, priests will only teach holy techniques to other priests."

All mercenaries are aware of this, mainly because they've all thought of learning the techniques themselves.

"What…? But Ares taught me, didn't he?"

"It appears to be part of their creed. I've heard rumors that it has to do with the Church's rights to the techniques, but people don't talk about it openly."

"But I learned holy techniques from Ares, didn't I?"

"That's because Ares is…unusual. He also uses bladed tools and eats monster flesh." A disgusted look appears on her face.

Before meeting Ares, Aria had only known priests who were very

strict about the creed, so this was a shock to her. Then when he offered her monster flesh to eat, she felt like her own faith was being tested.

"Do you think they'd make an exception for the Holy Warrior?"

"I don't know, but I think it's not likely. After all, the Church is uncompromising on certain points."

Toudou thinks on this, his expression grim.

Trying to encourage him, Aria says, "It is true that we need a priest. It might not be a bad idea to go to the Great Tomb. Right, Limis?"

"Well, I guess either place is fine for me...," Limis says indifferently. She had been listening with little interest. Glacia sits across from her, frowning.

"But...if you want to learn eradication techniques, rather than going so far away for it, why don't you just have Ares teach you? I ran into him just a few days ago—he's probably still in the village."

"?!"

Aria turns to Limis, a look of astonishment on her face.

Toudou has a similar reaction. Leaning his elbows on the table, he runs his hands through his hair in frustration. "We can't do that. I forced him out of the party. How am I supposed to ask him for a favor now?"

"I mean, I asked him if he could help us find a new priest."

"Limis—you did? You have more guts than me." She'd told Toudou that she ran into Ares but not that she went so far as to ask him a favor.

"I don't think it would be so bad just to ask him..."

"No way. There's no way I could... I told him I wouldn't have any men in the party."

Toudou rests his head on the table and slams his fist down. Limis jumps.

Aria looks down at him wearily. "On that point, to be honest...I've been thinking we may need to give it up."

"I know... I know." He slams his fist down again, hitting the table almost hard enough to break it.

Aria continues calmly. "It's going to be difficult to find a female priest, but that aside...there are other, more pressing issues."

"The overdone sense of justice is a crime."

"I said I know, didn't I?! Dammit... Shouldn't magical armor form to the body of the wearer? Why does it have magic to reduce its weight but not to adjust its size?! What idiot made this?! They summoned me here to be the hero, and look what I have to deal with!"

"Huh? What are you talking about?" asks Limis, looking confused. Aria tries to stop herself from smiling, but it slips out.

Toudou is still for a few seconds. He finally resigns himself to saying it.

"The hero's armor—the holy armor Fried...it's gotten too tight for me. It's because my chest has gotten bigger... It's already *so* uncomfortable. If I go on like this, pretty soon I won't be able to wear it anymore."

Limis chokes back laughter. Teary-eyed, Toudou grabs her shoulders and shakes her back and forth.

"This is bad, Limis! It's not something to laugh about—it's *terrible*! Until now, I've been able to hide it, since my chest wasn't that big to begin with...but the more I level up, the bigger it gets, and the armor doesn't fit me anymore."

"N-Nao—quit shaking me—I—I get it already—"

"No, you don't. You don't get it, Limis! This is the whole point. I'm a different gender than all the heroes who came before me. 'There's never been a female Holy Warrior before,' they told me. It's not like it's my fault—they're the ones who summoned me!"

"Please try to stay calm," says Aria. "We might be able to have it adjusted by a blacksmith or—"

"No, we can't! We can't! What if it's made with some kind of metal blessed by the gods? What kind of blacksmith could repair that?!"

"Well, um... There might be a...legendary blacksmith..."

"Where?!"

Toudou lays her face on the table and whimpers, her energy exhausted. "Plus, if they only fixed the chest part of the armor...they'd know for sure I'm a woman. This isn't a joke. They told me to make sure the kingdom and Church don't find out... But still, I'm the hero. I'm supposed to be humanity's hope."

Aria looks at the Holy Warrior sympathetically and consoles her.

"...But, Lady Nao, we've reached the limit with the binding. Isn't it already causing you considerable discomfort?"

"D-don't call me *Lady Nao*!!"

"All right, Lady Toudou, then. If we wait too long—"

"Don't call me Lady Toudou, either!! ...Anyway, I'll still be able to put up with this through the next level up..."

"But when you level up, it's going to get big—"

"Yes, I know! I know, already! *ARRRGH!!* I've had enough of this! Since when does leveling up have any connection to *that*?! I've always been a late bloomer, so why is it that as soon as I become the hero—"

"It's that the more life force you take in, the more your own life force increases in size."

"I GET IT, ALREADY! Now let's figure out a way to deal with this!"

Toudou stands up and narrows her eyes at Limis. At Limis's small chest, to be specific.

Feeling like prey being hunted, Limis recoils.

"Limis...switch with me."

"Um, no, that's not possible."

"No, it'll work. Somehow. I'll make it work. I won't...lose." Toudou reaches toward her. Limis hastily dodges and topples backward.

Watching the two of them scramble around the cramped room, Aria narrows her eyes and sighs.

Will this party really be able to defeat the Demon Lord?

Part Two

Still Continues

How the Hero Was Defeated

Toudou's internal clock is all mixed up. She isn't sure if it's morning or evening anymore.

A damp wind blows and brushes against her cheek. The only visible light comes from Garnet.

In Yutith's Tomb, there is only silence and the damp, heavy darkness.

Toudou holds her breath as she progresses forward, an uneasy look on her face. The stone path is easier to walk on than the forest floor, but their pace is far more sluggish.

Behind her walks Aria, looking serious as usual, followed by Limis and Glacia. Limis has an old map open in her hands.

The map, which looks like it has gotten many years of use, was given to them when they visited the church in the village near the tomb. It's covered with cautionary notes, the locations of traps, and the types of monsters that appear in each room and passageway.

Eventually, Toudou stops and looks back over her shoulder.

"…Limis, where are we now?"

"…We've only been in here an hour."

"…Oh… Only an hour, huh?"

"Are you all right, Nao? You don't look so good," Limis says, sounding shocked.

"I'm f-fine… Just not used to this yet." But there isn't much energy in her voice. She bites her lip.

Limis turns to Aria, who has been unusually quiet since they entered the tomb.

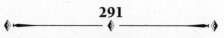

"You don't look so good, either, Aria."

"...I'm all right. Just not used to it yet." Aria glances around restlessly into the empty darkness without even turning to look at Limis.

Just then, a cold wind blows. Limis notices a shadow in the corner of the passageway and cries out.

"Ah—!"

"?!"

Toudou and Aria jump, then slowly turn toward the corner.

What appeared is one of the *living dead*. They are one of the weakest monsters to be found in the Great Tomb.

Still ten meters away, Toudou and Aria reflexively draw their swords.

The creature's skin and flesh are decaying. A nauseating, rotten smell drifts through the air, and a groan of sorrow and resentment echoes through the passage.

Its eyes aren't looking at them, but it moves slowly toward them, one step at a time.

Squinting at it, Limis says, "I *thought* I saw something moving over there!"

Ignoring her, Toudou and Aria look at each other. Toudou is the first to speak.

"Oh... Aria...you can take this one."

Wide-eyed, Aria bites her lip. "N-no, no—N-Nao, I concede this to you."

"Ah—a wraith!" shouts Limis.

"EEP!!"

Hearing this, Toudou and Aria both retreat backward, trembling. In their hurry, they trip over each other and fall on the ground.

A transparent form passes above the living dead. The thing has a body like mist and has vacant, ghostly eyes.

It doesn't move extremely fast, but it's much faster than the living dead that creeps slowly toward them.

A wraith—the second-weakest monster in the Great Tomb after the living dead.

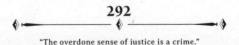

"The overdone sense of justice is a crime."

Toudou falls back in fright until she hits the wall. Aria readies her sword, her arm shaking. She prepares to attack the living dead.

"I-I'll take—the living dead. Lady Nao, y-you take the wraith."

"N-no, actually, *I'll* take the living dead."

"It doesn't matter—just hurry up!" shouts Limis, striking the floor with her staff.

At that moment, while Aria and Toudou argue back and forth, the floating wraith catches hold of them.

"EEK?!"

"Flame Lance."

At the sound of Limis's voice, a bright, burning flame in the shape of a lance shoots out, piercing the wraith and bursting on impact.

As it dies, the wraith's scream of agony echoes through the passage. Wincing, Limis covers her ears.

The scream has a sharpness that pierces the eardrum and shocks the brain. It causes Toudou to collapse on the ground.

"Nao!!" shouts Limis, rushing over to her.

"It's the *Scream of Sorrow*...," says Aria, her face pale. "A wraith skill that sends a jolt through the mind that can cause humans to lose consciousness..."

Suddenly, Aria's body goes limp, and she collapses on the ground like a marionette.

"Aria?!" cries Limis.

She looks at the two of them, dumbfounded. Though neither took a hit, they are both now unable to fight.

Limis nervously checks that they're both still alive. Pressing a hand to her forehead, she mumbles in shock, "...She's the Holy Warrior, but she can't handle the undead...? How does that even work...?"

The living dead groans as it draws nearer. It moves much slower than the pace a human would walk—in fact, you could probably get away from it pretty easily. The monsters in the Forest of the Vale were much more quick-witted and agile.

"I'm hungry…," mumbles Glacia sadly, looking neither at the pair collapsed on the ground nor at the approaching enemy.

For the first time since joining the party, Limis truly feels that she is in danger.

Lifting her staff, she points it at the living dead that stumbles toward her. *Even a beginner like me should be able to defeat something this slow.*

"Geez… Since I can't rely on anyone else… **Flame Lance.**"

The lance flies into the body of the living dead, and it bursts. Its fluids evaporate and emit an intense odor.

"Huh…?"

As she breathes in the vapors from such a close distance, the paralysis absorbs into her. In a moment, her consciousness starts to fade, and her entire body goes weak. As she passes out, Limis has no idea what just happened.

§ § §

"Why'd they even come here in the first place…?" I grumble, fed up with this group.

After only an hour in the tomb, the hero's party is totally defeated. Since they all seem to have completely lost consciousness, I immediately approach.

Toudou, Aria, and Limis lie flat on the ground, and only Glacia is left standing. The paralysis doesn't affect her. When she notices me, she jumps back and starts trembling.

"I…I'm not hungry," she says, almost like she's making an excuse.

"You don't even know what you're saying!" All she talks about is being hungry when clearly that's not even what she actually wants to say.

But I don't have time to deal with her right now. I go to Toudou and Aria to check their pulses and their pupils. They seem to have just taken some mental damage from the wraith's attack, which caused them to faint.

Next, I check Limis, who used her half-power flame magic to kill the undead enemy.

"The overdone sense of justice is a crime."

The paralysis caused by killing the living dead takes effect extremely quickly, but it isn't the type of thing that could kill you. For humans, who have some amount of divine protection from the God of Order, it's something that will fade over time.

After confirming they're all alive, I give them sleeping medicine to ensure they don't wake while I carry them out.

I tie ropes to Toudou's and Aria's wrists. Carrying Limis on my back, I grip the ropes and start pulling them toward the exit.

As I make my way out, using photon order to get rid of the low-level undead that appear along the way, I can't help but wonder—

Will these guys really be okay?

CHARACTER DATA

NAME	Ares Crown

【Level】: 93

【Occupation】: Priest (Crusader)

【Gender】: Male

ABILITIES

Physical Strength: Very High

Endurance: Very High

Agility: Very High

Magical Energy: Not Much

Holy Energy: Extremely High

Will: High

Luck: Zero

EQUIPMENT

Weapon: Wrath of God (barbed mace—able to kill)
Clothing: Equipment from Out Crusade—chain mail made of holy silver (provided by the Church)
Sub-Weapon: Daggers made of holy silver (blessed the silver himself)

EXPERIENCE UNTIL NEXT LEVEL   1,221,544,999

A priest of the Church of Ahz Gried and first-ranking crusader of the Church for the Eradication of Heresy, an organization whose primary objective is the extermination of the followers of darkness. Serious and cynical. Prefers to push through using brute force rather than carefully strategizing. He drinks, smokes, and sleeps with women—but not when he's on a job. Doesn't really believe in the gods.

NAME	Amelia Nohman

【Level】: 55

【Occupation】: Holy Caster

【Gender】: Female

ABILITIES

Physical Strength: Moderate

Endurance: Not Much

Agility: Moderate

Magical Energy: Extremely High

Holy Energy: High

Will: High

Luck: High

EQUIPMENT

Weapon: Sacred Prayer (combined mace/staff provided by the Church)
Clothing: Priest's robes (provided by the Church—comfortable)

EXPERIENCE UNTIL NEXT LEVEL   722,791

A sister of the Church of Ahz Gried and formerly Ares's operator. As a holy caster, she is a highly valuable member of the Church, and she requested to be assigned to support Ares. Although she doesn't let her emotions show on her face, she is a sensitive person. She likes quiet places and having a drink, and she dislikes work. Recently, she's taken an interest in dressing up a bit for Ares. A heavy drinker.

CHARACTER DATA

NAME	Naotsugu Toudou

【Level】: 27
【Occupation】: Holy Warrior
【Gender】: Female

ABILITIES

Physical Strength: Not Much

Endurance: Not Much

Agility: Moderate

Magical Energy: Very High

Holy Energy: Not Much

Will: Very High

Luck: Zero

EQUIPMENT

Weapon: Holy Sword Ex (lightweight—able to wield)
Clothing: Holy Armor Fried (extremely tight)

EXPERIENCE UNTIL NEXT LEVEL   32,657

The Holy Warrior summoned by Ruxe Kingdom to defeat the Demon Lord. A quick learner and a skilled warrior, she is a fundamentally serious and good-natured person, but she does sometimes act out emotionally and has a slight fear of men. Will go to any lengths to do what she believes is right. She likes justice and stuffed toys, and she dislikes ghosts and the undead. Recently, she is troubled by the fact that the legendary holy armor no longer fits her properly because her chest has gotten larger.

NAME	Limis Al Friedia

【Level】: 17
【Occupation】: Elementalist (Fire Only)
【Gender】: Female

ABILITIES

Physical Strength: Very Low

Endurance: Very Low

Agility: Not Much

Magical Energy: Very High

Holy Energy: Not Much

Will: Somewhat High

Luck: Moderate

EQUIPMENT

Weapon: Staff of Fire Flareshard (an old favorite)
Clothing: Sage's robes (made of soft materials)
Sub-Weapon: Revolver (low accuracy)

EXPERIENCE UNTIL NEXT LEVEL   7,523

The only daughter of Reider Al Friedia, the Mage King and a prince of Ruxe Kingdom. She is a prideful person and has received a high level of education as the daughter of the Mage King, but she has almost no experience in battle. Has only made a contract with a fire spirit she calls Garnet and, therefore, can only use fire magic. She likes magic and dislikes crude weapons and rude people. When she's bored, she whispers to Garnet.

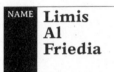

CHARACTER DATA

NAME	Aria Rizas

【Level】: 25

【Occupation】: Swordmaster
(Mixirion School)

【Gender】: Female

ABILITIES

Physical Strength: Moderate

Endurance: Moderate

Agility: High

Magical Energy: Zero

Holy Energy: Not Much

Will: High

Luck: Not Much

EQUIPMENT

Weapon: Magical Sword Lightning Soul (a treasure of the kingdom)
Clothing: Provided by the Church (equipment from Out Crusade—chain mail made of holy silver)
Sub-Weapon: Armor of Light (made with holy silver—the chest plate was remade to fit her)

EXPERIENCE UNTIL NEXT LEVEL   76,623

The daughter of Grand Swordmaster Norton Rizas, the leading instructor of the Pramia School of Swordsmanship and the chief officer of the Ruxe Royal Army. A gifted swordmaster with natural ability, she curiously was born with zero magical power. Has received military training but has little practical combat experience. Naive to the ways of the world and lacking in self-awareness. A bit self-conscious of her large bust.

NAME	Glacia

【Level】: Presumed to be around 60

【Occupation】: Wounded Glacial Plant

【Gender】: Female

ABILITIES

Physical Strength: Very High

Endurance: Very High

Agility: Moderate

Magical Energy: Very High

Holy Energy: Zero

Will: Not Much

Luck: Barely Any

EQUIPMENT

Weapon: Jerky (chews it when hungry)
Clothing: Linen dress (simple but slightly expensive)

EXPERIENCE UNTIL NEXT LEVEL   UNKNOWN

A glacial plant born and raised in the Forest of the Vale. She was driven out of her home in the deep part of the forest by a demon and began increasing her level in order to get her revenge. She encounters Ares and is beaten back by him, then transforms into a young girl. Has accompanied the hero's party ever since. Intelligent but mostly silent; even though she is able to speak human language, she rarely does when it is needed. Likes food and is completely submissive to Ares. Recently, Limis has been using her as a body pillow at night.

AFTERWORD

TSUKIKAGE

Thank you so much for picking up this book you have in your hands. My name is Tsukikage, and I am the author.

I first posted *Defeating the Demon Lord's a Cinch (If You've Got a Ringer)* on the website Kakuyomu, an online writing platform that started in 2016. After having the honor of receiving first place in the fantasy genre of the First Annual Kakuyomu Web Novel Contest, the fantastic illustrations were added, and the book was published.

To give a brief overview of the story, the protagonist is a professional priest who is assigned to support the somewhat incompetent hero's party on their mission to defeat the Demon Lord. You could call Volume 1 the prologue of their journey.

The hero's party consists of the hero, a mage, a swordmaster, and the main character, Ares. The hero is weak—she has potential but no battle experience. The mage and the swordmaster are also weak. They also have no battle experience, but they come from noble families and have natural talent. The main character, Ares, the priest, is strong. His natural talent is much less than that of the other party members, but he has a lot of experience in battle. The story is still at the beginning, and the hero's party has plenty of room to grow. I hope to continue the journey with Ares and the party for a long time.

Lastly, some acknowledgments. To everyone who takes the time to read this book; to bob, who created the beautiful illustrations; to my editor, Shukutani, who put so much effort into preparing the book for publication; and to everyone in the editing department. I express my deepest gratitude to you all.

I'm bob, the illustrator.
These two characters are
my personal favorites...I'm
looking forward to seeing
how the story develops!

bob